Jenny

Sara
Sweeney
545-3145

To Rod *ee
Kazoo
Hope for tee 1

Steve
Greenberg

ADAM'S
WILL

ADAM'S WILL

STEVEN GREENBERG

THE STREAMSIDE PRESS
Dobbs Ferry • New York

First published in the United States in 2000 by
The Streamside Company
221 Judson Avenue
Dobbs Ferry, NY 10522-3030
(914) 693-6792

Library of Congress Cataloging-in-Publication Data

00 - 191548

Book design and type formatting by Bernard Schleifer
Manufactured in the United States of America
FIRST EDITION
1 3 5 7 9 8 6 4 2
ISBN 0-940185-03-2

To Jerry and Millie for the nature; to Ben and Gladys for the nurture; to Eddie and Ro for acceptance; and an abundance of friends for tolerance and understanding. All of you have helped to mold the individual I once was and the writer I have since become.

To Louis and Fannie for Jerry; to Mart and Ellen for instruction, encouragement, and perseverance. And, most of all, to Deena for unconditional love, my model for the theme here embraced. Without you all, I would not have been the author of the volume presently in your hand. It is yours as much as it could ever be mine.

AUTHOR'S NOTE

Any work of fiction should be accepted as entirely imaginative. The present volume, however would seem to require a special and particular denial of any intent at the portrayal of actual persons and events. First, living—as I have done for many years—in a community very much like the fictional Bakersville, it is incumbent on me, and absolutely accurate, to state that the persons here depicted are not in the slightest particular related to individuals I have encountered in actuality. Only the area's topography is drawn from experience, and that should be general enough to offend only the professional geologist or naturalist, who may find a number of my putative scientific concepts flawed.

Second, I have played, if not fast and loose, then at least mildly accelerated and slightly unconstrained, with the physical layout of Bethesda, relocating Bethesda Avenue to the position of Woodmont, demolishing several rather large structures, and, in the process, adding several floors to the magnificent Hyatt Regency, which is such a pretty place it deserves them. This all was done not for purposeful inaccuracy, but rather to render the narrative more visually intelligible to the general reader not intimately familiar with the area in question. The test of my judgment in making these choices will lie in the imagery invoked and the effects produced by my words on the esteemed public. Preliminary input seems positive.

Finally, and most important, the watershed event on which the very heart of the plot turns, on or off axis, is entirely fictitious, based on no research whatever, but wholly on the requirements of the story. If it turns out one day to have the slightest basis in truth, no one will be more surprised than the author of this flight of fancy, who ever will remain:

truly and sincerely yours,
STEVEN M. GREENBERG

PROLOGUE

BETHESDA, MD.
MAY 1986

I T WAS JAKE'S IDEA TO USE THE BOY. HE WAS JUST AS SMART IN THOSE days, Jake was. Maybe not as wise as he would be a decade later, but still crafty, still resourceful. The Main Man. The one they got to handle all the major actions, those critical, delicate contracts wanting thought, decision, not just guts and muscle. Take care of it, they told him, and he set to work. Ten years later he still thought of it, played it out in his mind. The event matured him in a way, made him a better, wiser man, as cautious as an old stag.

They staked the place out for a week. Big, beautiful house, set back deep behind the foliage, so that they had a devil of a time getting to a spot where they could see and not be seen. They had to move around a lot, rent a couple of different cars, park them in front of other houses, dress in work clothes some days. But they found out what they had to, subtleties that needed mastering before they did the job: an easy way in, a guide to what lay inside. The boy was made to order.

Jake acted alone. The other guy was there to help, a specialist of sorts. On the seventh day, a Friday it was, Jake wore a suit, and told the other, Martin, he called himself—no last name—to wear one too. They followed the boy for a few blocks to a convenience store, then stopped him as he got out of his car.

"Young man . . . ," Jake called, mixing politeness and formality so deftly and with a tone and manner so sufficient to his purpose of sounding official that Martin rightly marveled at it. "Young man, can I speak to you for a moment?"

He was just a kid, really, seventeen, it turned out. Tall, almost six feet, brown hair neatly trimmed, athletic looking, with a pretty face, a girl's face, immature, scantily bearded, a smooth, unblemished face with fine and regular features. "Yes, Sir," he said, and stepped over to their car. Jake positioned himself so the boy would stand with his back to the car and to Martin within it, shutting Martin out of the interaction. He was a specialist, this Martin, and need not talk; needed, in perfect truth, *not* to talk.

Jake got his wallet out and showed the boy a card. FBI it said, with a name, not Jake, of course, but a credible name, unusual, not Jones or Smith, but Adonaldo, Roland Adonaldo. That was the kind of name one used.

"Son, we need your help."

"Yes, *sir*," said the boy—Seth, it was—very young and trusting. So Jake came up with an impromptu story, quick but not implausible. The house, he explained, was under surveillance, not for anything in the least bit bad the occupants had done, but for their protection. A crazy tale it was, but Jake could be convincing, and the FBI card helped. Seth was far too intimidated to ask for details. It was the FBI, for God's sake, and, more to the purpose, he was in love, poor thing, with the young girl—Sarah was her name—sixteen years old, pretty as a teen-age model, only child of Dan and Harriet Gruener. Seth's eyes were like saucers, as round and obedient as the family pet's, so Jake went on, explaining that he, Agent Roland Adonaldo, would really have to get in, look around, check on incoming calls, take the necessary precautions. Monitor those dreadful folks who might wind up hurting the nice Gruener family: union organizers, gangsters. Some bullshit like that. They—the agents, Roland and . . . and Fred . . . Frederick—couldn't say anything to the Grueners. Not yet, he told the wide-eyed Seth, lest they tip the rascals off unwittingly. A very bad thing for all of them, for Seth's beloved Sarah too. Agent Roland said it, so it must be true. They'd need Seth's help, to tell them when the family was out, give them a layout of the place. Sure he'd do it. Later Dan and Harriet would thank him for it—so said Roland—when they discovered how conspicuously he'd helped their saviors. Sarah would thank him too, and love him, and he, her.

On Saturday they met again, there in the lot of the 7/Eleven. Seth drew a floor plan of the house for them, for Jake, whom he knew as Agent Roland. Dan and Harriet Gruener would be out on Sunday at a party, from eight on, probably till midnight. Could Seth make sure that Sarah wasn't home? Sure thing. No problem. No one home then? No, absolutely. Dog? No, no dogs or cats. Nothing. No one. Alarm? Never turned it on when they were in town. Sure? Yeah. Absolutely.

They drove to Baltimore to do their shopping: fuses, kerosene; then filled the gas jugs on the way back. Just to be certain, Jake dialed the empty house from a pay phone, letting it ring a dozen times. There were lights on in the house, but that meant nothing, being normal for a big, expensive house in an affluent area outside Washington. Torch the place, they told him. Send a message. We want those papers. Send him a message through his son: the papers, *now*. Next time, someone gets hurt. Maybe bad. Maybe somebody you wouldn't want to get hurt.

Daniel Gruener had a migraine. He'd had one a couple of days before that went away with some strong coffee and a Darvon, but this one was a killer, drilling shrilly through his orbit on the right, clear up over the same side of his head to the occiput. At eight, Harriet brought him in another icebag. "Sorry," he said. "Don't be," said Harriet, "I didn't want to go anyway."

"Want the light off?"

"Yeah."

She clicked the lamp beside the bed, felt his forehead, which, of course, was cold from the bag of ice, unplugged the bedroom phone, and went to take a bath. A call came in while she was in the tub. Ten times . . . twelve, it rang. Persistent. Folks from the party, no doubt. Good thing she had unplugged Dan's phone. At nine, just dried and robed, comfortable on a couch, she heard the sound, thinking it was Sarah at first, but only for a moment. She should have called out: *Sarah? That you, honey?* Something like that. Anything. But she got up instead, moved across the silent carpet to the hall and looked down it, seeing two men, one heavily laden with plastic jugs—gasoline, it looked like. She didn't make a sound, but they saw her, Jake did, and Martin at the same time. So she ran swiftly, for she was an agile woman of forty, ran away from the two men in the hallway, back toward the rear of the house, toward her bedroom, where her husband lay with his freshened icebag, aching.

"Dan! Danny! There's someone in the house! Danny!" She turned on the light and locked the door, and her husband sat up, quickly, in confusion, for his head was throbbing, clouded.

"Danny!" she repeated, though he was sitting up now, as he reached over to the phone, his first response, as he started to dial 9-1-1, forgetting it had been unplugged. But there was a thud on the door, as of a body thrown against it, and it opened with a splintering of the jamb, and two men were there in the room, with guns drawn.

"Put it down," said the shorter man, who seemed to be in charge. So Dan Gruener replaced the unconnected handpiece in its cradle.

"OK, OK, whatever you say. Take what you want. We don't want any trouble. . . ."

Then the other man spoke: "They seen us, you know. That's it. They seen us." He looked over at the shorter man, who was silent and so seemed thoughtful, a little saddened even, with lowered eyes and pursing lips.

"Yeah. Yeah, I know." His voice sounded sad now, too.

"We got no choice."

"Wait a minute," said the shorter man. "Let me think." They watched him pause, the man, immobile, seated on the bed and the woman standing next to it. Then they saw the bigger man, the one who had seemed not to be in charge, point the long gun, lengthened by a silencer, at the person on the bed, at Daniel Gruener. "No," said the short man. "Wait!" He didn't, though, the tall man didn't. The woman saw him fire, saw her husband thrust backward on the bed. She wanted to go to her husband, to say something to the men, *Stop! Wait! What are you doing?* That was what she wanted to do, but she had never been in this type of situation before and really didn't know what one did, what exact words one used to make such men stop. Not that there was time anyway, a second or two, hardly more, for now she saw the gun turned, aimed at her. She wasn't frightened, just amazed. She never heard the sound of it, the shiny silenced pistol, for the bullet reached her forehead just before the dull thud of its firing had time to echo down into the hollow of her ear.

Seth took Sarah to a movie. But it didn't much matter where they went. He just wanted to be with her, his first and only love, that solemn, incandescent sort of love that children feel, barely out of adolescence, burning deep within them; burning painless at a time when love has never been fraught with pain, when the maturing child is unscarred yet, unaware of the course of love, of its outcome, of the grief, the hollowness of its end. She felt it too, the quickening of love. It shone in her eyes when she looked at him, visibly to him. Hypnotically.

He held her hand in the theater, then kissed her in the car afterward. Three months they had been together, three months of kisses, and still he couldn't get enough of them, though he wouldn't dream of anything more, being a polite boy from a good family, knowing what was proper and what was not. And she was an angel, this girl Sarah Gruener, who seemed to love him, incomprehensibly, for how could it happen that the exact person he loved so much, the absolutely perfect person, should somehow find it in her heart to love him back?

He put his arm around her in the car, and she leaned left, setting her thick black hair into the hollow of his shoulder. Roland had told him not to return before eleven. So he drove left-armed to a pizza place on Wisconsin Avenue, not far from the theater, ate a little, without hunger, then took her for a walk. They ran into some other kids from school and said hello, then turned back toward the car. *You know my folks aren't home*. She seemed a little sad, sad to be eating and walking when the house stood empty and the two of them could be alone in it. He couldn't tell her yet about the agents. Not yet. But he kissed her again in the car, looked at her, with just enough light coming in through the glass from a street lamp and a shop window to see her green eyes sweeping in their gentle pendular arcs across his face, to know that everything was all right, that whatever the reason there was for the pizza and the walk, she knew it to be good and sufficient and wise.

Then eleven came, and they headed back, straight out Wisconsin toward Bethesda. Seth saw it first, six blocks away, a dusty glow in the proximate sky ahead, just where the house should be. A policeman stopped them a hundred yards away, Sarah silent in the car, gripping his arm so tightly that he felt pain, though he would not move her hand away, smoke thick beyond the barricade, two trucks pumping queerly lit fountains into the volutes of flame.

"Oh my God," she said. "Oh my God!"

Seth thought about Agent Roland and hoped he wasn't hurt. What if the two men hadn't met him? Sarah might have been in the house. Thank God, thank God.

"What time were your folks supposed to get home?"

"Any time now. Oh my God! All Dad's papers and things, their pictures. . . ."

Seth took her to the Claymans' down the street, at the end of the block, friends of her parents. Then he went out, over near the house, to find out what he could from the firemen and the police. Sarah never saw him again. She called another house, the one her parents had gone to earlier, but the people there hadn't seen Dan and Harriet all night. Someone thought that they had called, Harriet had, to say they weren't coming, that Dan was sick, had a migraine or something; that he was in bed and they were staying home that evening.

Her aunt came in from Cleveland, Aunt Francie. Francine was her proper name, Harriet's sister, mid-forties, an elegant woman, aging nicely. She had been kind before and would be so after the event, but could not replace a parent. The police were kind too, in their way, not disturbing Sarah for two days, leaving her unquestioned, sheltering behind Aunt Francie in a darkened room, sobbing through the Valium. Then on Wednesday she emerged. Hollow-eyed, emotionless, she seemed, so that Francie worried for her. No, no more Valium, Sarah said. She had to know now what had happened, what the police had learned. Where was Seth? Why hadn't he called? How had the fire started? Were they sure her parents were in the house? How could they be sure?

A nice detective came over, kind and considerate, who looked at Francie and waited for her nod before divulging anything. Sarah seemed strong, strong enough anyway, so Francie gave her nod to it all. She'd have to find out sooner or later. Get it over with. At first the detective spoke, anticipating her questions. Yes, they were pretty sure the . . . that her parents were in the house. The dental records hadn't yet been verified, but . . . they found rings and . . . someone else had been inside that night, probably two men, and there was something else . . . gunfire, it seemed. . . . . The people in the house might have been shot. She wept now, Sarah did, despite herself. She had tried not to. He was a good man, the detective, dignified, well-dressed, soft-spoken, who knew when to proceed and when to leave a space for rest or thought. So he waited silently, letting Sarah have her cry, knowing it would stop, and when it did, he started up again.

But now he had to ask her some questions about Sunday: where had she been, when had she left home? Had there been any threats, anyone her parents had . . . her father had . . . talked about? People from the past? Was he a gambler?

She couldn't think of anything, anything at all. Her father was a car dealer. The detective knew that. Gruener Chevrolet. He'd bought a car there once. Then more questions, and more. She answered them all, all of them, and seemed to be finished now with crying. And then he asked her about Seth. Strange questions, about how he had gotten along with the Grueners, whether he had been in any trouble, about his friends, people he'd associated with. Francine had stopped nodding now, but it had gone much, much too far. Sarah had to be told.

So they both told her, Francie and the detective alternately. Seth might have been involved, the detective said. "No," said Sarah, "that can't be true," and her eyes welled again, so Francie leaned over and held her in her arms like a child. And the detective explained that they had found a paper with a floor plan of the house, in what looked like Seth's writing, and with his name and phone number printed on it. Found it in a car with a dead man in it, shot through the temple, found a gun in the car that might have been used in . . . well, used that night. Where was Seth, then? "He'll explain it. He can explain it," Sarah said. Then Francie held her close. "Seth's gone, honey," she said. "He's dead."

They found him in his car, a couple of blocks from where he lived. Shot in the head, right through the neatly trimmed brown hair, shot laterally, side to side, far enough back of the regular features of his face that he looked pretty even in death, executed with a bullet just the calibre of the long gun the other man had on him, the tall dead man with identification that said Martin Nesbitt. So there had to have been a third person involved. That much the police knew, though his location and identity, and any glimmer of a reason for his actions, remained for ten long years unanswered questions.

* * *

She went back to Cleveland with Francie, moved in with her and her husband, Mark. For a month she did nothing. It was summer still, and there was nothing much she had to do. She stayed in the room assigned to her, a pretty little bedroom vacated by her cousin Audrey, who'd gone off to Michigan State. Audrey came home once, two weeks after Sarah's arrival, to try her hand at rehabilitation, at counseling, with no more luck than Francie had, or Mark. Sarah just vegetated, mostly in her room, coming out to pick at food two or three times a day with the family, gazing at the television set with little interest and less comprehension, never leaving the house.

Francie gave her time, space, implicit love, making herself available but not intrusive, solicitous but not smothering. She was mourning too, Francie was, for a sister she had loved as much as anyone in her life. Having Sarah with her was a blessing. It de-emphasized her own grief, gave her an external focus, let her do this one more thing for Harriet, the single thing that Harriet would most have wanted, caring for her perfect child.

A rich child now she was, this new-made orphan. Half a million dollars, when everything was settled, the dealership sold, insurance money paid. Half a million, even after taxes. The Grueners' lawyer was the executor. He had the figures within a month, almost to the penny. Mark went over everything, all the details, being an accountant, the perfect liaison between Washington and Cleveland. They kept it in an investment account, all to be used later. Mark and Francie wouldn't take a penny. Sarah wouldn't discuss it, any of it, neither the money nor the investments. "Do what you want with it," she said. "Do whatever you want."

They registered her in high school, her senior year, afraid they would have a time getting her to go, as morose as she had been, as purposeless. On a Friday at the end of August, three days before the beginning of the fall semester, Francie went to Sarah's room to talk.

"Sarah? You up, honey?"

"Yeah, Francie, I'm awake." Sarah turned in the slender single bed, away from the far wall with its shuttered window, as Francie sat lightly on the minimal edge of mattress left vacant.

"Honey, we need to talk, you and me. I know you don't want to, but there's a lot you'll need to decide, and pretty soon. You know school starts on Monday. . . ."

"Yes, Francie." Her eyes were red and moist, no child's eyes, but wizened, prematurely aged, narrow and motionless as the eyes of a woman who had known the most profound pain, had wrestled with it too, in a month of casting out devils, of asking unanswerable questions asked anew by every generation of youth, pondered and pontificated over by every generation of elders, and solved only to the satisfaction of intellectual dilettantes and fools.

"Well, honey, do you think you want to go? . . . I mean . . . well, your un . . . uh, Mark and I are going to support whatever you want to do. Whatever. If you want to take some more time off, that's OK. Only you've got to decide soon. If you want to go, since this is a new school and all, it'd probably be better to start now at the beginning of the semester."

"Yeah, I know. I know. I *am* going. I am. I have to. I thought about it, and I *have* to go."

"Honey, you don't *have* to do anything. I don't want you to put yourself in a position where you're not comfortable...."

"No. No, Francie, I didn't mean that. I don't mean that I have to go to school.... Legally, I mean. Legally . . . I don't. People drop out all the time. I meant that I have to for my Mom and Dad's sake, that that's what they'd want. They'd want me to do something with my life. I'm all that's left of them, you know, the only thing really left, uh, biologically. I worked it out in my mind the past few weeks. I've got to do something with my life for them. I don't know what, exactly, yet. I'll figure it out later. But something.... I owe them that for all they did for me." Her eyes filled and spilled their overflow down her cheeks. And whether it was the tears, or the words, or just the full and final ripening of time, a month of denial, of suppression, whatever it was, a little dam burst in Francie too. A month, a great long month into her grief for a sister she had nurtured and grown with and held perpetually in her heart, she sobbed too, for the first time, uncontrollably, undistractedly. They clung to each other, there on the narrow bed that Audrey had slept in for eighteen years without a tragedy in her life, and cried for Sarah's tragedy, and for Francie's.

Sarah changed that day, changed not only from what she had become in the past month, but from what she had been earlier, in the innocence of her sorrowless youth. Gone were the moroseness and seclusion of recent weeks, so that Francie would no longer worry for her emotional state. But there was more. She seemed from then on purposeful. Not that she had been lax before as a student. That she had never been, always at the top of her class, Dan and Harriet's perfect child. But the new semester, in a strange new school in Cleveland, saw a remarkable young woman, aggressively brilliant, courteous, poised, mature. She was gifted in art, though she had never exploited the talent before. Now, with the encouragement of some interested faculty, her ability blossomed. Mark made a studio for her in the basement, with special lighting, counters, sinks, and abundant yards of space. One day, she asked him for a welding torch.

"You're kidding," he said.

"No, Mark. I really do need one. There's some sculpture I want to do. I can see it in my mind.... My mind's eye, I think they call it."

"Well, how would you know how to use it? I mean, it's not like an airbrush. Those things can be dangerous."

"Oh, Dad and I. . . . My dad used to take me to the dealership all the time. I used to hang out with the mechanics every weekend, and last summer, well, not this past summer, but the summer before, when I was fifteen, I practically lived over at the body shop. There was an old guy named Stan who did the best lead work anywhere. He showed me how to weld. Dad really got a kick out of it."

"You know, Francie and I both think you're carrying this academia a little too far. And the art. We love what you're doing and appreciate your talent, but you never seem to do anything else. You haven't been out on a date, or to a party. . . . That's not normal for . . . well, as pretty a girl as you are. . . ."

"No. No. Look, I'm just not interested in that now. . . . I've had enough of boys . . . enough of that one, anyway, to last a lifetime. This is what I want to do now. I don't know . . . the art, especially sculpture, it lets me . . . kind of . . . express things. I feel better when I'm working on something. I can't explain it, but it's helped me. Boys, though, I've had enough of that stuff. I've really had enough."

"Well, you're young. I guess you've got lots of time for that. Still, it wouldn't hurt you to get out a little, make some new friends. Boys can come later, when you feel better about it."

"Mark, I'll never feel better, not about that."

"Sure you will. People get over amazingly bad things, even what you've been through."

Sarah's face darkened. "Do they? I don't know. . . . Maybe I will. Right now I feel as if I never want to have another relationship like that again. . . . I don't know how to explain it. I opened myself up to him. He looked in my eyes, that night even. He. . . . I don't know . . . I don't even know how to tell you. I opened myself to him, my heart, I guess you'd say. There was a . . . an intimacy, sort of, like we were in each other's minds, and then, when he did that, you know, it was like the whole thing was a lie, a sickening lie."

"Well," said Mark, "sometimes people do things we can't understand, and really the reason we can't understand them is that there's something we don't know about the people. Maybe there's something you just don't know about Seth, or what he was told or thought he was doing, maybe. . . ."

"No. No, Mark, I know everything about him I ever want to know. Nothing more I could ever learn would make me accept what he did to me. To me and to my family. I trusted him, you know? All those things he said and did. How can I ever trust anyone again like that? How can I ever?"

"You will, in time. You'll see." He looked at this little niece of his, scarcely a niece, really; a niece-in-law, not even related by blood. What an extraordinary girl she was! Smart, frighteningly beautiful, talented, and suddenly mature, both intellectually and emotionally. *Does suffering do that?* he wondered. Maybe Audrey should have suffered more, his own Audrey, who was not what this young woman was. Suffering had done it, tragedy, but it hadn't stuck, hadn't broken her. There was anger in her, dark thoughts that had played themselves across her nascent woman's face when she spoke about the boy, the betrayal, but they dissipated in a moment, and she was animate again, eyes sparkling, with a quick and thrilling smile.

"You really want a torch?" Mark asked.

Two weeks later, the family cars were exiled to the driveway, and metal work, complex and quality sculpture—fine, admired things that found their way into a group of local Cleveland galleries—began emerging from the sole garage in the city now converted into the domain of a young orphaned sculptress working tirelessly late into the night, aspiring to unattainable perfection.

PART ONE

BAKERSVILLE, PA.
JULY 1996

CHAPTER 1

WHEN HE AWOKE, IT WAS SUMMER. THE LIGHT PROCLAIMED IT, FILING in with measured cadence through the window at his feet. July light it was, unmistakable. Chartreuse, the yellow of the sun, admixed with reflecting vegetation. The sound as well, and the scent, vegetal, fragrant. It was that he woke to.

Not that he had come to bed in any other season. No, the evening before had been summer, indisputably; warm and no less verdant. But he had slept long and fast, and what was odd now was not that it was summer, but that he had awakened to it, very late, in mid-morning, to full and ripening day, identifiable as to time of year. It was that he found exceptional on this last morning of his life.

He had slept profoundly, more soundly than in months, hungrily too, as if this one long night could fill the deep and hollow repository of sleep his disease had robbed him of. Slept on and on, long past his habitual time, awakening now from the enormous sleep languorously, unburdened of anything but the weight of his form upon the bed or the pulse of sense returning to his limbs. And it was only after minutes passed, when the liquidity of sleep had crystallized into fully sentient consciousness, only then that he realized, for the first time in months, that the signature of his disease, the great and remarkably accepted pain that had come to reside within him, had very nearly disappeared.

It wasn't gone completely. That would come later; a little later, nearer to the hour of his death. But so much had it abated, so diminished was it now, that he sensed his arms and legs again, stretched them and felt the pulse of life, unencumbered by pain, smelled the heated air, grass-scented, felt it upon his skin, the drifting air, the way he had before, before the pain, before the cancer cells had eaten at his spine, eroded the bone and left some rascally nerves exposed. A grumbling pain, it was, constant, gnawing, increasing in intensity over the months to an inferno, ameliorated only by its constancy, duration, and habitude.

It wasn't gone yet, but it was faint. And the other pain, less constant, the lancinating pain, jolting like a sharp poker when he stood or swiveled, an electric pain of little bone spicules broken free and meeting again with a clash when aroused by indelicate motion. That had left off too, as he found when he rolled a little to the left to fetch a book from the top of a bedside table. *Principles and Practice of Urology*, said the cover. He sat now, not painlessly, but not very uncomfortably either, sliding his legs over to the right of the bed onto the floor, resting the heavy book on his thighs. He took a pair of glasses from another table, this one to the right of the bed, and used them to scan the book, leafing through chapters filled with double-columned print, pictures, and diagrams, then to the index and back again through innumerable glossy pages. But there was nothing about diminution of pain. Nothing at all. So he set both book and glasses on the table at his side and raised himself on withered legs to a standing posture, slumping a little, but remarkably erect for a man who had been divested by disease of fully half his body mass. And it was then that he noticed the numbness down in his sacrum and around into his buttocks, and then that he realized just what this lessening of pain would likely mean.

But that was all right too, not unexpected. Only the timing had been uncertain. Just the timing. And it was uncertain still. Not weeks or months any longer, but hours, minutes. Maybe a day. Uncertain still, but there was something yet to do, something incomplete. So he stepped across the hallway into his bathroom, washed a little, rinsed his mouth, emptied his leg bag of accumulated urine, then reconnected the catheter. There was a robe folded over the back of a chair in the bedroom, and he slipped it on, tying it in front, then went into the hall and over to the stairhead adjacent to the bedroom door.

The steps down were interminable. Breathless, he sat for a moment on a chair in the foyer. The clock beside the front door read nearly ten. Extraordinary that he had slept like that, nearly to the time of Carol's visit.

She would be there soon, noon at the latest. He would have to tell her something, give her some minimal but sufficient information. Nothing in detail, certainly, but enough to warn her, get her away with her family for a time. He could hardly control events after his death the way he had controlled them these thirty years and more. Up to the very end, too, with the final things he had to do today: those last notes, some cash in an envelope for Carol, instructions. She should be safe—they all should be—but nothing was ever absolutely certain. Life had taught him that. Carol, at least, would need to know a fact or two, a smattering. Enough to take precautions.

He unbarred the front door and labored through the living room, past the shelves of books on either side, breathless, pausing once to rest, leaning on the big cherry dinner table, then, half-upright, stumbling into the kitchen. There sat the pie, Carol's pie, atop the counter by the sink. She had baked it for him a couple of days before, his sole sustenance for those two days, sweet but not at all inviting to his dulled palate. Food was no longer food to him, but fuel: calories for warmth, strength.

He cut out a wedge and sat at the kitchen table to eat it, meticulously, crumblessly, without hunger, or with the same sort of hunger that a stove might feel for the coal that feeds its belly on a winter day. He took some orange juice, too, from the refrigerator, and administered it to his mouth and throat the way he had fed himself the pie. Thirst, thankfully, had not departed wholesale with the rest. In a minute, the sensation of pressure below his throat diminished to a kind of vague fullness, perfectly tolerable. He rinsed the plate and glass and set the plate sideways and the glass upended to drain and dry, not really expecting to use them again, but set them so, meticulously, the way he had done things always, the way things were to be done.

In a minute or two, the food weighed more lightly upon him, though the juice came up sour in his throat. He stepped back into the living room, feeling stronger now for the pie or the juice or the moment of rest while he consumed them, sat down at the computer desk, and wrote out his final notes.

First came the letter to Carol. There was a bundle of crisp hundreds in the top drawer of his roll-top in the opposite corner of the room and he stuffed them into an envelope with her letter, sealing it, writing her name on the surface. Then he printed out the other things: the directive about his estate, a duplicate of the note and diskette for David, another card with Lesser's name and number. The packet to David was the crucial link and could not be left to chance without a back-up.

He set both envelopes on the desk, David's in the center of the opened roll-top's surface and Carol's stacked above it. She would spot them both there, take hers along and see that the other, the precautionary copy for David, got dropped into the box outside, or, better yet, into a proper mail bin where nothing could delay it; nothing, that is, beyond some postal strike or earthquake. So everything would be complete. Barring some bizarre occurrence, events would proceed as anticipated, even . . . well, human emotions apart, he had done about as well as he'd hoped he might, given the tumor and his incapacitation. The lines were written and the players in the wings. He was pretty much done with the whole of it. Time now for an hour or two of rest.

Carol came at twelve, a little late for her, but better so, for he had slept again, fatigued by exertion, lulled by painlessness. He awoke to that this time, to the utter absence of pain, but with increased numbness, extending down his right leg now. It was a palpable numbness, not uncomfortable, not really alarming, no more alarming than death itself, which was proximate, defined, and, in truth, not entirely unwelcome.

It was nearly noon, silent outside around the old farmhouse. He lay just a minute or two awake before he heard faint gravel sounds out at the far end of the access road, so distant and inconspicuous that he was sure the sound itself had not roused him from sleep. Indistinct at first, it might not have been *her* car or *his* road, but it was, and he distinguished the rumble of Carol's vehicle growing louder and louder still as she traversed the half mile to his property. She let herself in with a key he had given her a month before to the simple lock on the doorknob. There were other locks too, a deadbolt and the bar he had removed, but he had acquired the habit of opening them in advance these past weeks, when Carol's visit was due. She called first from the bottom of the stairs, then came up.

"Well, Charles, how are things today?" That was her customary greeting, familiar and comfortable. Two days a week another woman would come, and not always the same woman, but a series of less familiar and less comfortable voices and faces. On those days he would have to open the door, for only Carol had a key.

"Good, Carol. Pretty good today . . . considering. . . ." He was lying on his right side. Usually he lay perfectly flat, to ease the pain, but today he faced her, body and head alike, as she entered the room.

"Considering what, Charlie?"

"How are *you* today, Carol?"

"Just fine, Charlie, just fine." That would end her questions for a time. She was busy now, preoccupied with his pulse and blood pressure, both acceptably abnormal, then his temperature, routine, meaningless, a ritual. He undid his pajama bottoms, without embarrassment, for the cancer and the surgeons had neutered him months before. He must have smelled of urine, he or the room itself, for Carol wrinkled her nose, turning aside involuntarily. Nurses were supposed to be used to that. He was, his nose at least, used to the acrid odor. The indignity of it had been the problem for a while. No matter. Carol went about her business anyway, unplugging the catheter from his leg bag, draining both and irrigating them, letting the clots run into a basin. Then she walked out, and he heard her in the bathroom, pouring and flushing the fluids away. When she returned, the urine scent was stronger. He could sense it himself, not only from Carol's face, the look in her eyes, but in his own nose as well now, stimulated even in its habituation by the power of the scent. "You're wet," she said, and he was. He looked down and saw it, refluxed urine from the leg bag, pink-tinged, running into the fabric around him, beneath him. Well, this was the sort of work she did, what she was paid for. He'd taken care of her, too. The money was in the envelope.

First he'd have to tell her something, though. Not the whole story, certainly. But enough. Enough.

The room stank of urine, but that was nothing new to her. She had smelled her share of urine. Feces too, and worse. Gangrene a couple times. That was as bad as it got, gangrene. But that was always in the hospital. Home Health wasn't nearly as bad. Still, you saw a lot. People kept at home to die, draining wounds, tumors so exuberant in their growth that they came right through the skin. So this was nothing. After fifteen years of nursing, a little urine on her fingers wasn't going to hurt her.

What really got to her was the people, watching them suffer, watching them deteriorate. Not everyone. Not the women, for some reason. Women never fussed much about pain, or even death, just suffered and died passively, without expression. With men it was different. You could see their agony, even the strong ones who bore the pain in silence. This man for sure, just like her father, dying miserably, without complaint, but miserably. He got to her. He must have noticed it in her face, the shock of seeing him like that, wet through like an infant.

"Can I help you change, Charlie?" No, he would say. She knew that. He wouldn't want her help. Never had, from the first. Three months before, the doctor had insisted. A nurse would have to administer the medication. Dr. Arthurs had told him that, right there, with her in the room. "That's what the nurse is here for," Arthurs said, "to give the drugs." Supervise them, anyway, he said, though old Charles really could have done it himself. He knew enough from all those medical books he read.

"No. No need. I was going to get up anyway. Wash and shave and put something else on."

"Are you OK? You seem . . . different . . . different today."

"Yes, yes . . . different. I *feel* different." Medication, she thought, medication. What has he taken? She turned toward the bureau midway through his answer, rattling the little plastic vials spread out upon its surface as she took her inventory. When she added up all the pills, she found he hadn't taken anything, anything at all.

"*How*, different?" she asked, turning again toward him. "*How* do you feel?"

"Just different . . . Better in a way. The pain's better. Almost gone, really. I noticed it this morning." He rolled over on his side again, turning freely. He couldn't do that before . . . yesterday even. The last time he had moved that way was two, maybe three months before, and even then. . . .

"The pain's better?"

"Yes. Yes. Very little pain. I don't feel it at all right now. . . . Whatever that means. . . . I feel . . . I feel . . . uh, pretty good right now." *Pretty good?* . . . "You're off the next two days, aren't you?"

"Yes, umm. . . . Well, I'm supposed to be . . . but I could come by . . .
that is, if you need something. . . . You're not having any pain . . . at all?"
He raised his hand palm out and moved it slightly, side to side, then
propped himself on an elbow, weakly, looking at her, his gaze steady,
remarkably alert. His hair was full, but short, peppery, black and gray.
Probably smart not to have gone through chemotherapy. He was a handsome man, even now, thinned to a stick figure drawn with a fine-tipped
pen. Baldness would have been inappropriate on him. Neat and militarily
groomed, he had a barber come in every three weeks or so. Someone told
her he gave the guy a hundred dollars.

"Look, Carol, you've been very kind, and I appreciate it more than
you know. What you can do for me is have a pleasant weekend off, stay
away from here, and hug your kids and kiss your husband. Maybe get
away for a while. I left an envelope on the desk downstairs for you. Please
don't open it until later. Tomorrow, perhaps. You'll know when."

"I think we should call the doctor."

"For what purpose? What's he going to do, restore my health? . . .
Listen to me. In the envelope, along with a note asking that you do something for me, is a sum of money. I'd like you to get away from here for a
little while, with your family. Use some of the money for that purpose. Go
somewhere, even to Pittsburgh or Cleveland. Just go away for a week or
so, after my . . . after you open the envelope."

"Oh, I'm all right, Charles. I don't need. . . ."

"No, no, you misunderstand me. How can I explain this to you? . . .
I think you'd be safer to go away for a few days. . . . You needn't know
why."

Her thoughts came out in words, unaltered by cognition: "Safer! . . .
What are you talking about? What do you mean, safer?" *What was he
talking about? What the hell was he talking about?*

The old man lay silent for a while, his emaciated body stark against
the great square bed it occupied. The muscles around his mouth moved,
but without sound, as though worked in mental disputation. In a moment
he spoke: "What difference does it make now?" he said.

"What? What difference? I want to know . . . what do you mean,
safer?"

"No, no, I didn't mean that . . . 'what difference' . . . I meant *to me, to me. . . .* What difference does it make *to me?* . . . Carol. . . . Listen, Carol, you've been very kind to me. You've done more than any nurse could be expected to do for any patient, the food, things you made me, cooked for me. You didn't have to do that. . . . I haven't always been appreciative . . . *seemed* appreciative. I have been, though. I have been. . . ." He raised a hand and wiped one eye, though whether the moisture there had any emotional basis, she couldn't tell. " I wouldn't want anything to happen to you . . . because of me."

What was he talking about? Was he crazy? "Charles, what do you mean by that? This isn't funny. . . . You know. . . ."

"No. Hear me out. I'll tell you . . . I'll tell you what I can. What does it matter now?" He paused for a moment. Carol neither moved nor spoke.

"What do you know about me, Carol?"

She knew nothing, nothing about his life, his family, where he came from. He'd never talked about himself, not one personal statement about himself in three months. Oh, they'd talked. How could you avoid it? Five visits a week, thirty, forty minutes each. They'd talked about her, about his disease, about the doctor. Certainly the doctor. Charles had wanted to know everything about him, what Dr. Arthurs was like to work with, who his friends were, those kinds of things. He seemed to want to know about her too, her husband, kids, her recipes for pies and cornbread and meatloaf. He'd looked at pictures of her family, remembered the names of the kids, Danielle and Sandy, what they were taking in school. Everything. He seemed to remember every fact she'd told him. But what did she know about him, about this decrepit old man?

"Well . . . not much. . . . Nothing, really."

"Good, good. That's right. No one does. Not a soul, not a single soul. I've lived out here for ten years, since . . . yes, ten years, it's been . . . and no one knows a thing about me. Nothing but my name and address. The mailman knows me, and the tax collector. That's about it. Maybe I can die that way too. That's what I'd like, to die in perfect anonymity. You understand? But I can't control that. . . . I won't be here to control it, though I've made arrangements for everything else that I could handle with my limited abilities. The tumor . . . I didn't plan on this . . . this weakness, but I've done my best. . . . I've arranged to be cremated, obliterated, but until that's done, I can't be sure. . . . I just can't be sure."

She came over now and sat softly on the foot of the mattress. He was as articulate as he had ever been, and his manner seemed perfectly open and frank. He had suddenly become personable, approachable in a wholly new way, but he said these crazy things, *crazy* things, so bizarre that now she thought that if it wasn't his medication, it might be the disease within him that spoke like this to her, the tumor in his body and maybe in his brain.

"Listen, Carol, I have great enemies, people who can do great harm, amazing harm, things you can't imagine. If they find that I died here, here in this town, in this house, that . . . that you took care of me, in the house, you might get involved somehow. It's unlikely, but possible, and you should know about it. While I lived . . . while I'm alive, I'm . . . I would be their only target. But when I'm gone . . . when I'm gone, I can't know for certain what might happen, if my identity becomes known to these people . . . who I am, where I am. So you have to go away for a while . . . until you can be reasonably certain that no one has found out . . . for a week or two anyway, until you've seen that nothing has happened. You'll know, you'll know. . . . I can't have it on my conscience that you weren't told. The others I've made provision for."

It is *the tumor*, she thought, *cerebral edema, metastasis, some chemical in his body from the cancer. . . . The man's delusional from it.* This was crazy. What could she say to him? Nothing . . . nothing. But he was looking at her. She could sense it, see it in the corner of her eye. Awaiting some sign of comprehension, of belief, gazing steadily, with eyes as wide as eyes so shrunken could be opened wide.

"Charles," she said, feeling her way tentatively, "I'll try to do as you want. I'll try. . . . I'll have to check with my husband first. . . .You know, to see if he can get off for a few days. I don't know for sure. . . . But you seem worse to me today, weaker . . . you know . . . and I think maybe we should call the doctor. . . ."

He raised his hand and extended it toward her, down at the foot of the mattress. "Come here, Carol. Here, closer to me." She stood and moved to the bedside, level with the shrunken hand, a big hand, but atrophied, withered, yellow skin on a thick frame of bone absent any tissue between. The fingers opened to her, asking to be grasped, shaking noticeably from weakness. She took them, felt them to be cool, dry. Light too, the hand and arm, skin on bone with an exiguous thread of muscle between. Weightless, it felt, in her palm. She thought of an airplane wing, aluminum framed and surfaced, its outer tips trembling in flight, but durable, astonishingly strong.

"Look at me, Carol." She made herself do it, meeting his deep green eyes. "I'm going to ask you something, and you've got to listen very carefully; very, very carefully. . . . You may believe or disbelieve what I've said, and you may do what you wish with the information I've given you. That is, you may stay here in Bakersville or go somewhere else for a time after my death, as I would like you to do. But you can't tell anyone about it . . . about what I have told you. Not anyone, you understand? Not your husband or your children or anyone else. You have got do this for me. What I told you was for your protection. I took some risk in telling you . . . some risk to the plans I've made. You may do great damage in telling anyone. And it's important that you not call the doctor. . . . I've made arrangements to get in touch with him. You've got to give me your word that you won't call him or say anything. You must do this for me."

"Charles, I. . . ."

"You've got to do this for me. I've got to have your word." He squeezed her hand, more firmly than she expected. "I've got to have your word." He was peering at her and grasping her hand tightly, though his grasp was not uncomfortable to her. She thought of a surgical instrument, titanium, light but not malleable, capable of both firmness and delicacy, then the airplane wing again. She looked at his green eyes and the hair above, short, metallic in its silvery shading, and something made her say OK, OK, she'd do as he wished, not say anything, not call the doctor.

The old man fell silent now, but yet kept hold of her hand, and she would not be first to disengage. She looked about the room, with its dresser, little tables, one window at the foot of the bed and another to its far side, so much like the room at home where her father had died, twelve years before, just as withered as this old man, but younger, fifty-four, worn down by a life of laboring in strip mines and then a final bout with lymphoma. He'd called her over, too, that final day, not to the left side of the bed, like the old man, but to her right, There was something on the left side, a chair she thought it was, a big old lounge chair from the living room they'd dragged in so her dad could sit up a while when he had the strength. "C'mere, baby girl," he'd said, and she'd gone over, and he'd given her his hand the way the old man had just a minute ago, but it was twelve years ago for her dad. "Come down here." And she'd bent down to hear him, for his voice was weak. "Take care of Mom for me. Take care of Mom. Promise me." "Yes, Daddy. I promise." Then she'd said goodbye, and Homer Atherton, who'd been her dad for twenty-seven years, a good dad and a good husband too, died the next day, while she was at work, with her own second baby girl quickening in her womb. He died on the old bed she'd lain in as a child on winter mornings, between the two of them, Homer and Katie, and before that in Katie's belly, in the old room, not as elegant as this one, nor as desolate.

The old man dropped his hand and she felt the moisture on her face, so she turned away without another word, without a look, out through the door, never turning back, lest he see her eyes and think the wetness was for him, though maybe some of it was, some part of the fluid on her cheeks, for her father had been dead so many years. Then down the stairs, wet-faced and trembling, until she found a straightback chair in the living room and sat down at its forward edge, composing herself. And after a minute or two, having come to the end of her momentary sadness, for she was a strong woman, she rose and stepped to the open roll-top desk in the living room, where her envelope would be, set down her nurse's bag and patient chart, smoothed her hair, wiped her eyes, cleared her throat, and looked down at the desk. There, at its geometric center, precisely placed with edges parallel to those of the oak top, lay two medium-size manila envelopes, placed one upon the other. Hers was on top, printed by hand in block letters at its geometric center, FOR CAROL BOWDISH, and signed below, tremblingly, in the old man's script, Chas. Keller. It hadn't been there yesterday, so must have been prepared by him that morning, or the night before. Amazing, just amazing, as weak as he was, up and down those stairs, putting money in an envelope for her to go away somewhere. This was the saddest part, to see him like this. People after him! Thank God her father had stayed lucid to the end. *Take care of Mom, take care of Mom.* She picked up her envelope, put it in her bag, then reached for the other one beneath. It was thicker than hers, heavier, stamped with postage, and addressed to David Arthurs, M.D.

The sound of running water came from upstairs, rushing and whistling in hidden pipes above her head. Carol put her bag, with the envelope addressed to her in its side pocket, next to the packet for the doctor, then walked past the desk and past another, smaller computer desk through a dining area and into the kitchen. There was an apple pie, about half eaten, open in its container on the counter beside the sink. She had brought it over two days before, baked it for the old man along with one for her family. She looked in the refrigerator, then in the empty trash receptacle beneath the sink: nothing altered from two days earlier, nothing eaten but the pie. No wrappers, no empty cans, just some paper and what seemed to be a broken computer disk. How long could he survive on pie? Flour, sugar, Crisco, maybe eight hundred calories, reason enough for his weakness, his delirium. She walked back out to the desk and picked up her things, then stepped over to the stairway.

"Charles. *Charlie*."

The water sound stopped; then the floor creaked above as he came out of the bathroom. "What is it, Carol?" His voice sounded peevish, annoyed, perhaps that she had not yet left. That was good, good, more like the man she had known.

"Have you been eating anything? Besides the pie? Anything else?"

"Yes, I have. I'm really doing fine. Thanks for your concern. Now go take care of your other customers." His shortness, gruffness, reassured her. He was up now, washing. Dying men didn't do that. Her father hadn't. Just stayed in bed and died, not rising to wash, or shave, on those last interminable days.

"OK, OK." *What about the letter?* she thought. "Do you want this other letter mailed? The one to Dr. Arthurs?" She heard him move around on the flexing wood above, over to the stairhead. There, she could hear him clearly, despite the weakness of his voice, though she could not see him, for the stairway made a right turn six feet up at a yard-wide landing.

"Yes, I forgot. . . . Jesus, I forgot! OK, put it in the box outside. They'll pick it up. Or mail it, if you have a chance, if you're going near a mail box. Thanks. It's important. Don't lose it." He was composed again, stoical, a composure and stoicism in the presence of disease and pain that Carol had always found remarkable in him. Not the end, not yet. She would stop back tomorrow, her day off . . . bring him a hot meal. . . . No, no, not tomorrow. Tomorrow she had to take Danielle to the mall. . . . Sunday, then, Sunday for sure.

She called up again, goodbye, see you later. He didn't respond. Never did; never had. Not in three months of goodbyes. So she stepped out, locked the door, dropped the envelope to the doctor into the box on the porch, and got in her car. "Take care of Mom," Dad had said, and she'd done it, just as she had promised. Promises were sacred, spoken bonds of trust never to be transgressed. "Don't call," Charles had ordered, and she'd promised she wouldn't. . . . *Take care of Mom, take care of Mom.* . . .*Yes, Daddy, I will.* . . . *Don't tell anyone* . . . no, no. . . . A proper nurse would phone the doctor. Mr. Keller was different today, irrational, though free of pain. A proper nurse would report that. But it would be a betrayal, and to what possible good? He seemed all right now anyway, up and about. . . . He really seemed all right.

She'd bring him something good to eat on Sunday.

His legs felt a little stronger. The pie perhaps. Shaving had helped too, diminishing the gauntness of his face. He took off the robe, which would not do, and dressed himself in a fresh pair of pressed khaki slacks and a clean blue cotton shirt, long-sleeved, despite the warmth of the bedroom, buttoning it closed at the collar.

The stairs were difficult, but less so than earlier. He set the heavy bar back into the slots at the top of the door. He would rest better with it in place. Getting in would be a problem, but not his problem. Someone would figure it out.

He pushed aside the blinds and looked through the window at the wooden tray on the porch, the ersatz mailbox they had fashioned to save him the trip down his driveway. The envelope to Arthurs was in it, its yellow-ochre paper showing blatantly against the dark wood. Better if Carol had taken it. And she would have too, if he'd told her specifically. Not that it mattered all that much. Tomorrow was soon enough. The guy would fetch it, the mail man: what's-his-name . . . Dick. By eleven or so, he'd have it in his truck. Old Dick been taken care of too, three hundred-dollar bills a couple of weeks ago, slipped gratefully in a handshake. A good man, Dick, mail with a smile. David would have his packet Monday, Tuesday at the latest. He'd probably have the other one by then too, but duplication meant security. No point in taking a chance.

He closed the blinds fully, turning inward, toward the roll-top desk, bare now, its surface and its top drawer too, emptied of the hundred-dollar bills. His brow was cold, moist; he felt faint and very weak, too weak for much more activity, too weak for apple pie to be of much therapeutic benefit. So he labored back up the stairs, one step at a time, breathing heavily, scarcely reaching his bedroom.

He sat down on the soiled bed to rest, and rest invigorated him a little, so that after ten minutes or so he was able to stand again, less incapacitated. He managed to make the bed, neat and precise, with clean linen, forcing his impotent limbs to accomplish the work, for he would not be seen in disarray, not found in disarray. That done, he took up the vial of medication labeled "morphine sulphate, 10 mg,", stepped into the bathroom and filled a glass of water from the sink to wash the tablets down, then swallowed them all in groups of six and eight until he had emptied the plastic bottle completely, dropping it into a wastebasket. He stepped back into his room and lay back down on the fluffed pillow and crisply folded top sheet, feeling full, he assumed, from the water he had ingested, for the pills could not have taken up very much room. He willed them to stay down, willed the water to conduct them to an absorptive surface where they could take effect quickly, insensibly. He felt nothing yet, just the fullness, not a knot or quiver more.

The pain he had borne for a year had ceased entirely. Both varieties — the dull, intolerable pain and the sharp intermittent one — both gone, absolutely gone, replaced by an insistent numbness. But it was a sensory numbness, peripheral, localized to the bottom of his body, below the hips. His mind was lucid, unclouded by pain for the first time in months.

He thought of Pari. He always did, but now, in the absence of pain, she came exact into his mind's eye: Pari, her long black hair on the pillow beside him, her round eyes, black-brown, deep as the night. How he had missed her! But the pain had made him forget even that, even the last days of *her* disease and pain and their good-bye. "We will be together again," he had told her, not really believing it, never believing that absurdity, even as a child. *"Har che pich amad, khosh amad,"* she used to say: What will be, will be. She hadn't lived to see their son killed, or to know of his own black revenge for the killing. While she lived they were happy, affluent as royalty in Teheran, six servants in the big flat-roofed stone house, chauffeured about in their long black Mercedes beneath the sycamore trees. Nothing left of that, of the old life, nothing of his blood and Pari's except Sarah, who had her beauty, maybe her goodness too, for all he knew. He had done what he could for her. David would have to do the rest. David: He was perfect for it, hand picked, much like himself, *just* like himself, but more moral, or idealistic, or foolish. A good man, though who was he to judge? He of all people!

The room was light now, pure white from the midday sun, unaltered by angulation or greenery. He felt a sense of well-being, euphoria almost, his chest warm, no longer weighted by the fluid and morphine, but hollow, glowing. The ceiling was alive with light, dappled by it, the light issuing diffusely through the window, selectively reflected by the textured paper on the walls, the oak furniture, elegant, tasteful, the mirror to his right, above the dresser, the closet at his feet. *Sarah*, he thought, *she's all that's left of us*. He had done what he could, all that he could. David would have to do the rest. Just follow the directions. Just follow them, and now they were in duplicate, so what could go wrong? He'd seen to everything. The papers in the basement and the money in the closet. Too bad about the closet. David would balk at that. He'd meant to clean it out. Yes, most of it, anyway. The jar, the damned jar; he'd forgotten about it until now. What use was it? He had meant to get rid of it, but now he couldn't move, simply couldn't move. Well, David was a clever enough fellow. He'd figure it out. Everything would be quite all right. David would see to it.

He felt something beneath his hand, on the blanket beside him. It was an envelope, ochre manila, containing the final note he had written a little while before, after sealing the other two for . . . for Carol and . . . yes, for David. Of course, the extra one for David, though it was redundant.

He took up this other envelope from the surface of the blanket and set it on his belly, flat beneath his resting hands, one atop the other. He felt wonderful, like a spirit borne weightless upon cottony clouds, the bed itself an insubstantial vapor, the room about him suffused with fragrant air, grassy with riffs of floral scent, like the ripples of chocolate fudge in vanilla. Floating, ethereal, he drew in a long, sweet, perfumed breath and closed his eyes in sleep.

"I can't sleep."

"When?" he asked.

"When? I can't sleep, I said." Mrs. Daly looked pale and fevered.

"Yes, when? At night or in the morning? Do you have trouble falling asleep or do you wake up early and can't go back to sleep?"

"I sleep two hours or three and then wake up and can't sleep any more. I need a pill or something." She looked up at him for a moment, then away again. "I just don't feel right."

"OK, I'm going to give you something." David looked her over carefully, examining. Her hair was uncombed, her clothes haphazard. Stella's eyes were glazed, sleepless perhaps, but there was something else, an agitation. "Has your son been up? What's his name?"

"Patrick." Stella Daly stared persistently at the floor and its covering of flat gray and brown figured carpet.

"Has he been here lately to visit?"

"Two weeks ago, or three."

David set the chart down and sat beside her on the examining table, turning toward her.

"Which is it, two weeks or three?"

"Maybe a month," said Stella.

"Leave his number with Mae. I'm going to call him."

"Why? Don't bother him. He has his own life."

"Look, Stella. . . . Look, I spoke with him at the funeral. A full hour. He was pretty devastated. I don't think he wants to lose another parent just now."

"So I've got something bad then? Is that what you're saying?"

"Bad enough. You're depressed. That can be very bad. People die from depression, from just not caring whether they live or not. Major reactive depression we call it, and if you don't start getting out and getting your mind off the misery, you're going to make yourself really ill, physically ill, in a serious way. So I'm going to call Patrick and have him pick you up and take you down to his place so you can see your grandchildren and play with them and start getting on with your life. I'll give you some Elavil to take in the meantime, but it's only temporary."

"But I don't. . . ."

He stood and faced her, picking up the chart again.

"No argument. I'm the doctor. You want to argue, get a second opinion."

He wrote something on the chart, keeping a peripheral part of his vision on her. She relaxed perceptibly, her hyperextended foot and toes falling back into an attitude of absentminded passivity. Her legs hung freely there, within the line of sight to the left of the chart cradled in his forearm. She'd be all right. Just the fact that she had sought help meant she'd be all right.

"Reactive depression, major," he wrote. "Elavil, 50 mg. q.h.s. Ret. 2 wks."

"I'll see you in two weeks, unless you're still with Patrick. Leave his number with Mae. She'll give you the prescription when you give her the number."

He went out to the reception desk. Mae was on the phone. She turned to him, covering the mouthpiece.

"Get her son's number and make sure I call him today."

"Is she OK?" asked Mae. Mae had been with him for ten years; as had Stella, one of his first patients, in occasionally with the flu, and more persistently with her husband as he passed through the inevitably progressive stages of intractable coronary artery disease.

"Yeah," he said. "Just depressed.. Give her the scrip, but get the number first."

Mae smiled. "I can give you a ten-thirty," she said into the phone, though she continued to face him, her chair rotated away from the desk. David touched her shoulder.

"Hold on," she said, covering the phone again.

"Did Carol call?" he asked her.

"Carol Bowdish?"

"Yeah."

"No. No, just appointments. I haven't heard from her since, what, a couple of days ago."

"Good. Keller's OK, I guess. He can't last long though. I'm due to see him, when, Monday?"

"I think so. . . . Is he that bad?" Mae looked odd; expectant, perhaps.

"Yes. Any time now, I guess."

Mae turned away to her phone again. "Ten-thirty, Thursday, August . . ." She spoke in a low voice, having turned from him in his presence, unlike her, very unlike her, which made him wonder a bit, but just a bit, for he had so much on his mind now, what with the patients, Stella Daly and Charles Keller and all the others, and Cindy at home — that would have to be resolved—and he'd have to call Karen to see how she was and maybe find out what was new with Mom and Dad, though Karen might not have spoken to them lately either. It was four now, and he still had an office full of people to see, depression and diarrhea and heart disease. So it was no wonder if he occasionally forgot to return calls or check on patients. But he'd have to call Patrick Daly and, if he thought of it, maybe check on old Keller that evening or the next day. He couldn't last long now. He couldn't last long.

The old man died a little after four, neither dramatically nor convulsively, but in a simple exhalation, like an old watch with a broken stem winding down to silence. The evening passed and the night, all becalmed but for the faint and distant hiss of tires, or the growl of an exhaust out on the highway, and the sweeping of the trees, and the creaky measured sounds of crickets in the fields around. Three or four times during the night, some wandering animal would paw its way onto the shaven moat of lawn, first a deer, shortly after sunset, then a skunk or raccoon in the very depth of darkness. Each time, a sentry light would flash on, actuated by its motion detector, then blink off as the creature found its way again to sheltering foliage.

Perhaps some fauna had grown tolerant of the light, for one or two now lingered on the illuminated grass, where the old man had seen them many an evening, disturbing nothing but the floodlights. This night a raccoon family, mother and three cubs, loitered until nearly dawn, having perhaps perceived recent death, albeit unapproachable. Inside, the bedroom was silent, sealed against the minimal breeze. And when the morning came, nothing had been altered within it but the light, the yellow sunlight, and the July chartreuse of its reflection, now warming the house and the air outside, then progressively higher and hotter sun, heating the roof and the fields around, releasing fragrances of drying grass and hay and the musky odor of earth.

At eleven, Dick the mailman came and went, taking with him a freshly posted manila envelope addressed to David Arthurs, M.D. Then the hours passed quickly, noon, a full day now from Carol's visit, then two o'clock. Another hour lapsed, and another, and finally near five o'clock, the gravel road was stirred again and up drove Estelle Gallagher,

the visiting nurse *du jour*. She parked at the head of the driveway, adjacent to the porch, came up and knocked, waited, knocked again, waited,
then tried the bell, rattled the fixed knob, knocked more loudly, then
shouted and knocked again and waited. There was a cell phone in her car,
and she used it to dial the number listed on the patient chart. A phone rang
inside, its sharp, robotic monotone emanating distantly from an open
window somewhere upstairs, insistent like some intermittent alarm, ten
times, then twelve.

The sun had passed the hilltop now. The farmhouse was in shadow,
so quickly does the evening light recede in hilly land. Estelle moved back
to her car, then sat inside, agitated, hesitant. The old man's vehicles stood
to her left, off the driveway, outside a closed detached garage. She looked
back in the chart, at the entry, in Carol's hand, for Friday, the last nota-
tion, twenty-seven hours earlier. There was no way this man could have
left the house. No way. She started the car, took a cord from the center
console and plugged the phone into the lighter socket, then called the
home health service, knowing in advance that there would be no answer
on a Saturday after five, beyond the recorded message: "If this is an
emergency. . . ." She clicked the phone off, then on again, looked in her
directory and dialed the Bowdish residence. A child answered—Sandy,
she thought. No, Carol was not at home. Went to the mall with Danielle.

It was five-twenty now. So said Estelle's watch. The clock on the car
radio read five-thirty, but it was a little fast. She thought so, hoped so.
The shade had crept on now across the quondam farm's flat land, just
permitting a little glancing sun to dance among some treetops eastward
from the house. Some were aspen, and they caught a little wind descending from the hill and trembled as they're wont to do. The place looked
lonely, isolated. Estelle turned on the vent and touched some buttons,
raising the windows, locking the doors, then clicked a light on in the car,
not that it was dark, but the little yellow light felt better somehow. She
dialed her home.

Beth answered. "Honey, I'm going to be a little late tonight."

"Aw, Mom."

"Now Beth honey, open a bag of potato chips and put them in a bowl,
and get some of that chip dip that Dad likes from the fridge and set them
out for him before he gets home. You know how cross he gets when he's

hungry. And check to see that there's enough cold beer in there. If not, put some bottles in to get cold."

"When'll you get home?"

"Not too late. I have a little delay here and then two more calls to make. Maybe an hour late. Seven or so."

"Aw, Mom."

She clicked the phone off, then looked in her directory for Dr. Arthurs' number and dialed.

CHAPTER 2

CINDY WAS DRAPED OVER HER CUSTOMARY CHAIR, LEFT LEG ATOP ONE rolled leather arm, right shoulder against the other, in one of those characteristic postures of hers, unattainable by women less supple. It could not be said that she ever really *sat* in a chair, elegant Cindy, any more than a superb equestrian simply *sits* on a horse. But like a great rider, she decorated that which she occupied, becoming functionally, artistically linked with it, an embellishment, in the manner of a fine fabric gathered upon a surface, making that surface something greater than it had been before, more complete and more exquisite.

Pink, it would have to be, the fabric, imperatively pink. No other color would do. Delicate, floral would be the pattern, silk the material. The surface would not matter, being but a pedestal. Today it was a leather chair, but anything might serve as well to display her liquid form, and be graced by it. Like marble cladding on a brick wall or decoration on a cake, Cindy was the object of regard wherever she was, whatever she happened to be doing at the time. It was a property uniquely hers, accepted by the world as a portion of her being, neither good nor bad, but requisite. Unquestioned, by her as by others, and never really doubted as her due.

She was illuminated this afternoon by the dull light transmitted through a series of half-opened blinds. Otherwise kaleidoscopic glare from the television would have served, as it inevitably did at night, or when the sun was lower, toward evening, or when the blinds were closed. When she sat thus, whenever she sat thus, the television was on. She watched it perpetually, but often, as now, with that sort of rapt inattentiveness one might devote to the closest of friends, a pacifier of a friend whose companionship, whose mere presence in a room, gives far more pleasure than any entertainment his conversation might provide.

There was a drapelet of her, pink and silken, folded forward onto the floor; a delicate forearm, and then a hand fingering a remote, then another arm resting idly but elegantly, gracefully, on the top of the chairback. Later on, and not much later, when her loveliness of motion and of rest were gone, David would remember her thus, a drapery of a woman, trimmed and folded in all the proper places, as casual and impeccable as a springtime blossom, a perfect rose, though not without its pointed and inevitable thorn.

The telephone startled her a little, shattering the ambient audio drone. Not that calls were unexpected; they came in regularly once or twice an hour when David was on duty. But in that state of transport a half-watched video screen induces, it jarred her, awakened her really, from the tube's hypnotic glare, and from her thoughts too; mostly from her thoughts, black and troubled these past weeks. She set the remote down onto the carpet, lifted the phone from the top of a little end table beside her, and switched it on with that pink butterfly of a hand she used so delicately for phones and televisions and such.

"Hello. Arthurs'" For three months now she had answered as if that were her name too, Mrs. David Arthurs. It was a role that had fit her perfectly, quasi-spouse of an established doctor, the sort of man her friends would die for: well off if not rich, great looking, educated. Maybe a little older, her doctor, fifteen years or so, but no one would have known from appearances. They looked fantastic together, the cynosure of all eyes when anybody saw them—on those rare occasions, that is, when David took her out. Rare occasions bordering on nonexistent. Other men had loved to be seen with her. Alan had, certainly, flashing her about like a shiny red Ferrari. *Look at me, boys! Look who I'm with*. That achieved, he could hardly wait to drag her home and get her into bed.

David, though, he was a different story. Not neglectful, or even unaffectionate; no, that wasn't it exactly. Nothing you could really put your finger on. For he was unfailingly kind, thoughtful, a good lover—terrific,

really; maybe being a doctor and all. . . . But there was something special
missing, some deficiency in him. A detachment, perhaps; a kind of objectivity nowhere evident in her other men. That . . . that sort of hunger she
would see in their eyes, the desperation, the . . . the passion. David had
every desirable thing but that. Looks, brains, money, status; everything,
absolutely everything except that ravenous look in his eyes. And that single imperfection was enough to drive her mad.

She couldn't even make him angry. The worse she got, the more
bitchy, petulant, irrational, the kinder he became. She might have been
some hopeless psycho patient he was humoring prior to incarceration.
"That's O.K. I know you're not yourself today," he'd tell her. "C'mere,
I'll rub your back." Her *back*, for God's sake! How do you intimidate
some guy who doesn't even realize that you're upset? Worse than that, a
man who never gets upset himself, but keeps on smiling benignly through
even the most volcanic tantrums.

Then finally, a month before, it had all become too much. She'd had
her bellyful of bland detachment. No. . . . No, belly- and bladderful. Brain
too, and any other viscera they listed in those medical books he read at
night while she sat alone in front of the television. David Arthurs needed
a lesson—a shock really—and she was just the girl to give it. Shit, she was
Cindy Magnuson, for God's sake, the *objet d'art*. She knew how to handle men, the way to drive a guy to the perilous edge of his own personal
precipice. She'd done it often enough before. . . . With Alan, for example:
now there was a plaything, a puppydog of a lover, monotonously predictable, with that expression he got on his big round face, that narrow
stare and wet-mouthed gulp when she looked at him just the right way or
touched him in the proper place. Alan, yes . . . just the perfect ticket.

So she'd called him—three weeks ago, it was now—and up came
poor doe-eyed Alan to drag her back to Florida, to Miami, hot as hell in
June, so you could hardly go out, and she was stuck inside, where Alan
drove her absolutely up the wall with his doting. Really crazy, if not for
the big screen TV he'd bought for her last year when they were together.
She didn't let him touch her the whole three days. "Not till I'm sure what
I'm going to do," she whimpered, looking at him in the essential manner.
Alan went for anything she said; kind of pathetic in a way, making even
David's passivity look good by comparison. Three days of that had been

quite enough. Shit, she would have been in a loony bin in another day, even with the big screen. Anyway, David had suffered enough by that time, she figured. Three days without her: she knew what that did to a man; all she had to do was look at Alan to get the picture. Or look in the mirror, for that matter, or in the eyes of some guy she passed casually on the street, turning his head half way round to watch her until she turned a corner and passed beyond his line of sight.

Somehow, though, the plan with David hadn't worked out quite the way she'd thought. He wasn't desperate, rabid with jealousy, the way her men had always been before. Not even angry, really, or tearful, or even passionate on seeing her again. He charged her ticket on his credit card and picked her up in Pittsburgh, greeting her with a kiss on the cheek, as though she'd been away to see her folks in Virginia or on a shopping trip. It was maddening, incomprehensible. For all he knew she might have screwed Alan's brains out three days running. David never asked, and she was too angry to have told him the celibate truth if he had. But whatever connection there had been for them back at the beginning, back during the first few months, and even lately in a sporadic way in the weeks before she left, it was gone after her return.

Three weeks now, it had been. Even their meals together had grown uncomfortable. So when she answered "Hello, Arthurs," she did it with a note of unease. No longer was this her place too, but his alone. Both of them accepted that now, though he was far too polite and genuinely good-natured to say it. She was a visitor, present by his sufferance, some vagrant woman returned to the benevolence of her host. He had been kind before she left, and she found him no less kind after her return, but in a dramatically altered way. There was a sort of pity in it, pity for her! All she had to do was see herself in a reflection or photograph to see how ineffably absurd that was. Shit, he was lucky to have a woman like her, though he didn't seem to comprehend it. She had tried to get to him and failed. And it was precisely this failure of hers and that impassive kindness of his that rankled. Somehow she was going to find a way to set him straight.

The woman on the line seemed anxious, some nurse from Home Health. What did she care? They were always calling, nurses, patients, other doctors. She hated them all, hated talking to them, like some live-in secretary.

"Just a minute. I'll get him." She gathered herself up and headed for the kitchen, then through it to the utility room, opening the door to the garage. There lay David, flat on his back beneath the car, his outstretched legs in blackened denim protruding from a wheel well. Half his weekends had been passed that way, from the time their troubles began. Then, these last three weeks, ever since her trip to Florida, he rarely did anything his days off but work on the car or read, unless a patient called or he had to run up to the hospital for something.

"Dave . . . *David.* . . . It's the phone. For you. A nurse. . . . Home Health, she said." A tool dropped, echoing like a pitchfork on the concrete floor, as the legs moved, then the torso, scuttling out from beneath the car until David's long body first rose then slumped back into a sitting position, leaning against the propped-up fender, one knee bent, its begrimed skin visible through the tattered denim. David wiped his brow with the only patch of unsoiled flesh she could discern on his right forearm, thereby exchanging a little of the friable dirt from his head with some of the oily debris upon the arm.

"Goddamn coil spring." He smiled, but the smile looked synthetic to her, contrived. *Trying to be nice again*, she thought. Shit! What was the point? As he started to his feet, she saw his hands, black as a printer's, indelibly begrimed. Years ago, back in high school, some of the girls had liked that, a boy's blackened hands and fingernails, mechanic's hands; thought they were sexy. Losers, all of them, those cheerleader friends of hers; probably married to gas station attendants now, suckling kids on the back porch. That shit wasn't for her. Not now. Not even back then. What she'd wanted was money: a doctor, a millionaire. So here she was with what she'd always dreamed of, her doctor, this soulless son of a bitch, a grease monkey after all.

Better that he couldn't read that in her eyes, though he must have seen their focus, for he looked down now at his soiled hands and started to wipe them on his shirt, then apparently thought better of it. "OK, just a minute," he said. "I've gotta clean up a little first. . . . Tell her . . . tell her I'll get it in a minute." He stepped over toward the sink. "So," he asked, "what have you been doing?"

"Me? Watching TV. . . . It's not like there's a lot to do around here, you know."

"OK, OK, maybe we'll go out later. Go for dinner or something. That sound all right?"

"Whatever," she answered. He smiled again, or grimaced, but didn't say a word in reply.

She watched for a moment while he moved to the sink, looked at his profile and back. Tall and muscular, beautiful, a movie doctor, sexy, virile. Fiery and passionate too, to judge from appearances. Just her luck that appearances were wrong. There were a few strands of gray in his dark hair. Otherwise he might have passed for her age, twenty-five; hardly almost forty, though. No one who judged by looks alone would have guessed that.

"You feeling any better today?"

"I feel all right," she told him brusquely.

"Look, Cin. . . ."

"Yeah? You gonna take the phone or what?"

"OK, OK . . . uh . . . just let me clean up a little."

"I'll leave it inside." She turned and went back into the kitchen. "He'll get it in a minute," she told the nurse, who said nothing, put off maybe by her voice. As if she gave a shit. She set the phone on the countertop and went back into the den.

David turned on the water, using a paper towel to rotate the tap handles, testing the temperature with a little finger. He was immersed in grease, and not just any grease, but a blend of lubricants amalgamating all the way back to fifty-eight, when the old Impala had had its nether parts first lubricated. History it was, grease from the Eisenhower administration, grease spanning the course of his life from the age of one. A shame to wash it off, away down the drain for all eternity, like a memory lost forever by the world's collective consciousness. He reached out regretfully to a shelf beside the sink, popped open a plastic container, scooped out a dollop of viscid solvent and rubbed it into the skin of his hands and lower forearms, rinsed and dried, cleaning just enough to hold the phone and no more, then stepped through the utility room into the kitchen to take the call.

"Hello. . . . It's Dr. Arthurs." His voice was warm, open, something he made a point of—being unfailingly polite—even to the most inane callers, polite even at three o'clock that one memorable morning when a nurse had phoned to ask if she should give a sedative to a sleeping patient. "No, give it to him in the morning when he wakes up, so he doesn't have to eat the hospital's food," he had laughed. The nurse laughed too, out of embarrassment maybe, though he hadn't meant that with his teasing. There wasn't any reason to be rude to people, nurses in particular. These Home Health women earned their money, never knowing quite what they might encounter when they stepped through a patient's doorway. Damned if he would ever add a drop to their anxiety.

"Dr. Arthurs," said a woman's voice, "this is Estelle . . . Gallagher. . . . From Home Health?" Her voice rose in pitch to a question, seeking recognition.

"Yes, Estelle, how are you?" He would have known her voice if she hadn't told him. She was a nice person, Estelle, a good nurse. He knew her from the hospital, before she'd left for Home Health. He had taken care of her family, too, the kids and Bill. Now there was a case, old Bill, a real asshole. . . .

"I'm out here at Mr. Keller's place. . . . Charles Keller?" The inflection again.

"Uh-huh."

"I'm not getting any response. At the door, I mean. I knocked and rang the bell and didn't hear anything inside. And with as sick as he is, you know. . . . I called the house too. From my car phone. And I could hear the phone ringing inside, but no one . . . I mean, *he* didn't answer. . . ." She paused expectantly, the tactful nurse deferring both conclusion and instruction to the doctor. . . . So old Keller had died finally, alone in his secluded house; had died or was in the process of dying, mercifully, considering all the agony he'd endured. Poor, stoic old Charles. . . .

"Did you try the door, try to get in?"

"Yes. It's locked. And the front blinds are closed, so I can't see inside." Estelle had clearly done everything that could have been expected of her. She sounded eminently and appropriately agitated. He was too, a little. Not so much at the old man's death—it had been certain, imminent, for weeks now—but at the finality of it, and at his own sad inability to slow the progression of yet another intractable disease.

"All right, Estelle, I'll, uh . . . I'll call the sheriff, then come out myself." He looked at the kitchen clock. Five-ten. He could get there by five-thirty. "How's Bill?" he asked. *Take care of the living*: That's what he told himself whenever a patient of his had died; *take care of the living.* It helped him more than anything else in his inevitable and unequal contests with death. "He doing any better?"

"Oh, pretty much the same." He understood from the resignation in her voice, lingering over the last word, what that meant.

"I'll talk to him again," he offered. His heart went out to her. Half the nurses in town were married to men who were either abusive or alcoholic or both. Inscrutable women. . . .

"OK, then," said Estelle, "I'm going to do one more home visit and then come back here, so I'll see you in a bit."

He called the sheriff's department first, the number listed in the phone book. A deputy answered, Phil someone, a new man unfamiliar to him. Best to call the sheriff at home, Phil said, so he did. He'd known the last sheriff pretty well, but this was a different man, elected a couple of years earlier, Ronald Steele, a familiar name, someone he'd probably met at one time or another, though he couldn't remember exactly if or when. He had a gruff voice, not unpleasant though. "Yes, Doctor, what can I do for you?" David told him, gave him the directions to the old man's home. He was nice, the sheriff, deferential, said he'd send some men out right away.

He went back into the den and set the phone on the table next to Cindy, who straightened, disengaging herself from each chair arm. She looked up at him, unsmiling, but unalterably beautiful in any mode, a symphony of blond hair and pink skin, with just enough pastel blue of cut-off jeans and deeper-blue liquid dabs of eyes to set off the pink and gold. She had a halter top on, pink as well, just a shade more roseate than her skin, so she looked less bombastic than a symphony; rather more like a little sonata for two tonal devices, pink and yellow, yellow and pink, admixed and interwoven by the masterful hand of nature, casually splendid.

"I've got to go out for a while. An hour or two. Want me to get dinner?"

"So we're not going anywhere?"

"Uh . . . I don't know how long I'll be."

"Yeah, OK. . . . I don't care. . . . Whatever you say."

"How about Chinese?" Cindy never turned that down, however morose she was, whatever particular thing she happened to be morose about. That was her favorite food, fried rice and dumplings, same thing every time. The last dinner he had had at home with her—when was it, Monday night?— he'd picked up Chinese food, watched her eat it playfully, out of the cartons with a spoon, the way she'd done weeks before, months before, when they were getting along so well. God, it would be nice to have a pleasant evening together for a change, without tears and pouting. He needed that now, tonight of all times. . . . *Take care of the living.*

"I don't care. . . . Whatever," Cindy said, but he didn't hear the shrill-ness of her voice, thinking of the old man as he stood over her.

He had watched him shrivel, mummify, eaten alive by the tumor, uncomplaining though, even with all that pain, right up to the end. Three days before, he'd been out there. "David," the old man had said, "I . . . I'm grateful for everything you've done for me. . . ."

"O.K., then," he told Cindy, "I'm gonna go get washed up."

He passed down the hall and into the bedroom to change. There was grease under his nails, black and offensive-looking on the hands of a physician, though of impeccable provenance back to fifty-eight. He scrubbed his hands with a brush, getting some of the blackness out, then put on a clean pair of pants and dress shirt. Keller wouldn't care about his clothes, but this would be his last visit to the old man's home and it should be a respectful one. He'd been a decent old fellow and deserved that at least. He stepped to the closet for his shoes, just as the phone rang again. Cindy left it for him to answer, and he picked it up after the second tone.

It was the hospital, the emergency room: a Mrs. Chilcott, the clerk told him, complaining of chest pain. Yes, of course he knew her, Dora Chilcott, a sweet little lady with unearthly hair and a recurrently eruptive gall bladder. There was a new doctor in the emergency room, Dr. Thomas Greenwood. An appropriate name, that. David had met him: a recent graduate up from Pittsburgh, some cardiology fellow doing a little moon-lighting. Poor old Dora was in the midst of a cardiac evaluation, even Dora, with a heart every bit as potent as the fresh new water pump he'd bolted into the Chevy a month before. Like other inexperienced doctors, the putative cardiologist was out in search of some disease he might know how to treat. If the patient in question didn't happen to have that particular disease, well, so much the worse for her. Lucky for Dora that Dr. Greenwood was better versed in cardiology than neurosurgery. Otherwise she might have had her skull opened up by now.

It wasn't much of a choice: old Keller, dead or inevitably dying in the old farmhouse, or Dora, sweet and plump and frightened, and in pain. Double avoidance: a typical medical decision. Clearly, Dora needed him more. Not just to save her from the budding cardiologist, but to convince her, finally and definitively, to get that rattle of a gall bladder out. The old man would have to wait, death's obeisance to life. . . . *Take care of the living*. . . . OK, he told the ER, he'd be right over.

He went back to the den to get his keys and wallet. Cindy had shifted position, her opposite leg lay over the opposite chair arm, her foot on the little table touching the phone. There was a movie on the TV now, some film with teens and race cars, utterly devoid of meaningful content. No matter; the pretty pink and yellow head made no pretense of watching. He sat on the sofa just beyond the end table and put his hand on her perfect pink foot, fingering the lacquered nails. She looked teary now. Again. Dora would need to suffer for a few minutes more. He looked at his watch, retrieved from the top of the sofa table with his wallet and keys. Five-twenty.

"Well, Cin, what do you think? This isn't working. You're not happy here. It's hard for me to watch you like this. You know, I've tried, but neither one of us is getting much out of this . . . not lately. Neither one of us. Not for a while. . . . You've got to decide what you're going to do. I've got to know what you're going to do." His voice was serious but not sad. Not at all sad. He was past that.

She started playing with her hair, curling the long yellow strands around a finger, something she did when she was anxious, agitated. "I don't know how you feel about me. I don't . . . I don't really understand you. You don't. . . . You're different from. . . ." She paused, then seemed about to resume, but fell silent, playing with her hair.

"Look, no two people are identical. You can't compare me with other guys you've known . . . with Alan." She winced at the name. David looked at his watch again. Hell, Dora could wait a few more minutes. Maybe it would do her some good, convince her to let one of the surgeons yank that Goddamn gall bladder. Ten minutes more of that familiar pain and those incredibly normal cardiograms for a woman of her age and adiposity would hardly faze her. This was just as important anyway. Cindy was no less in misery than Dora.

"I shouldn't have come back," she said in a faint voice, barely audible.

"No? I . . . I'm not sure why you did."

"I thought . . . I thought . . . things might be . . . different. You know, that you, maybe, that you might have missed me and wanted to. . . ."

"Wait a minute." He was getting upset. He didn't want to do that, so he paused, collecting himself, letting the little bit of anger subside. "OK, I come home from the office and you're gone. No note. Clothes cleared out, without even a word. I have no idea what's going on. I was worried that maybe something had happened until I saw the clothes missing. Then I figured out pretty fast that you went back to your . . . your safe haven. You know, after three months—six months really—the least you could have done was leave me a note."

She looked him full in the eye, confrontational in her manner, defensive. "I was angry. You know I was angry. I sit around here all day by myself with no one to talk to. And then you come home and work for hours on that fucking car. . . . I just had to get away from here. . . . I had to get away."

"Look, I work, what, fifty-five, sixty hours a week. I just don't have the kind of time you need, apparently. This is what a doctor's life is like. So, O.K., I like to work on the car once in a while. . . ."

"Once in a while!"

"Yeah. That's all. Maybe three, four hours a week. . . ."

"Well, how come you never did it when I first moved in? You never even looked at it three months ago."

"You were nicer then, Cindy. You were fun then. *We* were fun then. . . . Look, I need the car now. It relaxes me. I have to carry around a couple hundred sick and dying people in my head all day, every day, and the car helps me forget them for an hour or two. It recharges the batteries. The rest of the time is yours. Or was. Now I don't know. I just don't know. I think you need more than I'm physically capable of giving."

"What is it you're capable of giving? Tell me that."

"Look, Cindy, I've tried to make things work, to be supportive. You say I don't spend time with you, but I do. You know I do. I try to be affectionate. . . ."

"You try? You need to try?"

"You know what I mean. . . . Look, nothing I do is any good. Since we've been together full time. . . . I don't know . . . things were better—a lot better—when you were working and commuting up here."

"Is that what you want me to do? Go back to work and see you on the weekend, or for a day or two during the week?"

"Do I want that? No. I like coming home to someone. To you, I guess, if things work out."

"You *guess*?"

"Yeah, I guess. . . . Look, why did you come back here anyway, if you were so miserable? Alan gave you plenty of attention, didn't he?" She glared at him, then softened, melting, an ice sculpture in a heated room. Raising a hand to her brow, she started to sob silently, shuddering with an almost indiscernible flutter of her arms and shoulders. That was something he couldn't abide: a woman's tears, much less those shuddering sobs. It tore him apart, fragmented decisions, resolutions, and a strong man's sovereign will.He went over to the chair and kneeled beside her, put his arms around her, in remembrance. She had been sweet once, and she was beautiful, ineffably beautiful, but just as capricious as the other women he had known, incomprehensible, capable of actions foreign to him, not only beyond his understanding, but qualitatively, culturally different from the manner in which he would act or think. So she had left him, walked out without a word, without a note. Someone else had done that to him once, long ago. Now it was Cindy, fleeing to Alan, as she had fled from Alan to him six months before. Poor good-natured Alan, a man she had never really loved, but used. Then, three days later, back here again, penitent. She was trembling now, weeping quietly, silent but for the sounds of her congested breathing. He felt the moisture of her tears on his neck. His firmness, his own reason, dissolved in her tears. *Take care of the living*, he thought, *the living. . . .*

"Listen, OK, let's try to work this out. I'm trying to understand your needs, your motivation. Try to understand mine. . . ." He straightened, kneeling higher, took her face in his hands, wiping her tears with his thumbs, cleaner now but still a little black around the cuticles and under the nails. "All I'm saying is, I'm willing to try again. I don't expect to own you or any other woman. You can do as you like with your life. I wanted you back for one reason: I enjoy being with you, or enjoyed it before all this took place. I don't care about Alan. You were with him before, and another weekend doesn't change things with us, as long as you don't change." She looked up, teary still, but slightly more composed. "OK?"

She nodded, seeming somewhat brighter. His watch said five thirty.

"Now I've got to go to the hospital to see that patient . . . uh, and then the other call . . . the guy the nurse called about. It shouldn't take long. Look, when I get back, we can talk some more. I'll get your fried rice, and we can watch a movie if you like. . . . Whatever you want to do. . . . If Alan calls again, tell him to fly in and I'll get an extra order of fried rice for him too. Pork or chicken, what do you think he likes? Shrimp maybe. Shrimp." He smiled to show that the sarcasm was benign, and it *was* benign. He had never been jealous in a relationship, never, even when he had cause to be. Once he had had abundant cause, yet he had seen the humor in even that, even at the time, and bore his former wife no malice. Perhaps he had never loved enough for passion to quench that objectivity that lies at the heart of humor, hence his perpetual good will. Cindy was evidently past that, though, past both humor and good will. She managed a mirthless smile, hollow-eyed, then looked away.

"I don't understand why you have to go *now*," she said. "This is more important than your patients. There's always some patient. . . . You're always gone, David. I'm always alone . . . always."

"I'm a doctor, Cin. You know that. You know what my life is like. You knew it when you moved up here. And you certainly knew it three weeks ago when you came back. We've been through all this before. It's something I can't change. Look, I'll be home maybe seven, maybe before. We can talk then. But I gotta go. I gotta go."

The side of her face was moist when he kissed it, and a little cold, for some of her tears had pooled there and evaporated. She felt the warmth of his cheek, then his lips, which touched farther back, almost at her ear, as she turned from his kiss. He must have felt the anger of her gesture, but it didn't stop him. He stood and headed for the door without another word. It was a joke to him, an amusement. She was too. Alan could have fucked her brains out those three days for all he cared. Cold son of a bitch; he hadn't even asked.

She wiped her face and stood up. The front door closed sharply, just as she stepped into the living room. From it, through the glass, she could see David get into the Buick, then drive off. She sat down on a blue sofa facing the window, sat properly, upright for once. The sun had dropped below the top of a tree across the street one house down, sending some sprays of light through the interstices between its leaves and branches, casting a series of dull green and yellow fingers of light into the room, signaling day's end. Despite its warmth, the evening reeked of finality, of looming darkness, of briefer days and summer's passing.

She rose and walked into the den, then switched off the TV. The phone rested where David had set it, on the little end table. She picked it up and dialed: zero-one-three-zero-five, then seven more numbers, familiar ones. An operator came on. Collect call, she said. Yes, for anyone who answers. There were two rings, electric clicks in the graphite speaker at her ear, then a man's voice. Yes, he'd accept.

"Alan," she said, "I made a big mistake in coming back here. I can't live like this. Come take me home."

"Want a ride home?" asked Edward, his head protruding beyond the glass door like some disembodied marble sculpture, Carrera marble, white and polished, for Edward abhorred the sun. She hadn't seen him approach, the motion of his passage through the outer office, the obligatory stop at Lisa's desk to say hello, so intent had she been on her catalogue.

"What?" she responded, surprised a little, for it was Saturday. Edward should have been at home. "What are you doing here? . . . . A ride? How come you're here on Saturday?"

"Me! What about you? I came to get my layouts. What, are you still working on the catalogue?"

She nodded.

"Look, I've got to go pick up Andrew. Out to Rockville, so I'll drop you at your place. You about done?" The head moved in, buttressed by the rest of him, the subjacent body, which then placed itself on the armless chair facing her desk.

"Uh, no," said Sarah. "No. . . . Five minutes, OK?"

"Sure." He leaned forward, inspecting the desk's surface. "That the catalogue?"

"Yeah. Three errors already. There'll be more. Look, they've got Boucher dying in 1970."

"Good for him. How old would he have been?"

"Two hundred and sixty-seven."

"That's a shitload of pudgy nudes."

They walked to the garage together, she with her briefcase, he with a large print folder, filled with full-scale floor plans, for he did a bit of interior design on weekends and evenings away from the Gallery. He took the Rock Creek Parkway, then a side road, coming out to Wisconsin at Chevy Chase.

"Any more calls?" he asked.

"No. . . . Nothing since that last incident. I don't think so, anyway. Sometimes it rings and there's no one on the line. Maybe it's nothing . . . unrelated. . . . Did you get in touch with the guy you know, the agent?"

"Left a message. Hopefully tonight. I'll call you when I hear, OK?"

"Sure," she said.

"You need to stop at Golden's? I'm going right by."

"Sure . . . if you've got the time."

The place was closed and locked, but Sidney Golden saw them from the counter and hurried over to open the door. "Well," he said to Sarah, "the reluctant artist!"

"Hi, Sid," she answered, smiling. "You know Edward..."

"Yeah, sure." He and Edward shook hands. "You got any more stuff done?"

"Why, did you sell the others already?" Sid frowned, looking comical when he frowned, pudgy and balding with his straight little Aryan nose, open-collar shirt and gold chain bearing that Hebrew letter that Sarah thought looked like a Greek *pi*. "Did I *sell*! Listen to her! Did I sell? Sarah, Honey, I got a waiting list for your stuff. You make more and we'll sell more. Wait, I'll get your check." He turned and went over to the counter, bringing back a sealed envelope.

"That's what I get for working with an affluent artist! I wouldn't wish it on you, but better if you knew what it was like to have to earn your living."

"Well, I *do*. I work anyway," she answered him. She knew what he meant, though. She didn't really have to work if she didn't want to, what with the trust fund and her inheritance. As for the sculptures, she couldn't turn out things she wasn't proud of, no matter how fast they sold or how much they brought in. "So everything is gone? The last of them are sold?"

"Sold, yes," said Sidney, "gone, no. The big one is sold but not yet shipped. It's going to a man in New York. He has another one of your pieces. Three more people would have bought it while it's sitting here over in the corner marked sold. You can't take some time and make me more like this? One a month, maybe?"

"I'll try, Sid, OK?" She stepped over to her sculpture. Six feet tall, bronze and stainless steel, semi-figurative, a bird-man, or an angel, with streamlined wings, an ornament of a head; it was pretty good, something she could scribe her name onto with satisfaction. It had taken her two months to fuse and shape the metal into something worthy of her parents' name, the Gruener patronymic.

"Oh, I almost forgot, some man was in asking about you." Sidney came up behind her, placing a gentle hand atop her shoulder. "He left his card. Said he wanted you to call him. Went to school with you or something, high school, I think. Alex . . . Alex something, nice looking young man.

"Alex Bender?" she asked.

"Yes, that's it, Bender. An old boyfriend?"

"Hardly. He asked me out once, in high school, but I didn't go."

"Well, he'd like you to call him. Maybe you should. He's a nice fellow, handsome, a lawyer I think, working for his father, lots of money. He was in with his parents. They wanted to buy your piece over there, even after they heard the price. He . . . he asked me if you were still as beautiful as when you were in school."

"I hope you told him he had the wrong person, then."

"No, Sarah, I told him the truth."

"Which is. . . ," said Edward, coming up on Sarah's right, taking her arm.

"Which is," smiled Sidney, his round face aglow with light transmitted through the plate glass window facing the recess of the gallery where he stood, "that whatever he remembers from his youth or imagines today can't possibly prepare him for the kind of beauty that Sarah Gruener now possesses. That's the truth." Sid went over to his counter and fetched the card. "Here you go," he said, handing it to Sarah. "Why don't you give him a call? Maybe a good you-know-what will inspire you to work a little more."

He let them out, and they headed for the car. Into a refuse can at the curb, Sarah tossed the business card Sid had given her. "Alexander Bender," it said, "Attorney at Law, Bender Trust Co."

"What are you doing that for?" asked Edward. "You know, it wouldn't hurt you to get out with someone for a change."

"No? I don't think so," she said. "There are two things I really don't want or need. A boyfriend is one, and memories of high school the other."

"That bad?" he asked, opening the car door for her.

"Worse," she said. Edward shrugged, started up the car, and edged onto Wisconsin, heading north to Bethesda and her home.

CHAPTER 3

I T WAS SIX WHEN THE DEPUTIES ARRIVED, IDLING UP THE FLATTENED GRAVEL to a little paved area adjacent to the porch. They drove a white Jeep Cherokee, new and clean, that looked like porcelain in the lengthening shade extending from the house, so bright and shining new that it might have seemed less a vehicle than some wheeled appliance, but for the lettering on its side, in silver figures on a yellow ground: Jackson County Sheriff's Department. Fresh from the dealership, a month old, courtesy of the fifty-thousand-odd county taxpayers, who had, at any rate, little else to spend their money on, what with the dearth of crime in this part of the state. Brian Clinger was behind the wheel, as far behind it as the seat permitted, for he was a big man, big in both height and mass. He stopped and waited in the vehicle while Phil climbed out and stepped up onto the porch, knocked, rang—an obligatory gesture—tried the door, then walked around to the back of the house, testing the door there too, returning quickly, shrugging impotently.

"What do you think, Phil?" the big man asked in his powerful voice through the open window of the Jeep. Phil shrugged again from the grass beside the porch.

"I'll check in," said Clinger; said it to himself more than to the other man, then dialed the sheriff's home.

"Locked up tight, Sheriff. No sign of life."

"Go ahead and break in," directed Sheriff Steele, two years in office, thus having served twelve fewer than his prodigious deputy. "I'll clear it with the judge."

So Clinger, who had done this sort of thing before, stepped out and around to the rear hatch, opened it, and took up a crowbar, black in color, but just as shiny and new as their immaculate vehicle. He tucked it under his arm and walked around the house, probing the windows, each of which was closed and locked. Then, having reached and having probed the last window of the house's north side, and having found it closed and locked as well, the two men heard the sounds of a car approaching on the gravel access road, whereupon they moved back around to the front of the house in ample time to watch Estelle Gallagher pull into the driveway.

Clinger recognized her. "That's the nurse," he told Phil, who might not otherwise have guessed it. After all, there might be other Kellers in the vicinity, kin to this man. For all he knew, this purposeful woman might well have been one. She parked behind the Jeep, got out, and walked over to them, Keller's chart in her hand; told them she'd called Dr. Arthurs; told them again what they already knew, what the sheriff had said, what their very presence bespoke, that something was very wrong inside the house, and they were the ones who would have to find out what it was. To do so, they would have to get inside.

The deputies smiled and nodded respectfully. Then Clinger, avoirdupois two hundred twenty pounds, mostly lean weight but with an incipient abdominal bulge at forty-two, took the crowbar in his massive hand and went around to the back door, which looked a little more negotiable. He started with the wood at the point of closure, broke the knob off with one end of the bar, then found the main lock, a deadbolt, still engaged. It was sturdy, steely-impervious, and not forceable even with the heavy iron bar. Pieces of the doorjamb splintered, but the door remained fast. Clinger pinched his nose between thumb and forefinger, a habitual gesture of his indicating reflection, then threw his shoulder onto the wood surface, again ineffectually, as if the door were metal or bore some inner reinforcement. Then Phil, who was thin and of moderate height, but wiry and strong, came around to help, two potent bodies straining, laboring, but nothing moved.

They returned to the front door. There was no forcing it, either. Then a window. They wrapped a towel around the crowbar to diffuse the spray of glass and struck a pane, one on the south side of the house, a few feet from the cars. It failed to break, so Clinger struck harder, now with the naked bar. The window flexed.

"What the hell *is* this?" said Phil, an exclamation rather than a question."Lexan," growled Clinger. "Or something stronger." He wiped his brow, wet from exertion, smoothed his hair, started to pinch his nose again, when Estelle called them out front again, to the porch.

She had watched the events without quite comprehending their ramifications. Locked houses were of little interest to her. What she did know was that she needed to get home, and soon. Forty minutes before, the sounds of a phone ringing, her call, unanswered, had traversed some open window, somewhere upstairs. The deputies peered up. There was one window partly hidden by the overhang above the porch. The younger man ran out along the drive, leveling his line of sight. He could make out an opening at the bottom, just above the sill. Phil rushed back. Clinger hoisted him up. He scrambled over the moderate pitch of the overhang, palms and knees on the asphalt shingles, reached the window, opened it wide, and put his left leg through, then his shoulder and head.

His left foot came down in an open hallway. The air was stuffy, thick. There was an odor: urine it was, strong but not oppressive. He sniffed for the scent of decay, not human decay, since he had never smelled that, but general fleshly corruption, the reek of carrion, familiar enough to him from hunting, from handling deer victimized by vehicles on county roads. No, there was nothing of that, just the urine scent. Perhaps the man was still alive. "Mr. Keller," Phil called out, rather softly, for he would announce his presence to the sick but not disturb inordinately the repose of the dead. The house was silent.

So Phil climbed all the way in through the narrow opening. The hall was half-lit, partly by the window he had just traversed, and partly by a sallow glow filtering in through an open doorway at the far end of the passage. He walked toward it, tentatively. "Hello," he called again, more quietly, more tentatively, "Sheriff's department. Everything OK?"

He reached the room from which the light emanated, entered it, and stepped to the bedside. The corpse was shrinking, desiccating, its neck muscles, thinned by disease, had begun to stiffen, retracting the death mask dorsally, toward the feet, as if to compensate for the impotence of gravity to act on the horizontal. The amber light had vanished with the sun's decline. Now the room was gray, gray like Keller's face, a scene drained of its color by the persistence of death. Phil breathed shallowly, afraid of the air itself, sweltering and pungent within the sealed chamber. He had never seen a dead man before, wasn't quite sure exactly what a deputy should do. He moved to the door, then yelled out toward the open window. "He's dead."

He walked back over to the bed. There was a spread turned down at the foot of the mattress, against the footboard. He lifted it from under the old man's socks and raised it, covering the body and the ashen face, a curtain shielding life from death. Then he backed out of the room and passed through the hall, over to the open window. Perhaps they hadn't heard him. He stuck his head out, unable to see them—Clinger and the woman, the nurse, there on the porch below the overhang—but conscious of their presence, and called again, "Brian. He's dead, Brian. Up here. In his bed."

"Come on down and open the door, Phil," said Clinger. "I'll take care of it."

Estelle looked at her watch. Six-thirty. An hour late now, and still one call to make. Her kids would be hungry soon, and Bill would have a whole six-pack down by the time she got home. She looked at her watch again, nervously, then at her car.

Upstairs, Phil moved from the window, passed the open door of the old man's room, and fumbled down the stairway beyond, down to the front door. It had a deadbolt with a key lock inside as well as out, but no key was visible near the entry. A small table stood adjacent, between the locked door and front windows. Phil picked up two sets of keys, vehicle keys, recognizably GM and Ford, corresponding to the car and truck outside. He opened a drawer but found no key to the deadbolt there either.

Clinger tapped on the door, an impatient staccato with the crowbar. "Open up, Phil," he yelled through the thick wood.

"There's no Goddamn key," responded Phil, his voice muffled by the sheer impenetrability of the door and wall and windows between them.

"Check the back door," said Clinger loudly into the crack of the jamb.

Phil was facing the door. He turned to his right, stepping into a large living room. The walls were covered by shelves filled with books, hundreds, maybe a thousand or more, most clothbound, professional-looking. He walked around a large roll-top desk, moved on into a dining area, fashionable, almost elegant, then pushed past a swinging door into the kitchen, neat and organized. A few scrubbed dishes sat on the counter next to an immaculate stainless sink, then a plastic rack with a single dish, positioned vertically and a single glass, upended. Beyond was a rear vestibule. Phil stepped into it and over to the door. From the inside it looked pristine, bore no evidence of the crowbar or the men's shoulders. The deadbolt was identical to the one out front, key-driven but keyless. Above the door there was a curious-looking valance, utterly out of place in so Spartan a utility entrance. Phil remembered seeing a similar valance on the front door, but there it had blended unnoticeably into the surrounding paper and drapery. He brushed aside the fabric and found a thick steel bar, quadrangular in shape and running across the upper door between retaining metal brackets secured to the door frame at either end. So that was why the lock had held!

Phil ran back to the front of the house. There were drawn blinds across the two contiguous windows looking out onto the porch. He pulled a cord and raised them. Clinger heard the movement and stepped to the window, looking in on Phil, who was sweating profusely now, not just from the apparent heat within the house, but from his activity too, and an anxiety legible in his countenance, the look of a caged animal, alone in a small enclosure, frantic with imprisonment and isolation.

Clinger raised a hand methodically and placed it flat upon the pane, a gesture of reassurance, of commonality. "Take it easy, Phil. Let's open the window." He spoke loudly, slowly, to be audible inside. The pane felt temperate, warmer than glass, palpably plastic. Phil looked at the top of the lower sash. There were two bolts with thick steel cylinders like those on old rifles he had used. He slid them open, then unclamped the standard simple lock at the center of the frame. The window lifted free.

But there was a bar too, a metal rod that ran horizontally across the window openings, above and below. Like the valance, it blended into the surrounding decoration, painted, as it was, the exact beige color of the blinds and walls and woodwork. Phil was trembling now. Clinger reached in through the narrow opening below the bar and clutched his arm.

"Listen, little buddy. Take it easy. No key?"

Phil pulled away from Clinger's grasp, then paused and felt himself drawn back to the thick arm, reassuring in its solidity. He touched it first, then held it in his two hands, exactly as a child would, then slid his fingers up to the enormous hand, clinging to it as to a lifeline. "I gotta get out of here, Brian. . . . There was a bar on the back door. . . . I can't go back upstairs. . . . I gotta get out. . . ."

Estelle stepped to the window. Phil had forgotten about her, or maybe thought she'd left. Seeing her there, he seemed to regain his composure, fashioned by an equal blend of embarrassment and bravura. It was six-forty now. Six-forty! And still another patient to see! This was bad, bad. . . . By the time she made it home, Bill would be out cold on the couch, and the kids. . . .

"Uh, Deputy?" she offered, in as sheepish and innocent a voice as she could summon. "What about the side window?"

Of course. Neither man had seen a bar there, just thick and impenetrable Lexan. Phil reached it at the very instant Clinger did. The bolts slid open, the window lifted, and Clinger pried his muscle, bone, and circumambient poundage through the opening into the house. Estelle, having made her contribution to the two several entries, drifted stealthily to her car, then made off down the gravel road. The old man was dead. Nothing more she could do here. Finish that last call and get home. There'd be hell to pay.

The deputies went up the stairs, Clinger following Phil, who had a second wind of courage, being not alone. They entered the old man's room. Clinger snapped on the light switch and went over to the corpse, lifting the cover from Keller's face. There was no question of life remaining, but he played out the exigencies of a death scene, in part for Phil's instruction, placing a ceremonious finger and thumb on the old man's neck, one over each silent carotid artery.

They looked around the room, among the medications on the bureau, on the bedside table, in drawers. No sign of a key. There was a closet at the foot of the bed; it too was locked.

"He locked the doors, Phil. He had to have the key on him." Clinger went back to the bed, pulled the cover back to below the dead man's hips. Keller was dressed in a blue cotton shirt and khaki pants. He ran his palms along the old man's legs. There was something on the left, a loose pocket that had fallen backward, over the hip. He reached in and found a ring with four keys.

"OK," he said to Phil, "go unlock the door."

Phil ran down and turned the deadbolt, then disengaged the steel bar from the brackets behind the valance. The door opened. Clinger heard the sounds and called down the stairway, telling Phil to go out to the Jeep and radio for an ambulance. The paramedics would have to declare Keller dead. It was nearly seven now. No sign of the doctor. Clinger looked around the room. Everything about this place was strange, but that locked closet at the foot of the bed looked singularly odd. Something about it. . . . There was a deadbolt on it too, not your normal closet door. It opened outward, into the room. That would make it less secure to forced entry, but the hinges looked unusual. He moved his fingers over them. Each pin had a cap welded onto its lower end. You'd have to cut them with a torch to get the door off.

He heard Phil come back inside. "They're on their way," he shouted up the stairs.

"Come back up here with those keys, little buddy. I want to see something."

Phil, glad for the company, sprang wirily up the stairs. Clinger took the keys. The first two didn't fit the closet deadbolt. The third slid in. The lock turned and the door swung open. There was abundant light in the room now, not filtered sunlight rendered amber by the lengthening day, nor the vegetal glow of morning sun reflected from a hillside, but two hundred watts of direct light, incandescent, nearly white. Charles Keller was bathed in it, supine in his blue cotton and khaki, undisputedly dead. The light poured over the room, filling every angle, every corner, so abundant that it overspilled the chamber, slanting out the open door to sprinkle the hall and glance from it too, gently flowing down the staircase. The brightness had played upon the locked closet, drawing Clinger's gaze, and now the open door had ushered light in there as well. The deputies looked in.

"Son of a bitch!" said Phil. "Son . . . of . . . a . . . *bitch!*"

"Phil," said Clinger, "go call the sheriff."

CHAPTER 4

DORA CHILCOTT LOOKED *IN EXTREMIS*. AT HER SIDE WAS SHARON, BIG-boned Sharon, quintessential ER nurse, hunched over her right arm, intent upon a blood pressure cuff. Otherwise Dora was alone, tubed and monitored, propped upon a gurney, the hospital gown strewn wide about her shoulders to accommodate a pasta plate of multicolored wires. She didn't see him at first through the glass of her showroom-windowed cubicle, attentive as she was to her nurse, or her pain, or the laborious task of breathing. There was a monitor above her, its luminous signal facing outward, displaying the electrical pattern of her heart, in linear traces and spikes of regular occurrence, rhythmic and monotonous.

"Do you know where her chart is . . . Chilcott?" he asked the secretary.

"Yes, sir, behind you, by the sink," said Stacy, smiling. She turned back to her paperwork.

He reached for the clipboard, sat down at the nurses' desk, and flipped through the records, stopping finally at the order sheet. A shadow appeared on the counter. "Do you see that shit? Do you believe this?" Sharon had come out of the treatment room and was looming over the desk, peering down at him.

"Did you see what that . . . that son of a bitch ordered?" she repeated, with further specificity. The "son of a bitch" had ordered a cardiac work-up for what was manifestly a recurrent gall bladder attack.

"Yeah, I'm looking at it now."

"This is bullshit!" said Sharon. "He's a cardiology fellow . . . not even that, but, like in the first month of his fellowship, and they get him up here to moonlight. It's bullshit, I tell you. If . . . I tell you, if I have anything to do with it, this son of a bitch, Dr. Greenwood, it is, Dr. Thomas Greenwood, is never coming back here. Not back here, if I have anything to say about it." Sharon would likely have much to say, and be well and attentively heard, being and having been for more than a dozen years the very bellwether of the emergency department.

"It's bullshit!"

"OK, OK," said David. "Where is he?"

"In the on-call room."

"Did you show him the chart?... The old chart."

Sharon gave him the *look*, open-mouthed, narrow-eyed, wrists on hips. "Do you really think I'm as stupid as your question is?" it said, in visage, posture, and silence. She was hardly a woman to be trifled with, five-ten, with arms and legs as thick as a man's, hands and forearms full-veined, like a surgeon's, furred too, though blonde, like her vast mane of hair, swinging athwart wide shoulders as she walked with that particular lumbering gait of hers that was her ambulatory trademark: one could spot her, moving uniquely, from a quarter mile away.

Her speech was just as notable; expressive and unambiguous, and funny when she wanted it to be. Three nights before, David had stopped in the ER.

"Hey, Doc," she had said, "you know how they practice safe sex on the farm?" Two patients flat on carts raised their heads to hear, for Sharon's humor was widely touted.

"OK, how?" he asked.

"They mark the sheep that kick."

Had Sharon been a sheep, she would have been marked, prominently and indelibly. It took a special kind of nurse like her to staff the ER. Every afternoon, like clockwork or the tides, she seemed to be there, through gunshot wounds, projectile vomiting, heart attacks, terminal malignancy, or a child in with the flu. She knew when to call, and whom, who was sick and who malingering, what to give and when to give it.

"Well?" she said. Dora was waiting.

"Let me just look at the strip." The strip was the cardiogram, likely normal, but *likely*, he knew, should never suffice to a doctor. Medicine is an inductive science. Just because the first five hundred clovers have three leaves, it doesn't necessarily follow that the five hundred and first won't have four. Five successive gall bladder attacks do not require that the next attack with similar symptoms cannot be caused by heart disease instead. Dora's strip was normal though.

"You want to get some atropine?" he asked Sharon.

"Already drawn up in a syringe. I couldn't give it till you got here."

He followed her in. Dora said nothing when he entered, just lay there semi-recumbent against the elevated backrest and pillow, her breathing labored by obesity and pain. She was a singular woman, as round as she was tall, with outlandish hair, a shade of pinkish-orange, less the coloration of coiffure than of plumage, or autumn vegetation. Some time back, he remembered, a year or two before, she had baked a plate of cookies for him in gratitude for some service rendered—he couldn't remember exactly what— then finished off the better half of them herself on the trip over to his office. Maybe it was those cookies that metamorphosed into gallstones, or the ham loaf she made for George, her reluctantly pampered husband, or the efflux of all those overstuffed fat cells. Whatever the cause, each attack was forgotten the moment it was past, that she might return to her cooking for George and plodding about with her three stout grandchildren. David knew them all, George and the grandchildren and the grandchildren's parents, Dora's two sons and their wives, all patients, or in with patients, through the past ten years. Small-town medicine is like that. If there's one thing that characterizes it, it's accountability. When a doctor does bad work, the whole family knows about it; then, before long, the whole town. But if the doctor makes people better when he can, and mourns with them, humbly and sincerely, when he can not, the family and the town celebrates him, as Bakersville celebrated Dr. David Arthurs.

Dora was his biggest fan, though not, perhaps, at the moment. He listened to her breath sounds, then felt her abdomen. It was the gall bladder, all right, indisputably. Sharon administered the atropine. In fifteen minutes, Dora turned her head toward him, smiled at him, curious-looking as ever, her pink hair in mild but unaccustomed disarray. His hand was in hers, right to right, as in a handshake, his arm upon the side rail as he stood beside the cart. He felt the pressure of her grasp lighten, then saw and felt her other arm come across, her other hand stroke the back of his hand, saying . . . what? . . . Thanks?... I'm all right now? Maybe both. He couldn't be sure, for she still didn't speak, out of fatigue probably. Passing a stone is hard work, miserable work. A few more minutes was all it took to convince her to agree to surgery this time. Dr. Greenwood had seen to that, useful for something after all.

"Who's on surgical call?" he asked Sharon.

"Dr. Nouri."

"Perfect. Call and tell him I found him some business."

"You got it, Doc. . . . Hey, do you know what's the worst thing about sixty-nine?"

"Yeah, you told me. The view, right?"

"Right. Good, eh?... OK, Doc. Have a nice day."

He drove out of the parking lot and down the hill, then left on the residential street that leads to Main. Main Street was and is the primary artery of the town. The route along it from the hospital passed and passes through the commercial center, such as it is, five blocks of shops and public buildings, some of them formidable structures of three stories, with a courthouse and its pre-eminent tower dominant over all. It is a broad street, with diagonal parking on either side, so that the unattended cars spread lateral to the stream of moving vehicles like a herringbone spine, divided down its center, rotated along a transverse axis, then stretched apart to allow for flow of travelers from half-kippery head to half-forked tail and back again.

Bakersville is set into the same geology as other Northwest Pennsylvania towns, where hills and streams provide the basic topographic features of the area. Farms beyond the corporate limits are sparse and few, for the land is stubborn. It is a country of unaltered forest, wet and thick with moss and fern. Here clouds predominate over blue sky, and rain is plentiful and frequent, sweeping in from the eastern border of the Great Lakes a hundred miles to the north, rain so abundant and regular that it has the wherewithal to wash away the topsoil in sloping areas carelessly denuded of trees. So level plains alone are cultivated, and they are few, invariably surrounded and bounded by densely wooded hills, rounded shaggy elevations maternally protective of their scanty garment of soil, in order that their seed-engendered vestments might have a chance to scatter, root, and multiply in turn.

The features of a town, of Bakersville or any other, are linked directly to terrain. Bakersville arose among wooded hills. Not mountains though, just hills, sometimes steep, but never insurmountable. Roads could have been raised straight up and over them, but it was easier by far to go around, and safer, if one had to go up, particularly in winter, to go up circuitously. There is hardly a straight street within the town's boundaries, and those one finds occasionally have the temerity to end well short of any place most people might want to go. Then there are the streams. Hilly land and frequent rain make lots of them, streams and rivers and rivulets, so that the roads have yet another set of obstacles to overcome. That they do with bridges, but those don't come cheap, so persistent streets will wind along the moving water to the next crossing point, the next perpendicular road-way, itself made sinuous by some rising ground beyond.

So it is a town of curves and dead ends, with each intersection seldom a factual crossing in the form of a plus sign, but more often an L or Y or T, or lazy italicized variety of one of these or some other letter, perhaps from a peculiar alphabet, perhaps indecipherable. Even Main Street swerves and branches in script. Though it stays fairly straight for the five blocks of down-town, just past it to the east it makes a Y, slightly italicized, the right branch of which runs up another hillock, then down the other side. Halfway down the declivity, Bakersville ends—its sewage and water and dominion. Drive past the boundary, three miles out, along the road that had been Main, and you will come to a gravel access road leading to two old unworked farms, one lately inhabited, and a group of hunting camps. It is an area few have visited, few remarked, silent at night but for the hiss of tires on the highway or the growl of an exhaust or the sounds of crickets in the fields around. On summer evenings, with the traffic at its ebb, the crickets reign unrivaled. As Dora Chilcott reclined pain-free upon her wheeled cart, as David Arthurs steered the Buick east on Main, they commenced their evening song.

He passed the township limits. The drive had become routine these past three months. Every week he'd been there, out Main Street and beyond to the old farmhouse, two times a week, or three, since the old man had been incapacitated. This would be the last though, the very last. An end of suffering it was, nothing more. Yet what he felt was sadness, only sadness. True, for the old man it would simply be an end to pain, a blessing really, this long-awaited death. But Keller was his friend; his, if anyone's. David would miss him. This last visit was going to be grim. If his luck held, the worst of the business would be over by now, taken care of by the deputies. Otherwise it would be his duty, his alone: the calls, the papers, whatever else the law required to process the remains of the human being he had known as a patient and a man, a human being who had suffered enough in the last months of his life to deserve a better death.

They'd met five years before at an antique car show. Keller, Charles Keller, he'd introduced himself, his big, lean hand out, a tall man, robust, handsome, with the bearing of a diplomat. He walked around David's car, a GTO back then, said something about the engine. He knew a lot about engines, about everything mechanical. He knew a lot about everything period, but never showed it, tried not to show it, so that you had to coax it from him. Never talked about himself though, where he had been, what he had done before coming to Bakersville, never talked about his politics, his philosophy, just asked questions, serial questions, one after another. If you asked him something personal he'd be evasive, change the subject, but if it was something else you asked about, anything at all, he'd tell you, reluctantly, hesitantly, but he'd answer. He'd know the answer, whether about a brake line or the species of a tree on his property or the details of a battle of the Revolutionary War. In the past two months he'd assimilated an entire textbook of urology and could converse in technical terms about ureteral obstruction and pulmonary metastasis. A remarkable guy. He'd miss him. There was an affinity between the two of them he felt, that neither had recognized precisely nor understood exactly.

Cindy saw it. She'd met Keller just once, six months before, one of the rare times she'd cooked a meal, back at the beginning, when she was in for the weekend and old Keller came over to look at the Chevy, then stayed for dinner. Cindy made ham or something, which the old man pretended to like but ate little of, whether it was the tumor or just the fact that he was used to food prepared by professionals. David thought the latter. Keller was a patient by then; knew what he had and when he was going to die, not to the month, but close enough. He made little of it though, as if it were a cold or a wart. Before dinner he looked over the Chevy, found a short in the the wiring harness and fixed a power window in ten minutes, something David had been working on for two weeks.

"He reminds me of you," said Cindy later. "Like somebody I'd picture as your father." She'd never met his father. If she had, she wouldn't have made the comparison. They barely knew each other then, he and Cindy, having met just weeks before. It was on a flight to Nassau. There was a captious passenger seated two rows in front of him, not an evil man, but a man uncomfortable with himself, thus a seeker of faults in others. Everything was unsatisfactory to him: the food, the seating, the cabin temperature, the sound of a child's crying. A flight attendant appeared, a pretty pink thing who placed a delicate butterfly of a hand on the man's shoulder and *thanked* him, thanked him for pointing out what the airline could do to improve its service, praised his perceptiveness, passed a surreptitious free drink to him, and smiled—most of all smiled. She tamed him. If she'd had a hoop, he would have jumped through it. It was a bravura performance.

Later on, stretching his legs, David bumped into her in the rear galley, complemented her on the way she had handled the man, did it, not because of her beauty, but because of her tact. And she had responded, responded in a way he had neither anticipated nor provoked consciously, but had welcomed nonetheless when it came, when she walked back to talk to him three or four times, during any momentary break, and finally concluded by asking him to breakfast the next day, for she had an overnight in Nassau. And they wound up having the breakfast, and dinner before it, and a memorable night in between. And everything had been good then for those three months of her weekly visits, and was still good for a couple of months afterward when they were together full-time, until the arguing started, as it always did with women, who wanted much more than he could give. Commitment they wanted, exclusivity. And that kind of doting love he couldn't even conceptualize, much less offer. If they spent much more time together, he'd make her progressively more miserable. Probably crazy as well. Miserable like all the other women he had been with, and crazy like most.

The car turned east on 302, through town and out along the two lane highway. Just past the borough limits came field and forest, low hills, rolling out to left and right sideways beyond the berm, hills carpeted with trees, diminished by distance into fibers, variously green. Flatter land there was, too, which had been farmed or stripped but which the vegetation had reclaimed. On it grew massive stands of rhododendron, black-green, digital and drooping, with the loveliest of purple blossoms, largely shed by mid-July, but here and there still scattered on some north-faced slopes.

He passed the charcoal plant, a trestle, now frequented by engines hauling coal, then right, onto a secondary route, and right again onto the final branch, gravelled and sprinkled at edge with colt's foot leaves and scented crown vetch and spiky yellow mustard. And trees everywhere, maple, hemlock, and beech, standing like solemn sentries on flatland and on hill along the route the dead old man would follow to his grave.

There was a rut at the entrance to the property, something Keller would have fixed three months before. David pulled far to the left to avoid it, just clearing an electric pole. The deputies' vehicle was in the driveway, down toward its end near the house. He steered the Buick up alongside, its left tires on the grass, then got out with his doctor's bag, a large black leather case with slots and cups for every type of medication and syringe, carried it with him, though in impotence and futility. It was evening now, yet light enough; warm enough too, though commencing to cool. The sky was pastel blue, a faintly grayish blue already muddied by the lowering sun. Off in the distance he could see some trees on hilltops shining yellow-green in the horizontal sunlight. He looked up at the house, dark now, isolated in the shaded flat plain, appropriately gray, a gray more drab than he remembered from his recent visits. The door was open, gaping wide, inviting entry. He stepped up on the porch and passed inside. There was a light on upstairs, and he heard some voices there, so he climbed up toward the luminance and sound.

The glow came from Keller's bedroom. David stepped through the doorway and saw two deputies, Brian Clinger and another man, younger, unfamiliar to him, thin and wiry, nervous-looking, agitated in fact. They must have heard him approach and enter, for they stood facing the door in expectation. Arthurs perceived them first, for life is stirred by fellow life, and then the old man, his flat form suffused with light and death.

"Hello, Brian . . . Deputy." David nodded to each, then walked over to the bedside and put his hand on the old man's brow.

"Not much for us to do here. He had a rough end." He smiled again, a sad smile. He felt it passing in an instant.

The deputies didn't smile back, but rather looked odd, uncomfortable. Not just the younger one, who seemed nervous, high-strung, but Clinger too. They eyed each other with expressions of arcane knowledge, mutual and exclusive.

"Ambulance coming?" He knew they must have called but asked anyway.

"Yes, sir," said Clinger. "Should be here in a minute." He was looking at the floor, at a vacant place on the floor, in fact, which rendered his face illegible.

That wasn't like Clinger. David knew him, not well, but adequately. He'd been a patient in the past, he and his wife and kids, before the divorce. Not that Clinger was ever sick, but he made it in for physicals, obligatory forms to be completed, an insurance exam once. He was manifestly not a shy man, rather one who looked you in the eye. A decent man too, not fond of lying, not the type of man who could lie effortlessly and hence effectively. Today, this evening, he looked remarkably awkward, and Brian Clinger was not a man who frequently looked awkward. There was something very strange here in this house, in this room; something odd and undisclosed between these men, some unexpected thing the deputies had come upon here in Keller's secluded home.

"What's going on, Brian?" David looked directly at the older deputy, unblinking; usually that worked. "You're not telling me something."

Clinger tilted his head and glanced up, intermittently and obliquely. "How well did you know this guy?" His voice was subdued, respectful, pointedly polite. There were beads of sweat across his brow, and his short hair looked moist and matted on the sides.

"Why? Did you find some bodies?"

The two deputies looked at each other again. There was a pause that seemed very long; then Clinger answered. "Not exactly, Doc, not exactly. . . . Look, do you think you could tell us something about him?" Clinger had an odd expression on his face, a sort of anxious semi-smile that looked remarkably and undoubtedly counterfeit. The other man, the slender one, put one hand up to his hairline, combing backward with his fingers. David noticed a subtle but visible tremor.

He thought for a minute. Clinger gave him time. He'd help if he could, but, after all, he could hardly know what it was they wanted, just what sort of information they might have in mind. What could he tell them anyway? What really did he know about the old man? What besides his body, the sound of his heart, the feel of his lymph nodes, the rectal hollow where his prostate had been. He knew the course of his disease, the organs it had spread to, supped on, consumed, the footprints of the cancer, the various letters of its signature upon his flesh. But of the man himself, the being who'd inhabited that fragile shell, he knew nothing. Oh, he had asked: about the old man's origin, family, career, life. But what had he been told? Nothing...nothing at all. "So, where are you from?" . . . "What's that? . . . "Where did you live, before coming here?" . . . "Oh, nowhere interesting. What about you, David. Where are you from, originally?" That was the pattern, the framework for every conversation with this man about whom the doctor—the town itself, so far as he could tell— knew absolutely nothing. But could he give Clinger anything of use, anything at all, tell the deputies the "something about him" they had asked for?

"Maybe I can. A little anyway. I've known him, who he was, for four or five years, and I got to know him a bit better in the last few months. Not much about his past life, but certainly something about who he was recently . . . toward the end, I mean. Nothing very exciting: interests, knowledge, that sort of thing. . . . Look, why don't you just fill me in on what you guys found, so I'll have a better handle on the kind of information you might need?"

He watched the two men in profile, Clinger and the other deputy, regarding each other as if in conference. But it was a voiceless exchange, and one-way to boot. This Phil was scarcely a participant. His face looked blank, dull. He must have been the one who'd answered at the sheriff's office earlier. "Call the sheriff at home," he'd said. "Don't ask me," was the corollary. "Don't ask me," he seemed to be saying now to Clinger. Obviously it was Clinger who was going to have to make the call. David stared at him, wide-eyed, looking as candid, as receptive as he could. *You can trust me*, said his face. *Whatever it is, you can trust me*. Clinger stared back, inspecting. He didn't look awkward any more. After twenty seconds he nodded, stepped over to the closet door, and opened it.

David saw the ear first, resting limply at the bottom of a slender jar. It didn't look real, not really like a genuine ear, being perfectly white and

considerably distorted by time and the opalescent fluid it lay within. So
the ear itself looked artificial, but for its margin, the severed edge, which
did indeed look genuine, and the sediment, bleached and friable, settled
crumblike at the bottom of the jar. It sat upon a shelf at eye level, alone
on the shelf but for one other object, something metallic, just alongside
the jar. Clinger reached in with a handkerchief and lifted it. It was a knife,
military looking, with a black handle and a serrated blade, maybe ten
inches long, blade and handle together. There was dirt on it; it looked like
dirt, but it was crusted, and not consistently black, but ruddy in some
spots, very much like blood, old and dried and remarkably offensive in
the way it had been consciously left in place on the blade—not that the
ear was any less so.

"Damn!" said David. He wanted to say something else but lost the
thought. "Damn," he repeated less emphatically, in place of other words
that had escaped him.

"Check out the rest," said Clinger.

"Yeah," said David. "I see it."

Below the trophy shelf, within the main section of the closet, and
above it, on another larger shelf, was an arsenal. Not a gun collection or
a cache of military souvenirs, but a storeroom of modern-day explosive
power sufficient to level a town. Some of the less exotic objects were recognizable as firearms. Others, Clinger knew and could identify, partly
from his long career in law enforcement, but mostly from four years in
the Marines: objects like grenade and rocket launchers, laser sights,
night-vision goggles. There were two full-scale assault rifles with filled
clips, then a dozen other clips stacked delicately on the top shelf—all told
a sum of two or three hundred rounds. Then two more concealable short
stock automatic weapons, and other things, one of which seemed to be a
U.S. Army M-60 machine gun, with long clips of ammunition, another a
small bore platoon cannon, an M-50. And items even Clinger could not
name: vials of some unknown liquid, and cakes of a plastic material, likely
an explosive, but unlike anything the ex-Marine had seen in service. Each
object was fixed in place, bracketed or strapped to the walls and back of
the closet door, ready to be used, nothing in disorder. The closet floor was
empty, clean. Not just orderly clean, but dustless, immaculate.

David moved back, away from the closet, off to the side of the bed.

"Jesus," he said. "Jesus Christ, what is this? What is all this? Do you guys know?"

He turned to the deputies. Phil shrugged.

Clinger stepped over, put a huge hand on his shoulder, still respectful, but supportive too, comradely. "Now can you tell us something about him, Doc? About all this?"

"No. No. I mean, I don't know, really. . . . I don't know." He paused. "I mean, I'm just as shocked as you guys probably were . . . are." He thought for a little while. Nothing made sense. Nothing in the room made any sense. "He seemed like a really peaceful man. I mean, not a murderer. Not the type who would be in a hate group. We talked about cars, machines. He knew a lot about mechanical things. We discussed his disease. . . . He never talked about himself, never gave me any information. I don't even know where he came from or what he did . . . uh, you know, for a living. He was intelligent, educated I think. He'd traveled a lot, read a lot. He seemed pretty normal. This stuff is. . . . God, I don't even know what to say."

He looked at Clinger, met his gaze. Clinger's expression looked pretty much the way his own face felt, dazed and dumfounded. A kindred spirit, he thought.

"I don't think he had any family. No next of kin, no visitors, no calls . . . you know, when he was sick."

"Maybe he stabbed 'em," said Phil. No one laughed, not even Phil. There was no humor in this place, no funny sorts of knives, or ears either. David felt claustrophobic, nauseated.

There were sounds outside, a car on the gravel. Clinger motioned toward the door, to Phil who stepped out into the hall and over to the window he had entered ninety minutes earlier. "The ambulance," he announced. Clinger closed the closet door, locked it, and put the keys in his pocket.

The paramedics came in a minute later, two of them. Clinger knew one from the Riverside Bar, having seen him there a few times: Richard something. A lousy pool player, but a kindly and sentimental drunk. The other guy was new, just trained. You could tell. He was awkward, bumping into Richard when he turned, following him like a shadow on uneven ground.

Their arms were filled with medical things: monitors, IV's, syringes enough to raise a dead Lazarus, but Keller must have seemed more dead than that, for they only felt and probed for a few seconds before grabbing their gear and plodding back out for a stretcher. They didn't pay the slightest attention to Clinger or Phil or even the doctor, just went about their business as if they were a troupe of actors playing demonstratively, with loud voices and exaggerated gestures, the way half-educated people carry on when they're trying to show off the half-education they've acquired. That sort of nonsense never bothered Clinger. He'd seen it all before a hundred times, firemen and lab techs and even the deputies when they first started, before he'd had a chance to kick their asses a little and show them that they had a job to do.

A door slammed outside, the ambulance's rear hatch, it sounded like. In a minute the medics were back with a canvas stretcher. They opened it widthwise and dropped it on the floor on the far side of the bed. Phil went over to help them, unsolicited, but not rejected either. "I'll get his legs," he said, and leaned across the footboard to lower the spread which lay across the old man's pants below mid-thigh. As he tossed it aside, something fell. Clinger saw it drop, drifting over to the left of the bed, off to his left as he stood facing the dead man. Phil lifted Keller's feet while the two medics, one at either side, hoisted him up and over onto the canvas frame. Clinger bent down and picked up the object that had dropped, flat, rectangular, and yellow-ochre in color. The two medics and Phil were busy securing the corpse to the stretcher. The doctor stood over in the corner watching them. Clinger slipped the flat object behind him, standing with his hands at his back as the stretcher passed. When they got to the door, Phil stopped and turned, while the medics clattered down the stairway and out to the ambulance.

"What's this, Phil?" asked Clinger, holding out a five-by-seven manila envelope, opened flat along a transverse fold

"I don't know. Where'd it come from?"

"Dropped on the floor when you moved the bedspread. Didn't you see it before? When you covered him? It had to be there."

"Mighta been," said Phil. "I was just lookin' at his face, but there mighta been something like that down by his hand. It mighta been there . . . I don't know for sure."

Clinger shook his head. "Go out and see if those guys need any other information for their forms. Make sure they take him to the hospital in case Wilson wants to do an autopsy, OK?" Wilson was the coroner.

Phil went out. The doctor stepped over, and Clinger opened the envelope. It contained a single sheet of paper that bore a brief statement, hand-printed in bold block letters, in a tremulous hand, but nonetheless distinct:

I, CHARLES KELLER, RESIDING IN THE GRAY FRAME HOUSE ON SWANSON'S MILL RUN, R.D. 6 BAKERSVILLE, PA BEING MENTALLY COMPETENT AND OF UNDIMINISHED INTELLECT, DO HEREBY APPOINT AS EXECUTOR OF MY ESTATE AND TENANT PRO TEM. OF MY PROPERTY DAVID ARTHURS, MD, OF BAKERSVILLE, PA. FULL DETAILS OF THE DISPOSITION WILL BE FURNISHED TO HIM UPON MY DEATH.

> (signed) Chas. Keller
> July 16, 1996

"Well, Doc," said Clinger, "looks like you got yourself a new job."

David took the note from Clinger's hand and read it again, disbelieving. There was a pulse in his ears, beating at a rapid rate, uncharacteristic of his generally placid state. Whoosh it went, whoosh, whoosh. Perspiring now, he moved to the side of the bed nearer the door and sat down at its edge, needing badly to sit somewhere, even on the dead man's bed. Even there.

Whoosh went the blood, somewhere around his ears, whoosh, whoosh. There was a darkened area at the center of the beige blanket, effected by the old man's buttocks and the urine that had pooled beneath them, but he sat well clear of it on a clean surface, for the rest of the bed looked immaculate. Outside, the ambulance clattered its diesel cacophony down the driveway and out toward town.

He was hot, his brow and hair thoroughly wet now, but the stale air within the room was hot too, so the moisture failed to cool his face. It was oppressive, that air, urine-scented, an efflux of the fouled blanket. Behind him and to his left he heard Clinger step over to the window, raise the closed blinds, and lift the lower sash. A breeze rushed in, cooled by the shade of the neighboring hill and redolent with the scents of nearby grass and crown vetch, subtly sweet, and distant pine, peppery and fresh.

"That's better," Clinger said. David looked around. "The air." Clinger smiled and pointed to the window with a thumb. *A kindred spirit*, thought David. *I'm glad he's here.* "Any idea what that note means, Doc? About more information—what was it?"

He looked at the paper. "Details of the disposition," he read. The cool air felt like an ocean breeze. "No. Jesus! Look, I haven't got a clue. No idea. . . . Look, I just can't do this, you know, be his executor. . . . I know next to nothing about the man. And the closet there. Jesus, I can't do this. No way! This is something that the state should be responsible for. Or his family, if he has any. I've got to get out of this. Can't I just refuse to do it?"

"Yeah, of course," said the deputy. "Let's just ask the sheriff when he gets here. He should be along pretty soon."

"OK, great. That's great."

"Hey, Doc, I was just kidding," said Clinger. "He won't know. . . . You don't know the sheriff very well, do you?"

"No. No, I think . . . maybe I met him once or twice. Shook hands, you know."

"Well, you're in for a rare treat, which is to say he's a real character. Not a bad guy, just a character. You'll see. Anyway, on the thing about not being the executor, you don't have to take on anything like this . . . anything you don't want to do. Nobody's going to force you. And I think you'd be crazy to take it on now anyway, after what we found in that closet. As far as I'm concerned, it's a police matter, and since it's county, the sheriff's department has jurisdiction, so I'll probably wind up with it, which is OK with me. You don't have to be involved at all."

"OK, then. That sounds better. . . . I mean, I would have liked to help in some way . . . you know, do something for the old man, but this stuff . . . that closet!"

Clinger paused, pinching his nose, then his face brightened. "Yeah, you're right, Doc. Let me see that note again. Then why don't we have a look around. If that's O.K. with you, Mr. Executor. Or Dr. Executor. Didn't you ever want to be a detective?"

"No. No, I really never did. Neither a detective nor an executor."

The room had cooled now, perceptibly. It was a lovely evening, with a little breeze rattling the blinds, freshening the air. Sly old guy he was, old Keller. Played a final joke this last day. He should have seen it coming, with all those questions, all those purposeless questions. What the hell. You had to have a sense of humor. He looked up at Clinger. "Yeah, Dr. Executor. Perfect. Maybe I'll find a new career in estate planning. What do they call that, vertical integration?"

"I think so," said Clinger. "Horizontal would be, what, selling clothing to your patients?"

"Used ears," said David. "Used Goddamn ears in bottles." Clinger came over and sat beside him on the bed, and David passed the old man's paper to him. There were sounds again outside, gravelly and automotive, louder through the open window, then a motor shutting off. Phil was downstairs at the open doorway and called up, announcing the sheriff's arrival, and then, in a moment, Ronald Steele was in the room.

CHAPTER 5

SHERIFF RONALD STEELE WAS SHORT AND THICK, OVOID. CLINGER LOOKED immense beside him. His face was not unpleasant, but curious, with little features: a tiny upturned nose, small eyes, dark but hidden, and a thin, straight mouth surmounted by a fine-tipped mustache, a thin brown line shaved down to linearity, just above the lip; all immersed, these little features, in a rounded head so choked with fat as to make the sheriff's ears all but vanish in the rolls and tucks of jowls and neck.

What little there was of neck was rudimentary, such that a frontal elevation of the sheriff presented to the eye no aspect of a neck at all, but rather a full moon face fit flush upon a flaccid trunk, itself cascading outward farther down into a great abdominal bulge. This was an appendage so immense and so prominent that it passed into a room before him, a preface to his presence, like a ship's figurehead or the nose cone of a jet. He clenched a cigar in his mouth, that hour as always, as if his face demanded a preface too, an object as long and diametric as a phallus, not exorbitant, but serviceable, and he pushed it around, the cigar, alternately to one side or the other of his linear mouth, talking, when he had to, around it. He had a tendency to light it for a while, when it was fresh, consuming half an inch or so, then let it smolder, stall, and cool, and chew upon it for an hour or two, until the nearer half was wet through with the moisture of his mouth, peppering the fine lines between his teeth and up above them, at their junction with the gums, with brownish residue, here liquid, there flake, lingering like flies upon a carcass, but less purposeful.

As he started to speak, his hand rose instinctively to the hair upon the dome of his head, gray-brown strands rising vinelike from a part an inch or so above the ear and swept, oily and insufficient, across his scalp toward the other side.

"So what's this all about, Brian, eh? Your man down there said I had to see something. Couldn't tell me on the phone." Though Phil had been a deputy for six months now, the sheriff could not quite yet identify him by name.

Deputy Clinger, with not another word, led him to the closet and opened it. The sheriff looked in, then turned back toward Clinger, an irritated expression on his face.

"What is that?" he asked, moving his eyes to the position of the lower shelf. "Eh? What is that?" There was something resting on the surface of the shelf that was attracting Clinger's gaze. The shelf was a little too high for anything on it to be visible. The sheriff stepped back. There was a jar there, just the top of it in view, with its lid. It had some sort of fluid in it, opalescent fluid, like dishwater. The closet below the shelf had a pretty fancy display of weapons. They looked shiny, new, never fired. It was an impressive display, but—he shrugged his shoulders—what did they want from him? On a Saturday night, of all times? Had he nothing else to do? "An emergency," the other man had said. "Something here you have to see." What was his name, the other deputy with Clinger, the new man? Paul something, he thought. Paul would hear from him! Calling him out on Saturday night to look at a closetful of unused weapons and a jar of water on the one evening he counted on being at home, the one evening he wouldn't tolerate being disturbed. What the devil did they want from him! What the devil was Clinger looking at with that Goddamn fool expression on his face!

"What is it, a jar of dirty water?" he asked again. How could anyone expect him to see it, sitting way up there on that shelf?"

"It's an ear, Chief." Clinger lifted it out and brought it down to eye level. It was an ear all right, pasty-white, in a granular liquid of some kind, alcohol maybe.

"An ear! Whose ear?" he asked. "Is it the dead man's?"

"No, Chief," said Clinger, "he had both his ears."

"Well, whose then?"

Clinger shrugged. He brought a knife out next, holding it with his handkerchief.

"Maybe it's from the war. Viet Nam, you know? They did that sort of thing over there, didn't they? Eh? Ears and things? Various organs, I believe. There's no evidence of a crime, is there?"

"Did you see the rest of the stuff, sir?" asked Clinger.

"Yes," said the sheriff. "Yes indeed. Arms. Military arms. That's all I see." It was a collection of some kind, guns and so on. Next week they'd call him out to view someone's carton of baseball cards. "I can't see that any crime has been committed, eh? There's no sign that any of this was used for an illicit purpose, is there? Is there? These weapons show no sign of use. No sign of being fired, much less for an illicit purpose. And the knife, well, the knife . . . well, it may be a war trophy, just like the ear."

Clinger didn't seem to have thought of it that way, and he was supposed to be a smart fellow, law enforcement degree and all. What were they looking for, some sort of foreign terrorist operation? Russians? Serbians? Kurds? It was getting so you couldn't depend on any of the men these days, any one of the deputies, even Clinger, even the infallible Deputy Clinger. Goddamn! He was irritated mightily, dragged from home for nothing. Nothing! Some imaginary misdeed even *he* could reason away securely, and he was just fresh upon the scene. If not for the doctor being there—for doctors are treated with respect in a small town, honored, really; more than that, they are regarded as nobility, considered, in fact, not just patricians, but celebrities—if not for the doctor being there, then, he would have told them a thing or two, Clinger and that new man along with him, Paul or whatever. Yes, he would have told them right then and there but for the doctor. Of course, there was always Monday. He could give them a good talking-to then, but on Mondays . . . on Mondays he always got soft and complacent, and never wanted to holler at anyone.

"Well, Brian, well?" He growled it. Clinger would know its meaning. He looked daggers at the other man, Paul or whatever. Paul averted his eyes and backed over to the far end of the room.

He was upset. Well, if they hadn't called, he would have been just as upset, maybe more so. "Who's in charge here?" he would have said. "Don't ever do anything like that again without clearing it with me." Some days you couldn't win for losing. He'd better straighten things out before they got chewed over and strewn about into something really nasty, like the sheriff's cigar.

"Chief," said Clinger, knotting his brow the way he did when he wanted to look earnest, ponderous, "we don't really know what all this stuff means, which is to say the weapons *could* have been used—we don't really know—and the ear might not be a Vietnamese soldier's ear, but maybe somebody else's, some missing person's, say. We don't know for sure, that is. We just don't know for sure. And if anything comes of it . . . you know, if it turns out to be anything bigger than what we're used to around here, I'm sure you'll want to say—to be able to say—that you were out here; in on the investigation, that is, from the beginning. . . . Plus . . . I needed your judgment on what to do with this stuff, which is to say what kind of investigation was in order. I know how quick you are to size up a situation. . . . No way we could handle ourselves it as good as you can."

The sheriff seemed to reflect for a minute. Clinger could see the tension drain from his face, the straight mouth curl a little upward at its corners, the vertical furrows above his eyes grow shallow. He'd seen that transformation a hundred times before. Ronald Steele had the capacity to look almost pleasant when he smiled, and his face had reached an aspect slightly on the pleasant side of vacuity by the time he finally parted his slender lips again in speech. "Well, Brian," he grunted, clearing his throat. The growl was gone now. "Well, Brian, it seems like a lot of fuss, a lot of fuss, but maybe you're right. Maybe you're right, eh?" His lips curled a little more, notching his visage full into the pleasant. "We never can tell what these little incidents may turn out to be." He lifted a plump hand and smoothed his lacquered hair again, then wiped his fingers on the side of a pant leg, depositing a trace of oil on the yellow fabric. "You two boys can't be held to account on an unusual case like this. Still, I can't see that any crime's been committed. Maybe we ought to just close everything up and check it out again on Monday. Can't we do that, Brian?"

It was a Saturday. "Date night" the deputies called it, winking at each other as the sheriff bolted out the door of whatever structure enclosed him at five p.m. on any given biblical Sabbath. The night, it was, that Mrs. Steele made pork chops, crisply fried in lard, with gravy from the drippings, and home-baked bread, and chilled a six-pack of Pabst for him, and opened a bottle of vodka for herself to mix with juice. Every Saturday. And he'd digest his favorite food, and drink his chosen beverage, and she hers, then the two of them would chase each other round the house like a pair of plump cherubs. So if you called him out on Sunday, unexpectedly, or saw him on a Monday even, in the office, he was as sweet and gentle as a lazy old cat full of cream that had just had its ears scratched.

It was something Clinger knew and worked with these past two years serving under a new boss. The previous sheriffs had had their foibles too. Part of his job was to please them, to keep them content and unintrusive, and to provide them with sufficient leisure to make themselves palatable to the voters, while the deputies handled any mischief in the county. The other deputies, past and present, had loved him for it, loved him still for his manipulative paternalism, and the sheriffs owed him, and realized they owed him, their very jobs.

"Chief," he offered, "look, why don't you head on home and let us take care of closing up and maybe looking around a little before we leave? I think I know just how you'd want to handle it."

That was good, that was very good. You could tell by his face how very good it was. The sheriff tapped his foot and nodded, looked around the room, at the doctor, and finally back at Clinger.

"Well, Brian, if you're sure you don't need me here anymore. . . . I suppose you fellows can take care of things, eh?" He must have thought of his pork chops and gravy, and Mrs. Steele too, equally plump and savory. A big wide grin enlivened his face now, ushering into view the brown-flecked teeth and gums. He turned to the doctor, smiling in a pleasant way but for the tobacco shards, nodded, reached up and patted his enormous deputy on the shoulder, and was gone.

It's not my problem, thought David. *Let Clinger handle it. I never bought into any of this. Crazy old guy, how the hell could he do this to me, involve me in his business? That's what you get for taking care of someone the way I did with him, treating him like an uncle, like a parent.* He sat on the bed, not really listening to the conversation, but absorbing enough of it to gather that the sheriff wasn't particularly impressed with what they'd found, any of it, the ear included. He stayed maybe ten minutes. That was it. Clinger must have known, anticipated his response. What had he said? A "character," he called him, a "character." That was pretty much right, an apt description.

Clinger stood facing out of the bedroom doorway as Sheriff Steele descended the steps, then turned back into the room. "Well, Doc, what do you think?"

He'd thought a lot, but nothing made sense. Not the old man, old Keller; that was for sure. Strange how you felt you knew someone only to find out that all your impressions were wrong. Half his life had been that way, half the people he'd known. Like Lynnie, cheating on him, telling him she'd done it because she loved him too much, and now Cindy, and then a dozen others in between, strangers really, after all.

"God, Brian, I don't know what to think. I thought I knew him. . . . Not *about* him, but his character, his nature. . . ."

"Oh, Keller, you mean. No, I meant the sheriff. What did you think about my boss?" asked Clinger.

"I don't know. He *is* sort of a character, I guess."

"You saved my ass being here, you know, which is to say you kind of defused the situation. He couldn't really come down on us, Phil and me, with you here. He gets over it quick though. By Monday he'll be sweet as chocolate. . . . Look, he basically dropped all this on me. I'm gonna look around here a little, with your permission. You know, technically you're in charge, being executor. The sheriff was right about that. We don't really have any clear evidence of wrongdoing, so anything I do here tonight needs your approval. Anything at all, until another executor is named, the court or whatever."

"Yes, I can understand that. . . . So what do you want to do?"

"Well, look around here. A lot of what we're gonna find out about Mr. Keller is in this house. Personally, I'd like to know some more about the kind of man who kept a devil's closet like that inside a house sealed up like some fortress. It's kind of my job to do this stuff, which is to say check up on things . . . the way you might try to figure out the cause of an epidemic, like a restaurant where some people got sick from food poisoning. So's other folks don't get sick, you know?"

Clinger was right. They couldn't leave without a look around. Not just the deputies, but himself too. He was curious. It was more than that though. He'd felt an affection for the old man, an ill-defined attraction, almost a commonality of thought. He had to find out something, anything. Tonight if at all possible.

"OK, Brian," he heard himself saying. "Yeah, OK, let's do it. I'd like to know what the hell was going on with him myself."

"Listen," said Clinger, "can you give me a ride back to town?"

Sure he could. The company would be more than welcome just about now, this guy's company in particular. He was a sharp fellow, this chief deputy. Ran circles around the sheriff.

"Sure, Brian."

"Well, OK, I'll run down and tell Phil to take the car back. Then we can have a little look around the place and maybe figure out what some of this stuff means."

He walked out of the room, his big feet sounding heavily on the landing and the stairs down, then, in a minute, creaking up again on the dry ancient wood. The Jeep started, crunched its way along the gravel, and in another minute was gone.

"I told Phil not to say anything about what we found . . . in the closet, you know? He's a good guy. He'll do what I tell him."

"OK," said David. "Where do we start?"

"Here's as good a place as any," said the deputy. It was a pretty standard-looking bedroom though. They went through the dresser drawers, the other closets, the two bedside tables, seeing nothing of much significance. Clinger found a pistol in a holster taped to the bed's headboard. It was loaded. "Hollow points," he told David. "Goes with the closet. . . . You ever see what a hollow point does?"

No, he hadn't, not really. His surgery rotation had been at a suburban hospital. Not much trauma, mostly hernias and gallbladders. Hollow points were nasty though. He knew that. Even the military didn't use them . . . the Geneva Convention or something like that forbade their use. Criminals used them; that was about it. Maybe hunters.

"They go in like a pea and come out like a grapefruit, leave a hole as big as your fist," Clinger explained.

A hole as big as your fist. What the hell had Keller been waiting for with those hollow-point bullets? Jesus! The old guy never said a hostile word about anything or anyone, even in the process of an agonizing and prolonged *danse macabre* directed by the tumor in his loins. None of this made sense. Nothing. Not the weapons or the fortress of a house or the disembodied ear. Especially the ear. . . . "You've got to love, David. That's all there is. Just that." "So who did you love, Charles? Your wife? Were you married?" "Oh, I'm not important, My life is over. Yours, though . . . yours is at its peak. If Cindy isn't right for you, then find the one who is. . . ." When was that? A couple of weeks ago? It wasn't a killer who uttered those things, suffered mutely. Not the kind of man who cuts off ears.

They went out of the bedroom and moved down the hall toward a window at its outer end, the one Phil had entered. It was open, and a breeze came through it toward the other open window in the bedroom, freshening the hallway with grass-scented air. There were two more doors upstairs, both closed and locked. They picked the one on the right, on the same side of the hallway as the bedroom. Clinger opened it with one of the keys on the old man's ring and switched on the light.

It was a medium-size room, almost a mirror image of Keller's bedroom. There were some filled bookshelves against a wall, the wall to the left, ending diagonally across the room from the door. Adjacent, along the wall opposite the door, stood a desk, orderly and neat and quite empty, and next to it a dark oak cabinet, with a large leather lounge chair and ottoman facing it. The cabinet looked new and expensive. It was filled with audio equipment, looking no less expensive, a large television, thirty-five inches or so, and a second TV stacked on a shelf above the first, smaller, maybe twenty inches in diagonal. There was a satellite dish decoder connected to the large-screen set, but the second, the smaller one, was wired to another little box positioned beside it. It had a small dial and an electronic numeral display, reading, when they switched it on, the figure three. David turned on the smaller TV, and instantly a picture appeared: the driveway near the house, with his Buick parked at its end. Channel four showed the rear of the house; five, the property outward toward the hill; and the rest, through ten channels, a complete, overlapping surveillance, with photographic clarity, of the home and its surroundings.

"He wasn't taking any chances," said Clinger. "Nobody gonna sneak up on him. This is a first-class security system, which is to say it cost a lot of money. Thousands. There's what . . . ten cameras?"

"Oh, he had money all right. You know, he paid cash for all his health care, surgery, radiation, everything. No insurance, just cash. Must have been fifty, sixty thousand altogether."

"So where'd he get it from, the money? Any idea?"

No, he had no idea, but he had wondered these many months, visiting the old man in his elegant home, where the cost of amenities and furnishings never seemed to be an issue. "Nope, he never talked about it."

"Maybe that's what we're looking for here. Money."

Money. Clinger was right. That made sense, what with the surveillance system and the impenetrability of the house. Maybe there was a fortune hidden someplace. In the house, possibly, or buried on the property. There'd be a note, in the mail or given to an intermediary, a note telling him how to distribute it, some carefully worked-out plan providing "details of the disposition." To pass it on to charities, perhaps, or to scattered relatives who never knew their benefactor as distant kin or, if they did, thought he was tucked away somewhere in an unknown cemetery, having scarcely had the funds to furnish his own burial. Clinger was right. The money was the key. The weapons and the security system had to be there to protect his hoard.

"What about the ear, though?" How the hell would that tie in? See if the deputy could come up with a plausible explanation for *that* stuff, the spattered knife and the jar. If not for that, seeing to the old man's final "dispositions" might not be so unthinkable, after all.

"Yeah, that's a problem," said Clinger. *Major problem*, David thought. They closed the door and locked it, then went across the hallway to the last remaining room upstairs.

It was a storage area, filled with boxes stacked one upon the other beside and in front of an old sofa bed. They pulled a few down and opened them, finding books, phonograph records, two boxes of electronic devices and components. They restacked the ones inspected and opened others: a carton of coins, silver and gold, forming a diverse and undoubtedly valuable collection, then more books, some of them foreign, printed in an Arabic script. One had pictures of the ex-Shah, dignified and uniformed.

"Must be Iranian," he told Clinger, about the books, written in Persian, indecipherable for the present.

"How does that tie in?" asked the deputy. "Did he say anything about it, about being in Iran? He must have been able to read it, to speak it, if he had all these books."

"No," said David. "He never even mentioned it. I'm sure he didn't . . . not a word about where he had lived or traveled. Nothing."

He pulled over some more boxes, three or four filled with books, Persian and English, and another cache of ammunition, various size shells in unopened containers. That was about it. Three feet away, Clinger was on the last of his own stack. He tossed a box atop five others, then suddenly dropped to his knees and clapped his hands on the side of a carton.

"Here we go!" he called out. David turned halfway round, toward Clinger, facing him, both of them kneeling on the floor with the box between them. It was just what they'd been after: a medium-sized carton chock full of photos, receipts, other personal records, and an old address book, with packets of correspondence tucked along one side, typed letters, mostly foreign, in an Arabic-type script like the books, Persian probably, and some manuscript notes, all in English, in a variety of hands.

There were a few more cartons, but nothing else of particular interest. Clinger picked up the box with the records and receipts.

"You off tomorrow?" David asked. He was, said the deputy.

"Let's go through it then. I know a Persian guy, one of the residents I trained with. We can fax him some of the stuff for translation if we need to."

"I thought you didn't want to get involved," said Clinger. He had a winning smile, exuding warmth and gentleness, a kind man in the guise of a bruiser.

"No, it's not that I didn't want to. It's just that I. . . ."

"The ear," said the deputy.

"Well, yes, I guess that made a difference."

"And you're over the shock of it now?"

"Maybe . . . I'm curious. Not about the stuff in the closet so much as the old man. . . . Keller. . . . I thought I read him better than I did."

"Well, who knows? Maybe it *is* a Viet Cong ear." Clinger smiled again and knotted his brow, in the exact way he had knotted it for the sheriff. "However," he continued, unknotting the brow again, "we're gonna keep you out of this until we're sure just whose ear it was."

They went downstairs and sifted through the lower floor, finding nothing of significance, pretty much as they had expected. Whatever secret things Keller had hidden, he wouldn't likely have hidden them in rooms his visitors would have access to, all those nurses and delivery people coming and going in the exigencies of his illness. There was a computer tucked away in the far corner of the living room, but David had no time to play with it for information. He'd check it when he could, tomorrow maybe. He looked over the mass of books on shelves in the room. History and technical manuals for the most part, surprisingly sophisticated stuff: electronics, materials science, organic chemistry, not older college texts but recent publications, altogether current. This man would make a strange malefactor, if that was what he was.

He followed the shelves around to the desk, a large roll-top, open, its surface entirely empty. Inside one of the drawers was a file of receipts. Another drawer contained some bank statements and a checkbook. He dropped the checkbook and a handful of receipts into the carton that Clinger had placed beside the desk. It was eight-thirty, the day finally lengthening toward dusk. The door was open, and the sounds of crickets blew into the room with the freshening air. David dropped onto a sofa in the living room and switched on a lamp resting atop a table to his left. Behind him were the long rows of bookshelves.

"Sit for a minute," he told the deputy. "Let's sit for a minute, then we'll head out." Clinger came over from the doorway and lowered himself onto the sofa. It was firm but not uncomfortable, a burgundy leather Chesterfield that must have cost a few thousand dollars. Clinger sprawled out on the leather, indenting it deeply despite the firmness of the tufted surface. His thick legs, spread apart, took up half the sofa's width, his left arm on the backrest reached nearly to David's right shoulder. Each of them sat slightly turned, facing one another in quarter profile.

"Look, I really want to thank you for helping me out with this stuff. It's more than I think I could have dealt with on my own."

"No, Doc, don't thank me. It's part of my job."

"Not at nine o'clock at night. I know they don't have you working thirteen hour shifts on Saturdays."

"Hey, Doc, what else I got to do tonight? It's not like I got a family to go to."

"No. No. I know. . . . How have you been doing, Brian? You see the kids?"

"Every weekend. Only Linda took them shopping today, to Pittsburgh. I give them money to buy things they need, whatever they need, clothes and stuff. It's Todd's birthday next week, and I wanted him to have something nice . . . from me, you know?"

"I still see Linda. . . . As a patient, I mean. I haven't seen the kids in a long time though. They been OK?"

"Yeah. You wouldn't recognize them, they got so big, even Mandy."

"Amanda, right?"

"Yeah. We call her Mandy. She's like a regular lady now . . . just like a regular lady."

"You been doing OK? Getting out?"

"Yeah, I see a couple of women. It's not the same though. Not like the way it used to be."

"I know what you mean, Brian. I've been there."

"You, Doc? You've got the world by the balls. I've seen you with that gorgeous girl, the blonde. And that one before her, the doctor from Clairville. What was she, an eye doctor?"

"An optometrist."

"Yeah. She was gorgeous too. You got the world by the balls. Not that I begrudge you. You earned it. You work hard for it. You deserve what you make. And you're a good-looking guy too. I see why the women are after you. Even Linda said that: 'You should see that young doctor. Like a movie star.'"

"Well. I've been through the same thing as you. Not with kids, thank God, but I was married once, a long time ago. Same thing happened as with you. You get over it."

Clinger looked surprised, really surprised. "Doc. I never knew you were married. Jeez, I never knew that. Nobody knows about it around here. You know how people talk about the doctors all the time. Everybody just assumed you were a bachelor, which is to say that you always had been. Jeez, how long were you married?"

"Eight years."

"What happened?... If you don't mind me asking."

"No, I'm not sensitive about it. We just separated. She met another man. . . . More than one, over the years."

"Wait a minute . . . and you knew about it? I mean, before the last one?"

"Yes, I knew. She'd come home crying and I'd comfort her. Tears really get to me. She was like a child, someone I'd take care of and comfort. And she was fun. We'd do things together. She was a good companion. I was sorry when things didn't work out, but I never got depressed about it. You can't dwell on it. I met someone else right away." "Yeah, but it wasn't the same, was it?"

"I don't know. Most of the women I've known *have* been the same. I've never been aggressive with women. I've always wound up in a relationship that a woman initiated. I just sort of go along. Then it lasts three months or six sometimes, and one of us gets angry at something, or bored, or both. Usually it's the woman. I can see that look in her eyes and hear the tone of her voice change. Then I know things are over. I have a theory that any woman really great is married by twenty-five or so. I'm sure there are exceptions, but I think the rule applies in most cases. That leaves anyone our age—you're forty, right? Over forty?" Clinger nodded. "Yeah, that leaves us with flawed choices for girlfriends. But I guess I never really make the choice. I just respond to someone who shows an interest in me. Then in a while they get bored or angry and it's over."

"Well, what about that pretty girl you're with now?"

"Cindy? Cindy and I are terminal. In the ICU on life support."

"And you're not depressed about it?"

"No, really, I'm not. . . . It's time."

"God, I wish it had been that way with Linda. I missed her in the worst way for a couple of years. Now it's better, more like I miss having the kids around all the time, but those first two years were tough. You never felt like that? Even with your wife?"

"No, not like you describe it. We got an uncontested divorce and in a month I had another girlfriend, Janet somebody. I don't even remember her last name. . . . No, Everett, it was. Everett. Janet Everett. She was a nurse. She called and asked me to a party."

"You know your problem?"

"OK, what?"

"I don't think you've ever been in love."

"That's not a problem. I'm not the one who's depressed."

"No, I'm OK now. I just get sad every once in a while. It feels good to talk about it though. Thanks for the concern."

"Any time, Brian. I still owe you . . . for tonight."

It was eight-fifty now. The sky was gray-blue, metallic, more gray than blue, with a golden glow from the horizon at the point of sunset beyond the hills. David popped the trunk and Clinger tossed in the carton with the old man's papers, then climbed into the passenger seat of the Buick.

He backed the car around and headed out the driveway. Halfway down, Clinger reached out, plopped his hand on the dashboard's padded top, and shouted "Wait!"

"What?" David braked to a stop, scrambling the gravel.

"Back up! Back up, Doc."

"What's wrong?"

"Uh . . . we forgot something."

He backed to near the porch. Clinger jumped out and scooted around the car, tapping its hood in passage. "Come on, Doc. Gimme the keys or open the door."

"What is it?" he asked as they stepped back inside, then over to the stairs.

"Come on, Doc."

He followed Clinger up and back into the old man's bedroom.

"The mattress, Doc. There's always something under the mattress. Always."

Clinger lifted it effortlessly, as though it were a coverlet.

"Reach in, Doc. Look under."

Right in the middle, flat against the box spring, was a large manila envelope, old and creased and mottled in that unmistakable fashion wrought only by years of handling, the accretion of oil and sweat from constant fingers, then periodic light and atmosphere to weather the lubricated ochre of the paper. David pulled it out, and Clinger set the mattress down, gentle as a girl with a piece of lace. "See?" he said.

They sat on the bed, unclasped the envelope and slid the contents out. Three photographs slipped onto the sheet, two feet from the yellow stain and slight depression in the center. Two were of women, one of a young man. The largest showed a beautiful dark-haired woman, perhaps thirty. She looked foreign, David thought, Persian maybe, like the books. The back of the picture was blank. Then there was a smaller photograph, a young woman, in color, a recent print, fresh and contemporary looking, on matte-finish paper. The girl, or woman, was extraordinary.

"God, look at her!" said David.

"Yeah . . . yeah, she's something."

"I wonder who it is."

"Well, if you wind up being the executor, you just might find out."

"I was thinking that," said David. Both men smiled.

Clinger picked up the last photo. It was a wallet-sized print of a young man, a graduation picture, wrinkled and dog-eared. When he turned it over, they found writing on the back: "To my Dad. My hero now and always. Love, Dan."

"His son," said David.

"I guess," answered the deputy.

"I think we should put them back . . . back under the mattress."

"Yeah," said Clinger. "I think you're right."

They locked the door.

"You keep the keys," said Clinger. "If I turn them in, one of the guys'll be out here to check out those weapons. Phil won't say anything, but I'm not so sure about the sheriff."

David put the Buick into gear, turning right onto the access road. The evening was temperate, and the outside air felt cool and smelled fresh, so they lowered the windows. The tires stirred a bit of dust from the gravel surface, but the summer air was more pleasant than the dust unpleasant. Neither of them spoke for a while, until the imminence of town was heralded by clusters of houses scattered on either side of the main road as it descended from Bakersville's enclosing hills. The sheriff's office was on Main Street, adjacent to the courthouse. It was just a minute or two ahead when Clinger finally broke the silence.

"Two things, Doc," he said, turning toward David in the seat beside him. "I told Phil to run a trace on Charles Keller. We should have something soon if he had any kind of record. The other thing is that part of the note about further details. You ought to check your mail at the office, or maybe see if Keller could have left something with another person for you. A nurse maybe, or someone else who knew both him and you. Can you do that?"

"Yeah, I thought of that too. I'll make some calls when I get home. Will you let me know if you find out anything from that trace?"

"Sure, Doc." They got to the office. David pulled up in front, along a strip of curb painted light blue with a sign beside it saying "Official Vehicles Only." Clinger had opened the door and started out with his thick foreleg when he had another thought and turned back toward the doctor.

"Those papers in the trunk—put them in a safe place."

"Sure, Brian."

"I'll talk to you tomorrow. We'll maybe have some information on the guy by then. . . . Listen, Doc." The deputy reached over and grasped David's arm, his right arm at rest upon the padded console between the front seats. "Listen to me. Don't *do* anything with those papers. I don't mean don't read them, but don't try to contact anyone whose name or address is on anything in that box."

"I won't, not now, but how else are we going to. . . ."

Clinger stopped him. "Look, this may be a wasp's nest. Keller was afraid of something or someone. Maybe it was the money he was worried about, but we don't know that for sure. Not yet. But whatever it was, from the looks of that closet it wasn't exactly a Girl Scout troop. We wouldn't want whoever it was coming here. After us. After *you*. Just sit on anything you find, and I'll talk to you later tonight or tomorrow."

"OK, Brian. I see your point." The deputy closed the door and tapped the roof in a sort of farewell mixed with benediction, and David started toward home, having forgotten completely about Dora and her gallstone, about the Chevy and its coil spring, and even about the encounter that awaited him next, the soon-to-be-departing Cindy and the Chinese food that was to be her final though hesitant request. What obsessed him now were pictures: a strange woman, an extraordinary girl, a smiling high school graduate's commencement message to his dad. "My hero, now and always."

Had the old man really been a hero, a hero in the sense that moral men understand the word? Had he done good deeds and armed himself mightily only to protect against the bad? Something told David Arthurs that in the next few days he would come to know.

CHAPTER 6

GORDON SAW THE LITTLE RESTAURANT FROM ACROSS THE STREET, HALF a block down. About what he had envisioned, coming from Edward: artsy, cute. *Dorothy's*. He could just imagine. There wasn't much traffic. He crossed nearly in front of the place, opened the door, multi-paned, nice wood, dark oak it looked like. Edward was seated at the bar, dressed in shirt and tie, without a jacket. He got up.

"Hey, Gordon! Great! Thanks so much for coming. How are you? How've you been?" Edward stuck his right hand out, putting his left on Gordon's shoulder. "Grab a seat. Sarah should be here any time."

He felt awkward, uncomfortable. Edward always made him feel that way, like he was being analyzed or something. He didn't know why. He tried to smile, but that felt awkward too, one of those mock smiles people find painted on their faces when they are excruciatingly self-conscious—too intimidated, that is, to summon a genuine tooth-some grin of good fellowship. Now Edward . . . Edward had the right kind of smile, open, sincere, now as always. His hand, as always, felt calm, steady, reassuring, and exerted just the right amount of pressure, just the perfect degree of warmth. A hard man not to like, Edward Kunselman, kind of heart, gregarious, ever cheerful no matter what the occasion, an engaging person, whatever his personal . . . well . . . *habits* were.

He took the seat next to Edward at the bar. Edward faced forward,
toward the front of the restaurant, sitting atop his stool, both feet tucked
up on a cross-rung, an elbow on the chocolate-surfaced wood. Gordon
saw that he had removed his sport jacket and placed it on the vacant seat
beside him. So he did the same, setting his gray suit coat on the surface
of the bar for lack of a better place, then sitting back down alongside
Edward, on the last vacant stool on the near side of the bar, between
Edward and the door.

"How have you been?" asked Edward for the second time. The open
grin still sparkled on his face . . . or maybe it had faded briefly then come
back. Gordon wasn't exactly sure.

"Good," he replied, meaning "well"; healthy, that is, rather than
saintly, though he could have answered *yes* in honesty to either meaning
of the word. Edward said something else: "You look great" or "You look
good," words to that effect. He didn't really make them out. There was a
strange ambience about the place, artsy, as he had expected, but something else distinctly palpable beside the artsiness. He glanced around:
pretty empty; only a handful of patrons eating—mostly drinking, really;
half a dozen or so, nearly all young men, sitting in pairs, fingering glasses
and little plates of snack foods, conversing quietly and making more eye
contact with each other than he was used to seeing among the men he
worked, commuted, and socialized with in his two decades of residence
in and around the Capitol.

"Andrew coming?" he managed to articulate after some seconds of
distraction.

"No," answered Edward. "No, he's home. Cooking, as a matter
of fact. . . . For tomorrow. . . . We're having some people over, some of
the. . . ." Edward went on talking about the dinner they were having, the
friends they had invited. Gordon had been to one of those dinners, just
one, a year before, feeling, from the time he stepped into the apartment to
the time he left, about as uncomfortable as a person could be capable of
feeling. Just the memory of it gave him the jitters. ". . . and Thomas. . . .You
may remember him. I think he was at the dinner we had last. . . ."

A pair of men caught Gordon's eye, an older and a younger, seated in
a booth across the width of the room, halfway between the door and the
rear of the restaurant. They were seated not across from each other, but

side by side, on a bench seat facing the entrance, and he could see them nearly frontally, though they were so piercingly intent upon each other that they would never have noticed his stare. The older man was middle-aged, maybe; it was hard to tell exactly. What Gordon *could* tell exactly was that the right arm of the middle-aged man extended down below the level of the table, and his corresponding hand appeared to be moving along the inner thigh of his seatmate. Gordon couldn't make out the hand precisely, but there was no mistaking the arm's trajectory, much less its effect. Both men were frozen, immobile but for that right arm. The younger of the two gazed downward, toward the hand on his thigh. He was a kid really, about twenty, with a flimsy reddish beard and three or more vertically spaced rings in the rim of an ear, not the lobe, but the hind rim, shining metallically against his sculpted, flesh-toned hair.

". . . the other ones were from the Museum, too, but. . . ." Edward stopped short and looked to his left, toward the two men at the booth, turn-ing his head clear around. He must have sensed Gordon's eyes attracted toward something. The younger man, twentyish, with the earrings, saw the movement. He looked over and smiled. Edward nodded back. The middle-aged man glowered, staring now right at Gordon, right into his eyes. *Jesus!* He turned toward the bar, his back to the two men, elbows on the polished surface, his coat pushed aside along the wood surface. The bartender appeared, a big, hairy man who looked as inappropriate in this place as a camel at a horse race.

"Get you something?"

"Yeah, a Heineken." Gordon's voice was hoarse. It sounded gruffer than usual. He cleared his throat. "A Heineken," he repeated, his voice still husky. Edward gave him a funny look and smiled.

"You're a character, you know that?" Edward said, in a friendly way.

"What do you mean? Why?"

"Nothing," said Edward. "Never mind."

"Look, couldn't we have done this somewhere else?" It occurred to him that he was starting to feel the way he had at Edward's party the year before, jittery, wishing he were home in bed.

"Just relax, Gordon. Relax, man. I come here all the time. Andrew loves it. . . . Look, the food is terrific, and no one is going to bother you. I guarantee it." He stared at Gordon, smiling. "I absolutely guarantee it."

"Still, it might have been nice to meet at a place we all felt comfortable in." His collar felt tight, and he put a finger up to loosen it. "We could have. . . ."

"There she is," Edward interrupted, turning first his head and then the rest of him in the direction of the door. Gordon turned around to see a dark-haired woman enter the room. She looked unusually beautiful from twenty feet away and showed reasonable promise of looking—unusually—every bit as beautiful up close. As she approached, he saw that she was . . . extraordinary.

"Sarah, my love, this is Gordon Tomcic. Gordon, Sarah." Gordon squeezed out a really pained smile, feeling now an even more exorbitant self-consciousness than hitherto. This Sarah was disarmingly beautiful. . . . Really intimidatingly beautiful. He stopped smiling and put his hands behind him, then into his pockets, then took them out again, and crossed them in front of him, over his little round belly, which he retracted to a degree. Edward kissed the woman, Sarah, on the cheek, and she took his left hand in her right, turning full face toward Gordon.

"Very nice to meet you." She smiled in a way that made him think about a picture of a girl he had cut from a magazine years ago, when he was just a young man, folded, and pressed into a book, then looked at periodically for maybe a year or two. He hadn't thought of it in twenty years, had no idea where it was, the picture or the book. Maybe at home in a box somewhere, an old geometry book, civics; something like that.

This woman, Sarah, transcended even the picture as he remembered it. She was extraordinary, breathtaking, though warm and gracious. He glanced over at Edward, hoping to copy his expression, wanting to give a grand and luminous smile like Edward's back to this remarkable woman, but he knew that it was futile. He wasn't cast like that, never would be. So he let his visage work its will into the absurd expression it had worn intermittently since adolescence, then more insistently in the past seven years of progressive baldness, ever since, at age thirty-five, insidiously and malevolently, his hair had started to shed in great furry clusters on his comb and in the shower. He took the proffered hand of Sarah and shook it two times, painfully, up and down. *Nice to meet* . . . he got out, in a voice that was no longer husky, but high pitched, squeaky almost. Then Edward cut in again, seizing the two of them by the arms and pulling them both toward an isolated booth at the far end of the establishment.

It was six o'clock, or just a few minutes after, now; a quiet time in Georgetown on a Saturday, when shoppers have departed to their homes to dine or to embellish themselves for dinner, perhaps back in Georgetown, after the embellishment. And it was hot outside, oppressively so, with that blend of intimate warmth and saturate humidity endemic to the District of Columbia in summer, so not a day for casual strollers down M Street, people who might drop in to a cool little restaurant-bar for a snack or drink. The place, in short, was as empty as it was ever likely to be, a perfect spot at a perfect time for private talk, with nothing but two distracted waiters to overhear, and the male couples equally occupied, and a hirsute bartender, so jaded with a decade of inebriate and grandiose dialogue that plain rational conversation, whatever its purport, was to him as water to a waxed surface, superfluous and unabsorbed.

The booths were ranged along the wide wall opposite the bar. Had the middle-aged man and his younger companion been seated one booth either fore or aft of their location, Gordon would have seen too little of their actions to remark them much, so private were the booths and so secluded from the restaurant beyond. Dark cherry and high-backed, they enclosed bench seats of black leathery material and adhered, at their far ends, to cherry paneling against the wall, elegantly finished wood that ran the circuit of the chamber, around the bar and past it to the front, above the split-paned door and windows. Surmounting that, from about six feet up to the black pressed-metal ceiling, the wall was papered dark green with an ill-defined overprint of black and sepia. Thus it was quite a fashionable and commodious little eatery that Edward had selected for their meeting, though assertively alternative. And quiet to boot. That he had thought essential. Gordon's heterophilia had not been a consideration.

Edward slid in to the recess of the booth, near the wall, making plenty of room for Sarah to his right. Gordon sat across, facing her and exactly opposite. A waiter came over with an extra set of utensils wrapped in a dark green napkin and placed it before Edward, rearranging the other settings on the white tablecloth and leaving three menus. When he left, Edward began.

"Sarah, dear, Gordon here is the man I told you about who can . . . uh . . . answer a lot of the questions you had about those mysterious calls and things. He's married to Andrew's sister Kathleen. . . . You know . . . Kathleen? . . . You've met her before. Over at our place? A couple of months ago?" Edward and Andrew were like an old married couple now, complete with friends and relatives of one or the other, who gravitated to their apartment as though it were a trendy coffeehouse or latter-day *salon*.

"Yes, of *course* I know Kathleen," she said. How could she forget? Kathleen was a force of nature, with the strength of will to have been a frontier lawman, or a frontier criminal, or an eremitic monk. St. Jerome, in his wilderness years, jousting with devils and discoursing with lions, might have had an equivalent strength of character, but definitely not a superior. . . . *So* this *is the man she's married to*, thought Sarah. *The government agent.*

"How could I forget Kathleen?" she continued, answering Edward with a question, but directing it toward Gordon, for the slightest encounter with Kathleen would go a long way toward elucidating just who and what Gordon might be.

She looked at Gordon, trying to catch his eye, to read his reaction. "It's very nice of you to take the time to meet with me today. I really do appreciate it. . . . Really." She smiled at him. Gordon pursed his lips into a quasi-smile, then turned his eyes down, arranging a knife and fork on the white tablecloth.

"No. No, that's fine," he said, looking down, then glancing up occasionally toward but not directly at her. "No need to thank me. I'm happy to help in any way I can." He seemed awkward to her, nothing like her mental image of an agent. To her they were James Bond types, suave and dignified, and here sat a somewhat pudgy, terminally balding, and thoroughly discomposed person, fortyish and untidy, with only a faint twinkle in his eye and a noticeably dexterous way of moving his fingers to hint at any level of skill that might be of benefit to her, or to anyone really.

"Edward told me a little bit about the problem," he continued, after a pause. "Just a little though. Why don't you run through it for me in detail?"

She watched him for a while, realizing now that he wasn't making any eye contact with her, but rather looking at her mouth or at the side of her face when required to confront her. She thought him very shy, quite nice, and nothing at all like the type of man she had expected. Not like an agent, that is, but, on the other hand, pretty much the type of man she had envisioned as the husband of a lioness like Kathleen Tomcic.

"All right," she said, "I'll start at the beginning."

As Sarah spoke, she looked down at the table, seeming to concentrate on her words, as though she meant to get them, the words, and the facts they contained, exactly right. And as she spoke, Gordon watched her, examined her remarkable face, exotic in its brunescence, Mediterranean, framed in thick black hair, not very long but very full, that melded seamlessly into the room's rich decor, as if a part of it. She could have been some accessory placed there by the decorator, selected from a thousand available objects for the uniqueness of its form and features, then custom-colored to suit the room, with black hair as elegant and definitive as the rich, dark fabric of the booths, and green eyes to match the paper, but much more green, a green of greater saturation. So green were they that the decorator had found it requisite to veil them, just a little, with some very long and very dark lashes, fringing the base of a nose and a tiny bump placed thereon purposefully, to make a perfect nose more human. Her mouth was rounded, with full lips, slightly larger than her other features, pouting centrally, so that in a position of rest they separated slightly at the center of her mouth, particularly when she spoke, requiring an effort on her part to close them tight. Though Gordon watched her intently for a minute or two, while she paused and finally began to speak, it was not until the minute or two had passed that he realized, despite the distracting beauty of her face, she had not a particle of makeup on her skin or eyes, nor a dab of artificial color on her lips.

"About three months ago," she began, halfway through his systematic study, "I got a call . . . a phone call . . . from a man who said he was . . . uh . . . a friend of someone . . . a relative, he said, I think . . . who had left him something to give to me."

"Left him, meaning he died?" asked Gordon, interrupting.

"Yes, I think so, but he didn't say that in so many words. Just 'left' . . . you know, without elaborating."

She looked up at him now, and he was able finally to meet her gaze, though haltingly. She seemed as diffident as one of the secretaries he worked with, seemed remarkably unconscious of her own beauty, not erotically beautiful to him, though she would have been to a more virile man, but beautiful like an exquisite child, like a remarkably gifted but vulnerable child.

"OK. Did he identify himself? Give you a name?"

"No. Not at all. Just said he or someone he sent would contact me. And then he asked me if I had a valid passport."

"A *passport*?. . . . Did he say why?"

"No. . . . No, he didn't elaborate on anything. But then, the strangest thing of all, he asked if I was happy. *Happy*. 'Are you happy?' Just like that."

"What did you say?... *Are* you happy?"

Edward laughed, not a vocal laugh, but a bit of a puff out through his nose. "Are you kidding?" he said. "She's about the happiest person I know." He turned to her. "Aren't you?"

Sarah smiled at him and nodded, but it was not a joyful smile, not the kind of smile she had illuminated the room with earlier. Gordon looked at her, at her upper eyelids now, for she was looking down at the table, and he didn't have to meet those green eyes again. Better not press his luck. Her lashes looked even longer in downgaze, seen from above, against the skin of her cheek. He thought she seemed less happy than Edward perceived, a little sad even, but he could see what Edward meant about being a happy person. She was a happy-*seeming* person, one who evoked happiness in others through the infectiousness of her smile and the sweetness of her manner. He could see how other people in her presence would feel a sense of well-being—happiness, if you like—when she was in the room. She hadn't answered the question he had asked, deferring to Edward's interjection, but he needed no answer now. He was beginning to form some concept of this remarkable but surprisingly candid woman. Was she happy? Yes and no, he thought, like all the rest of the world. He sat quiet for a while, watching, as the thoughts traversed her mind and their reflections passed, indecipherable, across her extraordinary face. Presently she continued: Was she happy?

"Well, I didn't know quite what to say, since I didn't know the man. But he seemed so serious that I could hardly make light of it. You know . . . treat it as a joke. So I said to him: 'Yes, I am happy.' Just like that. Then he was quiet for a few seconds and then finally said 'Good' and hung up."

"And you had a suspicion that it was—who, an uncle, that had died . . . that the man was calling about?"

"Yes. That was my first thought. My grandfather's brother on my father's side. We lost track of him years ago, had no idea where he was, or even if he was still alive. But that didn't seem right. I never really knew him and couldn't imagine him leaving me anything, or even thinking of me after all these years. He wouldn't have any reason to, that I can imagine. So I thought about it and came to the conclusion—well, conclusion is much too strong a word—to the idea, I guess, that perhaps it was my grandfather himself. You see, I thought—my parents told me—that he had died long ago, back in the mid-sixties sometime. He died overseas somewhere, they told me, around the same time as my grandmother . . . his wife, I mean. He was some kind of agent, too." She leaned toward Gordon and voiced the word "agent" in a hushed tone, as if concerned with divulging some vital state secret to the waiter, who was, in fact, at the far end of the exaggeratedly oblong room. Gordon smiled. He couldn't help it, so captivated was he by the enormous charm of the gesture, captivated, really, by her whole persona, a blend of feminine beauty and unfeigned diffidence he had never before thought compatible.

"But why would they tell you he was dead?... That is, if he wasn't." It was getting to be quite an interesting story to Gordon, who suddenly forgot his self-consciousness and intimidation, looking now right at her, into her eyes as she opened them toward him.

"There are so many things in my family history that are strange, unexplained, that almost anything seems acceptable in it." Her face darkened. *Happy*? thought Gordon: *yes and no. At the moment, no*. He'd best change tack.

"OK, OK, We'll skip over your family for a while. What happened next?"

She brightened a little, but only a little. "Well, after the call, for a few days I thought about it. About that voice, which sounded familiar in a way, almost like my father's voice. But he's been dead for ten years, my father and mother both. That I know about intimately." Overcast again. Her eyes didn't fill, but they looked just about ready to.

"Let's don't talk about that right now, Sarah," interrupted Edward. "We can come back to it later. Or I can tell Gordon about it myself after."

"OK, " she said. "OK, I guess that would be better." She composed herself and sipped some water. When she set the glass down, its rim, unfrosted, was otherwise clear, without a pink residue. No lipstick, as he had thought. She must have seen him looking, for she smiled again.

The waiter came over and took their drink orders, a Coke for her, a whiskey sour for Edward. Gordon got another Heineken. They stopped talking, not wanting to be overheard, and used the time to look over the menus. It was a good opportunity to take a break anyway. Sarah looked as if she needed one.

In a few minutes the waiter came back and they ordered: hamburgers for him and Sarah and a shrimp dish for Edward. The waiter, a skinny little student type who looked them up and down as though they were a group of homeless too infested for the local shelter, wrote up the order, nodded, and left them to their talk.

Sarah watched until he had passed beyond what she must have considered the range of her voice, subdued as it was, then went on: "So after the call, I started thinking that maybe my grandfather hadn't really died back in 1965 or whenever, but had been alive all this time, and had just died now, or hadn't died at all, and that maybe that was his voice on the phone. I don't know why that came to mind or why I thought about him after all these years. Intuition, maybe. . . . I hadn't really thought much about him at all before. He died supposedly before I was born. But you see, there's no one else left in my family. Edward will explain that to you later, or I will. I can't think of another person from the past, from my entire family—he did say a relative—who might really be alive and leave me something. Like an heirloom. And it would make sense that he might have been out there somewhere, for a number of reasons that I won't go into now."

"OK, tell me about the letters you sent," said Gordon. "Edward told me that you sent out some letters. . . ."

"Yes. All right. . . . I had a box of papers that had been in storage at the . . . uh, my father had an automobile dealership before he died."

"Oh, of course. I remember that. Sarah *Gruener*. Gruener Chevrolet. That was your dad's place?"

"Yes. Anyway, there was a fire, and all our personal possessions were lost. All but this one box of things in my dad's office at the dealership. I kept it, of course, all these years, but only looked through it once, briefly, maybe five years ago. So after the call I thought of it again and dug it out. And I found some letters addressed to my grandfather, nothing of substance, but with return addresses. So I wrote to them and explained that I had had a call from someone I thought might be my grandfather, that he might not be dead, and that I wanted some information about how I might reach him."

"OK," said Gordon, "what happened next? Did you get any responses?"

"Well," Sarah continued, "I think I sent out five or six of them, and a couple came back unopened, with markings like 'Addressee unknown' or 'No forwarding address,' like that, but no written response to any of them. But about two weeks after I sent the letters, I started noticing these strange things that I told Edward about, and then the break-in."

"Break-in!" said Gordon. "Edward didn't tell me about any break-in."

"Well, it just happened a couple of weeks ago. There's nothing much to tell. I came home one day and the box from the dealership was gone. No sign of it. And really no sign of anything else being disturbed. The locks were still locked, and no windows were broken, and they were all locked too, not that a person could get into unlocked windows on the seventh floor anyway. I still don't understand how anyone broke in, unless they had a key. Which made—makes—me feel pretty nervous."

"And what were the other strange things you noticed?" asked Gordon. "Edward mentioned some phone calls . . . after the other ones you told me about."

"Oh, phone calls with no one on the line. That sort of thing."

"Oh. OK. Do you remember hearing any funny sounds on those blank calls? Anything like . . . well, anything not like a regular phone call." This was his area of expertise.

"Yes. Distinctly. . . . I *do* remember, very distinctly. . . . On two of them. The first two. . . . I think it was the first two. . . . A sort of high-pitched sound. I remember it distinctly. And then a click, and the line went dead. What was that? Do you know what that was?" Sure, he thought. He nodded.

"Yes. Yes. Wait a minute. . . . Anything else? Did you hear from the man again? The one who called you the first time?"

"Just this," said Sarah. She opened her purse and took out a piece of paper. "It came a month ago to the museum addressed to me. Federal express. . . . Mailed from Pittsburgh."

"Wait a minute," said Gordon. "What museum? The Smithsonian?"

"No. The National Gallery. Sarah's on the staff. . . . She works at the Gallery, like me," explained Edward. "That's how we met."

Gordon nodded, then took the paper and read it. There wasn't much to it, just a single sheet of white paper, the kind used in copiers and printers, with the words written boldly, in block letters in a firm but tremulous hand:

TO SARAH GRUENER

I WAS UNABLE TO CONTACT YOU AGAIN. YOUR PHONE IS BEING MONITORED. DO NOT TRY TO GET IN TOUCH WITH ME OR INQUIRE ABOUT ME OR MY PREVIOUS CALL. DO NOT SHOW THIS LETTER TO ANYONE. I HAVE MADE ARRANGEMENTS TO HAVE SOMEONE CONTACT YOU. HE MAY OR MAY NOT DO SO. IF HE DOES NOT, FORGET ABOUT THIS AND THE PREVIOUS COMMUNICATION. I WISH YOU A GOOD AND HAPPY LIFE.

"That's it?" asked Gordon. "No signature? Nothing else?"

"That's it. Fed-Ex envelope mailed from Pittsburgh. No name. I have the envelope at home, if you need to see it."

"Well! Where do we go from here?" Gordon was hooked. "The high-pitched sounds on the first calls were probably a detection device, an older type. That's pretty certain. And the letter says that whoever wrote it knew there was a bug, so he wouldn't be likely to call you again if he didn't want to be traced himself. OK, since no one seemed to be interested in you or your phone line before you wrote those letters, it's obvious that someone is concerned with the person who tried to phone you, maybe your grandfather or uncle or some other person who has had contact with one of them. It'll be an easy matter to find the bug if it's in your home, but if it's outside, on an outside phone line, we've got a problem. That may be irrelevant though, since the interested party is probably only interested in your caller, and he isn't very likely to call again."

"So what would you suggest doing now?" asked Sarah.

"Well," said Gordon, "I'm tied up later tonight, but I could come over to your place, maybe Tuesday, and have a look around . . . check for the device, maybe, and find out just how infested you are. I have all kinds of monitoring equipment and can get a good bit of information for you, if any further contact is made by either party."

"Do you think you could disable the, umm . . . what did you call it?"

"Device."

"Device. . . . Could you get rid of it?"

"Possibly, but I don't know if we want to do that. It may not be wise to let these people in on how much we know about their interest. Sometimes that has a negative impact on what might have been a cordial investigation. I know that from personal experience."

"Do you think," said Sarah, diffident in the extreme, "umm . . . Do you think that it might be the *government* that's monitoring? You know, that the person who called, my grandfather or whoever, is in some sort of trouble with the authorities? Tax evasion or something?"

"Not likely," Gordon answered. "We wouldn't have done anything like the break-in. Besides, we have some pretty sophisticated electronics now. I doubt that someone out there like your caller would have been able to detect *our* equipment on the line. No, I think you've got some semi-skilled professionals about ten years behind your government." He spoke with some pride and sat up a little. Sarah smiled, and Gordon noticed the smile, though it was subtle, felt his self-consciousness return, and slumped again.

Their dinner came, and they ate quietly now, for there was not much more to Sarah's story. The present one, that is. The old one, the gloomy one that Edward had hinted at, was not to be related today, not by Sarah at least, whose nerves were frayed enough. She excused herself after taking a few bites of her burger and french fries, and went into the rest room not far from their booth. Edward then shifted over to his right, toward Gordon, who shifted over a little too. Then they each leaned forward to facilitate communication in the restaurant that was now filling up with voices amplified by the metal ceiling and paneled walls.

"I need to tell you about her parents." Edward spoke quietly. "It happened about ten years ago, when she was sixteen, I think. A couple of men broke into their home and killed both of them. Her mother and her father. Then they torched the place, burned everything. A young boy she was going with at the time helped them get in. They must have paid him or something. She never learned all the details."

"So how did she know what happened? Did they catch them?"

"No. It's still unsolved. Sarah was out at the time, with the boy. He took her home and they found the place on fire. I guess he brought her to a neighbor's or something. Then they found him dead the next day, and one of the men too. That's all I know. She won't talk much about it, but I got some of it out of her. I guess she feels comfortable with me for some reason. Maybe because I'm not a threat, you know, romantically or emotionally or whatever. I know she's never really gotten over it. I've never heard of her going out with anybody in the four years I've known her. Well, she hangs around with us, comes to our parties and things, but never with a date. Some of the girls have tried to hit on her—you can see why—but she isn't into that either."

"OK, she's coming." Gordon had seen her step from the rest room. Both men leaned back before she had a chance to notice that they had just been leaning forward. She sat back down and the three of them talked a little, casually, for a few minutes. Then Gordon excused himself. He had a soccer game to go to, something important—no, vital—to his sixteen-year-old son. He got up, then Sarah did too, then Edward, scuttling out from the recess of the booth. Gordon shook hands with Sarah, then with Edward, and departed. The other two sat down again, across from each other now, Sarah in Gordon's place.

"I told him about your parents," said Edward. "I hope you don't mind."

"No. He has to know that. Thanks for telling him. . . . I hate to talk about it."

"OK. Can I take you back to your place? Or would you like to come over to ours for a while? We could rent a movie or something."

"No. Thanks. I think I'll just go home. I can get back OK myself . . . take the train. You've been great to arrange this. I think he—uh, Gordon—can help. He's very nice. Very much Kathleen's husband though."

Edward laughed.

She offered to pay for the meal, but Edward looked so deeply offended that she knew better than to protest too much. He left the money on the table and they walked out. Edward got in a cab and waved goodbye to her, and Sarah walked up M Street, over the viaduct, and down Pennsylvania Avenue to the Metro stop.

The station was empty. It was after seven now, and nearly all the shop workers and diners-out had reached their destinations. She got on an Orange Line train to Metro Center, then transferred to the Red Line on the tracks above. There was a woman with a young boy on the platform in front of her as the train doors opened, a black woman, a little past middle age, attractive and well dressed. The boy was five or six, too young to be her child, but probably a grandchild. He dropped something as the few exiting passengers filed past, and the woman turned aside to pick it up, holding the child's arm firmly. Sarah stepped past and moved into the car, taking a seat halfway down the aisle to her left. Aside from her, the car was empty. A moment later the woman and child boarded, came down the same aisle, and sat directly across from her. Sarah glanced over, and the woman smiled. The child was quiet, snuggling close to the woman, who held him against her with a smooth arm, *café au lait* against his blue shirt and jeans.

The train started and the stations passed, with an occasional passenger entering, a rare one leaving. At Dupont Circle a tall man got on, well groomed, thirty-five or so, who sat in the first seat across the entryway from her, six seats away, facing her. He stared, unrelenting, for two stops, then got up and stepped over, taking a seat directly in front of hers. After a moment he turned back and said something indistinct, something about the Pentagon.

"I beg your pardon," she said. "I didn't hear what you said."

"Do you work at the Pentagon? I think I've seen you there."

She had been sitting with her arms crossed, avoiding his gaze, from the time he entered the train until a minute earlier, when he had taken the seat in front of her, but now she looked up at him, steadily, but with a blank expression. "No. I've never worked there. It must be someone else you're thinking of."

"Look, I couldn't forget a face like yours. I know I've seen you somewhere. Where do you work?"

"I'm sorry. I know you're mistaken. I'm sure we haven't met. Please excuse me. I have to get out soon."

"Where are you going? Which station?" Just then she heard a voice from her right. It was the woman with the child, calling over.

"Sir . . . sir," she called. "Could you show me where we are on this map?" She held out a map of the Metro system, held it over to the right of the bench in front of her, so that the man was forced to shift over to that seat, just across from him, and face the opposite side of the car to see it. He moved over, and the woman smiled again at Sarah. The train slowed and stopped at Cleveland Park. Sarah got up and stepped behind the man and out the door, then behind a sign board with a map of the subway system. She watched as the doors closed and the man turned toward the seat she had occupied, watched him look around the car in confusion, watched the woman pull the child to her with the *café au lait* arm and caress him with the other hand, smooth and lighter mocha against his chocolate skin. Then the train pulled out, the orange plastic of its seats, the yellow of its walls shining garishly through the windows of the cars as they passed through the gray and inconspicuous station.

She waited on the platform for the next train, the one continuing north, two stops to Bethesda. In ten minutes the signal lights, flush with the surface at the platform's end, blinked on and off dimly, announcing the next arrival. She boarded the car, picked an empty orange seat directly opposite the door, and sat down.

There was a young man in the car, a boy really, late teens, smooth-faced, sandy-haired. She saw his reflection in the glass windows as the car moved from the lighted station into darkness. Just an outline, a silhouette. Nothing like Seth, though she couldn't really see Seth's face in her memory after so many years. But the boy reminded her. Every day something did. And the voice came back, as it always did, sounding in her ear, *How could he have? How could he have?* as the train rattled its way through the tunnelled ground toward Bethesda, and the stations passed, alternating with the black and silent passages between them, till finally at Chevy Chase, with Bethesda just ahead, the doors slid clòsed, the train entered its final darkness before Bethesda, and when she looked up, into the black-backed, mirroring glass, the reflection and the boy were gone.

CHAPTER 7

CAROL DIDN'T MUCH LIKE DRIVING IN THE CITY, WHAT WITH THE TRAFFIC and all the noise. And the mall was always crowded on Saturday, way too many people for someone not much used to lots of people. But Danielle: she just had to go. What was it with teenagers and malls? And she had promised. Besides, there was Michael too, who needed some work clothes. In the twenty years they'd been married, he'd never once bought any clothes for himself. Never once. So they went, and it was crowded and hot, and a long, exhausting drive there and back. They got home at seven. Carol had picked up dinner, she and Danielle, some chicken, and the family ate as soon as the table was set, Carol and her husband and Danielle and Sandy, the younger daughter. Then she cleaned up a little, so it was nearly eight before she had finished with the meal and the cleaning up. And then it was that Sandy remembered the phone call: some other nurse, Estelle maybe. Around six or so, she guessed.

Now Carol wondered what in the world Estelle might want. On Saturday evening especially. . . . But then it came to her that Estelle might have been the one who picked up her weekend route, that she might have been at the old man's house that day. And if she had, and was calling because of that . . . She phoned Estelle back and found her at home.

"Did you call today . . . before?"

"Yeah. About the old guy. You know, Keller. I called to see if you. . . .

What a day I had! There wasn't any answer at the door, so I called the doctor: Doc Arthurs, you know? And he called the sheriff. Then a couple of deputies came out and one of them finally got in through a window and I guess, uh, found him dead. So then I left. Bill was out cold, and the kids were starving. What a day! Nothing more they needed me for."

"OK. Gee, that's terrible. I thought maybe . . . Do you think they need anything now? I've got a key if they have to open the front door, but I guess they're in already."

"Yeah. If they don't call you, I wouldn't worry about it. Give the key to the Home Health office on Monday."

Carol guessed Estelle was right. "Thanks," she said, and hung up. Poor old guy. Just like her dad; there was something she was supposed to do for him. "It's important," he'd said. There would be a note inside that envelope he'd left for her. *You'll know when to open it. . . . Promise you won't say anything. . . . Take care of Mom. . . . I will, Daddy. . . . OK, Charles. . . .* Poor old guy. She went up to her bedroom and dug the ochre envelope out of the dresser, then came down to open it with Michael, who'd be happy to find the money inside. They sat on the couch in the living room, and she pried the flap open. Hundred-dollar bills came out, thirty of them, when they counted, with a note thanking her and, at the end, a final request.

"WHEN YOU OPEN THIS," the old man had written, in his trembling block lettering, "IT WILL MEAN I HAVE DIED. PLEASE CONTACT MAE PLYLER IMMEDIATELY. SHE IS DR. ARTHURS' RECEPTIONIST. SHE HAS A PACKET WHICH IS TO BE DELIVERED TO HIM AT THE TIME OF MY DEATH. THIS IS VERY IMPORTANT."

"What is it?" asked Michael.

"Nothing. Just a call I have to make." She knew Mae from Civic Club. The number was in the directory: Aaron D. Plyler, on Preston Street.

"Mae?" she said, when a woman's voice answered.

"Yes."

"It's Carol Bowdish. From Civic Club. . . . I'm a Home Health nurse, and I've been taking care of Charles Keller." She paused.

"Yes. Yes. Mr. Keller. . . . Anything wrong? Do you need the doctor?"

"No . . . uh, Mr. Keller has died. . . . I found a note to let you know right after . . . um. . . ."

"Oh. Oh. Yes. . . . Oh, I'm sorry. . . .Yes, I have an envelope to give to the doctor. When did he die? I was supposed to give him . . . to give the envelope to him right after he . . . uh, after I heard he had died."

"I just heard it myself. They found him just a short time ago. An hour or two, I think."

Mae thanked her and hung up. Michael was sitting on the couch, bemused by the thirty crisp hundred-dollar bills, fanning through them with a thumb over and over again, as if to see if they were real.

"What was he like, the guy?" he asked.

"I don't know. A little like Dad, I guess. My dad, I mean. Sick like that, and . . . uh, uncomplaining."

"Well, I'm sure glad you baked him them pies."

"Me too," said Carol. Her eyes were moist, though Michael didn't notice, intent as he was on the banknotes. It was better, after all, that she hadn't called the doctor. The old man had wanted it that way, and she hadn't betrayed him. She'd kept her promise. Too bad she had to see him irrational like that on his last day, though: something he never would have wanted. People after him! Go away for a while! Thank God her father had been lucid to the end.

They'd bank the money and spend it on the kids; well, most of it anyway. And Michael . . . maybe Michael would finally buy himself a new suit.

Mae called the doctor's home.

"Cindy," she said to the voice that answered, "it's Mae. I need to talk to the doctor."

"So why call the house? He's never here!"

"Well, do you know . . . "

"No, Mae, he left around six. That's all I can tell you."

"Would you ask him to call me at home as soon as he gets in?"

Cindy said she'd leave a note, hung up, wrote it, then left it on the kitchen table. That was where he'd look for messages whenever he came in, notes to call the hospital or a patient or a pharmacy to order a pre- scription. And when he walked in an hour later, having forgotten the Chinese food until he was in the driveway, and then having gone back downtown to the little Oriental carry-out place down the street from the courthouse to get it, and having waited fifteen minutes more, until the food was done, and driven back again to his home—having done all of that in half an hour more, he came in to find the note on the table, looking for some other note perhaps, about something else, but not from Mae, of all possible callers, on her day off.

So he went in to Cindy in the den, sitting, as always, in front of the TV, and told her that the food was ready, all but the drinks and plates, which she roused herself to set out. Then, with her thus occupied, he stepped out to the car to get the box of papers from the old man's home. He carried it in, past Cindy, looking on elegantly from the kitchen table, and took it back to his office, this consisting of a desk and some shelves arranged in what a child-rearing family would have used as a third bedroom, up the hall from his master suite. He set the box on his desk, sat down in front of it, and reached for the phone to call Mae.

"Oh, good," she said. "I was afraid you wouldn't get the message." There was an envelope, she told him, something the old man had left with her a month before, on his last visit to the office before his final decline, asking her to give it to the doctor immediately upon his death. Mae didn't say that the old man had slipped her five hundred dollars to complete the task, didn't even tell her husband, but put it away for something special, found money. She'd stop at the office, fetch the packet from a drawer in her desk, then bring it over right away, if that was all right. Sure, said David, he'd be waiting.

So twenty minutes later she was there, walking in on the Chinese meal, with Cindy seeming a little preoccupied, she thought, and the doctor a little tense. He took the envelope and set it on the table beside the paper cartons of rice and noodles, thanked Mae for her efforts, told her he'd see her Monday, to have a nice day off. She said she would. It was a worry off her mind.

"What's that about?" asked Cindy, not seeming particularly curious, thus scarcely looking up from her dumplings.

"Charles Keller died. You knew him. . . . The elderly man who came over a couple of times to see the car. We had him over for dinner about six months ago, remember?"

"Uh, yeah. The guy who looked like that actor you showed me. . . . In the Western."

"Gary Cooper."

"Yeah. . . . He died?"

"Cancer. He had it for a while. It was rough. . . . You would hardly have recognized him at the end. Anyway, I have a box of his papers to go through, and I guess this note's from him. Written a month ago, Mae said. I'll explain it to you when I know what's going on myself."

"Is that where you were all this time?"

"Where did you think?"

"Well, I wouldn't really know. You didn't call. . . . Look, David, I know something's going on. . . . I'm not stupid. . . . If you're seeing someone else, you owe it to me to tell me. . . ." She paused, but he didn't look up, having had enough tonight, enough of everything. This was foolishness. He had no stomach for it now. What did she want from him? What had they all wanted? He took a bite of his egg roll, cool now, and greasy, tasteless to him, then wiped his mouth with a napkin as Cindy started up again, in a diminutive voice this time.

"I called Alan before. . . . After you left."

"*Did* you? How *is* he?... Will you be heading back south soon?" Cindy sat silent, expressionless, playing with her food. Jesus! Three weeks of this! No, more: it started back in May, maybe even earlier. Today, though; what a Goddamn time to pick! He got up from the table, took the envelope Mae had given him, and walked back to his study. He simply didn't have the strength right now; let Alan play psychiatrist for a while.

He closed the door and locked it, then sat down at his desk and opened the envelope. It contained a single folded sheet of paper, a photo, a business card, and a computer disc. Through the door, faintly, he heard water running, then the garbage disposal go on and off, grumbling its throaty roar. Well, she was functioning at some level anyway. And she'd eaten, and vented, so the basics were all covered for a time.

He looked at the paper. It was hand-printed in big block lettering, like the note they had found earlier. "DAVID," it said, "THE ENCLOSED DISKETTE CONTAINS INSTRUCTIONS FOR YOU TO CARRY OUT AFTER MY DEATH. FOR SECURITY, I HAVE PUT THEM INTO A FILE ACCESSIBLE BY A

KEY WORD KNOWN TO YOU. IT IS THE NAME OF THE GIRL YOU DATED IN HIGH SCHOOL. FIRST NAME ONLY. BEST WISHES. (signed) Charles."

He picked up the photo and the card. "Bernard Lesser" said the latter, with an engraved address and a hand-printed phone number. The photo was grainy, taken from a distance. It was of a woman, a close-up of her face, unposed, probably unaware of the camera; a beautiful face, exceptional . . . familiar. Familiar, yes: he recognized the woman. It was the girl whose photo they had found in the envelope under the old man's mattress. The same amazing face, just a couple of years older here. Black hair, full lips pouting a little, bright eyes, green perhaps, though you couldn't tell exactly from the photo. An extraordinary face, though. Extraordinary.

He turned the computer on and popped in the disc, fooling with the program for a minute. "Enter key word," it said. The old man had wanted to know about everything, even that, even her. "Have you ever been in love, really in love?" Keller had asked him two, maybe three months ago. He didn't really know. Puppy love, maybe. There was a girl once, in high school. First love, if that was what it was. Juvenile emotions, born of naiveté and adolescent fantasy, with a toxic brew of hormones thrown into the mix. Donna was her name. He'd thought about her once in a while, but only for an instant at a time, till the old man asked. A sweetheart, truly, certifiably. They'd licked at each other like a couple of puppies in eleventh grade, until her dad got transferred to California; broke his heart; led him to Lynnie on the rebound.

Shrewd old guy. Slick. The file opened, keyed by the letters of Donna's name. The screen came alive:

David,

This is being written on June 10. I would guess that I have a month or so to go. I plan to leave this with Mae to be given to you after my passing. I have tried to think of everything, every contingency, but I may have missed a few. You are a resourceful young man, and I believe I can trust you to see to anything I have overlooked.

First, let me say that I know you will be shocked at being involved in all of this, but I assure you that it will be amply rewarding to you. There is a large amount of money in my estate, and I propose to divide it equally between you and my single remaining relative, a granddaughter, if you can arrange to contact her and see that the 50% that is her share gets into her possession. This will not be as simple as it sounds. I myself tried to contact her some weeks ago, but found her line monitored and was unable to get back to her for that reason. I will try to explain some of this in the letter you have before you.

IT IS ESSENTIAL THAT YOU DO NOT TRY TO PHONE HER DIRECTLY. THE LINE IS BEING MONITORED AND THERE MAY BE CONSIDERABLE DANGER IN THIS BOTH TO YOU AND TO HER.

Many years ago, I was involved with the government in an intelligence capacity. I served in Iran during the 1952 disturbances caused by Mossadegh, and was able to make some valuable contacts there that served me well several years later, when I needed a safe haven. Most of the money I have accumulated came from my years in that country from the early 1960's until the 1979 revolution, when I was forced to leave, first for Egypt and later for the U.S. The money is all legitimate and none is in any way tainted by illicit activity. You and my granddaughter may enjoy it to the fullest extent without the least compunction. I will come back to this shortly.

In the late 1950's, I was assigned to a training program for Cuban exiles set up by the Eisenhower administration. I put my whole heart in it. Those men were truly good men, patriots, who had lost their country to a despot and a fraud. I lived with them for two years, out in the badlands of Texas and in the jungles of Central America, and formed friendships stronger than any I have known before or since. When the Bay of Pigs operation was launched, I was there with my friends, and I watched them get slaughtered on the beach for lack of support on the part of my country, which had sponsored them and made clear promises that they would be aided by us. They were betrayed and I was betrayed.

I left the service after that and went into what you might call contract work. I hope you learn no more details of my subsequent activities, but if you do, this will serve as ample justification. I got out on a boat and made it back to Florida. There were two attempts on my life by my old friends in the Service. I was pretty good in those days, and hard to kill. I got my wife and son out of the country, back to her home in Iran, to keep them safe. I stayed here though, for a while, but got into a nasty piece of business while working free-lance, and finally went back to Iran myself in 1964.

The nasty business is what the present problem is about. There are still interested parties who want the last memory of that episode silenced. I have kept in my possession a carton of papers which document that operation in great detail. I have kept it as a sort of trump card, but it will serve no purpose any longer after I am dead. I believe that if the people concerned get possession of it, with the knowledge that I am dead, and that no one else is party to the information in the box; I believe, under those circumstances, that any danger attached to me or to people associated with me will be ended.

I cannot stress enough the danger involved if this matter is not handled properly. Ten years ago, my son and his wife were killed as a result of an attempt to frighten me into releasing the papers I have referred to. The woman I want you to contact is the only child of their marriage and my only remaining progeny. Take care of her if you can and will. I managed to take particularly good care of the individual who ordered the death of my son, having paid him back in kind. At least he had a bit of his child's flesh to bury. I saw to that. No one need mourn the victim I sacrificed. He was an evil man and did not merit mourning.

Now we come to specific instructions for you. In the envelope containing this letter are three more things. One is a photograph of my grandaughter taken by me six months ago, when I first became impaired by my illness. It was taken from a distance with a 400mm lens. She, of course, was unaware of my presence at that time in Washington, where she works. I believe she was told I died many years ago, and I saw no reason to disturb her with evidence to the contrary at this late date. So I went to see her—that is, to see her from a distance and not be seen, to make sure she was the type of person who might put a large sum of money to good use. I convinced myself that she was. I should say that I made adequate provision for her some years ago, when her parents died, by purchasing an annuity. She currently receives $5000 per month from a fund deposited outside the country, which she has been told was set up by her father for her before his death. She therefore has no immediate need of the additional money I have left her, and if she does not receive it will be quite well off without it. Still, I would prefer that she have it if possible. Her name and address are on the back of the photo, but use them only in an emergency or after you have had assurance that there is no danger in contacting her.

The second item in the smaller envelope is a card with the name of an attorney in Chicago. He represents the parties concerned with the documents in the box, and can be relied upon to be an honest broker in the negotiations with them.

Now to the box. Just to be safe, I have put the instructions for finding it into another file on this disk. Go back to the Programs option and use as a key word the name of the car you were working on when I first met you, the red one. Use the model name, not the manufacturer. This second file will tell you how to locate the box of papers and a second box containing a sum of cash that should handle any incidental expenses incurred in handling this matter. Whatever is there is working money for you to do with as you wish. If you wish not to be involved in this any further, you may keep the currency you find for the trouble you have had so far. If you do decide to proceed, keep whatever cash you find in addition to the 50% of the account you are to share with my granddaughter. The account is with a bank in the Caymans. I took the liberty of forging your signature from a few examples I got from Mae, and my granddaughter's from some things I picked up in Washington in January. That was the primary purpose of my visit there. There should be about seven million dollars in the bank, around three million five for each of you. You need only sign jointly to get it out, or, if you want to leave it where it is, transfer it to separate accounts for the two of you. I would suggest taking it over to Switzerland or having it transferred there. You will need to contact the Caribbean International Bank in Georgetown, Caymans. The manager there, a Mr. Ansari, is an old Persian friend of mine. He can show you how to get money in and out of the U.S. without alerting the IRS, by buying and selling rare stamps and coins in international auctions.

David, you are a good man and a good doctor, and I know you did all you could to help me, but cancer is a difficult challenge to doctor and patient alike.

I wish you well in all you do, whether or not you take on the obligation I have dropped on you. If you do, please know that it gives me great pleasure to leave some of my money to you. I think you are the type of man who will put it to good use, the best use, by enjoying it. If you see my granddaughter, tell her that she was in my thoughts to the end, and that she is the single person in the world I would have most wanted to have known.

Charles Keller

(not, of course, my real name,

which is Adam Gruener)

David scrolled back through the letter, reading it again, line by line, selected paragraphs, then the whole again, scanning it. Unbelievable! No . . . surrealistic, the whole thing, as stark and otherworldly as a dream. And maybe it *was* a dream, the part about the money at any rate, the dream of a sick old man, some final delusion brought on by the cancer and medication. Such things were known, documented, the dissolution of reality in the face of death. Imaginary money, turned from wish into fulfillment, for him, at the end. But what about the other things? The ear, the weapons. They were real. The Persian books too, and that photo . . . that photo. He looked at it again. The old man's granddaughter: Charles . . . whatever his name was . . . whatever it had been . . . Keller, or Gruener. She had his eyes. The image showed that much. She was extraordinary. He turned the picture in his fingers. Her name was on the back, Sarah Gruener, with a phone number and address. He felt behind him; his wallet was still in his back pocket. Cindy had so upset him that he'd quite forgotten to take it out and set it on the sofa table, its habitual repository. His keys were in a pocket too. God, she must have really riled him, though he was over it now, the anger spent. And Cindy was all right now too, composed enough to wash the dishes, from the sound of things. Soon enough she'd be gone. He took out the wallet and slipped the photo in, back into the pocket with the banknotes. The card he stuck behind his credit cards. It slid in neatly, so nothing but a white edge showed.

He turned to the computer and brought up the other program. His GTO was the key, the red one Keller had seen at the car show five years before. GTO opened it, just as Donna's name had opened up the primary file. Two hidden recesses, one beneath the closet, one in the basement. Cash and papers. Simple. So simple he didn't have to take notes. He'd check it out tomorrow. If the boxes were as real as the ear, he'd have some choices to make. Tomorrow he'd find out, then get on with whatever he was going to do; decide that after he'd had some time to think, maybe talk to Clinger in the morning. He had a pretty good head, Clinger did.

Cindy was lying on the couch facing the TV, though not really watching it, when he came into the den. She didn't move. He stepped around the sofa to the chair she had come to associate herself with and sat down in it, facing her recumbent form, looking now less like beautifully arranged drapery than like a very lovely object set awkwardly in a very wrong position. She lay on her back, her head propped slightly on a pillow, at the opposite end of the sofa, perpendicular to his chair. Her face and eyes were turned in the direction of the screen, but now they rotated slightly toward him as he sat down. Her features were in shadow, so he couldn't quite discern her expression. No matter.

"You'll leave me a note this time, I hope, when you leave."

"If that's what you want, yes."

"What I want is a little civility. Just a little human consideration. I think I deserve that."

"Yeah?" she said, sitting up, peering at him, her face still in shadow, but her voice dripping venom. "Yeah, well, *fuck you*, David. I'll tell you what I deserve. . . . Who have *you* been fucking? Tell me who. It's sure not me. That I know."

There wasn't any point in talking to her, not when she was like this. No use reminding her that she was the one who had left, she the one who had phoned three weeks before, begged him to let her come back. Alan was crazy, insanely possessive, smothered her. She knew she'd been demanding, unreasonable. She'd change. She was sobbing, and he couldn't abide that, a woman sobbing a thousand miles away, down a thousand miles of cable, a woman he had cared for, shared intimacy with. OK, OK. He gave in, then, lubricated by her tears, though he knew he was being irrational, absurd. OK, come back; come back, we'll make it right. He picked her up in Pittsburgh, frighteningly cheerful when he met her at the gate, sobbing again two hours later when they entered the house. Three weeks of pouting, crying, draining him as he sat beside her, holding her; drying her eyes, her face, smoothing her hair, bringing her meals, anchoring her to reality.

The anchor hadn't held. It had broken loose today, finally and completely, when he doled out to himself a couple of hours to tinker with the car, mindless time to salve his raw nerves so he could take on another marathon effort at rehabilitation. Three weeks more, four . . . whatever. But this was hopeless, useless.

He heard her voice: "Well . . . did you? Answer me!"

"What? . . . What did you ask?"

"You heard me. I asked you if you ever loved me. You heard me!"
She sat up, forward on the sofa, her head turned toward him, tilted wryly.

"I . . . I guess so. Look, what's the difference?"

"What's the *difference*? Jesus Christ!..." She went on, but he wasn't
listening. What did she want from him now? Love? He'd cared for her,
taken care of her, enjoyed her company. Sometime long ago. Did she
want a deranged fool, all-consumed and all-consuming, like the two or
three doting women he'd known, impassioned, persistent lovers who
phoned day and night, parked outside his house or office to catch a
glimpse of him, spy on him, feeding their own frenzy. He wasn't like that,
never was and never would be. Come to think of it, neither was she.
Maybe Alan was.

"Maybe Alan loves you the way you want," he said, interrupting her
acidulous soliloquy.

"Yeah. Yeah. I think so," she said, and fell silent.

"Look, I've had a long day." He stood up and moved around the chair
that had been Cindy's to the sofa table behind her. "I'm going to take a
Tylenol and get some sleep. You keep our . . . uh . . . the king bed. I'll
sleep in the second bedroom. I'll just get some things out now . . . so I
won't disturb you in the morning." He emptied his pockets—change,
keys, wallet—on the sofa table. That was where he had forgotten to put
them before, rattled by this recently estranged woman. But he set them
there now, in the exact place he had deposited them each night, retrieved
them each morning, for months and years, since the furniture was new,
and he new too, a fresh new doctor in a house and town brand new to him,
with all his life before him, at the tip of his imagination.

With not another word, he left Cindy to her thoughts.

"Prick!" she murmured to herself, barely aloud. "Selfish prick!" She
heard a door close, then water hissing on its way to the second bathroom
he was using. Two days more, two long days here in this place before
Alan would arrive to take her south. He was a prick too, Alan was, leaving
her here, making her wait like this. For what? Some flight he couldn't
change, or didn't even try to. He'd have to fly to Frankfurt, he'd said, then
back from Frankfurt. That wouldn't be till Monday, Monday noon or

after. Then two hours from Miami to Pittsburgh, and two more to drive up
to get her; say, six, maybe seven p.m. Then they'd be out of there, away
from this asshole, this lying smart ass who wasn't worth the dirt on Alan's
shoes. Well, the dirt on her shoes. . . . Alan wasn't so perfect himself.
They'd get back to Pittsburgh by midnight, stay in a motel, and head out on
the first flight Tuesday morning. He'd feel it then. Leave him a note? Shit!

The sound of running water stopped. A door opened. Another closed.
Good. Go to sleep. Go to hell! Two Goddamn days and she'd be the fuck
out of here.

There'd be some incidentals on the trip, she figured, a drink or a magazine while Alan made arrangements or went to take a pee. She ought to
have a little money on her, change at least. Knowing Alan, she'd better
have a bit of cash. There wasn't much of anything in her purse, a couple
of bills maybe. David owed her something, owed her bigtime. She
reached behind her for his wallet on the sofa table, pulled out some bills,
a fifty and two smaller notes, then noticed something oversized, protruding past the leather edge of the currency pocket. A photo. She took it out.

"That . . . dirty . . . fucker." Now she understood it. Here it was. She'd
asked him if he loved her. What a joke! Did he love her? He was too busy
with this other bitch. She turned the picture in her hand, looking at the
back of it. Sarah . . . Sarah Gruener. Address, phone number. Convenient.
Goddamn bitch, she thought, *I want to hear her voice.*

A woman answered, after the second tone. "Hello." She sounded
sheepish. Good.

"Is this Sarah?"

"Yes?" Drawn out and hesitant, the wariest of affirmations.

"I'm calling about a mutual acquaintance."

"Yes? Yes?" She could hear the woman's anxiety. She smiled.

"David Arthurs? You know him? Dr. David Arthurs?"

"No."

"You don't know him?"

"I'm sorry. . . . What is this about?"

"Hey, do you know him or not?"

"I don't think so. Did he say he knew me? Did he give you this
number?"

"He has your picture here . . . in his wallet."

"Picture? . . . A picture of me? Are you sure? Look, have you called here . . .? You're not the one who's been calling. . . ."

Cindy stopped her, speaking crisply into the phone, spitting out each word, flinging them like quickly dealt cards from a new deck. "I found your picture in his wallet. Your *picture*. Do you understand me? Are you, like, mid-twenties, with black hair? Thin?"

Silence.

"Your *picture*. Your name, address, phone number. This is your fucking *phone number*, isn't it? You want to tell me you don't know what I'm talking about?"

"I don't . . . understand." Her voice broke, trembling. She made a sound, but it was unintelligible.

"Are you going to tell me about it?"

"Listen to me. I don't know. . . ." Cindy could hear her voice close off.

"So tell me. You must have been up here like three weeks ago. When I was gone. What did he do, call you when I left?"

"Listen to me. . . ."

"Listen to you? Fuck you. I'll fix the both of you." She punched one of the numbers on the phone, errantly, trying to hang up. A beep went off, metallic B-flat, mocking, infuriating. Then she found the right button and jammed the handpiece into its cradle, shaking with anger.

CHAPTER 8

H E DREAMED OF LYNNIE. ODD, DREAMING OF HER, NOT HAVING SEEN her in years. What was it, eight years? Ten? . . . Ten, he thought. When her mother died. Lynnie, of all people. He hadn't so much as thought of her in months, hardly ever thought of her really, since she left.

They were running down a hallway, he and Lynnie, *this* hallway, in *this* house in Bakersville, a place she had never seen, a town she probably couldn't point to on a map. And all their old possessions were there. *Here*. Here in this house, there, in the dream. Things they had bought as newlyweds: furniture, pictures. He couldn't see them all but knew that they were there, felt their presence the way one feels the presence of things in dreams.

She ran behind him down the passage, outside the room in which he now lay, running with him, a step behind, not *toward* something, but *away from* . . . what? That he didn't know, for the dream dissolved into awakening, and its imagery fled before him like a fluttering bird, just out of reach, ascending. He came awake, refreshed. So the dream had worked its magic, or sleep had, nine hours of it, harboring this dream, half remembered, and others, four or five more, entirely forgotten in the long night and lazy morning, till he woke to the bells outside and his surfeit of sleep, and the strange dream's end, and it was Sunday.

It was the Presbyterian church whose bells he heard this day, as David Arthurs exited his inexplicable dream. Six or seven blocks away it stood, down on Main Street, but the sounds it bellowed volleyed through the urban valley's bowl, reflected by a wall of hills, clear up through his window. Sunday sounds they were, summoning the town in time to eat some breakfast and dress for church.

He woke now, fully. Lynnie, of all people to dream of, a memory charged with not the tiniest scintilla of emotion, neither regard nor disdain, but absolute and utter indifference. He hadn't felt much more than that when she left him, eleven years before, walked out one day during the last year of his residency, moved in with another man, another doctor, a surgical resident she'd been furtively sleeping with for the six months before. Not her first time, and not much of a surprise but for the timing. Any other woman would have waited a few more months. She would have had some money from him then, alimony from a practicing physician, with at least the prospect of a comfortable income. Lynnie wasn't one to wait, though, so all she wound up with was the furniture. He'd shipped that off to her as soon as she was settled: china, silver, all their household goods. He had wanted no part of them, no memory. And, to his surprise, there was none.

He sat up and swung his feet over onto the soft carpet beside the bed. "Jesu, Joy of Man's Desiring" the bells played, now into the ninth measure. They weren't proper bells, of course. It would have taken a world-class campanile with ten tons of sonorous iron to play such full-fledged hymns as the Presbyterians turned out; heavy metal indeed. But they had a marvelous set of speakers in their steeple, and some *trompe l'oreille* recordings of actual bells that did about as well as the real thing. He rubbed his eyes and stretched his legs past the sixteenth bar, then gathered himself up to wash and dress.

He had slumbered past a lovely early morning. At dawn a thick mist had filled the hollow of the town, an earthbound cloudlet flattened at its upper surface into a broad shelf as visually distinct as a snowbank three stories high, level with the Main Street roofs. It was a frequent visitor, that gravitated cloud, settling into the saucer of terrain enfolding downtown Bakersville whenever rainfall or humidity wet the mountain air, after a thaw in winter or a storm in summer, or during a hot and humid spell, as at present. David had seen that sort of mist a hundred times from the hospital hill, spread out below him in the valley, always in the morning, just after dawn, before his daily rounds. Most days it burned off quickly, this day by nine, prodded by an eager sun. So the morning shone bright as new chrome to the waking town, all blue and gold and green.

He looked out through the bathroom window, out on a brilliant day, on one of those occasional mornings so brazenly beautiful that disasters just don't seem possible, that their occurrence would be inappropriate, an imposition. He washed and shaved, regarding himself in the mirror: fresh, open-eyed. A good night's sleep had served him well, that or the sunshine. What did it matter which or how? Last night's worries were not so much forgotten as neutralized, Cindy's departure accepted, the old man's business less a duty than a light diversion.

He stepped down the hallway to the room he had slept in. Past it, Cindy's door was closed, the one to the master bedroom. *She must have been up half the night*, he thought; *half the night, poor kid*. Quite a lather she had gotten herself into! As if he would have been seeing someone else! As if he'd ever had the inclination! Or the energy. That was hardly his style. She should have known it. All of his women should have, though they never seemed to. It wasn't something he was remotely capable of. One at a time: he'd always been that way, ever since Lynnie. Not that it made any difference in the long run. Not with a single one of them.

He slipped into his pants and shirt, the clothes from the evening before. They were still fresh, clean enough for the hospital anyway, and more than clean enough for the work he'd have to do at the old man's place. As for Cindy, when he made it home, the clothes wouldn't really matter. She'd hate him whatever he wore, however he looked, whatever he said. He'd try, but that was the way things always ended, with him harboring no anger, bearing no ill will, but the woman livid, implacable. What did he do to evoke that kind of hatred? What had he ever done? There'd never been a time he'd hurt a woman knowingly, guiltlessly. He was always generous, kind, affectionate in his way.

The pattern was invariably the same. He would meet someone, some aggressive female who would initiate the relationship. He rarely said no, liking the company. Sometimes he liked the woman too, or, even if not particularly attracted to her, he found himself incapable of hurting her feelings. They would enjoy each other's company, do things together, act like a couple eventually. Three months it would last, maybe six. Then something would change. The woman would grow uneasy, agitated. "You don't love me," she would say, or "You're different." Sometimes it was less defined: "You never take me out," though he always did, or "You never listen to me," though he always did that too, listened carefully, hoping to understand what was beginning to go wrong. He never did understand though, so the woman would leave, bitter, vengeful. And he'd think about her for a week or a month in remembrance but not despair, until her replacement appeared, calling him at home or running into him four times a week at the office or the gym. Eleven years ago he'd thought that Lynnie was the bottom of the barrel, but since that time he hadn't risen from the bottom all that terribly much.

He started the car, light in his eyes reflected from the Buick's hood. Two boys with baseball gloves walked by the open window, half skipping. "Hi, Dr. Arthurs," said one. "Hi, Doc," chimed the other. He smiled and waved, gave them time to pass, then shifted into drive, opening the passenger window. . . . Crazy dream, he thought. Lynnie, of all people! Well, if dreaming of her had made him feel even a little better after last night, he'd suffer through the dreams. Eleven years it had been, and here she was back in his mind, finally useful for something after all.

He turned out onto Main, in stream with the occasional cars dribbling in, heading to church. It would take an hour at the hospital, he figured, maybe a little more; then straight out to the farmhouse. By noon he ought to have a handle on the situation: how much of the old man's note was real and how much delusional, a product of those prostate cells gone mad. Well, if it was all fabrication, every bit of it, so much the better. He'd call the girl and tell her that her grandfather had died. Gently though; he knew how to do it. She could sell the house and get a decent sum for it. There likely was some money somewhere too. They'd find a bank account maybe; maybe even some cash. Then there were the coins, the ones they'd found in the second room upstairs. They had to be worth some-thing, just the gold alone.

Six patients in the hospital. He saw them quickly. *How are you today? Pain any less? Appetite any better?* He checked their lab results, wrote dutiful progress notes, appropriate orders. *Yes, of course, have your daughter call me at home. This evening.*

He stopped in the ER.

"Hi, Dr. Arthurs." It was Rhonda.

"Good morning," he answered. "What happened with Mrs. Chilcott?" That would be Dora.

Rhonda looked blank.

"Oh, that's right, that's right. It was after three. I saw her yesterday . . . in the ER. . . . You *leave* at three, *don't* you?"

"Every day." She sang that like a nightingale, "ev-ree-*da*-ay," then dropped into a contralto tone, sultry: "What did you have in mind?" She raised an eyebrow.

"OK, OK." He smiled back, polite but formal, thinking *Not today, Rhonda . . . not today.* "Can you check the chart for me?"

"You know I'd do *anything* for you, Dr. Arthurs." She stepped away from the reception area, then came back a minute later with some records from Saturday, a thick beige folder she held between her crossed arms and lavender blouse. When she passed the folder to his hands, the thin card cover bore a remnant of her body's warmth.

The notes from the previous day were atop the thick chart. "Dora Chilcott/ Dischg. from ER 7:35/ Stable, vitals nl./ Sched. surg. Tues./ Nouri. Lap. cholecystect." Good. Very good. By Tuesday night that incor-rigible gall bladder would be in a jar. One less problem to burden his mind.

"Thanks, Rhonda." He handed the folder back to her, smiled politely once again, started out, then turned back toward her, into her gaze.

"Oh, Rhonda?"

"Yes, Dr. Arthurs." Big wide eyes. Cute. Married to a guy with a gun collection, often used and kept in firing order. A five-act tragedy waiting for its victim.

"I'll be out for a while. Two, three hours. Could you let the switchboard know?" She smiled again.

The place looked lonely when he got there. Not that the day was less bright, the sky less blue, but morning sunlight, stark in its obliquity, seemed to emphasize the untended lawn, the ruts in the gravel drive. He parked near the porch and let himself into the house, deciding on the upstairs first. That part of the place he knew, from his visits to the old man and then the night before with Clinger. Familiarity made it less forbidding. He'd start there, with the closet.

He leaped up the stairs two by two, grazing the wall at the yard-wide landing three-quarters of the way up. The old man's keys were in his pocket. He found the proper one and opened the closet door.

The diskette had told him what to do. First clean out some of the weaponry, set it aside. OK. He moved the cannon, then the M-40, placed them on the floor gently, gingerly, then some of the ammunition clips. The grenades and explosives and liquid substances—whatever their nature—were up above. He didn't have to touch them, for which he was exceedingly glad. The closet floor was all that was important now, and now it was clear and accessible. Screwdriver in the bureau, bottom drawer, the diskette said. And it was there. The old man had thought of everything. Everything! Pry up the toe moldings. OK. Done. Now the carpet comes up. Good. Done. Then the floorboards lift together. And they were up, revealing a metal case, a courier case, up now, onto the bed. Lockable but unlocked, as the diskette had said. It snapped open.

Unbelievable! "Unbelievable," he said aloud to himself in the empty house. "Unbelievable!"—touching the surface of the money with a finger. The case was filled with it. "Working money" the old man had called it. Maybe for a factoryful of workers. He fumbled through it, fingering the pads of bills, shifting, restacking, counting quickly, roughly. Hundred-dollar bills banded in bundles of a hundred. Twenty-four of them. Then eighteen packs of fifties, twelve of twenties. Three hundred sixty-four thousand. Three hundred sixty-four thousand dollars! Then a few broken packs and loose bills, eight one-inch-long tubes of bullion gold coins, Krugerrands. Altogether around four hundred thousand dollars. He closed the case and took it out to his car. His hands were shaking, palms moist. The case slipped as he opened the trunk, but he caught it and set it down on the carpeted floor carefully, protectively.

He was perspiring briskly, round beads of sweat, brow and neck wet and running. He wiped his face, opened the Buick's passenger side door, and sat transversely on the seat, feet on the gravel. Jesus! That money! He hadn't doubted its existence; no, the note was too specific for that, too rational. But the amount! It gave a different scale to the old man's figures, making them less exaggerations than understatements. Like his printing, like the weapons, everything the old guy did was in boldface capitals. So what about the other things his note had spoken of, those millions in the bank, the papers, the men who wanted them so desperately? They would be just as real as the money in that metal case, not brain metastases or drug-induced delusions, but truths, inevitabilities.

Jesus! thought David. His heart sounds were beating in his ears, as through a stethoscope, as though he was listening to someone else's heart, racing, laboring. He was in it now, big time, though he could easily walk away. Or could he? Could he really? Did he already know too much to get out? And what about the girl, that picture in his wallet? What would happen to her if the old man's instructions weren't followed to the letter?

That was the problem: the plans had been so specific, everything arranged so meticulously, that it seemed perfectly natural just to do what the instructions said. What, after all, did he have to do to finish things? Dig out another box, make a few calls. A couple of days' effort, maximum. And the money: half of seven million the diskette said; enough to live whatever kind of life he chose, to take care of Karen and her family, to . . . . If he could only justify keeping so much for so little effort. Well, that he'd decide after talking with the girl. If everything went as planned, he'd phone her in a couple of days. By week's end he'd be finished with it all, a lot richer maybe, but, at worst, having lost nothing more than a day or two of time in the office

So it wasn't all that onerous, really, the task old Charles had dropped on him—Charles or Adam, whichever. Besides, it was kind of an adventure, a riveting story that was unfolding as he participated. What could it hurt to finish out the present chapter at least, then talk with Clinger, show everything to him, see what he thought best? David sat for a minute, thinking, took some deep breaths, trying to calm himself, stood, closed the car door, and went back into the house.

His heart had slowed now, the adrenaline storm past. He found a glass and took a drink from a bottled water dispenser in the kitchen, went to the door leading to the basement, opened it, and set the glass down behind him on the kitchen table. There was a switch just inside the door, and he flipped it up. The basement exploded with light, eight hundred-watt fluorescent bulbs, as he counted, now downstairs standing beneath them. Bright as daylight. The old man must have had a reason for that. There was a workbench off to the right of the stairway, and to the left he saw the washer and dryer, just where they were supposed to be, resting on a piece of gray linoleum that ran to, and stopped at, the staircase. He set to work.

He found a toolbox on a shelf beneath the workbench, exactly where the diskette had indicated, brought it over and set it down beside the appliances. Electric first. He unplugged both cords. Then the gas lines; tracing them up to a feed pipe, he turned a screw valve, then disconnected the two brass fittings with the appropriate wrench, detached the vent from the dryer, then the water and drain connections to the washer. Both free now. He strained to move them across the malleable linoleum, the footplates sticking in the soft surface, but finally freed and shifted, both of them, onto the far end of the gray covering near the stairs.

Then metal strips, screwed down, securing the linoleum to the cement floor. They came up, three of them, leaving the edge at the staircase still secured. And now it was free, and the gray material lifted, coiled, rolled back, and there was a break in the concrete with a wooden panel covering it, flush with the surface, directly underneath the floor space the appliances had occupied. The wood had a fingerhole. He lifted it easily. The fluorescent light shone on another metal case, snug within a recess in the concrete. He grasped the handle on its top and pulled it out. Thirty pounds, maybe a little more. He brought it over to the foot of the stairs.

It was sealed. Don't open it, the diskette said. He wasn't about to, wasn't even curious, just wanted to get rid of it, to get it to the lawyer, contact the girl, get on with his life with or without the money. He couldn't even think of that now. They were supposed to be able to tell—whoever "they" were—that the case had not been opened, that he was not privy to whatever perilous secrets it contained. The diskette had said that. He examined the metal box. It had a hinged top with a flange lock in front, secured there by a floppy combination padlock and sealed around its edge of closure with transparent packaging tape, like a safety seal. In front, adjacent to the lock, beneath the tape, was an envelope tightly glued down at all four edges and across its surface by the tape. David tilted the case back. The envelope was addressed to the old man, Charles Keller, in what looked to be his own writing, sent through the mail to his own address and canceled January 8, 1996, six months earlier. On its surface, below the address, printed in the same block letters, were the words COMBINATION INSIDE. Pretty smart, that old guy. Pretty God damned smart.

He carried up the sealed box and locked it in the trunk of the Buick beside the other case. It was hot now, thick and humid, nearly noon. He took out his keys and got into the car, then remembered the lights still on in the basement, the unlocked door. What was he thinking? He felt the presence of the cases behind him, back in the trunk, felt them as if they were cold metal pressing on his back, then lower, lower, like something cold beneath him on the seat, or something very hot. He opened the car door and stepped out. The fields about the house were silent, hot, windless. The door closed: Clunk! low and tonic, extended but echoless amid the thick green foliage. There was a hissing sound, familiar. He knew it: truck tires on heated asphalt, out past the trees, out on the highway, growing slightly louder though distant, then diminishing to silence again, the background silence of the fields, as some vehicle proceeded on its way to the interstate, or away from it toward Pittsburgh.

He had to think, to sit somewhere and think. The porch was adjacent, and he dropped onto its floor, onto the painted surface just above the steps, elbows on knees, palms on temples. OK, he thought, OK . . . Charles . . . but it wasn't Charles. . . . It was Adam. Adam, then. Adam . . . he worked on this for months, planned everything, down to key words and screwdrivers. Sharp sonofabitch, too. Knew what he was doing. So? What now? Well . . . let it play out, just the way he planned it. Do what he said to do, then extrapolate: do what he *would* have done, under any altered set of circumstances. Act like him, think like him. Do it for a few days at least, until the old man's drama had run all five acts out to its conclusion.

That would be the key. Old Keller—Gruener—had died in bed, his thousands in the closet, then maybe millions more beside, untouched. Died in peace behind an arsenal of weapons, never used. His way seemed to be the proper way, the only way. Just relax, play it out, and flow along with it.

He got up and went back into the house. It was inviting, cool after the porch, not an unpleasant place really, now that the mystery was out of it. What would the old man do? What?... He went upstairs.

The closet stood open, the floor boards still up, as he had left things an hour before. The cannon, or whatever it was, lay on the carpet beside the M-40. He replaced everything as it had been, as he remembered it, the floorboards, the carpet, the molding. Then the weapons, just as they had been oriented when the closet was first opened, not hard to do at all. The old man had so arranged the contents of the closet that everything in it seemed to fit perfectly in its appointed place, like an engine being reassembled. . . . *Just try to think like him, to do what he would have done.*

He smoothed the bed, erasing the impression left by the metal case. The room no longer smelled of urine. The summer had seen to that, what with its scents of grass and flowers, penetrating through the unclosed window. He looked about the room, at the round yellow stain upon the geometric center of the sheet, not at all offensive now, but comforting in a way, as if it represented the old man's presence. The carpet at his feet still showed the imprint of the guns. He rubbed across it with his shoes until the flattening blended with the marks of the deputies' purposeful steps, of the medics' theatrical prancing, of the sheriff's sluggish gait.

Then down the stairs again. He thought of calling Clinger, thought twice about it, carefully, turning the thought in his mind like a chess piece, then decided it was entirely appropriate. Was there a reason *not* to call? He couldn't think of one, nothing the old man would have objected to. The number was on a slip of paper in the car, but he found a phone book beside the old man's telephone on a table near the door. Clinger, Brian, 566 Walnut. He dialed.

"Hey, Doc, where are you? I called your place a couple of times this morning, but nobody answered. I figured you had to go out. . . . To the hospital or something."

Cindy! Either still asleep or just not answering the phone.

"I'm out at, uh, Keller's place. I came out an hour or so ago. After the hospital. . . . Listen, I've got a lot of stuff to tell you . . . stuff to show you. Can we get together sometime today? I'm going to need some help, or advice, at least . . . if you've got time. . . ."

"Sure, Doc. I don't know about you getting involved in this though. It's not. . . ."

"No, it's OK, Brian. Everything's pretty well under control. I got the, uh, 'full details.' He left them with Mae, my secretary. I just need some minor help."

"OK, then. I'll be around all day. Only thing is, I've got my kids today. The weekend, you know? We could all come out there if that's OK with you. I just don't like to leave them. Weekends are the only time we get to see each other, and they get upset if . . . well, you know how kids are."

"Yeah, sure, I know. I know. There's just some stuff here that maybe they shouldn't be familiar with. . . ."

"Yeah. Look, they're big kids, teens. They can entertain themselves and leave us alone if we need to talk or something. They're good kids. They'll do just what I tell 'em to do and won't bother us. You can come over here if you want to, but it's a small house, and I think where you're at would be a better place. More private, you know? They'd have more space to spread out."

"OK, Brian, OK, come on out, if you think that's best. I've got a little something to do first, so maybe half an hour from now would be good."

He heard voices on the line beyond Clinger's, a girl's voice, of indeterminate age, and a male voice, post-pubertal, gruffly adolescent, mocking, arguing, then Clinger speaking, muffled, away from the phone, not clear. "Hey! You guys are gonna get it!" Something like that. Then laughter, childlike from both, though faint, no longer adolescent but purely childlike and happy. "OK," said Clinger back into the phone. "OK, we'll be out in about a half hour."

He clicked the phone off. Plenty of time, half an hour. He went back into the basement, over first to the break in the floor. The wooden panel lay open slantwise across the recess. As he slid it back, he noticed something in the bottom of the concrete well, reached in and lifted it out. It was a small box, somewhat larger than a cigar box, swathed tight in transparent wrap. More surprises! Well, whatever it was, he didn't have time right now. He set it aside, replaced the wooden panel, took the little box over to the stairs, put it down there, and got to work restoring everything to the way he had found it an hour before: first the linoleum, then the metal strips, finally the washer and dryer, reconnecting all the lines and pipes. There were a couple of marks in the linoleum where the footplates of the appliances had stuck. They looked suspicious. He took a hammer from the toolbox and tapped them into generic-looking gouges, nondescript, no longer suspicious. His watch said twelve-ten. Five minutes left.

He seated himself on the second basement step and unwrapped the small case, stripping the adherent cellophane from its leathery surface, crinkling it into a ball, then opening the case. There was a gun inside, a sophisticated thing of shiny silver metal with an elongated barrel, nestled in a velvety depression in the case. Beside it, in a separate slot, was a cylinder three inches long. It looked like a silencer and it was, for the barrel of the gun was threaded at its end. The case was still weighted with the gun removed. He lifted the velvet material. Beneath it was a full clip and dozens of extra bullets, fifty or so, taped in a series of horizontal rows to the bottom of the case. Was this meant for him? He shook his head. How could it have been? What was he thinking?

He was perspiring again, but his hands felt cold: anxiety, more reflex than conscious. Well, that was normal under the circumstances. Perfectly normal. All in all, he hadn't done too badly for himself. The old man would have approved. Of course he'd check it out with Clinger. They'd be there any time now, Clinger and his kids. Any minute. He turned out the basement lights and went outside, scanning the gravel drive. No sign of them yet. He put the little case in the trunk with the others, then sat on the porch, thinking, waiting for his pulse to slow.

The top step felt hot beneath his body, the air hot now too, but it was a cheerful heat, humid, summery, and fragrant. His hands were warm again. There was a sound, distant, both unfamiliar and recognizable, chattering and popping; tires on gravel, vaguely louder in a moment, then more distinct, and more, and then the glint of light on painted metal, down deep along the access drive. Clinger. Once visible, the big red pickup became entirely an object of sight, its chattering sounds blending indistinguishably into the ambient song of nearer hill and farther highway. And then Clinger's truck was in the driveway, stopping up near the house, and he climbing out, down from the tall cab, with his kids scrambling onto the drive from the other open door.

Todd was the boy, husky like his dad, but less tall. David hadn't seen him in years, since he was eight or nine. He guessed sixteen now, and he was close. Fifteen it was, waiting for Drivers Ed. next fall semester. He looked like a weightlifter and he was, flexing his biceps whenever he thought himself looked at, or thought about being looked at, or, indeed, thought about his biceps. But he was polite, well-mannered. David shook his hand. He had a gentle handshake, respectful, like his dad's.

The girl's name was Amanda. Mandy, Clinger called her. Shy, awkward, exorbitantly adolescent, just fourteen, tall for her age, stringy, with naturally blond hair, a little too blonde and stringy too, but with a nice face that showed some promise of post-adolescent beauty. She shook hands furtively, looking away most of the time, trying to suppress a painful, silly little smile that lingered, nonetheless.

Clinger tossed Todd the keys to his Ford, told him he could practice driving along the access road, but not as far as the highway. "Take your sister." They giggled and were off down the drive in a minute, slowly though, and jerkily, with some grinding of gears. Clinger shrugged and smiled. "Still under warranty," he said. "So? What'd you find?"

David told him. It took only a few minutes. Todd was halfway down the access road toward the highway, quite visible. He slowed to turn around at a place where the berm widened. David walked over and popped the Buick's trunk, revealing the cases, then snapped open the one filled with money. "Jesus!" said Clinger, who moved his hand toward the open case but stopped short, as if incapable of touching the bills directly. David did it for him, pulling out a pad of hundred dollar notes and fanning through them with his thumb. "How much is in there?" the deputy asked.

"In the case?"

"Yeah."

"About four hundred thousand."

Clinger's mouth dropped open. "God *damn*," he said. Fifty yards away, Todd passed the gravel drive, heading out along the access road toward an old abandoned farm and some vacant hunting camps. Mandy waved through the back window.

"Could you . . . I hate to ask you this. . . . Do you think you could keep these things for me until I'm ready to unload them?"

Clinger pinched his nose between his fingers, thumb and index finger, up near the top of the bridge. "Hey, Doc, I can keep the two of them . . . put them away for you. Not the money, though. I can't be responsible for that. Not cash like that. I just can't do it."

"OK, I guess I can find a place to hide the money. But you'll be careful with the papers, right? They have to stay sealed."

"Come on, Doc. . . ."

"OK, Brian, OK, I'm just emphasizing the point. Sorry. Look, if things work out OK, and if I wind up keeping any of this money—I mean, after I talk to the girl—I . . . I want you to know that I'll take care of you. Make it worth your while for the trouble. . . ."

"Hey, Doc, I ain't about to turn down money, but I'll do what I can to help you with or without it. I don't need much for myself. Nothing much I want to buy. Just for the kids. College and so on. But I make a pretty good living, and we do OK. Let's get you out of this business, and we'll worry about the money later, if there's anything to worry about."

Todd had turned again and was heading back toward the driveway. Clinger waved both prodigious arms in wide arcs, summoning him, and he turned up the drive, bringing the pickup to an erratic stop two yards behind the Buick. Clinger took the big case with the papers and the small one with the gun and placed them back behind the seat of his truck. Todd and Mandy must have known from his look not to ask any questions.

"I'll talk to you tomorrow," said David. Clinger backed the truck around, waved from the window, and headed out the driveway. Mandy's head turned toward him, the silly smile still unsuppressed. David waved, and she turned away, then back again through the side window now, as the truck passed out of the driveway and down the access road toward town, the silly smile fading as the pickup grew more and more distant, and soon the truck itself was gone, entirely gone, past the last visible turn, but for its tires in the gravel, chattering and popping; then that faded, too, and all that remained was the vague sound of the highway and the shaggy hills and bees humming in the fields and the summer sun directly overhead, inching toward the western sky. He climbed into the Buick, its trunk laden with gold and banknotes, and left the old man's property, never to return.

CHAPTER 9

H IS NAME WAS LEONARD SISKIN. HE MIGHT HAVE BEEN A HANDSOME man once, long ago, but now, a couple of years out on the steep and footless slope past fifty, time and gravity had long since eroded any elegance he might have possessed in youth. From any distance he looked lumpy, rounded in the middle, with an awkward gait, awkwardly tall, and never agile, with oversized feet and hands, a rounded head perfectly bald above, reflective in its hairlessness, a face pear-shaped now for lack of upward elasticity.

A man named Isacco had hired him. By phone. Communicated with him that way, too. Isacco from Chicago, no first name, calling one night late, well after ten; he got the name from so-and-so, who'd worked with him at such-and-such a time and place. A thousand a week. You couldn't turn that down. Not for some simple surveillance anyway. It wasn't even full-time. Tap a phone and check the tapes. Rent a suitable place nearby, all expenses covered.

Gruener was the name. Sarah Gruener. She lived in Bethesda in an expensive condo, about three hundred thousand, he guessed; lived up on the seventh floor, alone. There was a rental available on two, for fifteen hundred a month. OK, Isacco said. It took a year's lease, so he gave a phony name; he would have anyway. Just leave when you're done, Isacco said. Let them keep the deposit, and split. He paid in cash, three grand.

Then five hundred extra, in bills: five hundreds, folded neatly in his hand, for the manager, and he was in the basement for the tap. He had to check up on his wife, he told the guy, record his own incoming calls. The manager didn't care.

He hooked in a basic system with caller ID. There was no need for fancy equipment. This wasn't the CIA. He went out and bought some furniture too, just for appearance sake; stayed there once overnight even, after he'd put down six Martinis at a topless bar with the boys and Betty told him not to drive back to Alexandria like that.

Leonard checked the machine every day at ten. He couldn't see any reason to get up earlier. The phone wasn't going anywhere, and nothing much had come in on it anyway. Nothing at all since that call from Pittsburgh a couple of months ago, a detection device it sounded like, with no voice on the line. He had the number on a little printout, phoned back the next day, got a Ramada Inn, told them it was a call from his sick brother, convincingly enough. They told him to call again in an hour; they'd pull up the records. He waited at the condo for a while, then called. From room 305, they said, a man, apparently alone, who'd checked out the night before, just after the call, paid in cash. No one could remember what he looked like. The name? Edward Teller. Bang! Cute.

Not a bite since then, not until today, Sunday, ten-fifteen, playback time. "He has your picture, your *picture*. Do you understand?" Listen for anything strange, Isacco had told him. Bingo. He called the number in Chicago, left a message on an answering machine. Thirty minutes later Isacco called him back.

"We got a fish on the line," Leonard told him.

"You got a number?"

"Yeah. Eight-one-four area code. Number's . . . ." He read out the other seven digits.

"OK, play me the tape."

"Over the phone?"

"Yeah. Play it."

He did, then played it a second time when Isacco asked.

"FedEx the tape to the address I gave you." Leonard guessed it was a vacant office with a telephone answering machine and maybe a desk and two chairs. He was wrong about the second chair.

"Did you check the number out yet?" Isacco asked.

"No, sir. I wanted to run it by you first."

"OK, good. I'll do it." He paused. "Look, I'll get back to you if we need anything else. You did good, real good."

"Yeah, thanks, thanks, Mr. Isacco. I . . . I kind of hate to see this job end though."

"Don't worry. It's not over yet. Plus, looks like you get a bonus if this seals it. A big bonus. OK?"

"Sounds good. OK. Yeah. I'll be home if you need me. I'll keep the tape on, right?"

"Yeah. Same as before."

It was Isacco who called the house. Nearly noon now, but she was still in bed, half asleep. She answered on the fifth ring.

"Arthurs'."

"Arthurs' residence, is this?"

"Yeah," said Cindy, remembering now who Arthurs was. "Yeah, it is."

"Is David there, the doctor?"

"Well, I don't really know. . . . If he didn't answer, I guess not. I guess he's not."

"OK, hold on, then. Maybe you can help me. We're looking for someone. An older man. Someone the doctor may know."

"Look," said Cindy sharply, "I don't really know who he knows or doesn't know. Who are you anyway?"

"Oh, sorry, ma'am. Agent, uh, Larsen. I'm with Treasury . . . the, uh, the Treasury Department. . . . It's very important."

"God, it must be for you to work on Sunday. OK, look . . . I was sleeping. Sorry. I don't think I can help you, though."

"Well, try to think, ma'am. It would be an older man. Someone the doctor might have had contact with recently . . . the past couple of months. We're looking for some papers . . . tax records and so on."

That rang a bell. Papers. David had mentioned papers. What did he have last night? The old man who died. Gary Cooper, that guy. . . . Yeah. . . . Yeah . . . she remembered. One of his patients; died yesterday, or that's when they found him. She didn't remember the name, but yes, there were some papers . . . a box he brought in last night, David did, a box of some-thing. . . . Papers, she thought he'd said.

"Are they there now?"

She guessed so. He took them . . . where? . . . into his study, she thought. Did he go through them, did she know? She didn't. He was in there for a while though. . . . Fuck him.Let him get in trouble with the IRS or whatever it was. . . . Treasury Department? Was that what the guy said?

"Well, thank you, Miss. . . ."

"Cindy."

"Yes. Thank you, Cindy. You've been a big help. You've done real good." *Real good, eh?* . . . Not too sharp at theTreasury Department, were they? What did she care? She'd be the hell out of there tomorrow.

She washed and put on a pair of cut-off jeans and a tank top, emerging from her room at twelve-thirty. He was gone, his wallet and keys absent from the sofa table, and when she looked out front she saw that the Buick was gone too. That was good, perfect in fact. She didn't feel like seeing him now, not today. Maybe tomorrow before she left. Or maybe not, maybe never again. Serve him right, the way he'd treated her. Leave him a note, eh? Fuck you, the note would say. Fuck you! She ate some of the leftover Chinese food, then went into the den, back to her customary chair, spread herself onto it, turned on the TV. An hour passed, thought-lessly, amid a kaleidoscope of Sunday juvenilia from HBO, Showtime, and Cinemax.

At two o'clock she heard a noise, the car it was, out in the driveway, then heard a door close, too close not to be the door of his car. She left her chair, warmed but unimprinted by her slight form. Left the television too, switched to Cinemax. Or was it HBO? Left it cackling and glowing, though it would have taken just a click of the remote to turn it off, so she must have left it on intentionally, to show where she had been and when. She made the hallway just as he was opening the front door, strode down it toward the bedroom, gracefully but fast, getting to it, too, before he was well inside the house, then slammed the door behind her with so much force and clamor that, coming from a motion of that slightest and pinkest of hands, it communicated in a nonverbal way just what she might have said, had she the gift of speech and presence of mind to cloak vituperation with intelligible prose, or the blackness in her heart with audible and lucid sound.

David turned and looked back at the car through the open doorway. Behind him, inside, another door slammed shut somewhere. Bam! He started at the noise, turning reflexly toward it, then realized that it was nothing but the sound of a door being slammed somewhere down the hallway, very loud and jarring, but just a door slammed shut. Bam! it went, and his body reacted, then relaxed, mindlessly. Cindy . . . Jesus! He took a deep breath, blowing it out in a puff of meaningful exhalation: Whew! Goddamn! Just what he needed now, frazzled as he was, irrepressible Cindy venting, making some kind of statement, Cindy in the midst of one of her tantrums! She'd picked the perfect time for it, with all this madness taking place and a third of a million dollars out there in the trunk of his car.

He dropped his keys and wallet onto the sofa table in the den, out of habit, then had a second thought and put the car keys back in his pocket. She never used the Buick, but why take chances? Of course, she'd have to walk right past him to get to the car, and she was no more likely to do that than to drive herself to Florida alone. She had made her statement, and it was as clear and candid as any such wordless communication can be: *I don't want to see you. Stay away.* She must have literally run out of the den when he drove up, leaving the television on in her haste. Or maybe the TV picture was another statement, like the slammed door and the weekend with Alan, but more cryptic, indecipherable. He stepped around the couch and turned it off, finding the silence welcome.

It didn't last long. As he sat on the couch beside his wallet, fresh sounds started from down the hall: the bedroom television, very loud, diminished only slightly by the closed door. Another message. She was like a spoiled child, like a Goddamn two-year-old, nothing like what she had seemed to be when they met.

It wasn't the contract he'd signed on to, or that any normal person would. Three months had passed since he'd found any pleasure in her company, though he'd gone through the motions dutifully. All the two of them had ever had in common was an obsessive interest in her wants, her needs. His days were consumed by them: cleaning up after her, seeing to her meals, taking her laundry to the cleaners, driving her around for clothes or for a manicure. "Why don't I get you a car?" he'd asked, more than once. "No, I don't like driving in a place I'm not familiar with," she'd answer. Not much point in arguing. She'd had guys fawning over her since high school, taking her orders, fulfilling her needs. He wasn't going to break those habits in a summer.

His needs were irrelevant, unregarded. Like today, with so much on his mind. It might have been nice to have a comrade, a sympathetic ear. There were times in a relationship when beauty didn't compensate, and this was one . . . this was a classic one. The more he thought about it, the angrier he got; irritable, like her, despite the best of his intentions. She'd simply picked the wrong time; an awful day, an awful couple of days. Discussion would be useless, a waste of words. . . . Better if he got away from her for a few hours, far enough away not to provoke her or to be provoked, far enough away not to hear that Goddamn television thumping through the insubstantial walls.

The telephone handpiece was on the coffee table in front of him. He picked it up. Maybe the Nouris were home. He dialed. Hassan answered. "David?" he said. "Sure, come on over. We'll be here." Good! Refuge. He switched the phone off. Down the hall, the television quieted by several decibels. So loud in there, inside the shut-up room, she couldn't stand it herself, or maybe she was listening now to see if he was still in the house. He went into the bathroom, the little one he had been using, and washed his face, urinated, flushed the toilet, pissing his presence in the house like a dog marking its territory, then stepped across the hall into his study, closing the door sharply but short of violently, locking it behind him.

He opened the closet. The box of papers he'd found in the old man's house—not the sealed case, but the carton of records, old checks, receipts, the one he and Clinger had located in the storage room upstairs—was inside, under some other cartons. He took it out, set it on his desk, and started sifting through it. Most of the documents were in an Arabic script, Persian he assumed it was, from the old man's note. Maybe Hassan could translate it, some of the words at any rate. They had to be at least remotely similar to Arabic.

There were hundreds of papers. Some bore the Iranian tricolor flag and lion insignia of the Shah's government, signed, for all he knew, by the Shah himself or his ministers, things that, translated, would have a lot to say about the sort of work Adam Gruener had done, the sort of employee he had been. But nothing in the box—not a paper, not a receipt, not a cancelled check, not a single shred or fragment—dated back to the early sixties, the era proper to the papers in the sealed case. What had happened then? What had Adam Gruener done? Sometime after Castro and the Bay of Pigs, but before the end of the decade.

David tried to work it out. He'd turned eight in 1964. The Cold War was on. Johnson got elected, beating . . . who was it? . . . Goldwater. Maybe something to do with that, electoral chicanery, like Watergate. Or maybe something cruder, like a mob hit. It couldn't have been Hoffa. That was later, 1970 or so. But mid-sixties . . . . Maybe a link to Viet Nam, or . . . or Martin Luther King . . . but the old man was no racist. The Kennedys, John or Bobby? No, both of those tragedies were investigated to exhaustion ages ago. . . . What, then? The answer would be in that metal case, but it was better for the girl and him—probably for the memory of old man too—if no one ever had a look inside.

He took out a few of the Persian documents, folded them, and stuffed them in a pocket. Maybe Hassan could translate a little of the text. Through the wall, the television audio ceased for a moment while the channel changed. A commercial came on. He heard it clearly, louder now: "Get rid of the zits with . . . medicated pads . . . face never looked so good . . . ." Then something about top soul videos, louder again, and the wall thumped with the basso profundo backbeat of a rap song: "You ain't nuffin, ain't nuffin. Ain't no one I want to be wit'. You ain't it. You ain't a thing. Don't put me on no string. You take me fo' a fool. But I'm too cool. You think you hip. . . ." Cindy hated that music. He smiled to himself. Good. She was locked up with it, a captive audience in the sealed room. Terrific! The joke was on her. As for him, the Buick with four hundred thousand in the trunk would be more comfortable. At least he could pick the audio and its volume.

He looked around for a place to hide the carton of papers. Not that Cindy could read Persian, not that she would make anything of the receipts and checks. But somehow he didn't quite trust her in the house alone with anything of the least importance. Other than that sealed case, which would remain inviolate, the carton held the only information anyone was ever likely to glean about the old man's character. The girl would want it— Sarah. He'd ship it to her later, maybe in a week or two. Meanwhile, the thing he needed now was a place of some security to store it in.

The closet wouldn't do. It didn't lock. He thought about the other rooms, but there was no place in the house at all suitable, certainly no closet or cabinet Cindy herself or they together had not been into. He thought of taking it with him, in the car, the trunk of the Buick, along with the case of money. That was an option, and he started out with it, down the hallway toward the front door, nearly to it on his way to the car, when he thought of the '58, up on jacks in the garage. It had a trunk too, an empty one, safe enough for the papers; maybe not the cash, but certainly the papers. Cindy would never go in there, either for curiosity or mischief. He turned toward the kitchen, then passed through it to the side door, and out to the garage.

The keys were in the ignition. He took them out and opened the trunk, tossed the carton in, closed the trunk, and dropped the keys into a rusting coffee can upon a shelf at the far end of the garage, pushing them down into the mass of bolts and nuts that largely filled the can. He turned off the lights, closed the door, washed his hands beneath the kitchen faucet, grabbed a couple of cookies—still to the distant sounds of video soul— and left the house to Cindy. There was Chinese food left. She wouldn't starve. Maybe he'd try again in a few hours. Or if not, if she was still her same intractable self this evening, maybe give it another shot tomorrow.

If not then either, she could leave the way she had before, without a word or even a scribbled note upon a scrap of paper. *Goodbye*, it might have said. *Have a nice life*. He deserved that at least, for all the time and counseling. Otherwise he was content. Let Alan have her, take her back to Florida on the first flight out Monday. What he wanted now was a little peace and quiet. He'd see to the old man's business, then take a couple days off to tinker with the car.

Hassan made tea. He was always drinking tea in little cups, with a cube of sugar that he took on the side, dipping it into the tea like an Oreo in milk. Jinan dropped her sugar into the tea, Western style. It went with her jeans.

"So he named you to be the executor." 'Execootorrr,' it came out. Hassan trilled his r's in a grandiose way, as impeccably as a Middle Eastern diplomat.

"Something like that."

"And there is supposed to be a great deal of money. . . ."

"Yes, but I'm not sure I can take it—my share, I mean. All of it should probably go to the girl. . . . His granddaughter."

"Why do you say that?" said Jinan. "He left a lot of it to you. I would keep it. You are crazy to give away a lot of money like that. This is crazy. Anyway, you are doing something for it, some work."

"I don't know that I can take millions of dollars for a phone call. Anyway, what do I need it for? I don't need it any more than you would. We've both done well here. Jesus, you've been here what, twelve years? You've got a million saved, just on my referrals alone."

Hassan laughed. "Your patients! They're all on welfare. Half of them never pay me anyway. They think doctors shouldn't charge them because you forget to all the time. That last one, with the gall bladder, she said she's going to make me cookies. Cookies!"

"Did she? Dora? You aren't going to get paid much then. The last time she made me something—chocolate chip I think they were—she ate half of them on the way over to the office. You'd better get the cookies up front."

"Ahhh! That's your referrals, anyway. It costs me money to see them. I'm doing you a favor, because you're a friend."

"Well, whatever. So, you want to look at the papers?" He took them out of his pocket and passed them over. Jinan moved over next to her husband to see, angling her head diagonally beside his shoulder.

"It's Farsi . . . Persian."

"That's what I said."

"I can't read it. . . . Some words, maybe. I know the sounds, but not the meaning."

"Can't you make any of it out?"

"No. Arabic and Farsi are different. Different kinds of languages. Arabic is what you call Semitic. Farsi is like Sanscrit, like Indian. . . ."

"Indo-European?"

"Yes, that's right. The words are all different except the Arabic words, like the French words you have in English. Here is one, *manazel*." Hassan pointed to the second paragraph in the paper he was holding. "It means 'houses.' Same in Arabic as Farsi. There are some other ones, but not enough to read it."

"Nothing, eh?"

"No, but let's call Parviz. I can read it to him, and he can tell us its meaning. Or we can fax it if you want."

Yes, Parviz was perfect. He had stayed in Philadelphia after their residencies. He'd been Hassan's friend, but they'd all hung around together. A couple of years before, he and his wife had been out to visit. "So, the streets of Bakersville are paved with gold," he said. But Parviz was happy in Philly, teaching at the university. It had been good to see him, like the old times. They laughed and drank whole quarts of tea and talked about interesting cases they had seen. And his wife was considerate enough not to ask about Lynnie. Nas . . . something . . . Nasrin was her name. He was sorry to see them go.

"Great!" said David, about the fax. "Let's see if he's home."

He was. Hassan went into the other room to transmit the letter.

"You should keep the money," admonished Jinan.

Parviz called back in twenty minutes.

"Salaam," said Hassan into the phone. "OK, OK. . . . Yeah, you tell him yourself."

Parviz sounded agitated: "Vere did you get these lehtters?"

"Why do you want to know?" David asked.

"They are Savak letters! Savak!"

"What does that mean?"

"Torturists! Murderers! Savak vas Shah's secret police. Like the Gestapo, you understand?"

Yes, he was beginning to: "The kind of men who would cut a person's ears off?" David prompted.

"Yes, and his balls too. Then mail them to his mother."

"What did he say?" asked Jinan.

"He said keeping the money is not an option. . . . I'm going to make one call, probably tomorrow, then take a couple days off to work on my car."

Nothing much changed that Sunday between them, after he returned. He had stayed away from her and she from him, she in the bedroom with the door closed, the television on loud, shutting out his sounds, letting him know through the door that of her two preoccupations in Bakersville these past months, of her two communicants in the lonely house, David Arthurs and the television, sentient and electronic, variable and constant, independent and manipulable, it was the second, the video tube, that had prevailed.

After leaving the Nouris he had stopped for dinner, an early dinner, alone, out at the Holiday Inn, where the chef was a patient of his, the manager a friend of sorts. Crabcakes, his customary selection, a few things from the salad bar, a couple of beers. He couldn't taste any of it, not with God knows what coming down on him and four hundred thousand dollars out in the trunk of his car. Art, the manager, came over to talk. Where was Cindy? Home, he said. At home. They had had a little disagreement. He looked up, across the table, at Art's awkward expression, saw mirrored in it his own face, warped with anxiety, not about Cindy, but how was Art to know that? The face above, across, turned perceptibly more awkward. How about some pie? What else could a food man say, burdened by a lack of information and a with culinary mind-set. The pie was as good as it had always been, as exemplary, in its way, of what is best in pies as was Art exemplary of what qualities are best in people, but neither offered what he needed, a clear mind, his life as it was before.

He got to his house at seven. From the outside, it looked as deserted as the old man's place had, lifeless, desolate. The door was open though, unlocked. Cindy must have opened it for something. Certainly not for him, but for something; maybe just to step out for a minute. Then back in, for she was inside now. He could hear the sound of the TV down the hall, muffled by the closed door. The Buick was in the driveway, sheltered as near to the garage as its bumper would allow, touching the door almost. He looked back out at it, out through the living room window, feeling still the presence of the money in its trunk, feeling it down low near the base of his spine, the way he had felt it before, like an ice cube in his sacrum.

Cindy never emerged from the bedroom. Nor did he seek her out; it was her tantrum and he was not about to intrude. He went into the den himself, watched the TV for a while, CNN, sitting in her chair, dozing in the dimly lit room. In a while the TV in the bedroom grew louder, less completely muffled. At eight he stumbled to his single bed with a book and a couple of journals, closing the door fast against the insistent presence of Cindy's trumpeting television down the hall. Soon he slept, fully clothed but for his shoes, bedside light on, journal in hand, mentally drained and physically exhausted. Once in the night a door slammed, rousing him. He dropped his journal to the floor, snapped the light off, turned to his side, and drifted back to sleep.

CHAPTER 10

G OOD AFTERNOON, CAPTAIN," MARISA SAID AT DEPARTURES CHECK-IN. It didn't sound like that though. More like "gewd ahf-tayr newng, Cahptayng,' Marisa being imperatively bilingual, though heavily weighted toward the Latin.

"Hello, Marisa." Captain Alan Hoffer was out of uniform, but company people recognized him at once in street clothes, knew his rounded face, stubbled blue-black below the beardline, dark within an hour of a shave, however close. They knew the full-lipped mustache, wide brown eyes, laterally retracting hairline, recognized him even from behind by the insular patch of flesh within his wiry black hair, like a precise tonsure, but downed over a little lately by the artifice of minoxidil. Stationed in Miami, an inveterate partygoer, a good twelve years in the air in one capacity or another, he'd met them all, from fellow pilots to baggage handlers, knew their names and families, if ever introduced. . . . Some, albeit, a good deal better than others. . . . One of a team he regarded himself, never pulling rank, waiting this afternoon obligingly in queue, like any other passenger. A brief wait though. This hour of the day, this day of the week, this month of the year, this end of the terminal, so remote were they all from the peaks of travel time and destination that the check-in counter was empty, about as silent as any place in Miami International ever gets through its hectic summer season swarming with Anglo-Hispanic humanity.

Captain Hoffer had just one bag, a small one, carry-on size, the type of case pilots use for overnight stays in airport hotels. Marisa asked him, in her Hispanicized rendition of English, why he didn't simply take it with him to the gate.

"Nope. Can't today, kiddo. I've got a firearm." He spoke in a normal voice, neither subdued nor exaggerated; matter-of-fact, rather, as if the object in question were an historical artifact or a tennis racquet. "I guess you'll have to mark it and put the bag through."

He opened the carry-on and removed a leatherette gun case, unlocked it with a key, took an automatic pistol from it, showed Marisa the empty clip, the vacant chamber. She made a strange face, a Latin strange face, worn gaudily for legibility, so Alan smiled, not just a little smile, but his wide, familiar toothy grin, mustachioed above, blue-bearded around, eminently reassuring, a face her expatriate Cuban mother would have loved, bless her soul, the face of a *caballero muy benigno*, a gun *owner* maybe, but surely not a gun *user*. Marisa looked happier, *simpatico*, stuck an identifying tag legible to the baggage scanner, into the pistol case, watched Alan lock it, then replace it in the carry-on. She tagged it, handed the claim check to Alan, and set it, more carefully than was her habit, on the conveyor.

"Peetsburgh, eh?"

"Yes, ma'am." He asked for the names of the flight crew. Marisa checked the monitor. René and a guy named John Sanderson that he knew pretty well. Did he need the other names, the flight attendants?

"No, sweetie, that's fine." He tapped his hairy hand on the countertop as a departing gesture of affection and thanks and walked out toward the gate.

He saw the crew in a lounge halfway down the concourse, sipping their Cokes and coffee. "Al! Whatcha doin' here?" René got up, grabbed his hand, threw his other arm around Alan's shoulders. "How are ya, buddy?"

René pulled another chair over and set Alan into it, directly at his side, put his slender pilot's hand on Alan's arm.

"How are ya, my friend? Everything OK? Where ya going?"

"I'm on your flight. Pittsburgh."

"Yeah? What for? What for, my friend?" René was French Canadian, thin and tall, with a hawkish nose and vertically furrowed foreface, exorbitantly French, and with a manner of speech and gesture rather French and very Canadian—that is, both gruff and friendly at the same time, a voice more gruff than friendly, words more friendly than gruff.

Alan answered not a word, but looked over at René with round brown sleepy eyes, eager and fatigued.

"Cindy again?" René pronounced *ah-gayn* like a loyal Canadian. *Seen-dee* was pure French.

Alan gazed downward, down at the little table with its four unmatched paper cups, mostly empty. He looked empty too, drained dry. René wondered how long, how many long hours or days, he had gone without sleep. Then, after a minute, the round brown eyes looked up again at René. "I love her, René. I love her."

René took him up by the arm, led him over to another little table ten feet away, smiling and nodding to the others. "I'm going to get you a beer, and you tell me all about it."

"Make it a hot dog too," said Alan, "I haven't eaten much. Here's some money."

Rene gave him the finger. That was his way.

"Ten minutes, René," said John Sanderson. René nodded.

Two hot dogs, a beer, a bag of chips filled the small round surface under Alan's chin, between his resting hands. He gobbled it down, all of it, hungrily, emptily, refueling. He had slept little and eaten less in the two days since Cindy's call, had flown to Buenos Aires two hours after hanging up with her, managed to lie down then for a couple of hours, sleepless, thinking of her. Yes, she did love him. Always had. Always. Then up again, ashen-eyed, but pumped up by his fantasies of seeing her, holding her. He found someone to take the home leg of his flight on Monday, so got out Sunday afternoon, through Mexico City, bummed a ride from there on a midnight cargo run back to Miami, getting in at six, then home for a few hours to wash and change. Next, nonstop to Pittsburgh at two-ten, and here he was.

The crew had five minutes left. John pointed to his watch and held up five spread fingers. René nodded.

"I'm going to get her. She's coming back to me, for good this time." Alan's eyes were wide with anticipation, beer, and sleeplessness. "You know, René, she's coming back to me for good."

"I hope so, my friend. I hope so. She hasn't been (pronounced *bean*) so good to you so far. You know?" René looked at his watch. "O.K., O.K., come on. You get on with us. Where's your bag? You got a bag?" They started walking.

"Checked it."

"Checked? Why? You got so much stuff? How long you stayin' in Pittsburgh? That's where she is, right? Pittsburgh?"

"Near there. A couple hours north of there. I got a car reserved. Remember Baker at Budget? He got a car for me. You know, Baker, that we took to Vegas a couple years ago."

"Yeah, Baker. Yeah, I remember him. When you comin' back from Pittsburgh?"

"Tomorrow probably. The late flight. Ten-thirty. Who's got that one? You know?"

He didn't, but it didn't matter. Alan had managed to change the subject. No reason to tell everybody in the airport that he'd checked a gun through. Not to use, not to hurt anyone, not even to threaten, but just in case he had to scare that smartass doctor, to show him how crazy this guy was for his woman, how dangerous it was to take that woman from him. It wasn't loaded. The bullets were at home in an unopened box, bought on a whim with the Smith and Wesson when all those airport carjackings were taking place. He hadn't touched the gun since then, hadn't handled one since he left the Air Force twelve years before. He bought the damned thing on a whim, and took it with him today in the same way, just in case . . . just in case.

He boarded with the crew. Angela was one of the flight attendants, a new girl he didn't know. She seated him in first class. The plane was less than half full. Fifteen minutes into the flight, John came out and asked if he would like to come forward and sit in the cockpit with them. He declined. Better to sleep a little; just a little, anyway. And he did, achieving a full hour of deep and concentrated sleep summoned from the depths of exhaustion and deprivation. He woke at two, dazed and cotton-mouthed, feeling all the worse for having slept enough to taunt his body but not enough to salve it.

They landed at four-forty. René had a little time, an hour or so, and walked with him toward baggage. "How about a drink?" he asked. Alan

declined. Had to get there. To see her. He had come so far and was so
tired, so very tired.

"Eh, my friend, you sure you OK? This woman . . . ."

Alan pulled him by the arm to a vacant row of seats at an unused gate.
"Look, René, look, man, I love her. Whatever she's done, whatever she
does. I can't explain it to you. Have you ever loved a woman like that?
Without reserve, beyond control or reason?"

"Sure. Sure. I'm French, you know?"

"You're French Canadian. You hate the French, remember? Look . . .
look, if you haven't loved anyone like that . . . . I can't explain it to
you. I can't control it. I just want her back, whatever else happens. You
understand?"

"OK. I guess so. Sure. Hey, you call me when you get back to Miami,
OK?"

"Yeah, sure." They shook hands, then René hugged him close with
one arm, let go the clasped right hand, turned briskly, and walked back to
his crew. Alan watched him, the back of his uniform, for a moment, slender, elegant, familiar as his own reflection in a mirror. René and he, God,
they'd had some sweet and crazy times together, ten years, all over,
through most of the inhabited world accessible to flight. In the old days.
Past life. Before he met her, before his life changed, before *he* changed.
God, what she had put him through! But she was so beautiful, so beautiful. He took the transport to baggage, found his case, got his rental car,
tossed his stuff in the back seat and himself in the front, and headed up
the interstate northward to Bakersville.

Had Alan landed three hours earlier, he might have seen another inbound
passenger, freshly arrived on a flight from Newark. They might have
glimpsed each other fleetingly, the way a thousand people glimpse a thousand others at a public place, registering for an instant a single constella-
tion of facial features, then another, and another still, in groups of two and
ten and fifty, slipping past like trees along a highway, distinguishable one
from the other if there were time enough and reason enough to distinguish.

They might have passed within a foot of each other, nearly face to
face, might have shared proximity for many seconds, for a minute maybe,

seen each other's eyes, expressions, gestures. But they would have seen without seeing, formed images without recording them. For neither bore the stamp of individuality, those singular marks of beauty or of variation from the norm that make a countenance worth preserving in the mind.

The one was very near the median in most things; height, weight, features neither inordinately pleasing nor displeasing, only a little hirsute beyond the average, but otherwise remarkable only for perfect mediocrity. Out of uniform at least.

The other was a little less generic, yet unmemorable. His purpose, his efficacy depended on that. Such men, if they are visually remarkable, singular, noteworthy, have very brief careers indeed.

He was tall, a full inch over six feet, and large, big-boned, but rounded, plump skinned enough to cloak any clear definition of musculature upon his frame; with thickened arms, juvenile and hairless pink below a short-sleeved shirt. His face was the same, pink and round, almost beardless-looking, with light brown facial stubble that would remain invisible even late that evening, when his work was accomplished, or the following morning, when it grew persistently on the visage of a dead man. Hair that color, hair of such transparent shade and paucity, hardly showed upon his head, receding as his hairline was, close-cropped an inch or so on top, clipped to oblivion on the sides, so that thick pink skin emerged through the exiguous strands of hair, like water in a pond, between the reeds. He had a childlike mouth, tucked down a little at its outer ends by buccal fat, not obese fat, but rather juvenile fullness of cheek. His nose was small and straight, nondescript, a little porcine, though, so that a pair of diagonally oval nostrils appeared in full face, unless his head was bowed slightly, as it rarely was. Above were narrow, deep-set eyes, hazel if frontally illuminated by sunlight or a flash, but otherwise black and absorptive, as if his pupils had expanded to fill both orbits, and each orbit opened into cavernous vacuity.

Had he been a little taller, a little more obese, had his hair been sparser, fuller, darker, his eyes brighter, his gait a little less burdened or a little more; had he, in short, been a fraction more mordant in appearance, not in every way, but in some way, had he been possessed of some discrete, solitary characteristic demanding attention, he might have etched his image into an onlooker's memory, into Alan's, for instance — that is, if Alan had been in Pittsburgh three hours earlier and seen the countenance of this unremarkable man. But the pilot arrived at four-forty, and Simon Fallaco—for that was the second nondescript man's name—was gone by then, well launched on his path, passing through the airport like a pathologic microbe in a stream of water, unnamed, unregarded, unrecorded, but lethal still.

He stopped, Simon did, on his way out, for a bite to eat, not really hungry but wanting something in his mouth, the taste and the chewing, halfway through the terminal, a Big Mac and fries, fed himself quickly, standing at a counter, then back for a second burger, biting at it as he walked, held in its open wrapper, a small carry-on case in his other hand, finishing the last bit of bun, meat, and special sauce on the train to ground transportation, satiated now, wiping the last bit of special sauce from the angle of his mouth with the nonabsorbent paper. He crinkled it and dropped it into a bin, properly. A declivity of steps led Simon downward to baggage claim, with a score of faceless others as uniform as their hand cases. He would be met there, and he was, ten feet out from the Avis counter, standing where he was supposed to be, unremarkable and receptive, shoulder against a thick, carpeted pillar.

Jake was trim, mostly gray these days, past midlife, looking sixty maybe, maybe sixty-five, but fit, tan, rugged, the type of man who might have been a boxer once. Unmarked though. Not averse to throwing a fight for the right price, the right patron. Clean-faced, even-eared, Roman-nosed, nicely aged, bronzed and silvered. "Renting a car?" he asked, peering obliquely.

"No," said Simon. He had a shrill voice, inappropriate to his height. "No, I'm . . . uh . . . I'm waiting for a ride. How about you?"

"Your name Simon?"

"Yeah. And you're ...?"

"Jake. Call me Jake." Simon took his hand, a little warily, Jake thought, as was fitting. Can't be too careful.

"Where to, Jake?"

Jake motioned with his head, and Simon followed. Up an escalator, across an overpass, down a corridor, out through an automatic door to short-term parking. They came to a white Ford Taurus, unremarkable, generic-looking, which the elder man opened with a keyless remote. They slid in, Simon's case in the back seat.

"You a Jew, Jake? That's a Jew name, ain't it?"

No, Jake said. His full name was Jacopo, Jake for short. "Maybe you don't like the name, eh?" No more though, no more. They had work to do.

"I don't give a shit, man. Jew, dago, all the same to me. I'm just here to do a job."

"Right. Sounds like you got the work ethic, eh . . . uh, Simon?"

Jake paid the parking attendant and drove out onto Route 50 north, an open Pennsylvania map beside him on the seat. Neither man spoke for a while, ten minutes or so, Jake looking down at the map from time to time, palming its flat surface, shifting its position on the seat very slightly, rotationally, as he came to a turn. The car reached Interstate 79, and Jake turned onto it, northbound.

"So, Jake, you know where we're going?"

"Obviously."

"Well?"

"On the map. Here." He pointed to a circled name, pushed the map over gently, a few inches on the seat. Simon picked it up.

"Bakersville?"

Jake grunted.

"So? What's the action?"

"What'd they tell you?"

"One, maybe two victims. Maybe a fire."

"Yeah. Yeah. Maybe." Jake figured he'd have to give the guy some information sooner or later. "We gotta get some papers. There's a hit on anyone who's been into 'em. The papers, they're private. Nobody looks at 'em. Nobody opens 'em. Got it?"

"Yeah, I got it. So what..."

"Nobody asks any questions about anything. Got it?"

"Yeah. Yeah, I got it. . . . So what gets torched? You gonna tell me that at least?"

"Yeah. Maybe nothin'. No hit, no torch. If we burn the place, it's a message. That we been there, our people. We burned a place ten years ago because of those same papers. Not to get 'em, but just to leave a message how bad somebody wanted to not have them fall into the wrong hands. Now, if we don't get them, or if they've been disturbed, you and me, we're gonna send another message. Loud and clear. Understand?"

"Must be pretty good stuff for fifty grand each. You're getting fifty too, right?"

"Me? No, I get . . . what you'd call a salary. I'm not a contract man. You they contracted out for the action, the hits, the fire, whatever. You do that, right? Torches, that kind of shit?"

"Yeah, mostly arson. Insurance work. Pays good. Victims too. Whatever pays. . . . Lets guys like you keep your hands clean, right?"

Jake didn't answer. They were well away from Pittsburgh now. Rural places, wooded land and farms, drifted backward past the side glass. Simon looked out at the scenery. Five minutes passed, then five more.

"Where's the hardware?" Simon asked.

"Up near where we're going. They left a car for us. I got directions. It's in the trunk, everything we need. They ask you what stuff you needed?"

"Yeah. I gave them a list."

"Good. We'll pick it up tonight, do the action tonight or tomorrow night. Depends on what we find."

"Sooner the better."

"You got the idea, kid. Get in, get out. Live a long time that way."

Simon leaned back in the seat, sliding his buttocks forward, spreading his knees. Right elbow on the door armrest, left forearm flat on the cloth seat, he closed his eyes. He was done talking for a while. Ten minutes more and Interstate 80 came up. Jake turned the car onto it, eastbound, and headed straight for Bakersville, fifty miles away.

CHAPTER 11

DAVID AWOKE AT SIX IN THE UNCERTAINTY OF DAWN, THE HOUSE SILENT, but for a clock ticking at his bedside and some appliance, amid intermittent chatter, humming leftward down the hall. To his right, opposite the kitchen sounds, the master bedroom door was closed, the room where Cindy slept, its door shut incompletely, being half an inch or so ajar, just enough for its latch to clear the jamb. He pushed it inward, without a sound. Cindy was asleep or, if awake, purposefully and sentiently immobile, crumpled in the middle of the kingsize bed. He moved past her in the darkness, felt for his things, a clean shirt, a suit, dress shoes. She lay motionless, soundless, even in her breathing, some obscure, inanimate mass of bedclothes sensed more than seen in the darkened room. He pulled the door back softly to half an inch ajar, as it had been before, feeling a mixture of sadness and relief. He'd be away that night, and Alan was likely due any time, so they might not see each other, he and Cindy, ever again. A little less than half sadness, he guessed; a little more than half relief. He'd try to call her later maybe, to say goodbye; say something at least in parting. If she answered.

He phoned Mae early from the hospital. How late was he scheduled in the office? Five, she told him. . . . He had something to do, wanted to be out by two or so. Could she move some patients? Yes, sure she could; OK for her to put them on for Wednesday evening? Yeah, that was fine, he said. No problem.

He got to the office half an hour earlier than normal, distracted, eager to get the day past him. He'd finish by two, head for Pittsburgh, stay there overnight; call the lawyer, the go-between in Chicago, today, before five, from some pay phone. Then, just in case he hadn't caught the guy in, he'd try again on Tuesday morning before heading back. Both calls—if two were needed—placed from Pittsburgh, so they couldn't trace the caller within sixty miles of Bakersville. That was the way the old man would have done it, near as he could guess. There wasn't any point in taking chances.

By noon tomorrow he'd be back in his office. Hassan could cover for him till then. So by tomorrow—tomorrow afternoon for sure—everything would be arranged: a place agreed upon to turn over the papers anonymously, the box deposited somewhere, a key or claim check somewhere else. Then he'd be free to call the girl, Sarah, talk to her about the money, arrange for her to get it. All of it, his share included, as far as he was concerned, if he could just get this nightmare over with. Back to the routine of small-town life, his practice and his Chevy, suspension work and all, and to his kingsize bed, alone if need be; back to sleep, undisturbed, free of demons, dreamless, restful, extended, awakening in peace.

Clinger called at one, Mae tapping faintly at the door of an examining room with her ringed finger to summon him, as was her habit. He told the deputy his plan.

"I'll call you later," said David. "Nothing on that trace, I bet."

"Nope, not a thing. . . ." Clinger paused. "A few Charles Kellers. Which is to say, guys with that name, but no one matching the old man's age or description. Not a thing."

"That's not his real name."

"No? . . . I figured it wasn't, but I thought if he used it long enough . . . ."

"It's Adam Gruener. Maybe it'd be better not to search that one though."

"Yeah. I think maybe you're right. I'm not going to . . . . Hey, you know where you're staying in Pittsburgh? In case something comes up."

"Hilton. Downtown. . . . I'll try to call you later though." OK, said Clinger. David switched the phone off, then on again. He was on time; a little ahead of schedule, if anything. He dialed his home.

"Cindy, it's me. Don't hang up."

"No. . . . I won't." She sounded reflective . . . maybe just a little sad.

"Look, I'm sorry about the other night. About everything, you know? . . . I mean . . . if I did anything to hurt you. I . . . . Look, I know you've been unhappy, but I think maybe one day you'll understand that . . . uh, that I never did anything consciously to make you unhappy. I know you're leaving, and I can deal with that, but I don't want you to leave with . . . . I didn't want you to leave the way we ended things the other night."

"Yeah. Yeah, no point in talking about that. . . . Look, Alan'll be here soon . . . ."

"You going today, then? Tonight?"

"Yeah. Prob'ly in a couple hours."

"OK, I figured that. . . . I . . . uh, I'll be away tonight. I've got something I have to do. . . . So I won't see you."

"Yeah, that's what I thought. She call you?"

"Did who . . .? Come on, Cindy. Let's not start that now. . . . Not now."

"Fuck you, David. And fuck her too. I'm out of here. Shit!" The line went dead.

He called back, but she didn't answer. An hour later he was on the road to Pittsburgh.

Jake stopped about twenty miles out of Bakersville for gas, pumping it himself, paying cash. Two rules among many: always keep a full tank, and never buy anything, gas included, in a marked town. There was a folded piece of paper in his pocket, and he took it out now, unfolding it, smoothing it down on the seat above the highway map. One of those computer printouts it was, a three-color detail map of small streets with names instead of numbers, houses marked on it, each with an address. One was circled.

They got back on the interstate, then off three exits later. Bakersville, the green sign said. Jake looked down at the little map, turning it slightly at corners as he turned the wheel. It was a quiet street they came to; the sort of place an unfamiliar car would be conspicuous. That was the problem with small-town jobs. Everyone in the business felt that way about it.

The house looked empty: no car in the driveway, nothing parked out front. No lights either, but it was daytime, four-thirty. They drove by without stopping, then came around again, slow enough to observe but not to be obtrusive.

"Better wait till dark," said Jake.

"Yeah, that's right. We've got to get the hardware anyway. I don't feel comfortable without a little metal on me. Not in a strange place like this."

Jake drove on, turning left now, down at the end of Chestnut, then two blocks more and right onto Main. He pulled over, parking diagonally along a block with twenty other cars. There was another little map in the glove box, computer-generated, three-color, like the one unfolded on the seat. He opened it, smoothed it, backed the car out slowly, courteously, and drove on, past the interstate exit half a mile down on the left, then turned left, without rotating the map this time, into a truck stop, filled with trucks and cars too, fifty, maybe sixty cars, strewn in rows irregular and incomplete across the full two acres of parking space.

He spotted the vehicle they were looking for, a green Taurus three or four years old, parked in the second row from the end of the lot, midway between two light posts. Jake pulled in a few spaces from it and killed the engine, then slid back his seat and turned his head and body toward the inside of the car, away from the driver's-side window.

There was nothing but time now, nothing but the hours until dark. Simon got out and walked into the truck stop, coming out with two cups of soft-serve ice cream. Jake declined, so Simon ate them both, sitting in the white Ford with the windows down, both men facing inward now, the backs of their heads to the open sides of the car.

By six the lot was filling: July vacationers stopping off to eat, in cars and vans, some in trailers, campers, the mass of them now outnumbering the trucks out back. Couples and families with kids, mostly, heading in to dinner, lingering, some of them, in the front entrance. No one would likely notice them now.

Jake motioned with his head, then put up the windows of the white Ford. The two men got out, locked the car, leaned against it for a minute, then stepped over to the green Taurus three vehicles away. Jake reached into the wheel well on the driver's side and pulled out something that looked like a sandwich bag, opened it, and took out a set of keys. He unlocked the door, got in, leaned over and snapped open the passenger door for Simon. On the first crank, the car started. Jake noticed that the tank was full.

"We'll use this one, then come back for the white one later, after we're done."

Simon nodded, either in agreement or in comprehension.

"Better check the goods," Jake said.

He backed out carefully and drove through the lot to the exit, then turned left up State Road 35 North. The first sign of farmland was three miles out. A road led to the left a mile north of that, and Jake took it, coming soon to forested land, then to another road, gravel surfaced, empty, with a fresh, unfrequented look. He turned onto it. Half a mile up the berm widened enough for him to pull the car off to the side. They got out and Jake opened the trunk.

"This what you asked for?"

"Looks like it," said Simon. The trunk was full: two five-gallon jugs of gasoline, a box of plastic explosive, some kerosene, fuses, and guns, four of them: two shiny silver .38 snubnoses and a pair of nine millimeter automatics with extended clips and silencers. There were two boxes of shells too, a hundred rounds, hollow point. They filled the clips, then the revolvers, hungrily, each loading his own two weapons, like a couple of children taking chocolates from a box.

"I gotta try it out," said Simon. Jake nodded. He snapped the clip into his Glock nine, screwed on the silencer, cocked the barrel, and fired at a tree.

"Ka-chock," went the gun, quiet as a footfall on dry grass.

"Nice!" said Simon, meaning, from his expression and gestures, both the sound of the gun and the heft of it in his hand. A nice piece was this Glock. Smooth. He smiled and raised his eyebrows. "I didn't know a nine could take a silencer."

"It's the bullets," said Jake. "They step 'em down. You can get about anything done if you've got the cash."

"Ka-chock." Simon fired again. "Clack" went the tree as the bullet struck it, the impact every bit as loud as the discharge. He picked up the empty shells and tossed them in the trunk, then popped the clip of the Glock nine and replaced the two spent bullets.

"Meet with your satisfaction?" asked Jake.

"Yeah, very nice." Simon pursed his lips and nodded. He set the black firearm, with its inordinately lengthened barrel occasioned by the super-added silencer, onto the trunk floor and picked up the .38.

"You ain't going to fire that," said Jake.

"I sure am. I don't carry a weapon I haven't used." Simon cocked it.

"You fire that fuckin' gun and you're on your own, you hear me? You got no silencer there. You nuts? Could be anybody around here. Anybody could hear it. You dumb son of a bitch! You fire it, and you'll walk back where you're going. You ain't coming with me."

Simon slid the hammer back in place and put the .38 in the trunk. Jake glared.

"Take your fuckin' Glock and get in the car," Jake said. He tucked his own gun under his arm and slammed the trunk closed. Each man entered and slid in, wide apart on the bench seat. Jake put the armrest down between them and slid his pistol under the seat. Simon did the same with his, silently, abashed.

"What the fuck's wrong with you?" Jake was fuming. *Where'd they get this guy?* he thought. *He's trouble.*

Simon wore a gnarled expression, embarrassment laced mightily with hostility. Jake knew the look, having seen it more often than he liked. Better get a leash on him now, before the guy did something really stupid, something that might interfere with what they'd come to do.

"Look, kid, we gotta get something straight. I'm in charge of making the decisions here. I guess you might say that I'm from the home office, the guys who write the checks. I plan the action; I understand the reasons for the action. You, you're here for a specific job. I tell you how and when and where, OK? If you got a problem with that, you better tell me now."

"All right, all right," said Simon. "You run the show." Predatory eyes he had, hollow and inscrutable. He kept them pointed far enough away though, far enough and low enough for his own good. You had to catch it early, nip it in the bud. Otherwise some guy like this could be a loose cannon, ruining a whole operation. He'd have to be watched now, put on a short leash. Then, if he messed up again, he'd simply have to go. Nothing much to that, though. Shit, with this guy it would be like pulling a bad tooth.

The car started and turned, heading back toward town. Seven o'clock. Time to have a leisurely meal, relax a while, wait for dark, then get the job done and get the hell out. Jake would, anyway. Simon? Well, you never knew.

Alan called about six-thirty from a gas station. On the tenth ring, Cindy answered. Traffic, construction. He'd get there around eight. OK? Sure, sure, just come. She couldn't wait to see him, she said. His heart contracted, turned on its axis in some indescribable way. By quarter-after-seven, he was twenty miles from her, past the construction zone with its orange-striped barrels and closed lanes, faster now, passing a few laggardly trucks; then the signs announced Bakersville, ten miles, then five, and he was there, turning onto Main, as his heart turned again on axis, his ears replaying the sound of her voice, his mind's eye the sight of her, her face and hair, and her nakedness, open before him.

He came in from East End, turning right onto Chestnut, so parked across the street, opposite the house. The porch light was on, though it was still bright enough outside, diagonally illumined with transverse shafts of dusky amber through the canopy of westward trees. The driveway was empty: no sign of Arthurs' car, a Buick he thought Cindy had said. Good, he wasn't home. And there was something on the porch too: mail it looked to be, unretrieved. That was better still.

He knocked, then tried the door, and it was open, so he pushed it in, seeing her inside, her form, moving toward the open door, and then stepped inside himself, toward her, nearing, and she was to him, against him, and in his arms, enclosed, her smell in his nostrils, her hair against his cheek. And he felt his heart turn again on axis, and again.

He bent his head downward to kiss her, without a word, and she opened to him, his tongue to hers, her breath exhaled in his nose, warm and scented of her, something that was part of her once, that had been in her, her throat and lungs, an essence of her now a part of him. She led him by the hand, voicelessly almost, all but for some words to tell him they were alone, and would be, through the evening. She led him back, down the hall, to her room, hers and the doctor's, but Alan couldn't think of that now, couldn't think of anything but Cindy, her face and her smell, and her nearness, finally in the unfamiliar house alone. His heart was turning, turn-

ing, on its axis, and his heavy eyes were closing with exhaustion and emotion. So he let himself be led back, trailing like a puppydog, back to the
big bedroom, seated, plopping ass first on the soft bed, with Cindy pulling
off her top, then dropping her cut-off jeans, and her soft big girl's breasts
and light pink nipples, and lack of contrast down there where the hair was
so truly blonde that it matched her skin in the scanty bedroom light

He drew her to him, her breasts about his face, leaning forward from
the bed in his sitting position. She recoiled. *Oh, the beard*, he thought, *the
Goddamn beard*.

"It's OK," said Cindy, rubbing the stubbled left side of his face with
her hand. She had a plan. The beard was a minor inconvenience.

"No, no. I'll shave. I gotta get washed up anyway." He stood, his
erection just enough diminished to the point at which it could be prodded
a little downward into a pant leg. "Stay right here. I'll be right back. . . .You
sure your . . . uh . . . friend . . . isn't coming back soon?"

"Not tonight . . . not tonight at all."

He walked down the hallway, through the living room to the front of
the house, looked out the window facing his rental car. No sign of the
guy—the doctor—or anyone else, for that matter. The street was empty.
Yes, it was crazy to stay around here, but he could hardly think straight
for wanting her. He couldn't drive like that, think to drive like that, not
without some release. And he was so tired, so very tired. . . .

His carry-on was in the back seat. He opened the door and took the
handle, tucked it under an arm, locked the car, and walked back to the
house, fast now, more eager now than tired, thinking again of Cindy's
smell, lying on the bed, the soft, smooth bed, Cindy, soft and smooth,
lying on the soft, smooth bed awaiting him.

The house felt cool when he entered from the heat outside. He hadn't
noticed that before, being so taken up with Cindy, so he couldn't notice
that it had warmed slightly, since Cindy had turned off the air. She was on
the bed, right in the middle of it, on her back, her knees up. He could
smell her fragrance in the still air but forced himself past it to the bathroom, flipping on the light after he had closed the door to shield her eyes
from it. He opened his little bag. The gun case was on top. He thought of
Marisa and smiled. He'd have to get her some perfume. He picked up the
gun case. What if the guy came home? That was what he'd brought it for.

Scare the shit out of him. He opened it, took out the gun; ten years since he had held one. Funny, you couldn't feel the weight of bullets in a gun. Though they had weight themselves, the gun felt just the same with a full clip as with an empty one. He set it on the counter by the sink, the impotent gun, bulletless but formidable nonetheless in its visual impact. He'd keep it handy, just in case, just in case.

Alan ran his electric razor. She heard it humming through the door. Perfect, she thought, then said it aloud, but very softly. "Perfect." Leave a little something for David, a little puddle in the middle of his clean sheet. A souvenir. He hadn't touched her in a month. Did he think no one was going to? Fuck him! Leave him a little wet spot, a little stain on his clean doctor's sheet. The razor sound stopped. Water ran and splashed. This was great fun, just thinking of it. Besides, she hadn't had anything inside her for a month, nothing but a tampon. She reached into a drawer and got some lubricant, rubbed it around inside the lips, around her opening, dilated a little now. It felt good.

Alan folded his trousers and shirt and placed them in the carry-on, then took up the gun, wrapped it in his jockey shorts, and stepped out of the bathroom. Cindy lay in the middle of the bed, back in the same position as when Alan had come in with his bag, flat on her back, her knees elevated and slightly apart, the covers pushed off to the side in the warming room. He dropped the wrapped gun on the floor beside the bed and slid onto it beside her, fully erect again. She turned to him and kissed him, her mouth opened wide, moved her hand to his erection, and he was caught up in a current, powerful, raging, uncontrollable. He grabbed at her, licked her, sought to touch every part of her, every soft surface and tucked crevice with every tactile part of him, seeking, not just the surface, but the inside of her, her essence, the vapors and fluids within her, and he was one with her, and inside her, drawn into the orifice of her mouth and down below into the orifice between her legs, now drawing forth *his* vapors, *his* fluids, until the torrent poured and swelled the roaring current, frothy now, white with agitation, swift along, but somehow in and out as well, then over some crest, illimitable now, beyond the will or force of one man to stay or alter, then down, down, into the void, falling, helpless, and out it poured, foam and froth, copious and abundant, into the calm below, spent and quiet and at peace.

He rolled from her and slept, fell into a sleep of calm, release, exhaustion. Cindy smiled. Didn't take him long. Never did. Finished fast and slept. That was OK today. Let him rest a while. They had a long trip ahead. She lay flat on her back, her legs a little apart, feeling the moisture gather in her opening, flowing warm out through the open place, dilated wide now, felt it pool and accumulate, flowing further down, droplet by viscid droplet, forming soon a miniature rivulet confined to its bed by the fleshy walls of her buttock crease, then dividing into two minuscule channels, one dripping softly down the right side of the crease directly onto the bed, the other running up still higher along the crease, up toward her spine, to flow on its inevitable pathway to the bed by a route an inch higher. She lay still, feeling each molecular movement, each delicate stream, distinctly. For David. From Alan. Courtesy of Cindy. Coffee, tea, or. . . .

Ten minutes passed. The flow diminished, then stopped. She squeezed a little more, but there was nothing left. As much of it was out as was going to come out, and, from the feel of it, a good broad pool. She slid to her left, away from Alan's sleeping form, breathing heavily in the warming air, now redolent with the moist effluvia of sex. It was nine-ten when she closed the bathroom door softly to wash. She'd let him sleep a little more. No rush. She liked to travel at night.

She turned the light off before she came out in order not to wake him, slid back into her pink top and cut-offs. Sex made her hungry, and she was famished now, thinking of the pork-stuffed Chinese dumplings in the fridge, of those and a glass of wine. She slipped out of the bedroom softly, softly closed the door behind her. Alan slept, breathing nasally.

Nine-twenty-five. The sky was dark now, charcoal gray. Cindy put the food into the microwave, punched in three minutes, poured her wine, a glass of cold chablis. Outside, through the kitchen window, she saw the Lincoln lit by a streetlamp. Nice for a rental car. She'd have to get him to buy one of those for her in Florida. She'd wake him in an hour and they'd head out. Leave the linen off the bed, all but the bottom sheet with David's present, right in the middle, right where her ass had been. Too bad she couldn't have shit on it too. Boy, that Lincoln was nice. She'd have to have him get her one just like it.

CHAPTER 1 2

J AKE'S FINGERS NEVER LEFT PRINTS. NOT THE WAY OTHER PEOPLE'S HANDS
do, clean, discrete whorls, labyrinthine, a circular maze of miniature
hedges rotating inward, then helically outward, leading nowhere.
Average fingers stamp them casually on everything they touch: drinking
glasses, forks, keyboards, books; little oily traces of themselves, characteristic of themselves, analyzable one from the other for their uniqueness,
for the way one tiny sinuous line swings left or right after two-thirds of
an orbit has been run; or possibly folds back upon itself; or even stops
abruptly here or there to make way for another something like itself; or
different, swinging off some other where, then round and round till it runs
off the flatness of the imprint onto the dimensionality of a finger, or inter-
sects a nail, or—and here's the magic of Jake's invisible art—up the finger, to its middle segment; or heroically beyond, to the proximal phalanx,
the nearest to the palm. Onto the palm itself if the diminutive ridge can
summon the tenacity, but by then the little ridge is ridge no more, but
crease; oily still, capable still of stamping a surface with its intricate
design, but no longer part of a signature. Indecipherable it has become by
then, a palm print, a proximal phalanx print, unrecorded, unrecordable,
useless to the analyst, to the identifier, to the law.

That was what Jake's hands left: nondescript smudges, nothing more
distinct. And it was simple. Effortless, in fact, for he performed the magic

unceremoniously, automatically, did it by simply never bringing those fingertips into use. Extraordinary, yes, but that was hardly all of it. For the uniqueness, the genius of Jake's ability lay in its ease, the transparent and facile grace with which he recruited into service all and every round and linear aspect of each digit, opposed and unopposed, flexed and extended, curled and coiled and angled, palm to digit and digit to nail and phalanx to web to crease, handling thereby virtually anything. Enlisting to his needs every manual part—every one, that is, except those distal print pads, which, to an adsorptive surface, he never at any time apposed.

Driving was simple, what with power steering, power windows. Why, a terminal leper could drive; a duck, if it could reach the pedals. The ends of a finger did nothing its flexed joint couldn't do, popping in a lighter, or pulling it out, with two opposing knuckles, turn signal flipped with the hook of a thumb, window lifts actuated with the edge of a little finger. Every part of the hand beside the inner pads of those distal tips. Those Jake never utilized, even to eat; even at home, where his fingerprints belonged, so accustomed had he grown to the technique. And if you watched him, watched his hands, that is, as he drove or ate or opened a door or turned on a microwave, why, you'd never notice a thing about that agile nonemployment of his fingertips. That was the genius of it; that, and not the printlessness itself.

Simon, for one, didn't notice a thing. He scarcely looked at Jake, so intimidating had the bronzed and silvered old boxer become. And, since Jake seemed to touch things, as Simon managed to perceive through the outer corners of his eyes, well, he naturally assumed that it was reasonable for him to touch things too. The green Taurus, notably, dash and windows and door handles, not that it mattered all that much in the end.

So Simon strummed the dash impatiently with his large fingers, and Jake grasped the gray steering wheel inconspicuously between a palm and thumb, as the two men drove neither very fast nor very slowly past the quiet house on Chestnut Street at just a little before ten, when the summer sky had darkened enough for streetlamps to predominate over the circumambient grayness of the waning day.

There were lights on now, a porch light, and others in the house, within the windows to the left of the porch and behind it, next to the door. But no car; no car either in the drive or out front at the curb. Only a new white

Lincoln parked across the street, in front of another house with lights on, thus accounted for satisfactorily. They passed just once now, the white Lincoln on their left, having seen all they needed to see of the house, then turned right at the next corner, then right again at the next, coming up another residential street, parallel to Chestnut, until they reached the point at which the marked house stood, but one block over, and parked there, along the curb one lot farther down, in front of a deserted looking house, with no lights and no cars and a For Sale sign on its front lawn.

Jake had a leisure shirt on, blue, abundantly large, with a straight bottom edge, made to be worn jacketwise, outside the pants. And that was how he wore it. He slipped the Glock from beneath the seat and stuck it into the space between his pants and underclothes, under the shirt, with the silencer resting on the lateral part of his left groin, the handle and trigger ring supported by his belt. Simon did the same, but pulled a jacket from his case to cover the long gun, since his shirt was inappropriate. Then they waited a few minutes until a car passed and the sky darkened thoroughly, too obscure now for Simon to see the hands of his watch. Jake's digital said ten-fifteen.

"We'll go across through the back yards." Jake motioned with his eyes, though Simon wouldn't have been able to see them, even if he'd been looking that way. "The guy ain't home. I'm sure of that. No car there, see? So it's probably just the woman, then. She'll know where it is, the thing we want. . . . One of our guys talked to her on the phone yesterday. That's why all the rush, why they called you late like that, last minute and all. . . . Anyway, the woman said she'd seen it, some box or carton with the papers we're looking for. If we get 'em, we leave clean. That's it."

"Still get paid the same though, right?"

"Yeah, yeah, you'll get your money."

"So we'll leave the stuff in the trunk now . . . for now." The gasoline and explosives, Simon meant.

"Right, right. Maybe we won't need it. . . . Better if we don't."

They got out and walked around the house with the For Sale sign, through the back yard, fenceless, diagonally across it to the other yard, one house to the right. Two windows were dimly illuminated near the far end of the rear facade, but the yard itself, just beyond the windows, was pitch black, utterly obscure. Jake got to a windowed back door, looked into a dim passage vaguely visible in the tracery of light coming from its far end. He could make out a washer and dryer in the opaque grayness. Nothing else. Simon stayed back, a dozen feet from the house, enveloped in night, waiting.

Jake moved along the wall to the right, to the next opening, to brighter light transmitted through what seemed to be a dining room, light emanating from behind it, from a kitchen. Then movement. A form passed some break in an inside wall, interrupting the light for an instant, a slender form seen in silhouette. Jake moved farther to the right, able now to see into the kitchen, the edge of a table, a chair. The form reappeared, moving past the light source, first transversely, in silhouette again, then beyond it, absorbing light, reflecting it, a woman, young, slender, wearing pink, with pink skin and gold hair. Jake raised a hand and Simon stepped over, slightly visible now in the window's transmitted glare.

A dog barked somewhere, not very close, not very loud, but the men crouched at once, instinctively, below the window, into the blackness. Soon the sound ceased.

"Looks like she's alone." Jake spoke in a whisper, barely audible. Simon nodded invisibly in the blackness. "That's perfect."

"We'll go in quiet through the back and look around. Got it?" Simon nodded again, crouching higher into the window's slanting emanation, slightly visible in the minimal light.

"OK," said Jake. He stood up and looked back into the window. The woman hadn't moved from the table. She was drinking something; wine, it looked like. Jake walked three or four paces to the back door. It took him thirty seconds to pick the lock, slow for him, but it was dark, and he had to be very quiet. The door opened smoothly inward. A good quiet door, Jake thought. Both men wore rubber-soled shoes and moved in silence, closing the door without a sound. The house too remained soundless, unreactive. Jake motioned to Simon to stay put, quiet, then moved carefully himself through the rear passageway, out through its far end, and around a corner, out of sight. Simon took the Glock out into his right hand. It had a bullet in the chamber, the one immediately beneath its fellow in the clip that he had fired into a pine tree three hours before. The gun reassured him to a degree.

Jake reached the dining room. He could see the woman's form reflected in a rear window, sipping from her glass, playing thoughtlessly with a little food on a plate in front of her. She was alone, a slight woman, harmless, vulnerable. This would be simple, smooth as glass. He felt it in his gut. He'd get the papers and head out, leave the woman alone. Simon was a costly backup, nothing more; he could stay right where he was, uninvolved. There'd be no need for fireworks.

Yes, thought Jake, he'd just take care of it himself. He stepped through the dining room and into the opening to the kitchen. The woman looked up, uncomprehending at first, for an instant, then agape with alarm, but speechless, unable to emit a sound in her shock and fear.

"Relax, miss," said Jake, extending a hand, palm down. "I don't mean you any harm. . . ."

The woman found her voice, came alive, shrieking, "What . . . get out of here. Get out. What is this? You . . . you get out of here right now! Get out . . . out now!"

Jake moved toward her. She stood and backed away, her cutoff jeans against the sink, one arm reaching behind for something, maybe a knife Jake thought. He scrambled over quickly, around the table, and grabbed her arms.

"What the fuck! Get your hands off me. What do you want? What . . . ."

That was it. Simon ran into the kitchen from the dining room, the gun in his hand hanging down. The woman struggled, trying to wrest herself away from Jake. "Jesus. What do you want? Let me go! Let go! Goddamn it, let go!" Simon came over to her, just beside Jake, an arm's length away.

"Shut the fuck up," said Simon. He raised the gun to eye level and pointed it directly at the woman's brow. "Shut the fuck up!" She stopped struggling, became limp in Jake's grasp, then started trembling.

"Listen to me, miss. Listen to me. We're looking for some papers." Jake spoke quietly, slowly. "We just want the papers. You hear me? We don't want to hurt you."

"Papers?" she said, looking down, avoiding their eyes. "OK, OK"

Alan heard her, first in dream-sleep, then waking, dazed. "Get out of here. Get out . . . now . . . get your hands off me . . . What do you want?

Let me go. Let go. . . ." He started up, groggy, naked on the bed, stood stuporous beside the bed, naked, sweaty, the hair matted, moist on his chest and groin. He reached down for his shorts. The gun fell out, onto the floor, with a dull thud. Son of a bitch came home, he thought, hassling her. He picked up the gun. Scare the shit out of him he would. Teach him not to mess . . . . He pulled on the shorts, inside out, wiped his chest and forehead with the sheet, and ran through the open doorway, down the hall, striding heavily, the gun in his right hand, past the entry to the den, where Cindy's chair stood vacant, the television silent, into the living room, visible now from the kitchen. And both men saw him simultaneously, nearing, with his hairy chest and inside-out shorts, though they couldn't tell that from where they stood. But they saw the gun swinging in his hand as he approached, and Simon turned to him and raised his own gun, which he had lowered from Cindy's forehead, and fired instantly, instinctively. Ka-chook. He felt the gun pulse firmly in the crook of his palm, a strong pulse, disproportionate to its diminutive sound, and Alan's chest snapped backward, thrust back in the direction of the hollow point's momentum, and he fell backward too, buckling at the knees, landing heavily as his shorts and head hit the carpet, with the gun still in his hand, outstetched in a splayed arm. And Cindy screamed shrilly, yelling "No! No! What are you doing? No!" too loudly for the men, so Jake put his hand to her mouth. And Simon rushed over to the prone man with just a trace of blood now issuing from the tiny hole in his chest, and put his foot on the outstretched gun, and leaned over, looking into the open eyes of the man, uncomprehending, leveled his Glock, muted as a footfall on dry grass, at his brow, and fired again. Ka-chook-pa. Usually you couldn't hear the bullet striking bone, but this Glock was so quiet that you could. A spasm closed the man's eyes, Alan's eyes they were, but the men didn't know that.

Jake would have started over to the wounded man, would have prevented, if he could have, the firing of the final shot, but he had hold of the woman and could hardly let her go. But his will to do *something*, not so much to preserve the man as a *man* but to keep him alive as a source of information, the will to act as an intermediary between Simon and his prey, loosened his grasp just enough for the woman to get her mouth open and get her teeth around a firm roll of the flesh of Jake's printless finger.

She bit down hard. "Shit!" he said, and drew his hand back reflexly, opening his other hand as well, so that her left arm was free, and she jammed it behind her into his chest hard enough to push him back. She was loose now, and she ran, out around a counter to the living room, then through it toward the front door. Jake started after her, but she was too far on her way, and would have made the door if not for Simon, who didn't take the time to think at all, but just did what his nature and his training bade him. He raised the Glock and fired again. Ka-chook, whisperingly quiet, but with a quick, strong backward pulse, and the woman fell hard into the door, then slumped down, taking a good long while to sink fully to the floor, but reached it, dropping like a delicate fabric onto the carpet, resting on her side, clothlike, pink and gold and blue, reached the floor before either man could get to her, Jake with his bleeding finger offering little hope, Simon with his smooth and silent gun offering none.

"You stupid fuck! You stupid Goddamn fuck!" Jake grabbed Simon's arm as it was raised to fire again. But it was useless, the attempt. The woman, just a girl really, was inert.

"What did you want me to do, let her go? Let her get out?" Simon backed away from Jake, intimidated. "What did you expect me to do?"

"Give me the gun. Give it to me!" Simon passed it over like a chastened child, and Jake stuck it down in his belt, on the right side. "You stupid fuck!" He turned the woman over onto her back, lifeless. Useless to him.

"Come on. We'll have to search the place. . . .Shit. Come on, come on." Jake headed down the hall, then stopped halfway and turned back.

"Look, I'll do this. I'll take care of this. I know what to look for. . . . We're gonna have to burn it now. You know? Go out and get your shit from the car." He passed Simon the keys. "Can you do that at least?" He struggled to compose himself, professionally. "OK, OK, just get the stuff." Simon took the keys and headed toward the back door.

So Jake searched. For thirty minutes, while Simon carried in the gasoline and plastic explosive and fuses. Jake searched under and inside and between, cut and tore and broke, scattered and upended in the pretty house that would soon be cinders, with two corpses freshly dead on the beige carpet, and Simon wiring blasting caps. But there were no papers. If they were hidden, they were hidden well and would be cinders too, which would be all right, perfectly all right, if only Jake could be certain that they were there and would be burned. That was what was wanted: not the papers, but the knowledge that there no longer were any papers. That was what they had sent him for, and he had let them down, despite his best efforts. He had failed.

They'd been here, those papers. Isacco had heard it from the girl herself. The doctor had found them, the woman had seen them. But both were dead now, the woman and the doctor, for Jake had no reason to believe the inert man in his absurd-looking shorts could be anyone other than this Dr. Arthurs. Had they told anyone else? Or passed the papers along? That he couldn't tell, and could hardly do a thing about it now.

So they poured the gasoline and set the fuses. And just before they left, Simon pulled the gas line from the dryer in the back passage near the door they had entered, letting natural gas run into the house, and he set a fuse there too, and some explosive, so that they had to exit through the front door. First Jake turned the inside lights off, and then the porch fixture, so the entrance was dark, and as they exited, Simon stepped on something, stumbling.

"What's that?" asked Jake.

Simon bent and picked it up. Mail it was, a nice thick packet, compressed within a pair of rubber bands. At the very top of the stack was a medium-size manila envelope, addressed, in its geometric center, to David Arthurs, M.D., though the light was far too dim for the men to read it.

Funny they didn't bring it in, thought Jake, but the thought was casual.

"You want it?" Simon asked.

"No," said Jake. "No. Shit! We don't want it in the car. Throw it in. Let it burn."

So Simon tossed the bundle in and closed the door. And the two men stepped around the house, to the passage outside the bedroom with its stained sheets, through the yard, past the dark house with the For Sale sign, to the car, the green Taurus, and drove away. Then, in ten minutes, there was a muffled roar, like a furnace being lit, heard all down the block with remarkably even intensity, and when some neighbors looked out, those who were awake and those who were wakened by the sound, shifting their heads to odd positions parallel to frontal picture windows, they saw an unaccustomed light, bright and yellow, like the setting sun, illuminating a single house, the doctor's house it looked like. And some called in to report it, this evident fire, and worried for the doctor and the pretty woman who stayed with him, and so came out to look, standing in their yards on the fine July night. And then the fire trucks came, quickly, for they had just blocks to drive, but there wasn't much left by then. Only the walls of the house, for everything inside was utterly consumed, charred or melted, long before the gas company arrived to shut off the methane flow and the last bit of smoldering combustion was finally extinguished.

CHAPTER 13

CLINGER HAD WORKED LONG HOURS BEFORE. TEN HOURS TYPICALLY, IN at eight, home at six. Once a week, twice sometimes, he'd have a meeting to attend; the county commissioners or a judge would need him for a statement, an opinion, an estimate. Then there were the semi-social gatherings, always after hours, the sheriff asking him to drop by for a chat, the other deputies needing a pep talk. He never balked, never complained, always made himself available. Inexhaustible Clinger, the rock on which the department rested, available to all, infinitely patient, the font of knowledge and decision. Selfless, loyal Brian, incapable of any action prejudicial to the Jackson County Sheriff's Department. The quintessential chief deputy. Up until Monday, that is. Monday was the day that did it.

He'd had a long stretch since morning, interminable, though it wasn't the length alone that mattered. This day, this Monday, that had turned out to be fourteen hours, starting at eight a.m., finishing at ten that night, when Clinger finally made it home. Fourteen hours. But that alone, exhausting as it was, that alone in isolation wouldn't have changed things all that terribly much.

It was the day itself that got to him. They'd spent five hours over at the courthouse, he and Phil, shepherding some low-life he'd arrested a couple of months before on a drunk and disorderly. Then papers, forms. That was one thing he hated, dry paperwork, not his forte at all. Even domestic problems were better than that, and they were the bottom of the barrel as far as law enforcement was concerned. But paperwork! That's what lit the fuse that day. And then to set it off, to fill his soul with dynamite, at three-fifteen a call came in that Sheriff Steele just had to see him, him and Phil, for something important, some task that turned out to be really special!

"So, what d'ya think he wants?" Phil had looked anxious, fevered, as if he might have been perspiring even without the heat, perspiring even if the hall outside the sheriff's office had been as cool, as marble-temple cool, as the office itself. That was where the power resided, there in that chamber, where vapor settled on the outside of the windows, thick as the moisture on Phil's brow, though extracted from the agitated air within by the sheriff's personally requisitioned cooling unit. Although the chief's particular power, cold and unchallenged, might just as well have precipitated such plenitude of vapor all by itself.

"Oh, nothin'," said Clinger. "Don't worry about it. Probably just wants to know about the old man's place. What we found, you know?"

"What we *found*!"

"Yeah. You and me, we were supposed to check it out today. . . . I haven't had a chance yet to tell him about going through it with the doc . . . you know, after the chief left on Saturday. If he asks about it, let me do the talking. Arthurs is kind of the principal here, and he wouldn't want everything out just yet. . . . Matter of fact, I don't know everything myself, and the sheriff sure ain't the one to tell even what I know. So just keep quiet. And try not to look like you've been sleeping with his wife or stealing his money or something, which is to say take it easy, little buddy. You worry too much. The sheriff ain't gonna bite you. He's not a bad guy really."

Phil said "OK, OK," then and wiped his brow. And barely a second after the moisture from his forehead had been absorbed by the khaki cotton fabric of his sleeve, dappling it a medium mauve, the door before them opened, and the Sheriff, round and cool and breathing smoke upon them from his narrow lips, protruded through the opening belly first to usher the two deputies into his presence.

"Well, well, boys . . . Brian . . . uh, young man, step in, step in, won't you? Step in, boys." There were two other individuals in the room, a thin,

pale man of twenty-five or so, with light brown hair and a scabrous com-
plexion, and a short, round woman, goiterous-looking, with bulbous eyes
and a perpetually open mouth. Clinger recognized them as the sheriff's
daughter and son-in-law. Once seen, they were not easily forgotten.

"Brian, I believe you've met Melissa and . . . uh . . . uh . . . Randy.
My daughter and her husband. They're in this week from Ohio for a
little visit. . . ." The room was thick with smoke from the sheriff's cigar.
A fresh cigar freshly lit, not long in the sheriff's mouth, exuding a
strong but not unpleasant air. Better, thought Clinger, than the scent of
stale saliva-impregnated tobacco that usually clung to the room like the
odor of rotting food.

"Yes, sir," said Clinger to the sheriff, stepping over to the couple,
greeting them with handshakes, manfully firm and gently respectful, each
in turn. "Yes, we met last year, when they were visiting. . . ." He turned
his head to the right. Then left: "... when you folks were visiting . . ."
Head right now. "Yes, sir. . . ." Then back to the left: "Very nice to see
you both again."

"Well, Brian . . . we've run into . . . that is Randy here . . . and we too,
on his behalf, you see . . . we too have run into a little snag, a little snag.
Seems that there's been some sort of a mistake, uh . . . well, it seems that
the boys out here in Bakersville—the town boys, you know—seem to
think that Randy here has some unpaid tickets . . . parking tickets. From
last year, they claim. Of course it's all some sort of mistake. But they've
just gone and made a big stink and said they'd take his license away. . . ."
He could see the sheriff's teeth now, speckled and outlined in sepia, as he
spoke, grimacing.

"Foolish things like that, you know, and all over a little mistake, you
see. So we thought that since you know some of those boys over there, a
number of them, maybe even this fellow Dixon who's making all the stink,
maybe you could figure what to say to straighten the matter out. . . ."

"Why, sure, Chief." Clinger glanced over at Phil for just a fraction of
a second, with maybe a half-wink, maybe just a little arching of one brow.
"I'm sure I can fix it. . . . Yeah, I'm sure I can. I've never known them to
make too much fuss over parking tickets. Which is to say, what with the
merchants on Main Street and all their worries about not losing any business in town for trouble parking. I'll go run over there right now . . . let's

see, it's four-ten. Yeah, they'll be there for a while. . . . Randy, why don't you come along, and we'll get this business taken care of now, the two of us."

But Randy declined, declined in such a way and so decidedly that Clinger wondered mightily what it was that he had parked, or where it was he'd parked it, to evoke such profusion of shamefaced reluctance.

"Let's just *us* take care of it," said the sheriff, smiling again. Better not to have smiled. The teeth did his countenance ill. "Us," he said. *"Us."* *Us* meant Clinger, in the sheriff's parlance. That was the way it had been for years, long before Ronald Steele won the approval of the Jackson County electorate. *Call Clinger . . . get Clinger . . . I don't know, ask Clinger. . . .* He moved toward the door, gathering Phil in his wake, but turning again, then, from the open doorway, toward the sheriff.

"Oh, Chief?"

"Yes, Brian my boy?"

"We took care of that other business. . . . At the old man's house. You know, Keller . . . Charles Keller."

"Yes, my boy, yes. I knew you would. Everything in order? I was sure it would be. No crime committed, eh? No crime?"

"No. No, sir. You were right. Dead right. Nothing to hide. Phil here was a big help in straightening everything out. He's a good man."

"Yes, my boy. I'm sure he is. Good job, Phil." Phil smiled in a painfully self-conscious way, exiting backward through the open door into the warm hallway, Clinger's big hand clutching the loose fabric of his shirt as he urged Phil's departure lest he stay for questions he had neither the capacity to anticipate nor the presence of mind to answer. Clinger closed the door behind them.

"Come on, little buddy. Let's go fix some parking tickets."

It was four-twenty, fiercely hot outside. Clinger wrapped his oversize arm about the smaller man's wiry shoulders and slung him along toward the municipal building, where Dixon and the others would be idling, waiting for the little hand to hit five. Seventy miles to the south, the flight from Miami was on its approach to the Pittsburgh airport, Captain Alan Hoffer aboard, though not in the cockpit. And closer, a mile away, a white Ford was landing too, in its way, fresh from the interstate, on its approach into Bakersville, with two strange men aboard, men who would go about their business unnoticed despite their strangeness, men unencumbered by parking tickets, scrupulous in their public habits, transparent men, invisible. For a few hours more.

It was four-twenty too when David got to Pittsburgh. Not quite to the city, but north of it, to Fox Chapel, ten miles away, near enough to his destination, far enough from his home. There was a Days Inn near the exit, and he stopped there, checked in under a false name, paying cash. He left an extra twenty to cover telephone expenses, then gave the clerk at reception twenty more. He'd leave right after the call.

By four-thirty he had reached his room and dialed. A number in Chicago, a law office it was, address, area code, and phone number hand-printed below the original engraving on the card in his wallet. A big firm, well established. Inconceivable that the line might be monitored, but why take a chance? Maybe they had caller ID. Why risk it? Besides, if everything went perfectly as planned, without a hitch—a time and place for transfer of the papers, a clear assurance of security, safety for him and for the girl—he might be able to call her too, to get the whole of it over with today. He knew *her* line was tapped. The old man's note had said that much. So calling her from home or from his office, or even from the Hilton, where he planned to spend the night, would flag him too soon. . . . Just a little bit sooner than safety required. This twenty minute Days Inn stop would be added security, something the old man would have recommended. It would make the call a tolerably comfortable one, though not one hundred per-cent free of concern.

The inevitable secretary answered.

"Yes, I'd like to speak with Bernard Lesser."

"Who's calling, please?"

"Well, uh . . . Look, I'd prefer not to give my name right now . . . if that's OK. It's very important, though, the call. Very important."

"Well, I can take a message. Mr. Lesser isn't available now."

"Can you tell me how I can reach him? Look, this is very urgent. Really urgent."

"Can you hold for a minute?"

Sure, he said, feeling very much better about calling from the Days Inn now. A full sixty seconds passed before a male voice came on the line.

"May I help you with something?"

"I hope so," said David. "Who is this? Who am I talking to? Is this Mr. Lesser?"

"No. Sorry. My name is Lewin. I work with Bernie . . . . with Mr. Lesser. Maybe I can help."

"Well, I don't know. Look, it's very important that I reach him. Very important."

"It'll have to wait a week, then. He's on a sailboat somewhere in Lake Michigan. I don't think the Coast Guard could find him till then." The voice, Mr. Lewin's voice, raised a little chuckle, emphasizing his *bon mot* about the Coast Guard. "If it's a legal matter, I'm sure I can help you. He and I work together all the time. I, actually . . . I do most of the legal work for the two of us, since Bernie, you know, is getting on in years. So I believe I can help you. If it's a personal injury of some sort, I'm sure I can be of assistance."

What the hell, thought David. "It's about some papers. He's supposed to see to their return. From a Mr. Keller, or Gruener. . . ."

"Papers? Papers! No. No, I don't know anything about papers. I don't do that kind of work. . . . I'll give you back to the secretary and you can make an appointment. With Mr. Lesser."

"No, wait. This is very important. . . ."

"May I help you?" asked the secretary. He hung up.

It was seven when he got to the Hilton, agitated and fatigued, but with forty minutes' driving time between the calls and the check-in, forty minutes to think things through. He'd done his best, called the three Bernard Lessers given to him by Information, then spent half an hour on the line with the Bar Association, hoping for some path to use in an emergency: Lesser's home, the number of a relative. No luck though, no luck with anything. None of the three Bernard Lessers he phoned was a lawyer, so *his* Bernard Lesser was probably unlisted. And the Bar Association wouldn't help, giving him nothing but the office number he'd already called. He thought about checking yacht clubs. After all, he really knew nothing about the man he needed to reach except that he was a lawyer and was presently on a boat. But it was after six when he got to that pass, after five in Chicago, too late for business calls. He'd have to try again in the morning. And then? Well, after thinking about it, he came to the realization that, even if he had no success, another week wouldn't make all that much difference. If the papers couldn't be disposed of this week, then next week wasn't all that far away. After all, things had been uniformly quiet since the old man died. Murderers were hardly after him.

So he checked in, and showered, and went down to the hotel restaurant for dinner, getting back to his room at eight-thirty. He phoned Clinger's home and left a message on an answering machine. Probably out with his kids, or at a Kiwanis meeting, or some place with the boys for a drink. He wouldn't be working that late, not the chief deputy, unless something unusual was going on. So David sat on the double bed in his shorts, looking over a medical journal with the TV chattering, just for company, and barely thought about Cindy. . . . Lovely Cindy, likely as not on her way to Florida via Pittsburgh by now, with Alan, poor Alan, who had loved that unfathomable woman in a way he could not even conceptualize, never having loved in a manner even remotely similar to it.

Someplace with the boys for a drink was where Clinger was, but not with his boys, not the county boys he worked with, Phil and the others. No, these were the borough boys, the ones who issued parking tickets. It was a business dinner, county business, since it was the sheriff's matter, though it was Clinger's own money he spent on their drinks and food, out at the Holiday Inn. Art, the manager, arranged for extra-thick steaks all around and plenty to drink. Dixon got a double shrimp cocktail, which was a good sign, he being the officer in charge, the one who held the cards, brought the case to prosecution.

Seemed that Randy *had* parked illegally, several times. Always in handicapped spaces. Well, acne was a handicap of sorts, so he probably thought himself justified. And that might just as well have passed with Dixon, except that he actually *had* a handicapped placard, Randy did. Problem was that it was stolen from another parked car, driven with some difficulty by a diabetic man with one leg. Dixon wasn't happy at first. He knew the one-legged man, lived down the street from him, a nice guy, he said. "Only an asshole would do something like that." Clinger couldn't disagree. But the steaks helped. Which is to say it loosened up the other borough boys. And who was Dixon to spoil their fun? Dixon, with a dozen jumbo shrimp inside him and some vast but indeterminate number of beers to float them in.

It was all agreed, then. They'd drop the charges. The sheriff would owe them one, meaning Clinger would. He was the guarantor, the one who could produce sometime, something they, any one of them, might need. He shook hands all around and left them to their pie and ice cream. Art charged him thirty bucks, his cost. Clinger had done kindnesses for him too.

Ten o'clock then, ten at night, Clinger got home: tired, but less tired than vexed. That was what his job entailed. His fault as much as anyone's: he had coddled these men, these lumpish elected officials, had run things for them while they sat in parade cars, pressed hands, pleasing the voters. The Goddamn Department would fall apart without him, go right straight into the dumpster. The phone was blinking, the answering machine. What did he care? More bullshit. He got into the shower.

At ten-thirty he checked it. *You have one message.* . . . "Hi, Brian. It's David. I'm at the Hilton. Give me a call if you get in by ten." Too late now. The doc sounded OK though. Maybe he got through to the go-between and everything was settled.

He walked into his bedroom and opened the closet door. There on the floor was the old man's box of papers, stowed for safety underneath some blankets. He lifted them and looked at the metal case below: ordinary, benign, unremarkable, lying flat on the wooden floor just the way he had left it yesterday. Nothing had been disturbed. Why should it be? Crazy old guy! Paranoid about something the doc said he had done thirty years before, something that had haunted him enough—more than enough— but had probably been forgotten twenty-nine years ago by everyone else. . . . Crazy old fool!

Clinger had had enough beer, so he sat down with a Coke and turned the TV on to catch the news. Twenty minutes he watched, too drained by the endless day to be patiently attentive. Then the call came.

"Brian?"

"Yeah."

"It's Dan."

"Yeah, Dan. What's goin' on?"

"Uh, there's a fire out here, a big one. At Dr. Arthurs' place."

"*What!*"

"Yeah. An explosion or something. It started all of a sudden. It's bad. There mighta been somebody inside."

"Jesus Christ! OK, who's there? Wait a minute. Never mind. OK, I'm coming out." He dropped the phone and ran to put on some clothes, jeans and a tee shirt, old loafers, no socks.

He made it in ten minutes. One truck was there, the borough pumper, spraying the house heroically, in vain. Then more came, the Stanleyville unit, and another from Emory, but it took a while to get things under control. The gas crew drove up around midnight. That helped more than anything else. By one they got to go inside, finding very little beside the two charred bodies, rendered unidentifiable. Just the walls were left, with the bathroom fixtures, a blackened refrigerator and stove. An enormous fire it had been, atypical, unusual, suspicious.

Dan was the deputy on night shift. Check on that car across the street, Clinger told him. Dan wasn't supposed to be around. County had no jurisdiction here within the borough. But he had nothing else to do and might as well be of use. Dan got on the phone, found where the Lincoln had been rented and to whom. Clinger took the paper with the name. It was three now, nineteen hours into this never-ending day. He headed home.

But not to sleep. He called Arthurs, waking him sometime after three.

"Sorry about this, Doc."

"Wow! Brian? Wait a minute." It sounded as if he turned on a light, evidenced by a barely audible click on the line. "OK God, what time is it?"

"Around three."

"Damn! What is it? What's up?"

"Do you know a man named Alan Hoffer?"

"Yeah. Jesus! What happened?"

"A lot. A lot's happened. There was a fire at your house."

"A what? A fire! Jesus! What the hell's going on?"

"Did you get hold of your contact?"

"What? No. . . . No, he's not . . . . He's on a trip for a week. What kind of fire? Look, tell me what's going on."

"Listen to me, Doc. Listen carefully. I can't tell you anything more now. You've got to stay where you are. Don't come back here tomorrow . . . today. Don't come back here. Let me sort things out and get back to you in a few hours. Stay where you are, and don't do anything. Don't call anyone, don't . . . ."

"Look, I've got patients scheduled. . . . What about the house? Did something happen to Alan? Oh my God! Cindy! Is Cindy OK?"

"Wait a minute, Doc. Listen. We're not sure about anything yet. But you've got to do what I tell you. You've got to do this. Stay where you are. Don't call your office. I'll do it for you. Don't do anything. Stay where you are. Don't come back and don't call anyone. Do you understand?"

"Look, I've got to know. . . ."

"Trust me, Doc. Trust me. I'll get back to you in a few hours. Don't ask me any more now. Stay put. Stay off the phone. I'll call you back in the morning. I promise you that. You'll hear from me. If you don't, then come here or call your office if you want, but wait till then. OK?"

Silence.

"Please, Doc, do what I say."

"OK," said Arthurs, and both men hung up.

Clinger pinched his nose between thumb and forefinger, the way he did when he thought things over. He'd have to sleep. He knew that. There was a lot he had to do, and he wouldn't be much good like this, without sleep. So he lay down in the living room on the couch, with the blinds open, knowing that the light would wake him early, in plenty of time to do what he had to do. And it did. At seven, with four hours sleep in him, enough, enough. He'd done OK lots of times on less.

He washed and shaved, ate a little cereal, thinking all the while. This was the real thing, the thing he had been trained for. Twelve years he hadn't seen anything like it, twelve years since coming to Jackson county. This was like the big time, like Newark, the three years he had spent there on the force after leaving the army. Heads cut off, body parts, drug deals gone bad. He never liked it, but it sure had held his interest. He left for the money, for Linda and the kids. Chief deputy, fifty grand, plenty for a family. The kids were babies then, and Linda was . . . well, better than what she turned into later. Fifty thousand with zero cost of living and a decent place to raise two children. So he took it. And wound up nurse-maiding pimply guys with parking tickets, pandering to assorted sheriffs, a glorified pimp at sixty-odd thousand now, without a wife, with a boy and girl he saw on weekends. Only. . . . Bullshit!

He sat at the breakfast table, pinching his nose. "Bullshit," he said aloud. "Bullshit!" It was seven-thirty. He went into the living room, sat on the couch he had slept on heavily for four hours, picked up the phone, and dialed the number of his ex. . . . Linda Byerly she called herself now, Mrs. Larry Byerly. Larry answered.

"Hi, Larry. It's me. I need to talk to the kids. To Todd." "Just a minute," Larry said. Not a bad guy, Larry. Linda had the better of the deal.

Todd came on, sounding sleepy, then Mandy in the background. Larry had roused her too. He must have struck Larry as pretty serious.

"Hey, big guy, sorry to get you up."

"Dad. Hey, what's goin' on?"

"Todd, listen. There's something I gotta do, and I may be away for a day or two. I just wanted to tell you kids I won't be home, OK?"

"What is it, Dad?"

"Nothin' exciting. Just some business I gotta attend to. You take care of your sister, OK?"

"What d'ya mean, take care of her? How long are you gonna be gone?'

"Oh, I didn't mean it like that. Just a day or two. I'll see you kids on the weekend, just like always. Lemme talk to Mandy. Is she there? Lemme talk to her."

Mandy got on.

"Hi, baby. I gotta go away for a day or two. Todd'll tell you. Just wanted to say goodbye."

"*Dad* . . . Where...? You didn't say anything yesterday. Where are you going?"

"Something just came up, baby. Look, I'll see you Saturday, just like always, OK?"

"Daddy!"

"Gotta go, baby. Take care of Todd." He hung up, then called the Hilton in Pittsburgh, Room 544.

"Doc?"

"Yeah, Brian. God, I'm glad . . . ."

"Doc, you haven't called anyone, have you?"

"No, man, I just sat here all night. . . . Tell me what's going on."

"I'll tell you soon enough. Just sit tight. Stay where you are. Stay off the phone. I'll be there in a few hours."

CHAPTER 14

ON MONDAY A BIT OF A STORM SWEPT INLAND FROM THE COAST. Devoid of violence, or even bluster, it was a summer rain, typical of July, placid and tropical, a mass of water siphoned from the sea and wrung out ashore. A little later in the year, in August, say, or September, it might have been a full-blown hurricane that blew in from the ocean to the land, but in July the mid-Atlantic had not yet felt enough of summer sun to heat it, or the land sufficient of the dregs of summer to begin to cool. The season simply hadn't ripened for a hurricane. So all the gentle stormlet summoned, drifting retrograde from east to west, was rain, though it was rain aplenty, cascades of it, not powerfully driven, but streaming down in perfect vertical linearity, like curtains of glass beads strung one upon the other in infinite succession from earth to sky.

It must have touched the continent around Annapolis, washing down the Georgian buildings, the ancient streets, rinsing salty encrustations from naval ships and smaller craft along the Severn and the South. Then slowly westward, urged on by the cumulated mass of enormous clouds, past Bowie and Mitchellville, Lanham and Cheverly, to the outskirts of the District. College Park would feel it first, the moisture of it, then Silver Spring, coincident with the Mall and monuments. By six p.m., it lumbered to Bethesda, drizzling at its outset, then spewing forth in quantity, quick rivulets of rain, slanting down brick walls, flowing through the streets. Tires of cars and trucks left transient bands of passage in the slick-ened asphalt of Old Georgetown Road and Wisconsin Avenue. Around, above the pavement, windward glass was studded with its vigor, precipi-tate water, refracting evening light in unaccustomed ways.

Sarah Gruener's windows wetted too, accumulating droplets, for they looked out upon Bethesda Avenue from the seventh floor, facing east-ward, frontal toward the storm's arrival. She watched it come in, listened to its random sounds all evening, then heard it from her bed, tapping at the window, whispering its cadence on the walls and streets, roofs and cars and citizens outside. It was that specific sound, natural and clean, that washed the echo of the phone call from her mind. Thus relieved, she slept, finally and deeply, that Monday night, aware of nothing but the rain.

"Your picture it had said, that strange voice, acid and accusatory, "*your picture, in his wallet. Are you, like, mid-twenties, dark hair, slen-der?*" It was a mistake. It had to be. Some odd confusion of identity between her and another woman. A mistake . . . wasn't it? Was it . . .? Was it just a mistake...? Or did someone really have her picture? Someone unfamiliar to her, a doctor, David . . . David somebody. David. . . . The last name started with a vowel. An A, she thought. Why couldn't she remember that, when she remembered everything else about the call? Everything.

He had her *picture*, the woman said. Who was that woman? Where had she called from? Pittsburgh? That was where the note had come from, Federal Express: *I wish you a good and happy life.*Was there a link between the woman and those other bizarre events? The note? The fright-ening calls with no one on the line?

That was what the rain erased; the rain or the fifty hours now elapsed from the shock of everything, from that initial feeling of confusion and helplessness the enigmatic phone call had evoked. Saturday night that was, two days and two hours before, though it seemed a week ago, a month.

Where had her strength gone? That was something she had taken for granted these last ten years, since the night... since the night her life had changed so dramatically. For ten years she'd been able to cast anxiety from her like a wet raincoat, once inside. Like the time her car was stolen from the airport while she was—where was it?—in . . . yes, New York. She had the space marked on her parking ticket, but another car was in it. So she reported it missing, took a cab home, got a rental car the next day, and bought a new car in a month, when the insurance check came in. She hardly thought about it, even at the time, just picked out a nicer car in a better color, a burgundy Mustang, pretty with its top down in the summer. Nothing like that had ever much affected her, not a querulous colleague or a torn dress or an unwelcome advance. Nothing. Not after all she'd lived through a decade before. Up until now.

Until this stuff. This had done it, this last strange phone call coming after all the rest. She'd been strong, but even the strongest metal has its fracture point, like a bolt that is turned and turned until it snaps. And if a bolt can break, then what about a woman? One who has suffered so much and lost so much and is so terribly alone at times. Will she not have a point of fracture too? A point where fear surmounts even the greatest resolve? For Sarah, the woman's call had been that point. She lay for two nights sleepless, sat for two days immobile, fretting over it, talking uselessly about it with Edward, afraid another of the dreaded calls would come to torment her again.

It never did. Not all day Sunday, nor most of Monday either. Then the sky grew gray late Monday afternoon, after a long week of blue and brilliant weather. By evening the steady rain had come, washing the woman's voice from her ear. She slept, dreamlessly or with dreams unremembered. Slept well into Tuesday, and the rain kept on, the distal edge of the storm, tapping and streaming on the glass, and a steel-wool blanket of clouds upon the sky, deadening it, neutralizing all the unknown terrors, as if to bid her sleep continue without end.

There was a pall of light within the room, vouchsafed by the sullen weather and the closed shades. And the scent of coffee. That was there too percolating thinly in the air through the crack beneath the door. That meant Edward, up and about at—what did the clock say?—nine-thirty? Ten hours she had slept. Nine-thirty already. Well, that was OK. Good, in fact, that she had slept, OK that she had slept late. She hadn't planned to go in today; had planned not to, sleep or no sleep. Edward had telephoned for her—for both of them, since he didn't intend to leave her alone. He had called the museum Monday noon to say they wouldn't be in on Tuesday either.

Monday had been obligatory. Two sleepless nights; she wouldn't have functioned at all. Not at all. And then that voice, still in her ear on Monday, that crazed voice, full of hatred. She couldn't have worked with that inside her head either, even if she'd slept. If not for Edward, she'd have been a basket case. He and Andrew, coming over first thing in the morning Sunday, staying with her through the day, getting her out for a meal, Edward sleeping over Sunday night, up with her most of the night, waiting for the phone to ring again, though, mercifully, it didn't. So Edward called off too, on Monday, then stayed all day as well. Both of them slept a little, napping after midday from sheer exhaustion.

She'd begun to feel a little better through the afternoon, distanced hour by hour from the call, and by Monday night, by eight, then nine, when no odd call came in, when two full days now separated her from the alarm of it, the eeriness of it, by then so far had she recovered her composure that she tried to send Edward home. "Nope," he said. "Not till I see you're OK." She was better, noticeably better, but not convincingly OK, so he stayed.

But Tuesday was different, different from the outset, in the way she felt, strong and resilient again. Still, she'd need a day for recovery, a day for diversion, for reading, art work, watching an old movie: re-entry into her little fabricated world. A day to escape entirely into it, safe within her sheltering walls for that one long, uninterrupted day. Nothing precluded it. There wasn't much doing at the Gallery, awaiting the new exhibit as it happened to be just then. Besides, she hadn't taken any personal time in months, a work ethic Edward couldn't seem to understand in a woman who, given her five-thousand- dollar-a-month trust fund, didn't really need to work at all.

She rose and washed and dressed, then followed the scent of coffee to Edward at the breakfast table, elbows on the surface, with the morning paper before him.

"How are you, sweetie?"

"Oh, great," she said, yawning, stretching. "I slept."

"I told them you wouldn't be in today . . . confirmed it, you know?"

"You didn't tell them . . . anyone . . . why. . . ."

"Now what do you take me for, some kind of idiot?"

She smiled. "Well, I didn't know there were different kinds. . . ."

"Oh, you!"

She put her left hand on his shoulder. "You were a sweetheart to stay with me. The neighbors are probably buzzing."

"Well good. It's about time you gave them something to buzz about."

"OK, OK. Enough of that. I think it's safe for you to go now. I feel better. I really feel better." She pulled out a chair and sat diagonal to him at the adjacent side of the little breakfast table.

"Yeah, I can tell you do. You're starting to look like a human being again."

"What, instead of a cockroach?" she said.

"A cockroach...? Oh, like Kafka. . . .What was his name? The guy in. . . ."

"*Metamorphosis*. . . . Gregor Samsa, I think."

"Yeah. Whatever did that mean, do you suppose."

"I haven't a clue. Maybe nothing. Like Dada art or politics."

"You got *that* right." He put a finger on her lip. "Hey, you smeared lipstick on your mandible."

"Right! First, I don't use lipstick, especially on my day off. Second, cockroaches don't use lipstick on their days off. And third, a genuine hundred-and-ten-pound cockroach would have eaten the lipstick and not wasted any of it on . . . uh, personal adornment."

"Speaking of which—the eating, I mean—stay there. I'm going to make you breakfast."

Edward took a couple of eggs from the refrigerator, along with some cheese and ham, and started an omelet. Beating the eggs, he looked up and winked at her, then turned away toward the stove.

For four years he'd been taking care of her like a personal servant, nearly since she'd landed back in Washington. "Want some coffee?" First time she'd heard that voice, four years before, she'd turned to see if she was the person the voice was speaking to. Edward was a little younger then but looked the same, or maybe her memories grew old in tempo with the people she remembered. Thin, nice features, well-groomed, same as now. "Yeah you, new person, whoever you are, you want some coffee?

I'm going down." She'd stammered something about not drinking coffee, but thanks anyway. Thought he might be hitting on her, until Rosemary Caldwell set her straight. "He's gay. Can't you tell?" How *could* she tell? Twenty-two years old, fresh from Hunter College, in her second year of graduate school at Georgetown with an externship at the Gallery, what did she know of the ways of Washington? She was sixteen when she left. All she remembered were the trips to the museums with her mother and school in the suburbs.

She'd not been very friendly to the guy—Edward, was his name, said Rosemary—so she made up for it the next time. "Maybe a Coke. Hold on. I'll walk down with you." They were instant friends; confidants, in fact, before many weeks had passed. Better than the closest girlfriend she had ever hoped to have, though she wouldn't have dreamed of telling *him* that. He took her everywhere with him, good as well as bad, parties at his place, where she'd felt strange at first, then progressively more at home, until now she was accepted and accepting, a member, but for the initiation and the rites. Sometimes she had to fight the women off, but she'd learned to do that too, with grace and empathy. The guys though, Edward pre-eminently, but Andrew as well and a dozen others, they were a delight, as kind and protective as her own kin. She was comfortable with them, and they with her, Queen Elizabeth with her courtiers, the universe around devoid of villains, benign at last. But that call, that call . . . .

The smell of the butter, the crackling sounds of it in the fry pan made her mouth moist, her stomach hollow. She hadn't eaten much yesterday, some crackers and soup. Now she was exorbitantly hungry. Edward was humming something, "My Old Kentucky Home" it sounded like. Of all things! She smiled to herself. He flipped the omelet over, to more crackling and buttery vapor. She pulled a leg up under her in the chair, crosswise, sitting on it, turning the newspaper toward her. In two minutes he set the eggs before her, with some toast and a can of Coca-Cola. That's what she drank for breakfast, then six or eight more cans during the day, burning it off with incessant activity.

"You can go now," Sarah said, when she had finished the eggs and toast and Coke, and then a dish of pistachio ice cream for dessert.

"You were hungry."

"I was. Now go home. Andrew probably took up with a woman while you were gone."

"That's disgusting. Yech! A woman! Now you've ruined my appetite for the day."

"Thanks a lot! Hey, go home. I'm all right now. Whoever that crazy was, I think I'm done with her."

He changed the subject. "By the way, how are your aunt and uncle? The ones from Cleveland?"

"Francie and Mark? Fine. I just talked to them . . . Why?"

"Oh, I know somebody in Cleveland who might need an accountant. What's his last name, your uncle?"

"Posner."

"They're nice people."

"Yes, they are. Now go home."

"OK." he said. "God, you've really ruined my appetite. Andrew . . . with a woman." He went into the guest room to collect his things. When he came back over to her at the table, he had his little hand case with him. "The thought of it! Yech! With a woman!"

She smiled. "OK, enough already."

He kissed her on the cheek, said he'd call later. "Or call me if you need anything, or just want to talk. I'll be home." They'd be back later, he and Andrew, dinnertime, when Gordon was supposed to come over to check her phone. Gordon the agent.

"OK," she said, "thanks for everything. Check Andrew's collar for lipstick."

"Yech!" he said.

The rain had slowed to a neat drizzle, and it was warm out on the balcony when she slid the glass door back and stepped out under the eighth-floor overhang. Edward was downstairs already. She watched him walk toward his car in the warm rain, probably still humming "My Old Kentucky Home," she thought.

She came back in and closed the door. The air inside was ten degrees cooler, maybe half the humidity. Two hundred a month for electric in the summer, all for air conditioning, but you couldn't live without it. Not in

Washington. Not in the summer. Besides, it was a big place, so two hundred in the summer wasn't all that bad.

It *was* big, nearly three thousand square feet, purchased outright with some of her inheritance. She stepped from the balcony into her living room, thirty-five feet across and twenty-five deep, carpeted in beige Berber. Off to her right was a dining area, to her left floral print couches; opposite, facing the windows, were shelves stocked with hundreds of folio art books, their brilliant spines dappling the room with color. The shelf-lined wall gave way on the right to a kitchen, on the left to a vestibule. The books were stacked between, on either side of a bathroom door. On the wall beyond the sofas was a portal that led to her master suite. Directly opposite, a hallway opened, running back to a lefthand guest room, lately Edward's, and, on the right, her studio.

That was what she needed, today particularly. She knew it when she woke that morning and would have found a way to get back into the studio even if Edward had stayed, excusing herself or dragging him back to sit beside her as she made her preliminary sketch. Working on her art did something for her; what or how she couldn't say exactly, only that it made her sound, always, miraculously, better than any psychiatrist or sedative could have done. Sometimes the art was distracting, taking her mind off troubles or vexations until they just resolved themselves or disappeared like bubbles, bursting from their own size and insubstantiality. At other times she'd think about a problem as she worked, pouring it into the paint or shaping it into her sculpture. Soon the piece she labored over would be transformed by some odd amalgamation of problem and thought, would come to contain them, so that they were hers no more, but part and parcel of the piece, which had come to hold, in a way, their solution. She never understood it, never tried to, but used it as a refuge at a time of need. Paint and metal were her mental balm.

Today paint would serve. Sculpture might have worked better, being more dynamic, more expressive. What she'd felt these past two days had called for that. But she kept her sculpture workshop elsewhere, in an unattached garage a mile away, rented from a woman who didn't own a car. She didn't feel much like going there today. Twice a week she'd drive to the place, shape and weld her metal segments. It helped her solve problems, helped her understand them, so that the solution came clear. More than that: it drew something from her; emotions maybe, making her objectivity that much more perfect and complete.

So each smooth and gleaming object was a sponge of sorts, absorbing and extracting the majority of her woes. Yet, at the same time, each piece was somehow enhanced by the problems it subsumed and had helped to solve, becoming thereby transformed into art. Those were works that sold; all she chose to make. Not that she needed the money, what with her trust fund and the salary from the museum. But there was an undeniable satisfaction in producing something really good, a satisfaction over and above the therapy it achieved. And they *were* good, really. The galleries snapped them up as fast as they emerged, then sold them to a list of eager buyers. She could have supported herself in reasonable comfort from the sculptures alone, had she worked a little harder on them. But then the quality would have suffered, and she wouldn't just turn out anything ordinary. Whatever she did had to be good, exemplary, worthy of her father's name.

Paintings sold too, but, unlike the sculptures, they took weeks, months, to finish. This one had just been started, sketched in with pencil on the yard-wide canvas, with not a drop of paint upon it yet. It sat upon a slightly slanting artist's table, level enough to draw on. She picked up the photograph next to it, a street scene in Alexandria, with a reflective window looking out on King Street. She'd taken it early on a Sunday morning when the light was perfect, yellow light from the ascending sun, desolate enough, but for a car reflected in the window of the little shop. The car was wrong somehow. It wouldn't do. She'd have to paint it out. That was what the other shots were for, a whole roll of them, none with the light so perfect, but enough that showed the window blank. It had to be that way, blank, empty. She didn't quite know why. The rest was good: lots of surface textures, glancing light, frozen transience, ideal for a photorealist canvas. It was a complex study, perfect for an exercise in technique. The photograph with the car in it was decent prose. A blank window looking out on King Street, very empty, made it poetry. She couldn't say exactly why.

She sat at the table and drew, some lines eased in, others penciled strictly with a ruler. It almost made her forget—almost; but the words had been so strange, and it was just three days before. How could someone have her picture, someone she didn't know? Was it hers? After the call, she had thought it might be a mistake. The woman had used her name, had her area code, thus knew her location. So she had checked the phone book for another Sarah Gruener in Bethesda. But there was none, no other Gruener in Bethesda at all.

She looked at the picture of the King Street shop. *Tobacconist* it said, in white letters on a green ground, above the window. Then the glass. That was the focal point, with masonry around it, as if it might have been an old brownstone redone for retail space. "Your picture," the voice had said, "your picture," but she put it from her mind, imagining the window as it would be on her canvas, with an empty street upon its mirroring surface, competing with the goods within, like some glassy double exposure. The street would have to be empty. Therein lay the poetry, though she didn't know exactly why.

Francie dialed the office. The phone rang once, barely once, before Theresa answered, as she did always, and with the same official tone each time.

"Hello, Theresa. It's Mrs. Posner. I need to speak to my husband."

"I believe he's in a meeting, ma'am. May I have him call?"

"No, Theresa. Get him, please. It's very important."

In a minute he came on. "Jesus, Francie, what's going on? I'm with the Houser Appliance people. . . ."

"Edward called."

"Edward. . . . OK. . . . Edward from the club?"

"No. Sarah's friend. . . . You know. *Edward.*"

"Oh, *Edward. That* Edward. . . . What's going on?"

"Look, Mark, we've got to tell her. We've got to talk to her."

"Why? What happened? What did he say?"

"She's been getting some calls and notes. I guess she wrote to some of Gruener's contacts. . . ."

"Jesus Christ! How did she get . . . how did she . . . Jesus Christ, Francie!"

"Look, honey, we've got to talk to her . . . go there and talk to her."

"Yeah. OK, I know. . . .OK, OK. . . . Just let me finish with this meeting. You know how big this account is to us, the Houser account. . . . I'll be out of here in maybe an hour and a half. Then we'll figure out what to do. I'll see you in a couple of hours, OK?"

"Yeah. OK," said Francie.

Thirty minutes later Mark was home.

They got on the road a little after noon, figuring seven hours to Washington, maybe six and a half if they grabbed some fast food on the highway. That's what they did, Francie running in for foil-wrapped hamburgers at a service plaza on the Ohio Turnpike while Mark got gas, both of them eating in the car. There was traffic on the Pennsylvania Turnpike, so they lost half an hour, but they made Breezewood by five, with Washington ninety miles ahead, straight down I-70.

Soon signs appeared for Frederick. That meant thirty minutes to Bethesda. Mark said it would be a good idea to call, to let her know they were coming, make sure she was home. "O.K.," said Francie. She dialed on the car phone. Mark listened.

"Hi, honey, it's Francie. . . . Fine. We're both fine. Listen, we're on our way to Washington. . . . No, just a visit. . . . Uh, just a day or two . . . just a day. . . . Yeah. We'll be there soon. . . . Uh . . . how long, Mark?"

"Thirty minutes. . . . Twenty. Twenty minutes."

"Twenty minutes. . . . No, nothing's wrong. . . . Yes, he did. This morning. . . . I don't know. Ten-thirty, eleven. Listen, he's your friend. He was right to call. You should have told us yourself. . . . OK, OK, we'll talk about it when we get there. . . . Yeah. . . . OK, see you in a few minutes. . . . Yeah. We love you too, honey. Bye."

They parked in the hotel lot a block away. Twelve dollars a day. Same as Cleveland-Hopkins Airport, Mark thought. Three men were at her condominium when they arrived: Edward, his friend Andrew, and another guy named Gordon. They seemed as though about to leave.

Gordon worked for the government, one of the investigative agencies, he said, but he didn't look the part, with his big belly and pink, balding head. Edward and Andrew were bantering like the three-year-married couple they essentially were. Mark had found it odd at first, a couple of years before, when he'd first seen them together, but he was quite used to it now. It was endearing in a way.

"Mr. Tomcic came over to check for a listening device," Sarah explained.

Mark asked if he had found one. No, said Gordon, not in the condo, but there was one in the building, probably downstairs, where the phone line came in. He'd come back in a couple of days and arrange to get into the basement for a look.

"Mr. Tomcic's married to Andrew's sister," Sarah explained.

"Yes," answered Mark, "we met her, I think." He looked over at Francie, who smiled and nodded. "Well, it's sure nice of you to help. What agency are you with, Gordon?"

Gordon tried to change the subject, which seemed peculiar, until it finally emerged that he did surveillance for the IRS.

"Oh," said Mark, "then we're opponents. I'm an accountant." It was sort of funny—at least it seemed so at the time—and he laughed, but in a moment realized it was not the perfect thing to do.

The poor guy looked uncomfortable . . . no, not just that; he looked miserable, in agony, wishing desperately that he were somewhere else, that he could crawl from the room beneath the carpet, unremarked. It was excruciating just to watch him, slumping in his posture, fumbling with a drink. Who knew what he had told them? Maybe that he was in espionage or something, a celebrated international spy.

Mark felt terrible, wishing he could recall his words, trying to think of anything to say that would ameliorate the situation. But nothing came to mind. . . . Nothing. Then, in a minute, Sarah stepped over and linked her arm with Gordon's, the arm without the drink, thank God, or Mark was certain Gordon would have spilled it over everything out of sheer agitation.

"That's the biggest agency of all," she said, in the most sincere and enthusiastic manner imaginable. "I had no idea you did anything that important. You know, it makes what you've done for me even more generous than I thought before."

It seemed to defuse things. Sarah had a knack for that: making people feel better about themselves. She'd been a blessing in their home.

No sooner had she'd spoken than Gordon seemed to become somewhat less tense, actually smiled a little, awkwardly. Then, a moment later, having apparently chosen to leave while he was even marginally ahead, he announced that he simply had to go, shook hands all around with the manifest pain and stiffness of a terminal arthritic, and walked to the door. Edward and Andrew followed him out, nudging each other, pinching back smiles, then Sarah behind, trailing them all to the elevator. For a moment the place was vacant but for the two of them, Mark and Francie, sitting face to face on the couch.

"What are you going to say?" Francie asked him, looking little less anxious than Gordon at his departure.

He shrugged his shoulders and looked into her eyes: "What choice do I have? I'm gonna tell her what I know."

Edward gave her a hug and kissed her on the cheek, Andrew just a hug, but a nice one. He wasn't very demonstrative. Her agent put his hand out, and she took it between both of hers and thanked him again.

"I'm glad I could be of help, Miss. . . ."

"Sarah."

"Sarah," he repeated. "Now remember . . . uh, don't touch any of the controls on the monitor. It will register the origin of any incoming calls and record them automatically. You don't have to touch a thing."

"No, I understand. . . . I hope you weren't offended at anything my Uncle Mark said. . . ."

"Offended? No, no. Why should I be offended. He just asked me where I worked. Why should I be offended at that?" He had that same odd smile on his face.

"It's just that he's very protective of me. I didn't even tell him about the calls and other things, because I knew he'd come out and make a fuss. He's been like that since . . . . since I stayed with them after I . . . . uh, left Washington."

The elevator made a tiny dinging sound, and then a dull thud, as the down light came on and the doors slid apart. Gordon got on first, nodding again awkwardly, then Edward and Andrew together, Edward's hand on Andrew's back, boarding like some outrageous quadruped. The doors closed and she headed back to Francie and Mark in visible embarassment on her pretty floral couch.

They looked painfully uncomfortable, which was odd for them. There was something going on, not just that she hadn't told them about the calls and things, but something else. She could tell. She knew them both well enough for that.

She went over and gave them each a proper hug and kiss, and they pulled her down between them. Francie smoothed her hair.

"Have you slept?" she asked.

"Last night I did. I look tired, huh?"

"Yeah," said Mark, "a tenth of a percent less gorgeous."

She got up to fix them drinks. Mark liked Sam Adams. She kept some in the fridge for him. One bottle and he got jovial; two, he fell asleep. She brought him one, and a glass of wine for Francie.

"I'm gonna make up your room. Edward stayed last night. . . . I just have to change the sheets."

"No, honey," said Francie, "I'll do it in a bit. You sit down with us. We've got some things to talk about." She hoped it wasn't a lecture: "Why didn't you tell us about the calls?" That kind of thing. How could she bother them with every little problem that came along? They'd done so much for her already, so much. Tried to be proper parents, and practically were . . . as near as anyone could be. She sat down sideways on the couch adjacent to theirs, perpendicular to it, facing them, a yard away from Francie.

"OK, tell us about the phone calls you got." Mark looked very serious, very concerned. She told them all of it, starting at the beginning, leaving nothing out, the initial call: "Are you happy," the man had asked, and her response, "Yes, yes I am"; then her suspicions about who it might be with something to leave to her . . . uncle, grandfather; her letters of inquiry, all unanswered; the FedEx-ed note; the disappearance of the box of correspondence; and last, the call on Saturday. Mark listened without a word of interjection or inquiry, leaning forward, his elbows on his knees, not a sound from him until she was completely through. Then he sat back and put his fingers through his hair.

"It *was* your grandfather. . . . At least I think so."

Sarah blanched, felt herself blanching. "How do you know? How could you know that?"

"I spoke to him once, just after you came to live with us."

"But . . . they told me he was dead. Everyone said that . . . that he was dead. Years before, they said. . . ."

"Yes, I know. I know all that. He wanted it that way. . . . But he was alive. He came to see me."

"Why didn't you tell me? God! Why didn't you ever say anything?"

"I promised him I wouldn't. I swore I wouldn't. Listen, he . . . he tracked me down. I don't know how else to say it. It was here in Washington, when I came to settle the estate with that lawyer friend of your Dad's. You know, Milner. The executor.

"I was staying at the Hilton, and when I came in after meeting with him—Milner—my message light was on, and the front desk said I had a note that I had to pick up personally, downstairs. I thought it was a . . . maybe a form to be signed, an agreement or something, you know, related to the trust. So I went down, and there was an envelope there for me, a little envelope, like a letter. There was a picture inside. It was of your father, one of those high school graduation pictures, wallet sized, and very worn and dog-eared, with an inscription on the back: 'To my Dad. My hero now and always. Love, Dan.'

"The note with it said something about it being the only picture he had of his son. He was risking it, *venturing it*, the note said, to guarantee to me that he was who he said he was, Adam Gruener. He said—well, the note did—that he had to meet with me about you, about his grand-daughter. It said to take a cab to the Lincoln Memorial. He'd meet me there. . . . I didn't know what to do, but the picture convinced me. It looked so worn and pathetic. . . . Anyway, I went. I was a little scared, you know, after what had happened to . . . well, after what had happened, but I went anyway. The picture looked so innocent and pathetic in a way. He must have been watching me and then followed the cab, because he was there in a car when I got out on that street that runs along the Mall."

"Independence Avenue?"

"Maybe. I don't know the name. . . . Anyway, I got in the car with him. I think I recognized him from some pictures I had seen. I hadn't met him before. Everyone seemed to think he was dead."

"They told everybody that."

"Yeah, well, Francie and I both thought so till that day. . . . So anyway, he drove me over to the botanical garden with all the trees. . . ."

"The Arboretum."

"Yes, that's it, the Arboretum. And we parked the car there and talked. *He* talked. He had a haunting presence, a big man, handsome, with deep green eyes, and the most penetrating gaze you can imagine. You've seen pictures, I know, but you really had to see him. He had this incredible presence . . . almost like a senator, or a movie star. He looked a lot like Gary Cooper, but without that sort of shyness. . . ."

"So tell her what he said, Mark."

"Look, Francie, I'm going to. Am I being timed, or what? I want her . . . ." He turned to Sarah again. "I want *you* to understand what kind of man he was. Or is." Sarah stood up and moved over to Mark, and he slid sideways on the couch so she could place herself between him and Francie. She sat in the hollow beside him and took his left hand in both of hers.

"OK, take your time. . . . I like the way you're telling it." Her body was inclined toward him, and his toward her, with Francie behind her, Francie's arm on the couch back just touching her shoulder.

"He said he knew who did it, you know, burned your house and everything. Not the actual ones who carried it out, but the ones who ordered it. It was someone he had worked for before he disappeared."

"But he worked for the government..."

"Yes, well, he didn't say who it was, whether it was the government or not, but just that he knew. He said he was going to get revenge for it. But it was funny: he didn't seem angry when he said it, just very serious and determined. He said he had some papers and things that he could threaten them with, the people he had worked for, and that you would be safe because of them no matter what he did. That as long as he had the papers and could bring them to light, no one could do anything to you, or really to him either, short of killing him. And he said this vengeance he was going to exact was something they would expect and understand. 'That's the way things are done,' he said. I remember that. 'That's the way things are done.'"

"So did he?"

"Did he? Oh, did he go after them...? I don't know. I never saw him again or heard from him, so I don't know whether he did or not, or what happened to him after that, only that the money was transferred a month later and you got your trust fund."

"My *trust fund*! That was from my father."

"Well, that's what we told you. He made me promise—swear to him—that I'd never tell you he'd contacted me. He wanted you to think the money was from Dan, from your dad. He said he'd be in danger if anyone thought he was in America, and that you might be in danger too, if I told you anything. So I never told a soul but Francie, and she agreed that it was better not to tell you anything about it. But you see why we have to now. I hope you're not mad at me. . . . You've been like a daughter to me the last ten years, the best daughter I could have ever had. Better than my own . . . better than my own daughter."

None of them spoke for a while. Sarah felt her eyes fill, that childish weakness that was of no benefit to her or anyone else, really. One could control that. *She* could. She blinked and blinked until the fullness was beaten away, somehow pumping it inward, so that nothing escaped but for two tiny dabs of fluid, one at the inner corner of each eye. Those she got with a thumb and forefinger in the act of pinching the base of her nose. No one seemed to notice. Mark was doing a lot of blinking himself, and Francie was making some furtive sniffling sounds behind her back. She was holding up better than they were. Mark's hand was still between her palms and she started rubbing it softly with her fingers, affectionately, in lieu of speech. . . . So he had been there all along, this progenitor of her father. She hadn't been alone all those years. If only she had known, even if she couldn't have seen him or even talked to him. It would have been enough to have the feeling that someone was alive, there for her if she needed him, someone of her line, half of what made up her father, a quarter of every gene within herself. All these years thinking he was dead, like everyone else. All these years. Her eyes welled again, and she beat them dry, just as she had before.

He was the one who had provided for her, this grandfather she had never known. The trust fund, all from him. She should have guessed, should have figured that out, the way it had appeared so suddenly after the estate had been settled. And Mark keeping it from her all these years, thinking to protect her, acting always in her interest, whatever he thought that interest to be. How could he have judged better? He had been a father to her, more than that, better really than any father, as if she hadn't been just a daughter, but a special daughter, selected from all the potential daughters in the world, displacing even his own, the natural daughter of his body and his blood. More than a father, but less too, at the same time, for he lacked that intimate bond of blood. Everyone did, even Francie in a quantitative way. So now to find that there was one alive who shared that bond and felt it just as strongly, as the trust fund served to show, shared it with her from some transcendent distance through the decade of her disconsolate orphanhood, had shared it with her through ten long years of abject loneliness but now was likely dead, with not a word of contact save a minute-long phone call and a half-page note; that was bitterly sad, maddening and ironic and intolerable, all at the same time.

"Are you OK?" asked Francie, rubbing her shoulder and neck so gently that it was almost indiscernible.

"Yeah. Yeah." She looked down and saw that she had worn a roseate stripe into the back of Mark's hand with the friction of her fingers, back and forth, back and forth, wiping away the solitude of a decade, wiping it from his skin or into it, as if his skin were a magic lamp and she could summon from it the spirits of all her amputated kinfolk by merely rubbing, rubbing. Mark didn't move. Nor would he have, neither moved nor made a sound to stop the motion of her scouring fingers, even had she scraped right through the skin to muscle and bone. She knew that when she stopped. She smoothed her hand softly over the redness, caressing the martyrdom of his soft skin, an accountant's office skin, unbrowned, hairless. When she glanced up at him, at his thin face, pale, fiftyish, and delicately lined, he did not meet her eyes, but looked down, down beside her shoulder at Francie's arm, on the sofa back. She could read the sadness in his gaze. Sadness at what? At hurting her? At not telling her something he had promised not to tell? That this good man was sad because of goodness he had done could not be borne.

"You were right not to tell me. You did what he wanted you to do, you and Francie both. I know that something must have happened . . . that I probably won't hear from him again. That must be why all of these things . . . the reason for all of the calls and things. I know that. I know that now. But I know that he wanted me to be with you. After arranging everything else, that's what he wanted. And he was right. You both have been more than parents to me. . . ."

They were good people. The best. As her parents had been, and this grandfather she felt the presence of, like an angel or a god, protecting her, sheltering her, though unseen, unknown. She would never know him now. She felt that, certainly, and the loneliness and isolation were unrelieved, unmitigated, as her eyes spilled over with liquid far too copious to be beaten back by mere eyelids, and her shoulders shook with sobs, and she wept like the rain, the July rain, warm on Francie's neck and hair, running vertically down her skin, moistening the fabric of her dress like the awnings over on Wisconsin Avenue. But the rain had ended, as the tears would too, in a brief while. Sarah would sleep dreamless again, or with dreams unremembered, and when she woke, with nothing there of Mark and Francie but their note upon her table, and the stormlet's moisture spent, and the sun low out in the East laboring to burrow through the last remaining clouds, the burden of her sorrow had passed. And all that was left was her work at the Gallery, and the nascent metal sculpture housed in a garage a mile away, and the yard-wide canvas in her studio with a central window painted in, reflective, looking out upon purposeful emptiness, though she didn't quite know why the empty-surfaced glass had to be painted in just that way.

CHAPTER 15

THE CLOSE-CROPPED TEMPLE OF SIMON FALLACO LAY FLATTENED TO THE window. For a cadaverous head, lifeless these seven hours, Simon's bore an aspect of remarkable serenity. His jaw, or that which had been his in life, sagged halfway down toward fully open, being in that state between flaccidity and rigor a corpse's jaw exhibits just seven hours out beyond its final pulse of blood. So gravity had left the mouth ajar a fraction of an inch, its leftmost angle, approximated to the glass, dependent. Fluid had gravitated there, a scanty amalgam of blood and saliva, gathered earlier in the throat and mouth, when the body had not yet cooled, nor its elemental fluids yet congealed. A narrow streak of coagulum, dark red, smoothly dried, so vivid that it looked like faux-gore wax upon a Revolutionary victim at Madam Tussaud's, inched down along a furrow cleaving cheek from chin. But that was the sum of Simon's brief exsanguination. Not a drop upon his clothing, upon the off-white shirt or charcoal slacks. Even the entry wound was clean, cauterized by the heat of the projectile as it burst directly from pistol through hintermost skull into his brain.

His left arm lay propped against the steering wheel. Buttresslike, it had helped to keep him erect, that and the minimal momentum of the bullet, for Jake had used the .22. It was known to Jake from many years of practice that your smaller bores were optimal for close range, causing no disarray at all, or very little. Just the entry, then the flattened pellet simply rattled through the brain, switching it off like a light, evoking neither protestation nor complaint. From the front, your clientele looked natural, peaceful in a way. Probably never felt a thing. The .22 was clean as a surgeon's knife. The Glock nine would have blown the fore part of the car into a war zone.

Jake had wiped the weapon down with alcohol, taken from a plastic bottle in the glove box. Then he let it dry and cradled it in Simon's other hand, his right, flaccid on the seat's black fabric. Unorthodox suicide that, from the rear. *Don't try this at home, kids*, thought Jake, grinning still. Rule number three was leave the weapon. Number four: have a little fun.

After that he'd left, around one, glancing back in resignation at the scene behind. A light blinked off, another on, as he turned the white Ford from gravel drive to gravel road, motion sensors mocking, lighting Simon's face against the glass of the second car in the driveway. Lighting the house too, its facing wall, the Goddamn puzzle of a house they couldn't find a way to enter. Not in an hour, going on two. That was all he figured they could spare—*he* could spare—by the time they got to it. And without tools, a drill at least,. . . it was impregnable. You couldn't break the windows—must have been Lexan, something like that. Couldn't even shoot out the locks. . . . Maybe with a cannon, if he'd had one. Oh, he could have probably found a way if there'd been a little more time: a day, a week. Gruener would have been amused to see it if he'd been alive, the sly son of a bitch; sitting someplace in there laughing like hell. Eluded them all until now, thirty years and more, and *even* now, with that fortress of a house. Thought of everything, even dead. Well, almost. He couldn't have planned on that woman, her and her loony doctor friend running around in his underwear waving a gun. Gruener couldn't have planned on them. Two such fuck-ups as one rarely gets to see in this world, odd choices for custodians of the type of sensitive material he had squirreled away. Slipped up there, old Gruener did, though he could hardly be faulted now, being dead. You can't plan on everything. That was in there too, in those rules. Top ten.

So that was it. No papers in the doctor's house, not that he could find. If they were there, they were toast now, which would be all right; better than all right. But if he hadn't seen them, hadn't inspected them himself with his own two eyes, he couldn't be certain. Not absolutely positive. Still, Isacco said the doctor had the papers. Isacco was sure. And he was careful, which meant he was usually right. The woman had seen them, he said, a box of papers taken from the home of a dead man. The right dead man, too, who'd passed along a picture of the right granddaughter to, unfortunately for them, the wrong two fuck-ups. Isacco had heard most of it, not about the fuck-ups, but the rest. And he was sure of what he heard. So those papers just had to be in the doctor's house, and had to have been burned. Everything was probably OK, but probably wasn't always good enough, not for the higher-ups anyway. You wouldn't want to get them riled, no matter what your rank or how high up you were in the chain. Seniority didn't much count in this business.

That's why Jake hadn't felt quite right about it, about not actually seeing the papers destroyed or getting them directly into his possession. And though he knew he'd better leave, for that was one of the cardinal rules too: *get in, get out*; though he knew that getting out was ninety percent of a job, though he sensed that time was inching in on him, quick minutes of it, unalterably, still he knew he wouldn't rest particularly well that night, or morning really, without taking one last shot at finding out where the papers had come from, and just possibly might still be: Gruener's residence. He wouldn't have a lot of time, but maybe just enough to check out the obituaries, see if there happened to be a dead man about Gruener's age with no relations, then maybe try to find his place and search it if he could.

So he and his asshole companion drove to the alley behind a drugstore, while the firetrucks screamed by and the rest of the town slept. He needed newspapers, a couple of days' worth, things a drugstore carried and discarded if there were copies left unsold. They found some too, just as he had figured, thoughtfully placed in a bin for recycling. No weekend papers in this microbe of a town, but the Monday edition had it: an obituary for a Charles Keller, with an address but little more. Fit the description, age just right, no relations, no past history. Not your Kiwanis Club member, in other words.

He drove to the truck stop, picked up the white Taurus, looked at one of the computer printout maps. Simon followed him to the place in the other car, down a dirt road. Damned hard to find though, but there happened to be a house with contemporary vehicles and a pretty sharp security system, motion-sensing lights and all, which had to be the one, and was.

But there was no getting into the God damned place. Jake was mad. First time in years. He prided himself on his control. And with this dumb son of a bitch pestering him: *Gotta go, gotta go*, and those fucking lights snapping on and off as they moved around the place. He knew they had to go, knew it just as well as Simon did. But they had a couple of hours before the fire simmered down and the law might figure there was foul play, as they liked to call it. He probably would have shot the son of a bitch anyway; yeah, he was pretty sure he would have. . . . But that pestering absolutely decided it. So he went into the back seat of the Taurus, the green one Simon was eager to drive off in, and put a little hollow-point .22 into the back of his head.

Then he left, about one o'clock, just as Simon's mouth was opening a little to emit the waxy track of blood and his temple was settling into the driver's side window. The night passed soundless, as it had for the old man three days before, here on the same property. Soundless, but for the crickets and the highway half a mile away, and when sunlight found its way into the car, about eight, surmounting a grove of trees to the east of the level former farm, it found Simon seeming rather peaceful and at ease, his temple flat against the glass. Clean-shaven, he looked. That was the way his beard grew, tawny and sparse, so that the hair seemed absent, though it had grown since eight the day before, grown a little during the night from dead skin which hadn't yet realized that it was dead. But for the track of blood, he would have seemed alive and sleeping, and when the deputy found him two hours later, popping open the locked door with his entry bar, he wasn't absolutely sure that Simon wasn't breathing until he felt the sparse-haired skin, cooled now to the morning dewpoint of the glassy comforter it lay against.

Clinger clasped the handle of the case in his enormous hand, lifting it from the closet. It weighed about thirty pounds, not far from the weight of his arm, his oaken arm, as thick across, midway between shoulder and elbow, as a slender man's thigh. Such an arm didn't allow for proper dress shirts, so he wore short sleeves, right on through the winter. Sometimes even those had to be vented at the side, like a jacket back, to let his biceps clear the hem. The case was nothing to that arm, a feather, a tissue, the atmosphere itself.

He took the other case too, the little one with the gun inside, tucking it up next to his biceps as he closed the closet door. Doc had found it with the papers, in the same intricate hiding place the papers had been in, so it had to be something special, some exotic high-tech firearm even the old man had thought important enough to bury with his stash. Shit! From what they'd seen in that closet, it would likely be special indeed. So Clinger dragged it along, figuring it might come in handy in such a situation as the doctor seemed to be in. Maybe the doc could use a gun anyway; so better safe than sorry, he figured, when he saw it on the floor. Besides, he'd been curious about it, eager to look inside, with the doc's permission. He'd check it out later, when the doc was with him, if he had the chance.

He set both cases on the carpet by the couch, sat heavily at the edge of the cushion, crushing it with his weight, reached for the phone, and called Phil.

"Hey, little buddy."

Phil could tell that something was up and said so with his tone, though not his words. He asked if Clinger had heard about the fire.

"Yeah. They called me last night, just after I got home. I went over; till around three, I guess." Had he slept? asked Phil. Yeah, he said, a couple hours. "I'm all right. . . . Yeah, I'm sure. . . . Look, I need you to cover for me today. I got something to do, and I gotta take off today. . . . Tell the sheriff something came up. He'll think it's with my kids or something. I got a lot of personal days I haven't used. He owes me anyway."

What about the parking tickets? The kid, Randy? "Yeah, I got Dixon to drop it. Tell the kid. Or tell the sheriff to tell him. That'll be better." When would he be back? "Maybe tomorrow. I'll let you know. . . . Yeah. Later. I'll call you tonight. . . . OK, thanks, little buddy."

He took up the cases again and headed out, leaving the door unlocked. No one locked anything in Bakersville, certainly not houses. And cars? Half of them had keys in the ignition. Shit, if your meter ran out, some passerby would put a nickel in the slot for you. Nobody ever actually took anything, except when the gypsies drove through every once in a while, and then that one crazy teen-ager who went around stealing women's underwear a few years back. That had been a big undertaking for the locals. They tracked him right to his door in the fresh snow: a real master thief he was, the cat burglar of Bakersville, with panties filling a whole drawer of his dresser, half of them extra hefty, large enough, each one of them, to accommodate a dozen normal, human-size buttocks with room to spare.

Well, thought Clinger, they could have his jockey shorts. That would be his personal contribution to local delinquency. Anyway, who was going to rip off the chief deputy sheriff? Maybe the gypsies. He got into the pickup from his unlocked house, the cases behind him in the storage bay. What an insurance claim! *Yes, sir, four pair of panties, two from the drawer, two from the hamper. . . . No, sir, not too soiled, just worn, you know. . . .*

He started the truck and headed out, feeling funny now about that box behind him. All those weapons the old man had. For this? Was it for this? Was this what they had come for? Blown up a house for? OK, so maybe it was an accident, maybe a gas explosion or something. But the timing bothered him. Hell of a coincidence. . . . Coincidence! That was just another word for bullshit, as far as he was concerned. He'd learned that back in Newark during his first month. A corpse had taught him, some blackened, puffed-out guy whose odor proclaimed his presence in the trunk of a car. Guy named O'Hara, Shawn O'Hara, but he spelled it Sean half the time and Shawn the other half. Happened to be on the racing commission. Some horses had just died in a fire. There were some other coincidences too, and he'd almost gotten himself shot checking out one of them. Newark went downhill from there.

He headed toward Arthurs' house on Chestnut. The street was closed off, but one of the local boys recognized his truck and moved some stanchions to let him through. He pulled in behind a trooper's car. No one seemed to notice.

There wasn't much left of the house. The bricks were standing, but that was about it. The roof was gone, and everything inside gone too, or maybe just changed, transformed into cinder and recongealed domestic lava, variegated alloys of plastic and glass and anything else that metamorphosed with heat into molten syrup rather than cinder and gas. Having cooled, it didn't much look like anything. Melted stuff, you'd call it. The State boys were milling around, three cars of them, with some forensics people. And Dixon, out front, leaning against his car. The locals always spent the day leaning like that, sometimes on Fords, sometimes on Chevys. Only thing that changed was the cars, and that depended on the discounts or kickbacks. Ford or Chevy, didn't matter so long as it was washed and polished. That way they wouldn't get their pants dirty.

"Hey, Brian, sheriff give you the day off for springing his kid?" Dixon was smiling, a nice wide smile with twinkling eyes surmounting it, indicating that the question was benign. Better for him. Nobody had the balls to say anything remotely *un*benign to Clinger. Not since eleventh grade, and even then. . . .

"It's his son-in-law. Yeah, I got the day off. Goin' fishin'. . . . So, what have they got here?"

"Big time. Double murder, arson. Professionals. Didn't take nothin'. They want to know if the doc was into drugs or something." He motioned with his head toward the largest gathering of state cops. They were the ones who asked about the drugs.

"What? That's bullshit! Look, did they even get a definite ID on the victims?"

"No, man, they was scorched. Gotta be the doc and his girlfriend though. They found exit wounds on both. Maybe .38. Quiet though. Nobody heard a thing. Big stuff for this town. You seen it before though. Where was you?"

"Newark." *So they thought it was the Doc in there.*

"Newark, yeah. Well, we're in the bigtime now. Nobody here never seen nothin' like it. That's why the state boys took over. We're just watchin' now. Let them big shots do the work." He motioned with his head at the troopers again. "Big shots."

So they thought it was the doc. . . .

"Me, I just come over to see what's goin' on. . . ." Dixon kept rambling on about his lack of jurisdiction, though he was probably happy to be watching from the curb. Nobody had any idea what they were dealing with, how big this was, how high up it might go. For an instant Clinger thought of turning everything over to the state cops: the box of papers, the

dead guy's name, the one they thought was Arthurs. Alan somebody; he
had it written on a slip of paper in his wallet. That's who they'd carted
out, not the Doc, who was in Pittsburgh at the Hilton, sleeping or maybe
unable to sleep for what he'd been told or what he hadn't. These guys
were looking for drugs. Shit, what did they know! Not half of what he
could give them.

If he had the sense to do it. But he didn't, or had more loyalty than
sense. He'd made a promise to Arthurs. More than that, he'd advised
him, counseled him. What was he going to do now, turn him over to the
Keystone Cops? Flag him for whoever it was that had meant to kill him?
These troopers wouldn't protect him. How could they? They had a million other things to do. This was a bigtime operation, maybe even had the
Feds involved, one of those clandestine agencies the law enforcement
people whisper about. No, why take the chance? Best thing to do was go
down to Pittsburgh, go over things with Arthurs, then let him decide. It
was his call. He was a smart guy. Let him make it. If the doc wanted some
help, well, he'd do his best. Otherwise just drop off the box and haul his
ass back to Bakersville. That seemed right, and that was what he was
going to do.

It was around eight now. Phil would just be getting to the office,
ready to tell the sheriff his son-in-law was off the hook, loosed on the
populace to make some other mischief. Maybe he'd steal the diabetic
man's fake leg this time, or his crutches. Shit, what difference did it
make? Ronald Steele owed him, now more than ever. He could take off
a month if he wanted. . . . Hell, what would he do with a month
off? Probably go in and hang around the office. What else did he have?
What else?

One of the state troopers came over to talk to Dixon. Clinger turned
from them and headed for his truck. He'd heard enough, more than
enough. Now he'd have to tell Arthurs, tell him that the fire was set, that
two people were dead . . . murdered . . . that girl, that pretty girl who
lived with him. How do you break that to someone . . .? Still, he'd said
they were splitting up, the doc and his girlfriend, and she *was* with that
other guy . . . Alan. So maybe the Doc wouldn't take it so bad. . . . OK,
he'd head down to Pittsburgh next. But something else needled him, one
more thing. What if . . .? What if . . .? The old man's place, Keller's

place. . . . It would only take ten minutes to check it out. He'd drive by. Just to be sure.

He saw the green Taurus from fifty yards out along the access road. It was parked halfway down the drive, facing out, looking empty at first, silent, the house and the car both, as if someone had abandoned the car there and left sometime back. But Clinger knew enough to be cautious. He slowed and then continued down the road, slowly, slowly, past the drive, glancing over, seeing a figure in the driver's seat, indistinctly, so that he wasn't sure about it, whether it was a person or something in the windshield and over flat against the tinted side glass. He kept on, passing the farm, then stopped a hundred yards beyond the property, parked there, and went on foot through a grove of trees to the edge of cleared land that marked the old farm's natural boundary. He had his gun, his .38, stuck down under his belt. No time to strap a holster on. No need. This was purely unofficial.

The house looked deserted, doors and windows closed, no signs of entry, at least from where he stood. Maybe someone had tried to get in and couldn't. . . . Yeah, he could relate to that. . . . He inched toward the clearing, still within the last layer of foliage. The car was visible now, seventy yards or so away. There was clearly a person in it, up in the front seat, leaning into the window, maybe asleep. Not a sign of movement or awareness. He waited. . . . A minute passed, then another. Nothing moved. This was odd. Strange place to take a nap, unless he was . . . .

Clinger drew his gun. He was a great shot, but a great target too, for somebody else with more firepower. These people would have it. He stepped along the ring of shrubbery at the outer border of the property, just within the road, keeping his head and eyes moving alternately back and forth between the house and car, car and house. No movement. None. The man in the car stayed motionless. He could see it was a man now, his pale head pressed against the glass, inert. Clinger reached the head of the driveway, then moved on past it, within and beyond the line of sight formed by the house and car, so that a shot fired at him from the house would be screened by the vehicle. Just one direction to worry about now. So he moved up toward the car, slowly, crouching, like a man who's been shot at more than once. Nothing broke the stillness, not even when he reached the car and tapped at the window, the passenger-side glass, with his .38. Nothing. There was a gun on the seat, in the man's right hand, with a silencer on its barrel. That settled it: only bad guys had silencers. Them and the Feds. So he was right. They'd been here. For that box . . . all for that fuckin' box!

He ran back sideways to his truck, all the time keeping car and house in view until he passed the grove of trees. Still nothing moved. It took a minute to get the entry bar from the storage bin and then he was back into the farmland clearing, walking upright now, striding toward the Taurus directly, for still there was no sign of life from either house or car, and he reached it, and unlocked the driver's side door, holding it in a little, so that the body wouldn't fall out onto his legs. He pushed the body inward, onto the seat, felt the coldness of it, then saw the entry wound, an inch or so around the back from the right ear, execution style, strictly professional. Just like Newark: shoot 'em in the back of the head with a .22, clean the gun, put it in the victim's hand. *Here it is, pig, try to find me.* He looked around the car a little, knowing there would be nothing there, not even a second set of prints.

Then he went over to the house—less cautiously, for these were professionals and would hardly stay around long enough for a body to cool to ambient temperature. He stepped up on the porch, treading heavily, making the wood floor creak in flexing, aware that he was safe to do so now, and saw the bullet holes and pits in the door beside the deadbolt and in the front window, that Goddamn plastic or whatever the hell it was. Whatever in the hell it was that old guy had put in there instead of glass, as if he knew these men would come one day. As if this was what he'd been waiting for, with his remote cameras and cleared land and grenade launchers. The old man knew. He was laying for them. And if they'd come a few months ago, these guys, when old Keller was healthier, stronger, he would have popped open his closet and given them quite a welcome party with that arsenal of his. Then what? Would he have had incoming cruise missiles next, or napalm? These were the big leagues now. These fellows weren't playing for nickels and dimes.

So what the fuck was in that box? He pulled back the seat as he got to his truck and looked at it again: shiny cobbled metal with a padlock in the front and a whole roll of tape across its lid. It didn't seem that formidable, but it was; no doubt about that. The authorities, *some* authorities, would have a field day with it more likely than not, but that wasn't his decision to make. It was the doctor's. He'd have some difficult decisions to make in the next day or two.

He started his truck and got out on the road. There wasn't much traffic, so he made it to Emory in twenty minutes and stopped there at a pay phone to call the office. Phil answered.

"Go check out the old man's place. There's a body there, in a green Taurus. . . . Never mind how I know. Don't mention me. Just check it out. See if you can get an I.D., any information. I'll call you later."

Phil said OK. He'd take care of everything. He knew better than to ask any more questions.

The door sprang open almost between knocks. Doc looked ashen.

"Jesus, Brian, Jesus! What's going on?" Clinger had the big metal case in his hand. He saw the doctor's eyes move to it, his mouth opening to speak, though no words came forth. Arthurs made way for him to enter, closing the door behind.

"OK, Doc, let's sit down, and I'll tell you what I know."

Arthurs moved over to the far side of the room, where a table and two chairs sat between the king-size bed and window. Clinger turned a chair toward the doctor, facing him at the outer edge of the mattress. He looked awful, pale and perspiring, wide-eyed, as if he hadn't slept.

"You brought the case."

"Yeah. It's what we thought."

"What do you mean? That somebody . . . ."

"Yeah."

"They burned the house?"

"Yeah."

"Somebody burned the house?"

"Yeah."

"Cindy was gone though, right? She was gone when it happened. She wasn't . . . ."

Clinger had no idea what to say. He hadn't really thought about the language he'd use or what sort of reaction he'd be confronted with when he finally got it out. But his face must have spoken for him the words that stuck there on his tongue and in his throat, because the doctor got crazy, his wide eyes widening even more, his nostrils flaring so roundly that Clinger's eyes were drawn to them, and then to the skin of his cheeks and lower face, now pasty wet and alternately pale and livid as his rage suffused its surface.

"What happened to her? What happened?" His voice notched higher and louder, not dramatically louder, but discernibly higher in pitch, sounding throttled, agitated. You could hear the harsh tonality, the agitation.

"OK, Doc, look, take it easy. I'll tell you everything I know. Just try to take it easy. This is hard for me too, you know. None of this has been much fun."

"Was she hurt? Was she burned, or . . . or the smoke, maybe...? Look, where is she? Why did you ask me about Alan? I've been up all night, Brian. Jesus!"

"OK, Doc, OK" He put his massive hand on Arthurs' shoulder, steadying him. "They killed her, Doc. She's gone."

There was a mirror on the outside of the bathroom door, and the light reflected from it onto a facing wall as it opened, swinging rotationally. Arthurs came out holding a towel, wiping his brow, his neck and the hair of his temples soaking wet. He looked awful, but maybe a little less awful than before, a little more composed—controlled maybe was the word— gazing down at his feet as he returned to the indentation in the covered mattress he had made a little while before. He looked up at Clinger, straight into his eyes. The vertical elongation of his stare was gone, and his nostrils had assumed their original oval shape.

"OK, tell me what happened."

"You're sure you're OK with it?"

"Yeah, I'm OK. I'm OK."

He still looked bad, pale, and with a wet brow again, though it had been dried not a minute before. But Clinger told him anyway. Hell, he had to find out sooner or later. Both of them were dead, he told him, the girl and that guy Alan, shot before their bodies were burned. And the fire: it was set, with explosives and the gas lines open. He told him about the dead man out at Keller's place—Gruener's it was, he remembered now—and the bullet holes in the door and in those plastic windows. Were they sure, Doc asked, about the people inside? Could it have been someone else, not Cindy or Alan, but two other people? Could somebody have made a mistake?

"I don't know. Maybe they're not sure. They don't know too much yet. . . . Not half as much as we do." Clinger felt hot now, his brow sticky and tingling from the moisture.

"You mean the box, the old man's things?"

"Yeah. . . . I didn't say anything. . . ."

"Well, we've got to turn it in now. It's evidence. . . . Jesus, that poor kid. She had nothing to do with all of this. . . . I killed her, you know, just as much as if I'd put a gun to her head. Shit. I can't believe it. I can't."

"You didn't do anything."

"No. That's right, I didn't. I didn't even tell her there might be something wrong. I left her there alone. . . .You told me, Brian. You said something like this might happen. . . ."

"But how though, Doc? How could anyone have found out about it so fast, that you had the papers? You didn't call anybody from your house, did you?"

"No, no, you know I wouldn't do that. Why would I do that? . . . I can't figure it out. Nobody knew about that stuff but you and me. I can't figure it. You're sure? You're sure about . . . that it had to do with the papers? I can't handle the guilt if I did this to her, left her there alone to. . . . It couldn't have been an accident? I mean, the bullet wounds, how could they be sure, with the fire and all?"

"No, Doc, no. You can't make a mistake about that kind of thing. Not with hollow points. . . ."

"Jesus, that poor kid. I killed her, you know. I killed her. Just as if I'd put a gun to her head. . . . Look, we've got to go to the police, turn all this stuff in."

"OK, Doc, whatever you say."

The doctor picked up the towel again and wiped his face. "Look, Brian, I've got to think. Give me a little time to think about all of this."

"Yeah, Doc. Sure. . . . I'm not gonna leave you, though, not like this.

You've got to straighten things out in your mind, then decide how you want to handle everything. I'm not gonna leave until you do. OK.?"

Sure, the Doc said. He'd like the company. "Can you stay around tonight? Go with me tomorrow to the police or wherever?"

"Yeah, I guess so. . . . Sure!"

Arthurs went over to the phone and called the front desk. He cleared his throat, coughed, sort of, but whatever it was that happened to throats at times like these couldn't quite be cleared or coughed out, so he sounded odd, congested maybe, or a little hoarse. He asked for an adjoining room, 542 or 546, clearing his throat again. "It's important," he said, then: "Nothing at all? Are you sure . . .? Look, can you send somebody up?" He hung up and sat on the far side of the bed, away from Clinger's chair, next to the phone, his head in his hands, moving not at all except to breathe. After a couple of minutes he got up and went to the closet, reaching up on a shelf for the metal case that Clinger recognized from the other day, the one with all that cash inside. He set it on the bed and opened it, then took something out, some bills. There was a knocking, thin, as though made by a slender hand. Arthurs closed the case and went to open the door. A young man came in, wearing a blue hotel blazer with a matching blue tie, well groomed. Arthurs asked him if there wasn't something he could do to get an adjoining room, 542 or 546, handing him the money he had taken from the case.

"Oh, no, sir, you don't have to give me anything," he said. Something to that effect.

"I insist," said Arthurs, and the young man left and in a few more minutes a bellman came up with a key to 546. Arthurs handed him a bill from the case. It looked like a twenty.

Then they talked for a few more minutes, the doc beside himself with sorrow and guilt, Clinger trying to be comforting, with a modicum of awkwardness and no success. He had to be alone for a while, the doc did, and that was OK now with just a door between them, so Clinger went to his adjoining room and closed the door, one single door, not locked but closed, and turned the television on, its volume down to indistinctness. In an hour the single door opened and Arthurs came in, looking a little better.

"Brian?"

"Yeah, Doc."

"I'm a dead man if they find me, these guys, right?"

"We don't know that for sure. They might . . . ."

"Come on, man. Level with me. I think I understand it now."

"Well, it's trouble. That's for sure. These guys are pros. They can be . . . I guess you'd say relentless."

"Even if I turn the case over to the cops, the papers, I mean. . . . They'll come after me even then."

"Yeah, maybe."

"And if it's a government operation, if these guys are from some crazy clandestine outfit, even the police won't be able to protect me. So if I'm alive, I'll be running from it the rest of my life, wherever I am. I'll never have my life back the way it was. . . . Never."

"That might be true, but we don't know for sure. . . ."

"OK, but the girl, Keller's . . . Gruener's granddaughter. They'll go after her, too, won't they? She's just as dead as I am if I turn the papers over to the law. Right?"

"Maybe that's right. . . . Yeah, maybe."

"Well, I was thinking about it, and I can't kill another one. I can't be responsible for her death too, so I've got to get to her and warn her before anything else happens. I can't kill another one like that. . . . Do you understand?"

"Yeah, I think so, Doc, but you didn't . . . ."

"I did, and I'm not going to do it again. I can't call her. He said not to. But I can drive there, to Washington. It's what, about four hours? I can find her and talk to her and see that she at least knows enough to protect herself, that she knows what happened and why."

"How's she gonna know why? We don't even know why."

"I'm going to tell her."

"But you don't know. We don't know."

"We will."

"How's that?"

"We're going to open that box. That is, I am. You can leave if you want. It's not your problem."

"Me! After what I've lived through? . . . Shit! I'll get it." Clinger went into the doctor's room and brought the case back, setting it on the table.

"It doesn't look like something people would kill for." Arthurs ran his fingers over the top of the case. "See this?" He pointed to an envelope stuck down beneath a thick layer of transparent tape. "The combination to the lock is supposed to be inside."

"Looks like a hundred yards of tape. Package tape, it looks like. . . . I got a knife, if you're absolutely sure you want to do it."

"Yeah, I do. See if you can get it open. I've got to make a call."

"A call?"

"Yeah, my sister. She'll be crazy if she hears about the fire. Look, don't worry. She lives in Atlanta. Nobody's going to trace it."

He would have called her last night, absolutely would have, if not for his promise to Clinger. Now it couldn't be delayed. If she heard about the fire, that there was a dead man in the house, that he was missing . . . well, he didn't know what she might do. Fly in, maybe. Put herself at risk. No, that wasn't an option.

Once a week he phoned her, then she'd call him too, every week or so. They filled each other in on everything they did, almost. All but the intimate things that brothers don't discuss with sisters, and even some of those. That's how close they were, how close they had been ever since her birth. He was ten when she came home from the hospital, wrapped in that tiny pink blanket, with feet and hands so small they looked like a little pink possum's or a doll's. She was like his pet, his own child, a special being to protect and nurture. A companion in the lonely house, always there when he got home, with whatever nanny they had hired to stay with her. He'd run in to see her first thing in the morning and put her to bed at night, most of the time, when Mother was out late to a party or playing cards at home or at the club. And as she grew, faster than he seemed to grow at first, and then a little more slowly, so that she came to just keep pace with him; as she grew, his role changed from nursemaid to protector to teacher and confidant, and hers changed as well, from plaything to protege to friend. She was thirty now, with two kids of her own and a decent lawyer for a husband, a kind and ethical man she wouldn't have stayed with for an hour if he hadn't been kind and ethical. She was raised that way. David knew that, as he should, for he had been the one who raised her.

"Hi, baby": that was how he greeted her every time, whether he called or she did, day or night for twenty years. "Hi, baby." But he couldn't bring himself to say it today when she answered.

"Karen?" he said, and she knew something was wrong.

"Davey? Dave? What is it?"

"I wanted to call you . . . to talk to you. There's been an accident here, a fire. My house got burned, and I just wanted to let you know I'm all right."

"Oh my God, what happened? . . . You're OK?"

"Yeah, yeah, fine. Look, I might be away for a while. Make sure you tell Mom I'm OK when you talk to her. . . ."

"When's that going to be? You talk to her more than I do."

"Well, call her and tell her I'm OK. Can you do that?"

"Sure, I'll page her at the club. Maybe I can get her caddy and he can give the message to her."

"OK, OK, be nice. . . . Everything OK with you?"

"Yeah. I'm worried about *you* though. You don't sound so good."

"It's been a rough day. Look, you might hear some things about the fire. Some people got hurt. I wasn't there though. I'm away from home. I . . . uh . . . I wasn't there when the fire started. . . ."

"Who was, then, Cindy?"

"Yeah. Cindy was there. She was home."

"Figures."

"Yeah, you never know. . . . Look, I've got to go. Just wanted to tell you I'm OK, in case you hear otherwise. I'll try to call you in a week or so."

"Where can I reach you?"

"You can't just now. Look, I'll call you, baby. OK?"

"OK."

He hung up, pulled his legs up on the bed and lay down. Four hours before, he'd sent the maid away, not wanting his room cleaned. The bed was still in disarray, the pillow still indented where his head had rested. He hadn't slept more than an hour or two, thinking about Clinger's call, about Cindy, worrying, but even in his fears, the worst of them, the oh-my-God,-what-if anxieties that had kept his consciousness alive through the never-ending night, even in the ghastliest of his imaginings, he'd never pictured this. She was a beautiful thing, like a flower or a lovely fabric. He couldn't imagine her otherwise, couldn't conceive of what Clinger might have seen.

She had been his ward, under his roof, in his protection. As long as she was there, she was his responsibility, and he'd let her down, abandoned her in the most egregious way. How could he live with that? How could he ever? Now there was another woman entrusted to his care—left to him, moreover, by a dead man. *Take care of the living*. He thought that, but the thought rang hollow, for Cindy was no dead patient whose heart gave out a little sooner than nature would have chosen. She was a woman he had kissed and held and lived with, and ultimately abandoned. And Alan too, poor Alan. Never hurt a soul, incapable of it, but certainly capable of being hurt. How he must have loved that girl! Loved her so much that he might even have died happy just to be with her in death. Not the kind of man you wanted to take a woman from and try to sleep at night, and, after all, a woman that you didn't love yourself, but merely played with for lack of someone else, anyone else, to feel about as Alan had about Cindy, as poor Alan had about poor, poor Cindy.

So he had killed Alan too, just as if he had put a gun to his temple, killed them both for all his pride and apathy. And now his head was heavy with it, with the weight of it, spilling over into unconsciousness, like a glass, brimful, beneath a faucet, dripping, dripping, its excess urged upward, over the edge, until its mass was too much too, like his head. But the pillow was soft beneath it, and the air around him temperate, and the little noise, faintly rasping beyond the closed door at his feet, the faint sound of peeling, something being peeled, tape perhaps, tape being peeled or stripped, all those things merely adduced to his comfort, being soothing to his senses or diverting to his mind, and he was so tired, so unconquerably tired, that he let the whole of it spill over and loosed his heavy head and arms and legs in sleep, and finally his mind.

He seemed to have slept for hours, but that was illusory. The light was just as it had been from the window to his right, so the sun was just as high. A quarter of an hour had passed, no more. There was sound, a startling sound, beneath him. No, not beneath, but down somewhere—at his feet, it was—and an opening, an open door with someone in it, saying "Doc, Doc, Jesus, Doc . . . Oh, you sleeping? Jesus, Doc . . . ." He raised his head. Was it Cindy? No. He had just seen her, sitting in her chair—well, not sitting, for she never really sat, but that wasn't where he was. . . . He was in his hotel room, and it was Clinger there, and Cindy was dead. He knew that, so it must have been a dream.

"Jesus, Doc," said Clinger, who looked a little wild now, standing over him, so he raised himself part way up on an elbow and shook his clouded head.

"The box, that box. . . ." Clinger was talking about the box, the one that they were going to open.

"Your old man, your guy, he shot the President."

"What President? Who? What do you mean?"

"The President . . . . Kennedy . . . . He fuckin' killed John F. Kennedy!"

CHAPTER 16

THE NIGHT WAS PALPABLY EMPTY, EERILY EMPTY, BLACK OF SKY, OF foliage, and of road, ineffably obscure, but for the silvery cone of light projected by the Taurus' headlamps. A hundred yards or so they reached, sweeping and bouncing along the pavement, catching up on the berm as the road swung left or right, then following in turn when the vehicle circumscribed the same arc. Light defined the highway, gave it form, provided some assurance that there was manifest existence out beyond the vehicle, a hundred yards out front at least, where the highway was illumined, where bright reflector panels on swaying guide posts and on low-slung guardrails flew by like strings of Christmas lights along the road's edge, left and right, quick and straight as tracer bullets, spaced with mathematical precision. Beside the car, behind it, and out beyond the utmost reach of the automotive lamps, nothingness closed in; black nothingness, relieved only by the occasional taillights of another four- or eighteen-wheeler traveling in equal isolation through the still and somnolent hours of the predawn day.

Once along the way, a brilliant truck came into view, alive with color, bristling with chains of purplish bulbs along the outer edges of its trailer sides, a chartreuse fluorescent glow beneath its cab. Gaudy, blatant, as dazzling as a tenanted ship in interstellar space, it was a peacock of a vehicle, its alternator laboring to strew pastel upon the night, to no known purpose. But it was slow, as slow as it was singular, thus readily passed at seventy. And when the final traces of its two sharp headlamps, and the fainter glow of trailing color, purple and chartreuse melding into a neon phosphorescence, when those final receding traces faded from a speck in the rear-view mirror into oblivion, the Taurus was alone again, separate from all the world on the two-lane strip of pavement leading out of Pennsylvania to the west.

About twenty miles short of the Ohio line, some signs announced a truck stop. And abruptly it appeared, up on the right, an oasis of light along the silent interstate, lighting the black sky amber gray. Jake pulled in, drank some coffee, half a cup or so, just enough to stay awake an hour more, ate a doughnut, bought himself a good cigar. Ten bucks it cost, and worth it, a nice cheap thrill for the forty minutes left to drive. Forty minutes more, just past the Pennsylvania line, into Ohio. Youngstown, maybe, or Niles: as good a place as any, and just about as good as home. Six, eight hours sleep, then up and make it back to Chicago in seven hours more, then, the next day, stay home and rest, order something in, watch TV.

The cigar was sweet and pungent, fragrant with the windows down and the cruise now set at sixty. The Taurus hauled itself along, requiring nothing but a gentle nudging of the wheel, done expertly with the sides of one's fingers and knuckles, automatically. The car was environment, the cigar entertainment. Jake played with its sweet smoke, curling it in his mouth and nose, blowing it leftward into the warm stream of moving air.

Soon enough there were lights and many vehicles, town succeeding town, with neon signs and streetlamps, brighter but less singular than the purple-sided truck. By three-fifteen he turned off south toward Youngstown, found a Ramada there, and checked in under an accustomed name, one that he had used a time or two before. He carried Simon's case with him up to his room, poured the contents out onto the king-size bed and sifted through the little pile, finding nothing but a change of clothes, nothing specific to Simon. Only Simon's wallet, slipped from his pocket after the .22 had had its play. That and his keys, tossed into the case; no point in making the identification any easier. The wallet was brown leather, new and nondescript. He weeded through it before he slept, shredding some cards and pieces of identification, flushing them down the toilet, burning a couple others in an ashtray out on the balcony. Then he got into bed, just as his coffee rush was petering out, and slept, oblivious as a child.

In the morning—late morning by then—he dialed the number he had memorized months before, Isacco's latest number in a string of them changed twice a year by the calendar. An answering machine took the message, and in twenty minutes more, Isacco called him back at the pay phone outside a convenience store.

"Where you at?"

"Youngstown."

"What happened? You get it?"

"Not exactly." He told him the rest.

"Well, you got 'em then. The papers were there. That woman told me. She seen 'em. They're burned for sure."

"Yeah, I hope so. But I didn't see anything like that, and I looked around pretty good. If not for that stupid fuck they set me up with, I woulda had the girl to ask, even if we had to do the other guy, the doctor. . . . He had a piece, I told you."

"Sounds like it couldn't be helped though."

"Maybe. . . . I don't know. . . . Better clear it for me with the top."

Isacco said OK. He'd check right away, have an answer in an hour maybe, maybe two. "How about I call you back at two, two-thirty?"

"Make it two-thirty. I'll come back here then."

"OK. Pay phone, right?"

"Yeah. Convenience store. I don't answer, hang up, then I'll call you later."

Jake went to an Italian place for lunch, a fancy-looking restaurant near downtown with plaster statues out front and a little fountain in the entrance. He was hungry and ate too much, especially with the wine. It made him feel heavy, tired. The bill came to fourteen dollars and change, with the glass of chianti and coffee. He left a four-dollar tip, generous but not conspicuous.

Isacco called at two-thirty on the nose.

"That you?"

"Yeah," said Jake.

"I talked to the brass."

"Yeah? And ...?

"OK, they don't give a shit about the man and woman concerned in the business we discussed."

"OK. . . ."

"And the other gentleman. The, uh, professional associate . . . ."

"Yeah?"

"They don't give a shit about him either."

"No?"

"No. In fact they said it saved them fifty grand." Isacco laughed. He had a pretty good sense of humor, but it wasn't so funny if they really did say that.

"OK."

"But you got another assignment."

"Another *what*? Look, I'm not going back to that shitball town again. It's too hot now. . . ."

"No, no. Take it easy. They want you to go to Washington, where that woman lives, the granddaughter . . . see if anybody gets in touch with her. You know, to be sure there's no contact. They figure anybody who had Gruener's stuff would try to get to her."

"Washington! Jesus! . . . . What about the guy you hired there?"

"He's not what you'd call reliable."

"No, I'm the reliable one who gets to do all this shit. . . . So what do they want done with her, with the lady in question? If she don't have any information, I mean. We can leave her alone, right? You know, this is the one . . . . What I mean to say is, I've been to Washington before on this matter, and I sort of met the family. . . . You know the story."

"Sure, sure, I know. Hey, I don't make the rules. They don't like to leave any loose ends though. You know that. Plus, I think they still want some satisfaction. You know, for what the old man did."

Satisfaction. Everybody wanted satisfaction. He wanted to say that *that* was satisfaction too, what the old man did, satisfaction for the death of his son, but Isacco knew it already. Besides, there was no point in arguing with *him*, with Isacco. They were both employees, good, reliable soldiers, valued and rewarded for their loyalty and brains. Both qualities told him not to say another word.

"Call here when you get in," said Isacco.

So much for the couple days off. He looked at a map. The Ohio Turnpike led to the Pennsylvania Turnpike, and that led to I-270 straight to Washington. Four hours, maybe five. He'd driven it before, more than once, but once more memorably than the rest. "Send him a message," they'd told him. "We want those papers." After ten years he still thought about it. The event had matured him in a way, made him a better, wiser man, as cautious as an old stag.

They read the papers all afternoon, bundles and packets of them, clipped together or slotted into file folders, coherently disorganized, detailed in particular areas, vague in others. They read and passed along for each other to read, straight on from the time that David's transient sleep was interrupted, past the time their stomachs growled in protest, so that they called down for room service, dropping mayonnaise on one manuscript, spilling a drink on another. They read while Jake was on the road, on his way to Washington from Youngstown, and Sarah was at work in the administrative offices of the Gallery, feeling that things were a little better now, a little less threatening. Mostly they read in silence, but for the shuffling of papers, Clinger speaking hardly at all, being a slow and labored reader. David talked a little more, scanning quickly through the pages, pointing out passages that Clinger hadn't come to yet or had seen but couldn't quite decipher.

Dear Lee, one photocopy of a letter ran, *You're doing a great service to your country. You were hand picked for this job, and we have the greatest confidence in you. This goes for me as well as the people at State and National security. That goes all the way up to the top, although we can't of course mention any names. You understand what I mean when I say that. . . .*

"Look at this one," David said, passing the paper over. "It's to Oswald."

"*Oswald!* Jesus Christ! A note to him? Who wrote it?"

"Look at the signature."

"Yeah ...?"

"It's Keller's . . . . Gruener's."

"You sure?"

"Yeah. I know his writing. From all those checks and papers we found. . . . It's the same. Just a different name."

"Albert Greer, it says."

"Right, same initials."

"Maybe he had monogrammed shirts."

"Yeah, could be. . . . Are you reading it?" Clinger was, but slowly.

"What the hell does it mean about helping the country?"

"He was a patsy," David explained. "Maybe he thought he was shooting at someone else. Maybe they convinced him that aliens had taken over Kennedy's body. Who knows? It's probably in here though. . . . I think if we keep reading, we'll find out."

There were hundreds of papers: letters, photos, plans and maps, alternate routes the procession might take. Everything was there. By evening they had a reasonable understanding of the plan and the part of it that had been carried out.

There were three teams of shooters, stationed at various places to cover not just the anticipated route the motorcade would take, but two others as well. Each team had a patsy, told he was firing blanks toward the Presidential limousine. A dead Cuban would be found there, shot by security, after the event. That's what they told them, the patsies with military cap guns. An attempted assassination: the perfect pretext for a military ouster of Castro. All phony though, no one would get hurt but the dead Cuban.

Oswald thought he was working for the Feds. He was the most easily convinced of the three shills and lived the longest, a full day. The other two had reservations, questions, but not that misguided soul. He was fervent, messianic. After all, he'd been to Russia, a stinking shithole if there ever was one, in his words. He probably loaded the gun himself with blanks and almost shit himself when some real bullets struck home. Then he must have run, knowing something had gone terribly wrong. For him, it had. Not for Adam Gruener.

Albert Greer he had called himself back then. He had planned everything, recruited the teams of marksmen, all equipped with silent weapons, all positioned in safe, sheltered places. All except the patsies, that is. He positioned one particularly talented marksman a floor above poor

Oswald; two others, less skilled but competent, in buildings across the plaza. Oswald had ordered a rifle, a Mannlicher-Carchano, from a catalogue given him by Gruener. Then Gruener had taken the gun and had the firing chamber duplicated three more times. He did that with each weapon of the three nonentities he had recruited. Projectiles fired from any of the four firearms would be identical. A Swiss gunsmith had done the work. Twelve thousand dollars was his fee. There was another item: twenty thousand dollars for the gunsmith's execution. Couldn't be too careful.

Each gunman was promised half a million dollars for his work, or intended work, and safe departure from the country. Four million five for the shooters or would-be shooters. It looked as if all of them had gotten away. Their names were in the documents, along with everything else. Four of them were Latino, maybe Cubans after all. One little slip and Castro might have had his island bombed back to the Stone Age anyway.

But everything went as planned, right down to the main team seeing the action. Oswald was the leading patsy and clearly had to die. All three patsies did. Gruener saw to it. Two of them were put out by the three-man teams they didn't know existed. For Oswald, now in custody, he made special provision, one of the guards in the Dallas jail. Convinced him it was his patriotic duty, gave him something undetectable to put in the food. Then Jack Ruby went and saved him the effort. Gruener must have thought he had an angel on his shoulder, so perfectly did the whole operation go off. He left Dallas the day after Ruby did the final cleanup for him, the perfect stooge, killing co-operatively for his country.

Each man traveled by a preplanned route; ten men, some through Mexico, some across the gulf to Jamaica. Gruener got out after all the rest, having shepherded his last man off domestic soil. He apparently spent a month or two in Athens: some of the correspondence reached him there. Then he made it to Iran. His stipend of two million dollars must have been waiting for him when he arrived. Patmos Trading was the agent, patron and sponsor, with a Chicago address. Find out who ran Patmos and you had the individual or group responsible for the assassination. That was nowhere in the papers, neither the reason nor the person behind it all. But it could be learned. It could definitely be learned.

David set the last of the papers on a ruffled pile and pushed it over toward Clinger, alongside the stack the deputy had been sifting through. "How could they have kept it quiet all these years?" he mused, half to himself.

Clinger dropped the paper he was reading onto another stack, rubbed his eyes, and looked up in manifest relief. "Your old guy probably took care of it, at first anyway . . . . Gruener. He did everything else, so I'd guess he arranged to keep everybody quiet, himself included. Then something must have happened, something he thought of as a threat, which is to say . . . maybe they tried to go after him, the ones who hired him, I mean, or didn't give him all his money. And then he kept this stuff for insurance or blackmail. Somebody knows he had it. That's for sure. So he must have told them about it, that he'd saved everything and would use it if he had to."

"I guess that sounds right. He did get paid, it looks like, so I'd bet that he was threatened in some way, he or his family. . . . You know, I just can't believe he was involved in this kind of thing. It just wasn't him. I don't know, he was a neat old guy, not like . . . . Well, he said he had his reasons, though. In that letter he wrote to me."

"Yeah, well, he couldn't have been too concerned with your welfare. . . ."

"Oh, I don't know. He didn't plan on this. That's for sure."

"Hey, I didn't know the guy, but it's hard for me to believe he cared a lot about you or anybody else after what he did."

"Yeah, I know, I know. I've been thinking that too. Maybe . . . . Maybe sometimes people do bad things for reasons that are better, or that we don't understand. . . . Not that I'm defending him. . . . I wouldn't put myself in that position."

"So what are you gonna do? You still want to go ahead with it? Try to get to the girl and all?" Clinger dropped the paper he was holding and leaned forward, his elbows on the table.

"What choice do I have?"

"Well," Clinger held up a thumb and index finger, "you got two choices: head to Washington or go to the law, which is to say go public with it. The FBI maybe, or the papers, the press."

"So, what do you think? I'd bet I'm a dead man the minute I open this stuff up and anyone finds out who I am and where I am. . . . Besides, how do we know that Patmos Trading isn't linked to some governmment agency? Maybe even the FBI. I know there were all kinds of theories to that effect when they were investigating."

"Yeah, that Warren Commission. . . . Wasn't that the one? It was a joke. Gruener probably arranged that too."

David leaned back in his chair: "I was just a kid when it happened, you know? They say people remember what they were doing the day Kennedy was shot. I remember being in school and going home early. They closed school early. That's all I remember. That and the funeral, watching it on TV. I was, what, about seven? I remember watching the boy, John Jr., saluting the casket. That's the main thing I remember about it. Of course they've shown that so many times . . . ."

"Yeah, I remember that," said Clinger, "that part, the little kid, and Mrs. Kennedy with that black veil. I was eight, I guess. Our school let out too, right after it happened. Somebody came into the room and told our teacher. I remember her starting to cry and then telling us that something had happened to the President. Then they sent us home. . . . My dad worked for the electric company, up on the lines or driving truck. He did-n't have much use for Kennedy, said he was a crook and his family were all crooks too. He said he had it coming to him. But I remember him sitting there and watching the funeral and just sort of shaking his head, the way he did when somebody let him down, like one of us boys getting bad grades or getting into some mischief. It was as if he was ashamed of the country, ashamed of everybody. . . . Himself too, maybe. You know, for all the things he said about him—about Kennedy—I remember thinking that afterward: how he didn't say anything, just shook his head. I don't know why. I guess I never really understood exactly what it meant when he shook his head like that, the way he did it. . . ." Clinger started to move his head slowly side to side, perhaps the way his father had. He was solil-oquizing now, opaque to any other presence in the room. "I guess people really do remember where they were that day, those few days. Even young kids . . . even people who were kids then."

David nodded, thinking *yes, yes*: There was something very odd about it. Something almost incomprehensible about an entire generation's fixed obsession with a single event, as though it had shattered their lives in a way, like the death of a parent or a child. Maybe it had. Maybe that one extraordinary action *had* changed their lives, the lives of all people in the world since that watershed in history. For Johnson had followed with his war in Viet Nam and the Great Society. And then the counterculture started, a reaction to the war, with exaltation of civil disobedience and recreational drugs; and the Great Society brought welfare expansion, and dependency, and the dissolution of families, and crime. There had been much good too, civil rights and health care and an enormous enrichment of culture with the explosion of diversity. Adam Gruener had changed the world in many ways, though whether ultimately for good or for evil would take the perspective of another century to decide.

Clinger was still musing, far off in his own fantasy, sitting motionless, unblinking, his eyes fixed on the littered table. *His father*, thought David. *There must have been much unspoken love between them.* He got up and went back into the adjoining room, into the bathroom, washed his face, looked at its reflection in the mirror, haggard, unshaven. Not that he'd forgotten to shave; he just hadn't cared, waiting all morning for Clinger, unable to think, let alone wash or groom, just waiting, with wet palms and a dry mouth, then hearing the news, what he had most feared but had not let his consciousness imagine.

It was the *way* they had killed her, gratuitously, the way they had come for something that wasn't there, then gone ahead and killed the two of them with no purpose. The two of them, innocent of everything. They likely hadn't even known why the men had come, why they were being killed. For nothing, it was. Nothing they'd done, anyway.

So he hadn't cared much about shaving then, didn't care much what he looked like now. Who was going to see him? The maid? The fellow from the front desk? Shit, that kid had hardly minded a little beard growth on a patron who'd passed him a fifty dollar tip. Still, he did look like hell, his image in the mirror, just like hell, just as awful as the way he felt. Could he function that way? Think and act with the level of sophistication required by the world of trouble he was in? He'd have to. After all, getting himself killed wasn't going to help Cindy in any way, bad as he felt about her and Alan too. It wouldn't help anyone really: not his patients, nor his sister, nor Gruener's beautiful granddaughter whose picture lay snug in his wallet. No one, other than the folks from Patmos Trading, whoever they were. He looked at his ragged image in the mirror.

No, he didn't want to die like that, supine, passive, and disheveled, behind some ineffective barricade of his own inept device. He plugged in the razor and plowed off the full day's beard, then wet and combed his hair. When he stepped back into Clinger's room, the deputy looked up at him and smiled.

"Good, Doc. That's better. Now you look like the guy I came down to see."

He got into his chair again, an elbow on the table. "Well, Brian, what do you think? I need your professional advice here. What should I do? Somebody's gone to a lot of trouble to keep this stuff quiet. What would you do if it were you? Yesterday I killed a couple of innocent people. Maybe bringing all this out would be the best way to atone for it. I don't think my life's worth much now anyway. . . . So, you tell me, what would you do?"

Clinger pinched his nose. David noticed that he had a way of doing that, holding the base of his nose, up by the brow, between his index finger and thumb. Whenever you asked him a question he had to think about, he'd sit silent and put his hand up to his face that way. David had seen him do it before, two or three times, always when he was thinking about something, thinking hard about it. Whatever it did for him, concentration or whatever, it seemed to work. He was a bright guy, experienced and sensible, with a penetrating understanding and unerring judgment. He'd help figure it out, maybe not come up with an answer where there was none, but at least help clarify the question.

"Doc," he started after two full minutes of pinching, "I can't figure any way for you to get out of this safe by going public. OK, look: that old man, look what he did. He knew what to do better than anyone, right? Kept himself alive long enough to die in bed, peacefully. What did he do? He took off and went to live in Iran, then finally came back here like a hermit with a new name, which is to say he didn't go on TV or write a book. Maybe in a few years all of this shit may come out. But you're not safe doing it yourself, letting this stuff out. At least that's what I think. Besides, what good's it going to do you or anyone else? It's thirty-what, thirty-three, thirty-four years ago? Who really cares now who killed anybody that long ago? I say take care of yourself. You didn't kill that lady friend of yours any more than I did. I knew just as much as you and didn't say anything either. Just to you maybe. But I could have warned her too. Nobody could have known. Nobody could have.

"Look, I say go try and find that woman, the granddaughter you're supposed to split the money with. Then go and get the cash and disappear. You can live a long time far away from here on that much money. Shit, the old guy owes it to you now, after what he did, not what he did thirty years ago, but what he did to you, now, today, by getting you into all of this."

"Maybe you're right, Brian. Yeah, you're probably right, but I've just got to think. . . . I might be able to do it though. I might . . . maybe follow her, meet her someplace when she's out, if nobody's watching her. How can I tell that? What do you look for, what kind of things, to tell if it's safe to contact someone, whether someone else is watching me and her both?"

"Jesus, Doc, that's no problem. With the two of us on it? Shit! Nothin' to it."

"What do you mean, 'the two of us'? How do you figure that? Look, this isn't your problem. And it's sure not safe for you to make it yours. Hey, I'm grateful for all the stuff you've done for me already, but . . . . Look, Brian, you've got two kids at home to raise. I'm not about to be responsible for putting you at risk after what just happened. . . . That's it, you're going back to Bakersville tomorrow, tonight if you want. I can get myself to Washington—Bethesda or wherever—and figure out what to do when I get there. I could use some pointers though. Maybe I'll call you if I need advice on something. OK?"

"Doc, I've got to show you something." Clinger got up and walked into the other room, then came back a moment later with his travel bag. It wasn't very big, somewhere between a small checked bag and a large carry-on. He put it on the table, atop and among the papers they had gone through all day. Then he opened the case and pulled out some things, socks and underwear, a few shirts, short sleeved, with enormous girth for chest and shoulders.

"What's in the bag, Doc?"

"OK, all I see so far is clothes. What, you've got a gun in there?"

"No, just clothes. My gun's in the truck. Yours is too. The one the old man left you. . . . What I'm showing you is clothes. I knew pretty well

what was going on when I left home today. Not everything, you know, not
the stuff about Kennedy and the dead guy at the old man's place. But
enough. . . . I knew enough. I knew there was somebody who tried to kill
you and wound up killing somebody else instead. Now I know there's one
less somebody, but I don't know for sure how many we started out with,
so that doesn't count for very much. Which is to say, I had a pretty good
idea you were in a good deal of trouble, and I packed about a week's
worth of clothes and got that much coverage to come along and help you
out as much as I can. So you can't possibly think I'm afraid of a little
action for a change. I was on the force in Newark for three years. There
were crazies there, I'll tell you. Crazies. Now, these guys are professionals. They act rational. You can predict how they're gonna do things. If
there were crazies after you, well, maybe then you could count me out,
but with professionals, this might be fun. Look, I'm just a whore back in
Bakersville, in Jackson County. A pimp for the sheriff and a whore for the
County, taking money for dressing up in a uniform and driving around
and making deals. It's gonna feel good to *do* something again, to get you
out of a scrape, maybe even kick some shit out of the guys who burned
your house and. . . . Shit, you know what I'm saying. I'm tired of feeling
like a whore when I visit with my kids. I'm tired of the whole Goddamn
thing. . . . I'm going with you to Washington. Just not to Iran . . . . There
I draw the line."

He put out his big hand, so huge it scarcely seemed real. Clinger was
looking at him, into his eyes, and he into Clinger's, round blue eyes with
lots of lateral creases, laugh lines, smile lines. Those eyes had laughed
and smiled a lot. They were kind eyes on a gentle face, despite its size and
the troubles it had looked upon. This man had deserved better than he
got: an errant wife, two kids he never saw enough, a living humiliation of
a job. How could he be put at risk? How could anyone? But he was a
mountain of a man, indestructible. What would it take to injure such a
man? A tidal wave? Thermonuclear war? What harm would it do for him
to come along? Just make sure he wasn't exposed to any possible danger.
It couldn't be too hard for David to see to that, maybe help to keep himself safe as well. Clinger's hand was opened wide before him, thumb
cocked back, fingers straining to grip. David took it in his grasp, and it
was gentle as a child's, like a huge mechanical claw machined to microns,

capable of crushing a car or lifting a moth by the wings without disturbing so much as a particle of its powder.

"OK, Doc. Great! We're gonna kick some serious ass." Clinger's teeth shone brightly in the middle of his jutting smile. His eyes creased, accentuating the lateral lines, deepening them, slotting off the circular blueness of his gaze. He brought his other hand to bear on David's, enveloping it, cheerfully, protectively, like a giant claw holding the wings of a moth, benignly. "Thanks," he said. "Thanks, Doc," and squeezed the smaller hand with the gentlest hint of pressure, though what there was to thank him for was just as obscure as Adam Gruener's past and just as doubtful as his own bleak future from this day forth, as far as he could imagine.

PART TWO

TO BETHESDA AND BEYOND

CHAPTER 17

ARLY TUESDAY EVENING JAKE PULLED OFF THE INTERSTATE SOUTH OF
Frederick, looking for the proper phone, isolated, inconspicuous,
accessible. Some unattended pay booth in a sheltered spot where
he could place his call in peace, leave a message for Isacco, then park
unremarked nearby, sit unnoticed with the windows down, close
enough to the phone to answer before the third or fourth ring. For years
they had communicated that way, he and his contacts in Chicago,
Isacco and the ones before Isacco. Just different numbers to dial, different office space to house the mostly silent phone. Someone would
take the message—some person in the old days, but lately a machine.
Then the call would be returned. Twenty minutes on average, usually a
little less or more. One night late, it took four hours. Nothing you could
do. Just sit tight and wait: not the sort of call you placed or took in
comfort at a Burger King.

Half a mile out beyond the generic strip of highway food and lodg-
ing, straight on Maryland Route 26 in the direction of Urbana, the
frontage turned industrial. A few blocks more and he found a solitary pay
phone at a muffler shop, a franchise sort of place that would have closed
at five. Not a soul around. It was nearly eight now, but seasonally bright,
a gold and horizontal sun at play upon the easterly facade of the building.

Custom Pipes, said the sign, black on yellow, *Foreign and Domestic.*
When he dialed, against all expectation, Isacco answered.

"Where are you?"

"Past Frederick . . . . uh, about maybe twenty, thirty minutes out of
Washington."

"You made good time."

"Yeah, yeah. Look, I'm kinda tired, Carmen. What's the plan?"

"OK, I was thinking you might as well stay at the place we rented
there. It's in the same building the woman lives in. . . ."

"Wait a minute . . . just wait a minute, OK? . . . Do you think I want
to be seen there if . . . if they made up their minds they're gonna, you
know, carry this thing through? That's nuts. That's just plain nuts."

"OK, yeah, I know, I know, but nothing's definite. I mean, nobody
made any definite decision that I heard of. Anyway, you can go in and out
at night, right? So as not to be seen? I mean, you know what to do. You're
the expert at stuff like this. . . . If you're right there, in her place, you'll
get a better feel for the situation, won't you?"

"Yeah, yeah, I guess so. OK, say I do it. Say I look it over and figure
I can get in and out OK. . . ." He paused for a minute, thinking. "All right,
say I look it over. . . . Where is the place? How do I get a key?"

"That guy we hired, I'll have him meet you. . . ."

"Are you fuckin' kidding me? Another one? I had enough of the ass-
holes you guys hired! Jesus! That last son of a bitch, you know . . . ."

"OK, OK, hold on. This guy is straight. He's no shooter, that's for
sure. You look at him cross-eyed, he'll shit himself. But he follows
orders. He's OK. This one's OK."

"This what they want?"

"Who?"

"What do you mean, *who?*"

"Yeah, yeah. This is how they'd want it handled."

"How they *would* want it handled or how they *do* want it handled?
You talk to anybody about it?"

"Yeah, I did. Sure I did. Hey, why you bustin' my balls over this? I
didn't hire that other guy, Simon whatever. That's over my head too. You
know . . . I do what I'm told to do. Like you. We're on the same side,
remember?"

He got the local contact's name and number, Leonard Siskin in
Alexandria. His wife answered. "Lenny! Lenny!" She had a whiny voice,
strident, like a spoiled bitch. Then Leonard came on, deferential, an ass
kisser, which was a vast improvement over the personnel he'd been given
in the past. Meet him in the lobby of the Hyatt, he said, just a couple
blocks from the building the woman lived in. Great, thought Jake, soon
enough he'd be privileged to say that he'd known the whole Gruener family, three extinct generations worth.

In forty minutes he was there, circumambulating the lobby, with its
dappled pink marble floor and walls. Leonard was standing over by some
potted plants. You couldn't miss him. He looked the way he sounded, like
one of the plants, a pear with legs, two-thirds of his loose flesh heading
south. Light from the ceiling fixtures reflected off the top of his scalp,
making it look wet or maybe greasy. Jake walked up to him and nodded.
Leonard's face was pear-shaped too, bejoweled and flaccid, even in the
putative animation of speech.

"You Mr. . . . ."

"Jake. Call me Jake."

Leonard stuck out a hand. Jake took it. It was cool and moist, ichthy-
oid. There were little beads of sweat on Leonard's forehead, stopping
where the hairline might have started once, as though baldness had obliterated all the functioning sweat glands in the process of uprooting his
hair. He had a rumpled suit on, a loose tie half an inch askew in the collar of his shirt, and obtrusively scuffed shoes.

"Mr. Isacco said you're going to stay at our place."

"Yeah, maybe. I'll take a look at it first." That was all he had
promised. If it was a dump, half as unkempt as Leonard, he could always
come back to the Hyatt. For an extra fifty, they'd invariably find a room.

"We can go right over," Leonard said. "Whenever you're ready,
Mr. . . . ."

"Jake."

Jake looked at his watch. Eight-forty: an hour and a half till very dark.

"Let's have a drink first."

Leonard nodded, smiled sociably.

They went into the bar. Jake was buying, of course. Leonard had lots of bourbon, lubricating the exposition of his autobiography, personal philosophy, and political orientation, all in sequence. When he got to religion, Jake noticed that the streetlamps were illuminated just outside the window to his left.

"Let's have a look at that place of yours," he interrupted. Leonard seemed chagrined.

"Are you a Catholic?" Leonard asked. The bourbon had turned him melancholy.

"Used to be," Jake told him. Nobody ever responded to that.

Jake left his white Taurus at the Hyatt and rode the three blocks in Leonard's Toyota. It stank of spilled coffee and its plastic dash was torn. They went in through a remote-activated entrance, then parked in an assigned space in the substructure of the building. After Jake slid out, working the handle of the car door with the inside surfaces of his thumb and little finger, Leonard locked it up and set the alarm.

"You know which car is hers?" Jake asked.

Leonard pointed out a burgundy Mustang convertible.

"Nice," said Jake.

Leonard nodded. He looked a little wobbly from the bourbon. Jake came up with a mnemonic for the Mustang's plate: lucky lotto winner seven and eleven plus two.

"Elevator's over here." Leonard started walking toward it unsteadily.

"Hold on," said Jake. "I'd like to have a look around . . . uh, outside." He walked up a ramp toward the garage entrance, Leonard behind him.

"Which unit is ours?" he asked from across the street, around the corner from the exit. Leonard pointed to a window on the second floor.

"And hers?"

Leonard pointed again. "Up there. With the light. Seven-oh-five."

"Nice," said Jake. Tough nut, he thought. If he had to shoot her, the best place would be the garage.

They left at six Wednesday morning, Clinger following the Buick in his bright red truck. He'd need it to get home, he said. "OK," said David, "let's go." They took the turnpike, staying close together. David had the maps; Clinger, the guns. By noon they were in Bethesda.

David parked the Buick. Clinger thought someone would be looking for it by now, the police for sure, then maybe others too. So they used the truck. They drove past the address printed on the back of the woman's picture, a high-rise condo on Bethesda Avenue, then looked for a place nearby to stay. The Hyatt was the closest. Two adjoining rooms, he told the girl at reception.

"Anything facing west, upper floors?" He passed her fifty dollars. Fourteenth floor, high enough to see the upper half of the condo, though not the street in front. Best they could do. They checked in, then went out for a walk.

The trick was not to be conspicuous, not to hang around the same place too long. Clinger told him how to do it, though David had figured out as much already. There were two streets of shops and restaurants adjacent to the entrance of the building, perpendicular and parallel. That helped, providing lots of options. They went into a coffee shop and waited for a window table, David with a cup of tea, Clinger with black coffee. David gave the boy at the counter a ten to cover a check for two dollars and change. He expressed his thanks effusively, then left them alone.

Through the window, David faced out at the east facade of the building. Unit seven something, the address read: seventh floor. He wondered which window, which balcony. Two people entered in an hour, an older couple, well dressed, through the front. Then a car drove up, activating the garage door. There was a man behind the wheel, dressed in suit and tie, middle-aged it looked like. The garage door closed behind his tail-lights. It was two-fifteen. He and Clinger got up from their table, and immediately the clerk came over.

"Anything else I can get for you?"

David smiled and shook his head *no*, then reconsidered. "Yeah. Yeah, maybe you could hold this table for us in case we want to come back in a little while."

"Sure thing," said the boy. "Leave your cups there. I'll keep it open for you." It paid to tip up front. Gruener must have lived that way too, passing out fifties by the handful, plucked from his metal case. David dropped another ten onto the table, then turned and followed Clinger out the door. Behind him, chair legs grated on the tile floor as the clerk pushed them inward, collecting his gratuity.

Two doors down they stepped into a bookshop, both men browsing by the window. Across the street, a young woman exited the condominium with a child of six or seven; light hair, though, on the mother, so not like the photograph at all.

David bought a map: DC and Suburbs. It was nearly three now, the air hot and thick. They went outside again, going up the block, around the corner, the building still in view, walking up a hundred yards, then back down the other side, into an ice cream shop for an hour, sitting by the window, then a little grocery near the coffee shop, their front table still vacant. At five-fifteen they slipped into a front booth at a pizza place diagonally across from the entrance to the condo, among the row of structures that blocked their view of Bethesda Avenue from the Hyatt.

"I don't know about you," said David, "but I'm getting hungry."

Clinger smiled. "Yeah, I could eat something." He went up to the counter to order. Two cars drove in now, through the valvular garage door, one behind the other, both with men at the wheel, as far as David could tell, but he couldn't tell for sure. This amateur surveillance was going to be trickier than he'd thought. Clinger must have known that. Sarah Gruener might be sitting all the while in her living room, maybe having been in all day; maybe having come in unnoticed through a back entrance. Shit, she might be out of town, for all they knew. This was futile. . . . Futile.

A glass door opened on the second floor of the condominium and a man stepped out onto the balcony, late fifties, early sixties, tan, trim, silver hair; looked like an athlete, tennis player maybe. Rugged though, almost like an old boxer. He was smoking a cigar, looking around in a funny way, a strange way, as if the street were new to him, as if he had lived there for a year but had never been outside until that moment. In a little while he went back through the open glass door and slid it closed.

"I got you a Coke. That OK?" Clinger passed the drink to him, a thirty-two-ounce styrofoam cup.

"Yeah, sure. Here's some money."

"No, I got it. You've been paying for the rooms and all. . . ."

"Brian, this is not negotiable." David passed him some bills. "Hold on to the rest, and tomorrow you can buy lunch. How's that?"

Clinger looked up in an odd way, not immediately recognizable, neither consenting nor argumentative, but expressive of something . . . sort of sheepish and awestruck, a peculiar conjunction in this monolith of a man. David examined him, his face, for a second or two before he realized that Clinger wasn't looking at him at all, but past him, slightly upward toward the door. There was a distinct sound of the door closing, clicking closed, as the small pneumatic arm pushed it to. A shadow passed leftward, from someone coming in. Clinger tilted his head slightly, then motioned to David with his eyes. He was about to turn around, when Clinger motioned again, this time to the right, Clinger's right. David turned his head that way, to his left. Twenty feet away, over at the counter, stood a woman, young, it seemed, though she faced away from him. She was neatly dressed in a white top and long blue skirt, and had beautiful thick black hair.

"Hi, Tommy," she said to a man behind the counter. "I'll take a tuna sub, no cheese."

"Yeah, yeah, I know. No cheese, lettuce, no tomato, vinegar and oil, right?" said Tommy.

"Right."

She reached into her purse, turning, as she did, in near profile. Her face was extraordinary, both delicate and exotic in some incomprehensible way. David couldn't pry his eyes away from her.

"That might be her," he said to Clinger, almost whispering. "That might be her!"

Tommy handed her a bag, and she passed a bill to him, then took her change.

"Thanks, Tommy. Thanks a lot. See you later."

"OK, Sarah," said Tommy, "have a nice day."

David watched her cross the street. As she entered the building, he saw a form move in the window on the second floor where the bronzed and silvered man had stood, but the glass remained closed. For an instant he thought about the man, how he had looked around, orienting himself it seemed. But the thought was lost, swamped, obliterated by the vision of that woman, that girl he had driven here to meet, yet couldn't approach, not today, so near her home. She stayed, exact and vivid, in his thoughts and eyes and memory through the interminable evening and restless night, and, when he arose on Thursday, light upon his window reflecting off the building where she slept, he found his mind obsessed with thoughts of seeing her again.

Isacco called at three.

"So, what are we doing? What's the plan?" asked Jake.

"You're off the hook."

"Yeah?"

"They got a couple of the guys coming in to take over. When they get there, you head home."

"What happened?"

"I told them what you said, you know, about being there before. In Washington."

"Bethesda."

"Yeah, Bethesda. They said it would be too much for you to have to . . . uh, do some more business with the same family."

"That it, then? They still want satisfaction?"

"I don't ask that. I don't know the other guys' orders."

"Since when?"

"They're from the business, these guys, management level."

"Who?"

"Caplan and Fontana."

"Holy shit! They'll blow the whole place up!" Jake laughed. "Hey, I'm gettin' outta here now."

"Soon as they get there, you're off."

"So, what do they want me to do in the meantime?"

"Just keep tabs on her, check the calls. You know, see if anything turns up. A couple of days, that's all. You ain't gonna be involved, that's for sure. Go take a walk, if you like. She don't know you."

Jake sat around for a while, then fixed himself a drink. When he finished it, feeling nice and loose, and a little flushed, he tore the wrapper off a good cigar and lit it. Good, he was a caretaker now, an observer. That was a relief. He didn't know why, exactly, having done worse things than execute somebody, male or female, good or bad, the organization wanted put to sleep. Never question orders. That was right up there on the list of cardinal rules. And he hadn't, not in thirty years and more. But there was something about this job, something about that family. . . . Ten years it had been, and still he thought about it. It had made him a better man, wise and cautious, but still, still . . . .

The room was saturate with smoke, so thick that the cigar had lost its taste. What it required was a palate freshener, like sherbet after rich and pungent food. Air, it required, summer air. Jake was off the hook, and he slid the glass door open and stepped out on the balcony, breathing deeply to clear his nose and lungs. This was new to him, a new place, seen for the first time as a participant in the scene, not just an onlooker through insulating glass. There was a pizzeria across the street, and the summer air was scented with its exhalations. Sweet it smelled, redolent of baking flour and cheese, though laced with soot and diesel from the streets. It cleared his nose and throat, and when he took another drag from his cigar, the rich gray smoke seemed quite as good to his reawakened pharynx as any fragrant odor he had ever tasted in a breath.

Phil was at home.

"Brian, where ya been?"

"Oh, I've got some stuff going on. I guess I'll be another day or two. That O.K.? The sheriff OK with it?"

"Yeah! Are you kiddin'? He loves you, man. He said you could take off as much time as you want. Hey, you know what? That ugly sombitch son-in-law of his left today, and the chief's missin' a whole box of them cigars he got from Canada or wherever. I was laughin'. . . . I said to myself, you got to tell Clinger. . . ."

"Yeah, yeah, I should have told Dixon to lock him up for a couple of days." Clinger laughed. "Listen, Phil, If I ask you to do something, can you do it without askin' any questions?"

"Sure. Yeah, sure."

"OK, I need some information on the . . . . Hey, did you check on that homicide I told you about at the old man's place?"

"Yeah. *Yeah!* They figure he done the, uh, the fire and stuff, uh, the shooting. Him and somebody else."

"OK, good. Where are they working from, the state people? Where's their headquarters?"

"Right at our office. The sheriff made room for 'em."

"Yeah? Great! Listen, I need some stuff, some information . . . uh, on the investigation. Can you get it for me?"

"Sure, sure. It's all in the back office. You know, by the records room. What do you need?"

"Everything, which is to say anything you can get."

"OK, sure, but . . . . I can't ask why, right?"

"Not now. I'll tell you some time."

Phil did what he was asked, went down to the office—just two of the night men were there now, in and out—got the key from the sheriff's smoke-stained sanctum, opened the door that the state boys had locked upon leaving, took out the sheaf of files, and faxed them to Clinger in Bethesda. At fifteen seconds a page, it took nearly half an hour, Clinger standing at the fax machine in a booth behind reception. Nobody minded, least of all the young guy out front at the desk with a freshly folded fifty in his pocket. Clinger rolled the paper into a loose tube as it issued forth. At eight he came up to the two adjoining rooms on the fourteenth floor.

"Doc, I got some stuff to go through. Phil faxed it."

They sat down at a table by the window and pored through it, maybe a hundred pages of scrolled fax paper, as inhospitable to perusal as an old parchment, so Clinger tore the linear roll into sections. There wasn't much there: diagrams, a few bad pictures, notes taken from interviews. Nothing on the dead man. They must not have identified him yet. The car they found him in was stolen, the plates on it taken from a different car. The only prints they found in it were his. Clinger had expected as much.

"These must be your phone records." Clinger passed them over.

"Yeah, looks like it."

"Go through it. See if anything stands out."

"Yeah. 313 is Florida. That must be Alan's number. Cindy called him on the eighth, I guess. That was what, Saturday? When I went out, to the old man's place. Jesus, I just can't believe it, that they're dead. Both of them. Jesus! She didn't deserve that. Alan didn't either. He was a decent guy, you know?"

"I'm sure he was, Doc. . . . Anything else on the phone bill?"

"No . . . not so far."

Clinger labored through the coiling paper, holding it flat as he read.

The state boys had interviewed all the neighbors. No one had seen a thing. That alone was incredible. It took two, maybe three trips by two guys to bring in enough gasoline and fuses. The place burned in an hour, like a napalm bomb. So maybe there were more than two men. Or just two who knew what they were doing. He got up and walked over to the window. The sun was very low now, flaring blatantly in his eyes as he looked across onto Bethesda Avenue, immersed in dusky shade made darker by contrast from the setting sun. Beside him, Doc was scanning his strip of paper, scrolling to the next sheet.

"Wait a minute! Brian, look at this! . . . Jesus! What's the area code here?" He reached for the wallet sitting on the table beside his keys, took out the photograph of the woman, and turned it face down, reading: "Sarah Gruener . . . here . . . forty-six-oh-six Bethesda Avenue... two-oh-one. . . . Jesus! It's her number! How the hell...?"

"Whose number?"

"The girl's: Sarah. . . . The granddaughter."

"What? On your phone?"

"Yeah, yeah, on my phone! Here, look at the number." He passed it over. It was placed on Saturday night, 11:44, P.M., and lasted four minutes.

"Well, *you* didn't call her, did you?"

"Me! Are you kidding? Me? No way! Not after what that letter said."

"What? About it being dangerous?"

"That and her line being monitored. . . ."

"So who else could've called her?"

"From my phone? Nobody. Nobody else was there besides me and . . . ."

"Yeah?"

"Cindy!" The Doc looked down at the table. His wallet was sitting on it and the keys he had used to move the Buick to the Hyatt garage after their little excursion, slanting it in next to the big red truck on parking level one. After a minute he put five spread fingers up into his hair and leaned forward, his brow now on the palm of his hand, one elbow on the table, mumbling something indistinct, *wallet*, something, *my wallet*, then: "Jesus . . . I can't believe it!" When he looked up half a minute later, his expression had an enlightened look about it, as though he had just discovered a vaccine for stupidity.

"Cindy called her, Brian. Jesus Christ, it was Cindy!"

CHAPTER 18

ETHESDA WAS THE HOME OF HER CHILDHOOD. IT WAS A QUIETER PLACE then, a residential town of diners and low-rise motels, with curb parking on Wisconsin. There was an old movie house they'd walk to, she and her parents, with a full-size screen and a real marquee that advertised the one feature film being shown. One day it read *Bananas*, in big black letters against a white ground. She could make it out by then, phonetically, *ba-na-nas,* sitting in the back seat at a traffic light. Her father was incredulous: "Did she read that?" "Sure," said Harriet, her mother, who had taught her the letters. On Saturday he skipped his golf game so the three of them could go to a matinee, and she laughed her cheeks wet when Woody Allen strolled into a little restaurant and ordered a thousand sandwiches to feed his army. She laughed so hard it made her hungry, so they got butter popcorn, sopping with yellow oil, and she ate it till her favorite white dress was smeared with its residue, and her dad's cheek too, from the kisses she gave him on the way home. They fixed her a bath and put her to bed, and she dreamed about Woody and his big glasses and funny way of talking, and when she got up in the morning, her favorite dress was sitting at the bedside, white and clean and ready for another day.

When she was in third grade, the Metro came in. There was construction everywhere, a barricade around the place the station would be, and two big holes in the ground that soon would be hotels. Their favorite diner closed. The one across the street from it had watery gravy and french fries that were nowhere near as crisp. But the trains ran straight to the Smithsonian, and her mom would take her there on Saturdays to look at the bones and planes and paintings. She discovered art that way, Whistler's Peacock Room in the Freer, the strange sculpture in the Hirshhorn garden, the walls of paintings in the National Gallery. Before long, her dad bought her watercolors and brushes and signed her up for courses to supplement the tedious hours of violin and ballet she never really acclimated to.

She took the Metro to her art course. Everyone took it everywhere. Not just *from* Bethesda, but *to* it. People from the District rumbled in and rode the never-ending escalator of Bethesda up and up and up until they found themselves at the corner of Wisconsin and Old Georgetown Road. They discovered Bethesda the way Bethesdans had just rediscovered the District. All on the Metro, all because of the Metro. Everything changed. The diners closed, then the big movie house with the marquee. High-rise hotels sprang up like mushrooms on a fallen tree. Parking inflated to eight dollars instead of a dime. New restaurants opened, not diners, but sushi bars and Afghan grills. There came to be four Oriental carpet shops in the city and three health clubs, too, but one had to drive a distance to the mall in White Flint or Rockville to find an article of hardware or get some school supplies. Bethesda's main street, Wisconsin, didn't look the same anymore.

Sarah watched it change, watched it grow as she grew from toddler to schoolgirl to young lady. By the time she entered junior high, her dad was a celebrity, Daniel Gruener of Gruener Chevrolet, successful even by modern Bethesdan standards. She had everything: well-off and doting parents, recognized talent, a brilliant mind, and sufficient beauty for a hundred pageants. There were parties and boat rides and a dozen white dresses, if she cared to wear them. It was a time of security, of complacency, in a pillared house a few blocks off Wisconsin. The three of them, with not a worry in the world, their three charmed lives open illimitably into the future.

It was something she could never return to. Six years passed before she came again to Bethesda. Then, in 1992, she traveled home. She came with a degree in art history, some repute as a sculptress, and a position at the Gallery she had visited with wonder as a child. But the theater where she'd laughed at Woody was gone, and that diner with the soggy french fries, and the pillared house a few blocks off Wisconsin. She found the Metro unchanged, underground, though there was a towering Hyatt atop it. And the post office, two blocks down: it was the same too. And the thick heat of August, and the biting wind of winter, and the flowering of trees in early April; those she remembered from her youth. They gave off a sense of permanence, of neonatal memory, of closeness to the things that she had loved. But there was something vital missing, something more essential than the buildings that had vanished, more important even than the scents and sounds of childhood that could never reappear. She would dream about it asleep and search her deepest thoughts for it awake, like a familiar name just beyond the reach of recollection, but what it was, or why it had eluded her for so many, many years, she never did discover till the day it came again into her life.

There were no more calls, nothing ominous anyway, only Edward checking in to see that she was feeling all right. And Francie phoned on Tuesday morning, having made it home OK, she and Mark. They were good people—the best—and had done what they thought proper in not telling her. Still, it would have been better for her to have seen him, that grandfather she had never known, better to have heard his voice just once in all those empty years of isolation. He had been there all along, alive all along, the old man who was her nearest kin. He had provided for her without wanting her to know it, looked after her from a distance without wanting to be seen. Just once to have been with him would have been enough. For all she knew, he'd been as much alone as she. Why, then? How could he not have wanted to see her, touch her, talk to her until the end?

If it really was the end. . . . He must have had his reasons. Mark said he did. If he were still alive, if she could communicate with him now for an hour or a day, they'd make up for all the time that had been wasted. One thought cheered her: No one knew for sure that he was dead. For now, that would have to suffice.

Coming home on Wednesday, she grabbed a sandwich at the place across the street for dinner, then read a while and went to bed early, making up for the sleeplessness of the weekend. Thursday was supposed to be nice, the rain having cleared and, with it, the last of the clouds. She woke early and showered, washing her hair and letting it dry. Thick hair, like her mother's. She never had to touch it. Just wash and wear, the way her mother's hair had been. From the back, you couldn't tell them apart. Her dad had said that, laughing, a month or two before he died.

. It was a pretty morning, sunny, warm. Not yet hot, but it would be. She walked out to Wisconsin, then turned left toward the Metro.

Some days she ran into Evelyn Clarkson and rode down with her. She was there today, at the foot of the escalator, buying a ticket. It was a relief to see her. There was a man a dozen steps behind her on the escalator who looked as if he was going to approach her, tall, well built, nice looking, one of those Washington types so taken with themselves. She had learned to spot them, the aggressive ones about to pounce. It embarrassed her, that type of contact, some strange man coming up to her in a public place as if he knew her. The guys at the Gallery were all OK. Once she'd established that she wasn't interested in dating, they'd pretty much left her alone.

It was the strangers who were the problem, young men and old, old enough to know better, saying offensive things in a nice way or nice things in an offensive way. Why her? She dressed like a professional, never wore a bit of makeup, left her hair to dry straight from the shower, however it felt like drying. Lots of girls she saw were pretty, blonde, big-breasted. That was supposed to be the type that men went after. Every day she saw them, flashy girls, blatantly available, judging from their dress and makeup. But then she was the one some strange man was always starting up with. Maybe it was the challenge. Yes, yes, maybe that was the problem.

She tapped Evelyn on the shoulder. "Hi, Ev."

"*There* you are. Let me just get my ticket and we're off."

The man behind her on the escalator got in a short line at one of the other ticket machines. She made out his shape and movements from the corner of her eye, a tall man, casually dressed, glancing at her occasionally, but not staring the way some of them did. There were a couple of people in front of him. That would mean a minute or so to get a fare card. Not that it mattered all that much now: she'd be perfectly safe with Ev.

They started toward the trains, the man well behind her, out of sight. She'd been lucky to run into Evelyn that way. Not that the guy would have hurt her or anything, but it was always so embarrassing.

"You ready for the show?" asked Ev.

"Getting there. The lettering is done. The stuff comes in next week."

"How many paintings? A hundred?"

"Hundred and thirty-something, thirty-five I think."

"All Boucher?"

"No, some Fragonards and portraits, Largillière, that sort of thing. All rococo. Mostly Boucher though. Ninety percent."

A man's voice broke in behind her: "Do you work at the Gallery?" She closed her eyes, shook her head with the most inconspicuous of motions. . . . *Here it comes*, she thought. . . . Why her, why always her? . . . She turned around and saw an elderly man, not at all what she'd expected, a dignified sort, probably in his seventies, well dressed, with a gray mustache, possessed of an inordinately deep and youthful voice. "Are you working on the Boucher show?"

"Yes. Yes, sir." That was a relief . . . not what she'd expected at all. The other man, the one from the escalator, was nowhere to be seen. "Are you planning to come?"

"I never miss a new exhibit. Are you a volunteer, Miss?"

"No, sir. Gainfully employed. I'm on the staff. . . . The show is supposed to be pretty good, but we haven't seen the paintings yet, just the slides. It's been in Paris at the Grand Palais."

Other eyes were on her now, a couple of people from the crowd, casual observers, innocuous, benign. But there was something else; she felt it. Looking up past the gray hair and mustache on one side, past Evelyn's lacquered orange on the other, she saw him, the tall man, spotted him two rows back in the crowd on the platform, his eyes on her, attentive enough to be conspicuous. She didn't want to meet his gaze, but did, for a second. It was awful, *awful*, that thing with strangers' eyes, like an electric shock, like having your mind penetrated. She hated it, always had. But it was the man who looked away, instantly, even before she'd had a chance to. Odd . . . but good; not at all what she'd expected. Usually they stared you down, leering. This one was less aggressive, a window shopper, shy or married. Guys like that were easier to deal with, less persistent in the face of rejection. Tell them *no* just once and they left you alone. She looked back at the gray-haired man, his temples crinkled in a smile.

"Well, good luck to you, miss. I'll look for you at the show."

She smiled at him and nodded. Past him, two rows back, the tall man's eyes gazed forward, not toward her, but forty-five degrees away.

"Here we go," said Evelyn. The platform lights were blinking. In a minute the train was in, then open. Two women got out. She and Ev were right in front of the entry door and boarded first, getting a seat. The tall man entered the same car, stepping down the aisle past her, behind her, where she couldn't see him. That made her feel uncomfortable. Better if you knew where they were, what they were up to. But she was a little curious about him too. He hadn't acted like a lot of the others, pushy guys impatient to make a score. He looked a little like a tourist really, with his casual clothes, a shirt and khakis, a pleasant-looking guy, handsome, and the way he'd stared at her, then turned his gaze away when she looked up, not like the arrogant, insistent ones. . . . Maybe she'd misjudged him.

"Nice man," said Evelyn.

"What? . . . Who?"

"That man who asked about the show."

"Oh, *him*."

"Yes. Who did you think?"

"Nobody. . . . Him, I mean. Yes, he seemed nice." Nice or not, he had vanished completely, having perhaps entered another car. That was funny; he was right behind them when they entered. . . .

"You know, Connie's dating that guy from . . . ." Sarah didn't have the heart to say she wasn't interested. Six months they'd been riding down together: six months in which she'd had a thousand facts and fables told to her without ever really hearing a single one. God, if she wasn't interested in her *own* love life, she certainly wasn't going to be interested in someone else's. So all the time she'd nod and smile, indicating . . . what? . . . maybe complicity, participation. And Ev would go on with her stories, never seeming to notice that they hadn't registered in the least. Sarah would think about work, or her art, or listen to the music of the train, using Ev as background noise to block out the other passengers. Today, as usual, she turned and nodded and smiled reflexly, still a little bit lethargic from her plenitude of sleep. ". . . I don't even think he has his degree, but that's not what he told. . . ." Ev paused for a second, smiled back, then just went on. It was eight thirty-five now. Edward would be meeting her for lunch, then Dr. Spivak would be around to finalize the text of the audio guide. The recording was Monday. She'd have to get the re-edited text to . . . .

". . . Did you know him?" asked Ev. Sarah smiled and nodded. . . . Should be finished early today, maybe get some sculpture done, that tubular array. . . . The train stopped at—what was it?— Friendship Heights. She turned her head just a little to the left, searching with the very end-point of her vision for the man behind her. She couldn't pick him out. He didn't exit there, at Friendship Heights, so he had to be in the car still, somewhere behind her, seated maybe. The train started.

"Spivak told Peter Angelonis you were his most promising assistant curator."

"Did he? Now why would he say that?"

"Why! Because you're so damned smart, that's why. And he probably wants to get in your pants too."

"Evelyn! He's married. His wife's a pretty woman. I've seen her. You think everybody . . . ."

"They do, all of them. Look, you get it all the time, those guys after you. Sometimes I think that's why you look for me to ride with you, to kind of screen you from them."

"Evelyn!"

"Cleveland Park," said the intercom, "doors opening on the right." She looked for the man, but he didn't leave. Now the car was filling, people standing in the space between the doors and in the aisles. If he was going to get off soon, he'd have to move up closer to an exit.

". . . . Do you know if he's been tested?"

"Tested?"

"Yes, for HIV. You hang around with him so much. Don't you think you should know?" Edward . . . . She was talking about Edward.

"Well, it's *his* business, but I'm pretty sure he *has* been tested and he's negative." Not that it was Evelyn's concern in the first place, but Edward wouldn't want her even thinking . . . .

"Woodley Park, National Zoo, doors opening on . . . ." Anyway . . . there was still no sign of the man. Not in the part of the car she could see.

More people got on. When the train left Woodley Park station, entering its lightless passage, she turned her head to the far window on the left. She thought she could make out his reflection, three seats back, facing forward.

They changed at Metro Center. She tried not to turn around, but found herself powerless to resist it. He was behind her, walking in the same direction, ten or fifteen feet away. Down the escalator too, and onto the Blue Line train, two stops to the Smithsonian, this time ahead of her in the car but not facing her, maybe looking at her in the glass of the darkened window, for he stood that way, near the door, peering into the darkness, fully visible in profile. A nice-looking guy though, clean-cut, handsome, black hair with just a hint of gray. Maybe a little older than she thought, mid-thirties, but trim, athletic. Evelyn saw her looking.

"Cute, eh?"

"What?" said Sarah.

"That guy." Evelyn indicated with her eyes, rolling them toward him, arching her brows.

"Don't make an issue of it. He's been behind us since Bethesda."

"Not another one! I swear, you ought to do this for a living!"

"*What?*"

"I didn't mean *that*! I meant like a recruiter, to bring men in, you know, like for the army. A man magnet."

Sarah laughed. It was kind of funny. The man didn't seem to notice though, staring out through the window, or into it. She thought she could see his eyes for a second in the glass, then they turned away; or she thought they did. She couldn't be sure.

"Smithsonian," said the intercom, "doors opening on the left." The man stood away from the door. She rose and exited, Evelyn at her side. When she turned, he was behind her. They walked down the Mall toward the Gallery. Ev was headed to the East Wing and said goodbye at the Gallery staff entrance.

"He's still back there," she said, looking over Sarah's shoulder.

Sarah hurried past the guards. Cyrus was at the door, fiftyish, dignified, built like a wrestler. He didn't need to check her badge. Cyrus was about as far as the guy was ever going to get. That was the last she would see of him, unless he waited for her all day outside the building. Unlikely.

He wasn't the type for that; she could tell. She was a little out of breath when she stepped into her office. Lisa was sitting on the top of the desk talking to Jonelle, George Rimet's secretary from down the hall.

"Mornin', Miz Gruener. You look like you *run* to work today."

Sarah smiled. Lisa talked like South Philly, but somehow her type-scripts came out Edwardian English. In the absence of Sisters, her speech would tend toward the Edwardian, too.

"Oh, some guy followed me from the Metro."

"Another one?" said Lisa. "Girl, you nothin' but a *man* trap. I never seen *nothin'* like it."

"That's right," Jonelle joined in, "Just send 'em on down to me if you can't use 'em, I'll show 'em what to do with them dinky little things *they* got." Lisa curled up on the desk in a spasm of unfeigned laughter, explosive but soundless, holding her belly in evident pain.

"Girl, you gonna make me have a *accident!*" she said between her teeth, her cheeks wet with tears.

"OK, come on, you two. If Spivak walks by and sees the two of you, you're both going to be sweeping floors. . . . Jonelle, shouldn't you be in your office before Dr. Rimet gets in?" Sarah laughed. "It's lucky for the both of you we've got Affirmative Action."

Lisa's laughter stopped abruptly. She wiped her face. "That guy . . . your guy today, what did he look like?"

"Why?"

"Just curious. I bet he was cute." Lisa chuckled a little.

"Well, he was, kind of. I mean, you'd probably say so. Tall, black hair, maybe thirty-five, athletic looking . . . ."

"Was he, like, six-two, curly hair, kind of dark, superfine, with khaki pants and a blue shirt?"

"Yeah . . . . Yeah! How did you know that?"

Lisa's voice deepened to a contralto, approaching the Edwardian in syntax and inflection: "Because, *Miz* Gruener, I'll bet that's him standing right behind you in the doorway."

Sarah swung around, turning right into the face of the man she had tried all morning to avoid. He wore an adolescent expression with an embarrassed little smile, closed-mouthed, open-eyed, knot-browed; all told, a sort of bashful, anticipatory face, totally out of keeping with his presence, uninvited, in the room, and his persistence in getting there. Behind her, abruptly and in unison, Jonelle and Lisa exploded in a cacophony of riotous and unfeigned laughter.

She had spotted him back in Bethesda, noticed him looking at her, probably thought he was some kind of creep following her like that. He would have said something at the station or on the train, if not for that friend of hers. *Pardon me, miss, your grandfather sent me to tell you he left you several million dollars, and, by the way, some men just tried to kill me.* He'd have to think about that a little.

They got out at the Smithsonian. He followed. At the near end of the National Gallery, the friend left. The girl, Sarah, went in through the side entrance, a staff entrance it looked like. He went in after her.

"May I see your badge, sir?" said the guard.

"Uh, no. . . . I mean, I don't have a badge. I'm here to see someone."

"Well, the Gallery don't open until ten, you see. Why don't you wait till then and go in the main entrance. You can arrange to see whoever it is you need to see at the desk."

"Uh, yeah. . . . Look, this is really important. I mean, it's worth a lot to me to get in early."

The guard's badge read *Cyrus*. Cyrus' face showed a trace of interest.

"It's worth quite a lot."

"Well, sir, I can't just let you in. Without some sort of ID or somethin'. You got anything like that?"

"I have a picture of the person I need to see."

"That would help," said Cyrus.

He took out his wallet, took the picture from it, and a fifty. Cyrus looked reluctantly undecided. He took out two more fifties, handed them to Cyrus with the photo. Cyrus turned the photo in his fingers, pocketed the fifties, and handed the photo back.

"She just come in. You might still catch her by the elevator."

He didn't though. No sign of her. There was another guard inside. "Miss Gruener?" he asked.

"Ground floor," said the guard, "down the hall to the right, four or five doors down. Name's on the door."

Sarah Gruener it said in black lettering on the glass, *Associate Curator, European Painting*. There were two other women in the office, secretaries he thought, laughing uncontrollably. One of them was facing him.

"Because, Miz Gruener," she said," I'll bet that's him standing right behind you in the doorway."

Sarah turned full face toward him, bright-green eyes and jet-black hair. God, she was beautiful.

"I'm sorry to barge in on you like this. . . . You're Sarah, aren't you? Sarah Gruener?"

Her mouth was still smiling. Her whole face was—Lisa and Jonelle had seen to that—and she wanted it gone, that residual smile. You can't just wipe them away though, smiles of joy and laughter like that. They have to wear down gradually, when the joy and the laughter are spent.

His wore off faster, that sheepish smile he had brought into the room. It was gone in a second. Now he looked serious. Nervous maybe, too. Yes, nervous it was, *he* was. *He should be*, she thought. A lot of gall to come in here, into her workplace! He *should* look nervous, *be* nervous. She was going to tell him! Some nerve, some damn nerve, following her all the way from Bethesda!

And the name too. How did he know her name? Ask about her? This was her office, not some cocktail bar. It took a lot of impudence to pester someone you didn't know, someone you'd followed around with not the least provocation. And then to use her name! But then she remembered the lettering on the door, so that was probably it: he must have just read it and walked in. "You're Sarah, aren't you? Sarah Gruener?" That took gall. That took arrogance. . . . But the funny thing was—she couldn't quite figure it—he didn't act the part, didn't seem remotely like the other men who pulled this kind of stunt. Not conceited at all, from first impression, nor pushy, but almost reticent, as if he actually *was* sorry to be barging in on her. A decent sort of guy he seemed, respectful, polite. Yet here he was, in her workplace no less. Sometimes these men really hard to understand.

"Yes, that's my name, same as on the door. May I help you with something?" She folded her arms. Her smile was nearly gone now. She didn't want him to think she was laughing at him. There was no need for that.

"Look, I've got to talk to you. It's not what you think, what you might think. . . ."

No? she thought. "OK, what is it, then? How did you know my name?"

He took a deep breath, his mouth slightly open, then swallowed, hard and visibly. "My name is David Arthurs." *Arthurs . . . David Arthurs. . . . That was the name . . . .* " I took care of your . . . ."

"David Arthurs? . . . *Doctor* David Arthurs?"

"Yeah. *Yeah* . . . how did you know that?"

"I got a phone call. . . . God! . . . OK, OK, come on in." She led him back to the inner office. Lisa had stopped laughing. Her normally wide-open eyes were open wider than usual, darting between Sarah and this man David. A photograph of her taken at that moment would have resembled a caricature, so exaggerated were her features with amazement. Sarah peered at her angularly through the glass, then closed the door. "Hah!," said Jonelle, in a voice loud enough to be audible through the wall. It wasn't funny. Lisa would hear about it later. Yes, both of them would.

"Sit down, if you like," said Sarah, when she turned toward him from the closed partition.

He took the chair facing her desk. She walked around and sat behind the desk, her arms crossed on the slick wood surface, empty but for a stack of exhibition catalogues. Through the glass she saw Jonelle leaving through the door this strange man had entered a minute earlier, then Lisa stepping back toward her own desk, out of sight now behind a tall metal cabinet. The man waited a minute, until Sarah was settled in her seat, before he spoke.

"She called you. . . . Cindy called you, right? When . . . . Saturday?"

"Is that her name? Cindy? Yes. That's when it was, Saturday night. Who is she?"

"It doesn't matter. . . . She caused some trouble for us, though."

"For *us*?"

"Yeah. Yeah, unfortunately, for both of us. There's a lot to explain. . . .

I, uh . . . I took care of your grandfather. Adam Gruener. He didn't go by that name. Charles Keller, he called himself."

"You know him? Are you sure?"

"Yes, I'm sure. Look, I'm sorry, he died on Saturday. . . . Maybe Friday night, but we found out on Saturday. He'd been sick a long time . . . months . . . almost a year from the beginning. I'm sorry. . . ."

"Oh . . . oh. . . . He *is* dead, then. . . . I didn't really know him, but I was hoping . . . I was hoping that he might still be alive. . . ." *All those years, and he maybe a few hundred miles away. . . .*

"I'm sorry," said the man, David Arthurs. His face looked sad, but handsome too, clean and chiseled. Such faces weren't customarily sad, nor were they anxious, customarily.

"And you were his doctor?"

"Yes. . . . Look, do you have any idea what's going on?"

"No. . . . No, I got some strange calls and things. . . . Somebody's been monitoring my phone."

"Yes, that's what the letter said."

"The letter?"

"Yes. Look, he's left you quite a bit of money; *us*, actually. He's left a lot of money to *us*."

"And that's why you've. . . ."

"No. That's not all of it. It's not that simple. . . . uh, there were some papers. . . . I don't think we should talk about it here. It's a little too public."

"The glass partitions, you mean?"

"Yeah, I guess. . . . Can we go someplace else more private?"

"OK. . . . Say, how did you get in—I mean past Cyrus?"

"I showed him this." He reached into a back pocket for his wallet and took out a photo. It was of her, grainy, taken from a distance. She was wearing a yellow coat, her yellow coat, her hair about the same as now, so taken within the year, maybe six months ago or a little less.

"Where did you get this?"

"It was in the packet from your grandfather." Her eyes started to moisten, but she beat back the tears with a dozen blinks.

"OK, come with me." She led him out. Lisa was now the picture of composure and professionalism. She was typing something into the word processor and didn't look up.

"How about a Coke . . . or coffee, if you'd like?" she asked him in the corridor. She wiped the corner of an eye with a little finger, inconspicuously.

"Sure." He laughed. "My mouth is kind of dry. You looked like you wanted to shoot me back there, when I walked in."

Sarah gave him just a little smile of reassurance. She led him along a corridor to the public part of the Gallery. There was a snack bar there, not open, but they were setting up, and a woman gave them a couple of Cokes. He passed her a ten, then put his hand up, palm outward, refusing any change.

"Big tippers where you come from," she said.

"Bakersville, PA." He said it like that: P . . . A.

"That's where he was, then, all that time, in Pennsylvania?"

"Ten years I guess. . . . Yeah." *Ten years. So he had been there all along, even when . . . when she'd gone to Cleveland and thought she was alone. Right there a couple hundred miles away, while she was spending the money from the trust fund he'd set up for her, thinking he was dead and the money was her father's.*

She took him to the ground floor conference room, unlocked the door, and led him in, not very proud of herself, the way she had misread him. He was a decent man, as far as she could tell. Maybe some of the other men had been like that too, just trying to be nice, to be friendly. God knows, she could have used a friend a few times. There'd been no one like that for her until Edward. She hadn't given anyone the chance though. Like this man, following her for something other than what she'd thought. Probably didn't even think she was attractive; not that it made that big a difference anyway.

"Nobody will bother us here."

She ate her lunch there sometimes, a lovely room, twenty feet by thirty, with medium oak paneling and a matching conference table, inlaid in the center of its six-yard span with a wreath and Liberty head. Not a public room at all, it was available to the staff for business meetings, a gorgeous place to hold them, really a work of art in and of itself. Roosevelt had been there once. There was a picture of him somewhere, leaning on the prow of the gorgeous table, maybe in his wheelchair, but you couldn't tell that. One could smoke here then—he could, anyway—

and he had that ubiquitous cigarette holder in his mouth, smiling, celebrating perhaps the flagrant humiliation of Andrew Mellon.

Mellon had donated the Gallery, along with his priceless art collection, to the people of the United States. A year or two before, he had left office as Secretary of the Treasury under Hoover. Now in private life, he was hounded by Roosevelt's Congress for the putative peculation of fifty thousand dollars during his years of tenure. Fifty thousand dollars — by a man who was in the process of giving away a hundred million to the nation now represented by his persecutors. It didn't matter. He went ahead just the same, arranging for his hundred-million-dollar gift. His legacy meant more to him than vengeance. Perhaps the legacy *was* his vengeance. There were no pictures of Mellon sitting in the lovely room, just Roosevelt, smiling, smoke curling upward from the tip of his pedunculated cigarette.

They sat beside each other at the edge of the massive table nearest the door. The man, David Arthurs, set his Coke can on a napkin atop the aged oak surface.

"Is it OK to drink in here?"

"Yes, of course. I eat lunch here all the time. Roosevelt used to smoke in here. Probably dumped his ashes on the carpet."

He smiled.

"What was he like, my grandfather?"

"I'm not sure. . . . I'm really not sure. Let me tell you the other stuff first."She nodded.

"There was a letter from him. . . . I don't have it with me. . . . Maybe—probably—it doesn't even exist any more. . . . Anyway, the story is, he left a lot of money, several million dollars, which he arranged to have us split. I don't know why he picked me to share in it, but he did, somehow. I didn't expect it and didn't really want to be involved in this at first, but things have changed since then. I may . . . uh . . . I may need some of the money now."

"Well, if he wanted you to have it, you should. He took pretty good care of me all these years without my knowing it, and I'm sure he had good and sufficient reason for leaving whatever he did to you too. I just wish I had known him. You know, spent time with him and talked with him the way you did. . . . I never met him though. Never. They told me he was dead . . . had died back in the sixties, around the time I was born, or before."

"He did, in a way."

"Did what?"

"Die. . . . He did something back then, something that caused a lot of trouble. He had to be dead as far as anyone was concerned."

"What kind of trouble?"

"Different kinds. Trouble for himself though. Big trouble for him. He had to go away, leave the country. He went to Iran. I think he worked for the government there, for the Shah. There were a lot of letters among his things. I wonder if they're still there. . . ."

"What did he do . . . that caused all the trouble?"

"Better for you not to know too much about that now. Maybe I'll tell you some of what I know another time, but now . . . now wouldn't be a good time for you to hear all that. . . .OK?"

"No. I'd like to know. I've been through a lot in my life. Believe me, I can handle it."

"Yeah, I know. . . . About your father being killed. That was in the letter, the computer disk he sent me. Look . . . uh, Sarah . . . . Look, I just can't tell you about what he did, your grandfather. I just can't tell you now. Maybe I will later, when it's safe, but I can't now. I'm not going to. You'll just have to accept that. OK?"

"It has to be OK, I suppose. . . . Well, tell me what you can, then."

"OK, he left a box of papers. I guess they implicate some other people in the thing I mentioned, the thing that caused all the trouble. And they know somehow that the papers are out in the open. That's the problem. When Cindy called you, they must have traced the call to my home and figured I'd been into the papers. I don't know how they arrived at that conclusion, but they did."

"How do you know? Have you talked to them?"

"Talked to them?" He puffed out a little laugh. "No, I didn't have a chance to talk. They . . . someone . . . came to my house on Monday before I had a chance to talk to anyone."

"To your house?"

"Yeah. Cindy was home, and someone else with her. They went there, whoever it was, went there and killed them and torched the place. . . ."

"Oh my God! You said they . . . they burned the house, your house?"

"Yes. . . . Hey, take it easy. It was *my* house, and my. . . ."

"Oh my God! They were shot? Were they shot?"

"Yes, that's what the police said. . . . I wasn't home, but. . . ."

"Oh, God! Oh my God! They were shot and then the house was burned!" It couldn't be, but it was, from what he said. Just the same, exactly the same, two people killed, shot, and then the house burned down on top of them. There was smoke for two blocks or three. You couldn't see the sky, the moon even, and all those people standing out on the street. No, that was ten years ago, but it seemed only a month, a week, so vivid was the memory. She started shaking, not merely trembling but shaking convulsively, her shoulders and her head. She couldn't control it.

"I'm sorry," she said, "it's just that . . . ." She couldn't continue, for her voice was breaking and her eyes were running over. She put her head in her hands and her elbows on the table for support, feeling now an arm upon her shoulder, a hand up by her neck.

"No," she said. "No, don't," moving her shoulder so that the arm slid off. "Look," said the voice, "I had to tell you. . . ."

"Yes." The words came slowly from her lips. ". . . it's all right, it's not that, only. . . ." Then the arm was back, on her left shoulder, so she pushed it off, not looking, but shaking now, with her face in her hands still, and her elbows on the magnificent table where Roosevelt had sat. The arm didn't return.

"Are you OK?" the voice asked.

"Yes. Yes, only . . ." He seemed nice, the man, decent, but he shouldn't touch her like that. She didn't want to be touched like that, even if he was nice. Even if he meant nothing by it. You couldn't trust . . . you couldn't trust anyone really. He probably didn't even find her attractive, not that it made the slightest difference.

"I'll be back in a little while." She stood and walked out of the conference room, down the corridor to a staff lavatory. It was half an hour before she regained enough of her composure to listen as the man continued his extraordinary narrative.

CHAPTER 19

SEYMOUR CAPLAN WAS A DILETTANTE OF SORTS, DIGNIFIED IF NOTHING else, his taste impeccable. He caused it to be known and bruited about that those durable goods worthy of his possession, whether they be cars or clothing, dinnerware or furniture, those consumables requisite to his delectation, whether food or drink or grooming aid, must be nothing but the finest of their kind. Not a suit among the vestments in his wardrobe could be reproduced by any clothier in Chicago for a nickel under twelve hundred dollars, even on a sale day in the slowest season. He drove a BMW 740i, the finest driving machine in the world. Not by his imprimatur alone—he had driven nothing less estimable to compare it with—but by the general consensus, that which the most respected automotive enthusiasts asserted, the finest vehicular guides proclaimed.

He dined at The Cart, the Cape Cod Room, Mindy's, the Top of the Hancock, washing down his Wellington with Bordelais, Foucault Frères, 1974, his veal Oscar with Pinot Noir, Jacques Picard, 1987. Once a wine steward spilled a bit of Stellenbosch Burgundy. Fluting the glass rim, it splashed upon his cuff, dappling the monogram, wetting, transiently, the pearl and lapis link. Seymour smiled and wiped at the droplet with his starched and perfect napkin, soiling it, so that he required another. Later he made a casual call and had the steward summarily dismissed.

On Thursday, July 11, it was, midway between Independence and

Bastille Day, thus a date entirely appropriate to armed intervention, he left his faultless home at nine a.m., the Bimmer's pearl-white paint frosted by mid-morning sunlight. Angelo Fontana was expecting him, short and dark, beneath a green canvas awning at the lakeshore entrance to his condominium. The sun was in Fontana's eyes, so that he shaded them with the visor of his hand. He looked rumpled, as if he had just awakened. There was a vinyl case in his opposite hand which looked, to Seymour, cheap and exorbitantly used. When Fontana closed the Bimmer's passenger-side door, having entered, its quality latch, a miracle of German engineering, made an estimable sound. Seymour was delighted with it.

"You still drivin' this piece of shit?" Angelo liked to get his goat.

"Perhaps walking would better suit you, Ange." Seymour spoke with a quasi-British accent. That is, it sounded British to Chicagoans. Really it was something halfway in-between the dialects of London palaces and Providence mansions, the speech pattern of a literate but hypothetical city in the mid-Atlantic, five hundred miles west of the Canaries.

"No, sir, no more walkin' for me," said Angelo, "not with all that dog shit I just stepped in." He made a wiping motion with his shoes, as if to clean their leather soles upon the Bimmer's immaculate gray carpet. Seymour took the joke good-naturedly, smiling, without comment. Both men knew that, had the carpet been willfully stained, one of them would never return to Chicago.

They planned on a day or two. Arrive there today, finish tonight, return tomorrow, the next day at the latest. There was little to it: locate the house, burn it if the papers weren't found. Clean up the mess the other men had left. They were back in the field for a change, back in action. It might prove entertaining, enjoyable in a way, a sort of vacation.

Nine was early for Angelo. Grinning still about the dog shit, he hit the switch and set his seat back at an obtuse angle, closing his eyes. Seymour counted on him sleeping for a while, and he seemed to, lying silent for twenty minutes or so, then awakening with a kind of fluid motion just as the vehicle veered onto the Interstate.

"You talk to Jake?" Angelo asked, having raised his seat again.

"No. Isacco did. Jake is getting old, I fear, unable to complete his assignments. I believe that management may be coming to the same conclusion."

"Who's management? . . . *We're* management."

"Yes, but *higher* management."

"Oh, *higher* management! Higher than us, huh?"

"Yes," said Seymour, "just a trifle higher than us."

"Yeah, but Jake, *Jake*. Hey, he's been their main man for years, *our* main man. All that stuff that management, us and . . . and . . . *higher* management . . . don't like to do."

"Yes, well, we're doing it now, aren't we?" Seymour looked at his Movado. Ten-forty. The Bimmer's time indicator on the sound system had jammed, blinking out 12:00 continuously in a luminescent green stammer. It had come from service that way, sent out for a skipping CD player. *JDM* said the bottom of the repair slip. That would be the technician who had done the work. He was going to find out just who JDM was and cut out a separate bit of flesh for every time those fucking figures blinked.

"What's the matter with the clock?" asked Angelo a moment later.

Seymour didn't answer. There was a pulse in his ears, drumming out a rhythm that was synchronous with the clock. When he noticed the concordance, the drumming intensified, then quickened, speeding past the static rate of emerald 12:00 ebb and flow over to the right, in the center of the dash. He bit down hard, over and over, pumping out the muscles of his jaw, crushing his molars together arrhythmically, or in some strange rhythm incompatible with both the drumming and the flash. Angelo must have heard it too, the drumming, for he stayed silent. Seymour hit a switch, cracking the driver's-side window a fraction of an inch. A stream of warm air whistled and whooshed above his left ear, drowning out the pulsation. He swept his left wrist with a pair of fingers, pushing back the gray silk fabric of his suit coat, bringing the Movado into view, not so much to see the time as to see the watch. Somehow it didn't please him. Better perhaps to go back to a Rolex. When he turned his head to the right, the seat was reclined further, and Angelo appeared to be asleep.

At one o'clock he turned north from the Interstate.

"Lunch," said Seymour.

Angelo had recently awakened and was cerebrating slowly. "I gotta take a piss," he said, zipping his seat back up to near the perpendicular.

The River Grill, it was called. It had valet parking, even at lunch time. Seymour had eaten there a couple of years back. He unlocked his door, then waited for an attendant to open it for him. Angelo was standing outside the car when Seymour exited.

"You know if there's a Bimmer dealer in the area?" he asked the kid who had swung open the door.

"No, man. I don't know of none."

"Who would?"

"The boss maybe. Over there." He indicated a uniformed man at the parking desk. Seymour walked over.

"Say, do you know if there's a BMW dealer in the area?"

"Sure," said the uniformed man, "right downtown, ten minutes from here. Toledo Imports. They come here all the time to pick up cars, you know, when they won't start. You got trouble?"

"No, no, just the clock."

"The clock?"

"Yes, that's right, the clock. Do you have a problem with that?"

"No, sir, no problem at all."

"You're sure!"

"Yes, sir, no problem at all. No, sir. Should I call to have the car picked up, sir?"

"Are you mocking me?"

"No, *sir*! I mean it. They'll pick up the car for you and have it back in a few hours. Lots of people get their service like that. I'll call 'em if you like."

"No, that won't be necessary." *Necess'ry*, he said. "Just draw me a map of how to get there, if you will." The man's name was Alvin. He had a name tag on his green jacket. Seymour smiled at him, a wide grin with all his teeth exposed, top and bottom, front and back. "Leave it in the car, if you would." He handed Alvin a ten. Least he could do.

"Yes, sir," said Alvin. "Thank you. Very kind of you, sir."

All the waiters wore gloves, and the tablecloths were starched. Angelo's face bore a pained expression.

"I'll order for you, Ange. What would you like?"

"Pizza," said Angelo.

Seymour's choice was Portobello mushrooms and steak *au poivre*, medium rare. "My friend will have a pizza. I assume the chef can accommodate him?"

"Yes, sir," said the white-gloved server, menus tucked between left white glove and chest, the other glove professionally absent, thrust militarily behind his back. "May I suggest the freshly baked focaccia bread dressed with goat cheese and lamb sausage, perhaps? That makes a splendid pizza."

"How about that, Ange?"

"Whatever," said Angelo. "Just bring some ketchup. If it tastes like shit, I can douse it with that."

"He's kidding," said Seymour. The waiter smiled obligingly and left.

"I gotta take a piss," said Angelo.

He liked to spray a little on the wall. He didn't know why. Maybe the dog in him, the animal, scenting its territory. There was no one else in the john, just him and the shiny green marble and the gurgling urinal with the plastic fresh-scent dispenser in its flanged receptacle of a bowl. So he did it, pissed a stream of liquid splat against the marbled wall, running down to the floor. Let some dickhead clean it up. Maybe that fairy waiter.

He zipped his pants and rinsed his hands, dropping the paper towel on the floor. The mirror was flattering, making him look younger. The bags were still there under his eyes, but his hair looked better, less thin on top, though you could still see the light reflecting off the vertex of his scalp. He wet his hands again and smoothed back the hair over his temples. That always made him look ten years younger, for some reason, but didn't last. The water would evaporate and the hair on the side of his head bush out again, dragging his face down, renewing middle age. He took another paper towel and dried his temples, dropping the paper on the floor and pushing through inner and outer doors into the grilled meat ambience of the dining area.

Seymour was drinking a glass of wine, dark red, looking like blood. A full wineglass was set before his place too. He sat down and tasted it, dry and sour, like old blood, old blood gone bad.

"Where's the fag waiter? I'm gonna get a beer."

Seymour snapped his fingers and the man appeared.

"The gentleman requires something?" asked the server crisply.

"Yeah, bring me a beer. You got Bud?"

"Certainly, Sir. Shall I remove your wine glass?"

Angelo blew a laugh out through his nose. "Yeah, feed it to the fish."

The waiter took the glass and left. Less than a minute later he was back with the bottle of beer and a pilsner glass crusted at its edge with ice.

"I'll pour it," said Angelo, brushing the waiter's gloved hand away.

The food came in a little while, and they ate. The pizza was pretty good, all but the goat cheese, which was a little too creamy and sour. Seymour ate his meal with relish, though when he finished, there wasn't a crumb or droplet of liquid on the tablecloth in front of him. Angelo never understood how he did that—or why.

"Can you fetch the maître d'?" Seymour asked the waiter, paying cash and tipping generously.

"Anything wrong?" the waiter asked.

"Not with the food or service, no."

"I have a complaint," he said when the man came over. "The head parking attendant was very rude to me. I assume you'll register the complaint to the management." Angelo saw him pass the man a hundred-dollar note. *Guy must have told him he didn't like the color of his car*, thought Angelo. *Didn't know who he was dealing with.*

"Yes, sir, I'll take care of it."

"You ready?" Seymour asked, standing and straightening his jacket.

"Yeah, in a second. I think I'm gonna take one more piss." Fuck this place, he thought. Piss on it.

He followed the little hand-sketched map, not a straight line on it, but he found the place anyway, ten minutes from the restaurant, then drove into the open service entrance.

"Can I get someone to have a look at this clock?" he asked the service manager.

"The clock?" he asked, smiling stupidly.

"Yes, that's what I said. Do you have a hearing problem?"

"No. No, sir. Sorry. Look, we're kind of busy today. Can I make an appointment for you? We can arrange to pick up the car . . . ."

"No. No, I'm not a local resident. I'll make it worth your while if you can get someone to fix the clock for me now." He had a hundred ready and handed it to the man.

"No, sir, that's not necessary. I can't . . . ."

"Take it. Just take it and see if you can get someone to . . . ."

The manager pocketed the hundred. "Let me have a look," he said, climbing into the car and fumbling with the audio controls between dash and console.

"It's the main processor in the unit. This . . . this isn't a factory system, you know. We'll . . . . It'll have to be sent out."

"Can you disconnect it?"

"Yeah, but you won't be able to use the radio. The way it is, everything works except the clock. Why don't you just . . . ."

"Disconnect it, please."

"I'll have to take the unit out. We really can't get to it now."

"Can you cut the wire?"

"Sure, but that will make the . . . ."

"Cut it, then."

"We can't just . . . ."

"Cut it."

"Look, you don't want to . . . ."

"CUT IT!"

"They fixed it," said Angelo, when he got back into the car.

"Not exactly, but they got it disconnected."

"Hey, you must have tipped 'em pretty good. Usually they don't do nothin' that fast." Angelo had a smile on his face. He looked like a cat with a canary in its belly. "Nice classy dealership, nice lounge. . . ."

"Was it? Anyone else in there?"

"No. Nobody but me. Nice bathroom too, marble, like the restaurant, only . . . ."

"Only what?" asked Seymour.

"Only some asshole had pissed all over the floor."

Seymour glanced over at him. The seat was back again, halfway down. Angelo had his eyes closed and his arms crossed over his chest. His lips were curled up in a smile, a real delighted grin, though what he found so funny in a restroom floor befouled by urine left much to the imagination.

"You do what I say! You do whatever I say!" Bill Gallagher was drunk again and always repeated himself when he was drunk.

"I can't get it. I told you that. I couldn't get it even if I wanted to," said Estelle. "Carol turned it in." She shouldn't have told him. "Where was you?" he had asked, waking from his chair drooling, hungry. "Some guy died," she'd said, "a patient." Then she'd gone on about the house, the signs of wealth, thinking it would distract him, get him off her back for a while, long enough to fix dinner and see to the kids. It was a mistake though, a big mistake. You couldn't tell Bill anything provocative like that—not when he'd been drinking, anyway—without giving him ideas he might never have had.

"Call her and check. You don't know for sure that she turned it in. Call her and check. You don't know that for sure." There were twelve empty bottles on the kitchen counter. Any more than six and he got mean.

"She doesn't have the key now. She told me."

"Fuck you," he said. There was foam at the corners of his mouth, beer and saliva in equal measure. All of his bodily fluids seemed fashioned of the two, in equal measure, foaming and bitter, sucked in and spat out, beer and saliva, foaming and bitter. "Fuck you!" he said to Estelle, his wife of fourteen years.

She knew better than to argue. "I'll see what I can do," she told him. God, she couldn't have called Carol anyway. They'd gone away somewhere, she and her husband and the kids, suddenly called in to Home Health, when? Tuesday it was. Day before yesterday. Said they had to go away somewhere. A death in the family or something. No point telling that to Bill. No point. Just get the heck out. The kids were already dressed.

She got them out to the car while he was in the bathroom, the door open, his stream of urine audible throughout the house, gurgling and splashing in the bowl, twelve beers' worth. She'd sleep over at her parents' place. He'd never bother her there, not with her dad and his twelve gauge shotgun looking out. In the morning he'd be penitent. "Honey, I'm sorry. I'll never touch another drop." At least he only said it once when he was sober.

He heard the car start and ran out without flushing the toilet, his fly unzipped, though he had managed to tuck away his penis. There wasn't any point in following the bitch. She never listened to him. Never listened. In five minutes she'd be over with old Roy and Mabel. They'd never liked him, never given him a chance. Thought he was beneath them, a farm boy. So what the fuck was the difference if he hadn't finished school? He made a decent living hauling coal. Better than her old man had made, better than old Roy.

What did he care? What the hell did he care? She never listened to him. Thought she was better than him, educated. *Educated.* Big fuckin' deal, educated. He could have been educated if he didn't have to make a living driving ten ton of coal down two-lane roads. Shit! She never listened to him. Winter and summer he had to drive that fuckin' truck. She never listened to him, just to Roy and Mabel. Whenever he asked her to do something, she never listened. There was something he'd just asked her to do, too. The key, it was, the Goddamn key. Carol had the key, that Goddamn bitch. That's what he wanted, that Goddamn key, that and another beer, for his mouth was dry now and his bladder empty.

It was cold and tasted good. He'd finish it and go. He was going somewhere . . . somewhere. Not to Roy and Mabel's, that was for sure! He laughed out loud: HA HA HA, in big round hissing H's and open A's. He wiped the corners of his mouth. Not to Roy and Mabel's place! That was for sure! No, it was . . . it was. . . . He took another swig of beer. That guy's house it was, the old guy that had died on Saturday, that fucking house with the doors you couldn't open and the glass you couldn't break. Last night he was there and couldn't get in, couldn't break the fucking door, couldn't break the fucking . . . the fucking windows. Shit! "Get the key," he told her. "Get the key!" "I can't," she said. "I can't."

OK, OK. That was OK. Now that he knew about the windows and the . . . the fucking DOOR, he'd go prepared, take his drill and a big-ass axe.

There was cash in there. There had to be, lots of it, lots of cash, as rich as they said the old guy had been. That old guy, he was rich and didn't have nothin' in the bank that nobody'd heard of. Nobody around to lay claim to it that anybody knowed of. So why shouldn't he take a shot? A couple thousand bucks maybe, and nobody the wiser. Hey, somebody else had tried it, some stiff they found, wanted to get into the house, that body they found dead out there the other day. Left bullet holes in the door and couldn't get in hisself. Why shouldn't he take a shot at it? Why shouldn't he?

He finished the beer and headed out to the garage. All the lights were blurry and moving a little. He banged his knee on the garage door jamb. It jarred him but didn't hurt much, not like banging your knee when you didn't have a couple gallon of beer in you. HA HA, he laughed out loud. A light went on at the house next door. *Nosy old bitch*, he thought, saying it under his breath: "no-zee-o-bish."

The axe was up against the far wall, and his drill was in the tool chest. He'd need an extension cord too. He threw them all into the truck and started off, backing down the driveway, spinning the wheel left when he hit the street, following the route he'd followed the night before. It was easy now; he knew the way. But the road was moving, swinging all over the place, the center line shifting too, back and forth. You couldn't hardly follow it. *Can't hardly foller it*, he thought to himself. Lucky there wasn't but a handful of cars out.

When he got to the overpass, then the tipple, he knew to turn right soon on the dirt road. That's where he'd missed it the day before. It was dusky, near-dark, when he pulled up to it, parking in the driveway up near the house. If somebody come along, he'd just tell 'em he was lookin' out for clues to help the cops. A citizen got to get involved. "Involved," he said out loud. HA HA!

The garage was open. No deadbolt locks on *that* door. He plugged in the extension cord and ran it over to the porch, like a skinny orange snake, then plugged in the drill. There was bullet holes in the door, four of 'em, clean through, right around the lock, and he started drilling between them. It took all of twenty minutes, and he had the area of the door around the lock looking like a piece of Swiss cheese, or like a postage stamp, with all them little holes around it. Then he got the axe and give it a couple good taps, and the door popped open. Bill turned around, scanning the horizon: not a sign of life, nothing but the crickets and the floodlights going on wherever there happened to be movement, which meant over on the porch now, right where he was, giving him plenty of light. There was nothing any more between him and the money, so he strode on in. Maybe he'd find a beer inside. He was commencing to get thirsty.

Angelo was all for going right there, but Seymour thought they'd better wait till dark. Seymour had his way. They hung out at the truck stop. Nobody notices strangers at a truck stop. People never make eye contact there. The truckers don't like it.

By nine-forty, the first signs of darkness were gathering, a burnishing of the sky that fringed the gray clouds copper to the west. Seymour got into the car and took the nine millimeter from its holster, snapping a bullet into the chamber.

"Right out of here, then left at the light; can you follow it?" He passed the letter-size map to Angelo.

"Yeah. I got it."

They passed along the road to Bakersville's valley, then through the quarter mile of Main Street urbanity.

"Straight through," said Angelo.

"What is it, about three miles from here?" asked Seymour. Angelo grunted in affirmation.

They came to a gravel road. "This it?" asked Seymour.

"Yeah. Yeah," said Angelo. The BMW was silent even on the gravel.

"Plastic in the trunk?" asked Angelo. The explosive, he meant. They had been told the house was difficult of penetration.

"Yes," said Seymour.

"So what exactly are we looking for? They tell you?"

"Papers. Some sort of papers."

"You know what's in 'em?"

Seymour laughed. "I haven't the foggiest idea. All the boss said to me was that he wanted some papers returned to his possession, that they were possibly in the place we've been sent to, that we were not to examine them, and that they were all from around the same time period, the same year."

"And when was that, exactly? What year was it?"

"1963."

"So what the fuck happened in 1963 that the organization might have been involved in?"

"I don't have a clue," said Seymour. "Who won the Series that year?"

"I don't know. Probably the Yankees."

"Well, perhaps something to do with the Yankees," said Seymour.

"You think so?" mused Ange incredulously.

"Yes, that would be my guess."

"Pretty impressive," said Angelo.

There was a truck in the driveway and some lights were on upstairs, so they parked the Bimmer just past the property in a gravelled turnoff. Seymour got out and closed the door softly. "Don't slam it," he told Angelo, who didn't, leaving the door wide open so that the interior lights stayed on. They headed toward the house, its amber windows now rendered prominent by the looming darkness.

The first room was open, the bedroom, but there wouldn't be no cash in there, nowheres but behind a locked door, so he started with the second room down. In a minute or two his drill chewed clean through the lock and the door popped open. There was a lot of boxes in there. Looked like pay dirt. "HA HA," laughed Bill, didn't need no fuckin' key anyway. The bitch could keep it, what's her name . . . Carol . . . and his bitch too, who never listened to him. He'd show her now, shove some cash in her face, buy her something with it, too 'cause she really was a decent mother and took pretty good care of him too. If she only listened to him a little bit better, instead of goin' back to Roy and Mabel all the time. Fuckin' Roy and Mabel . . . .

His head hurt, right up above one eye. He wished he had a drink. Maybe there was something downstairs. He'd go and look pretty soon. He pulled some boxes open. A bunch of shit, electronic stuff, shit like that. Books too, fuckin' books and records. Shit. Then he found it. Pay dirt! A box of coins. Looked like mostly silver and some gold. Shiny silver dollars and some old-type half dollars and quarters in books. That had to be worth something. A bunch of foreign coins too. Arab or something, silver and some little gold ones about the size of dimes. Had to be worth something. He put the box over by the door and kept on, but didn't find nothin' else. No money, cash, like that. Nothin', just the fuckin' coins, but that was something at least, and well worth the trouble.

He picked up the carton of coins and headed down the stairs, running his hip into the handrail below the yard-wide landing a third of the way down. It hurt this time, not numb like his knee when he had jammed it earlier. He needed a drink.

He put the box by the door, then walked around through the living room. There wasn't nothin' there. He'd checked it before. But there was a kind of cupboard in the dining room, a shelf that opened and had liquor in it. Beer would've been better, but there wasn't none in the place, so he opened a bottle of Cutty Sark and took a long pull on it. It burned like fire.

He sat down on a dining room chair and rubbed his head. It felt a little better. . . . The whiskey maybe. He took another pull.

OK, he thought, the upstairs was done, the room with them boxes and the one with the TV. That was just about it, other than the old man's bedroom and then the basement. The drill was still sittin' upstairs and he'd have to go up for it anyways, so's he figured he'd and check out the bedroom first. There was a noise, sort of like a car on the gravel. He looked out and saw a pair of headlights, but they drove on past and went out right away after they went by, so he knowed nothin' was out there to worry about. He went back up, watching out for the handrail this time.

The drill was sittin' on the floor outside the room he'd found the coins in. He yanked on the extension cord and dragged it back into the old man's bedroom. The light was still on from before, when he'd plugged in the drill to use down the hall. There was a closet down near the foot of the bed. He pulled on the door hard, but it was locked up tight. The drill was over on the bed. He picked it up and jammed it into the lock, triggering the drill. *Whirrrr!* it went. Sparks and little metal fragments flew out—your ordinary metal ain't nothin' to a diamond-studded bit; nothin' at all. The lock popped and the door pulled open.

"Holy shit!" said Bill. "Fuck me!" He reached in and put his hand on the M-50. There was an ear or something in a jar on the shelf above, but you sure couldn't get nothin' for it.

"You hear that?" asked Angelo."

"Yes. Yes. It's . . . ." Seymour turned his right ear toward the stairs.

"It's a drill or somethin'," said Angelo.

"Yes, certainly."

The sound stopped. Then some words came down to them, fractionally distinct: " . . . *shit!* . . . *Fuck me!*"

"What do you think?" asked Angelo.

Seymour smiled. "I think we'd best oblige." He took his gun out of its holster.

The man was seated on the bed when they got to the door.

"Who the fuck are you?" he said. He had an Uzi in his hands but didn't make a move to point it. Seymour leveled the nine millimeter at him.

"Drop it," he said. The man looked dazed.

"Hey! The gun! Drop it," he repeated, aiming the barrel between the man's eyes.

"OK, OK. Shit, man, OK." said the man. He put the Uzi on the bed. Angelo went over and snatched it up, pushing past the open closet door in the process. When he had the automatic in his hands, he glanced into the closet.

"Get a load of this!" he said to Seymour.

"Face down on the bed, hands behind your back," said Seymour to the man. He did as he was told. "Cover him."

Angelo nodded, then stepped over to the bed and sat on the prone man's buttocks, his pistol out now and pressed against the back of the man's head.

"Amply prepared, old Adam, I'd say. . . . It's best we came here after his demise. What do you think?"

Angelo turned, but kept the bore of the gun against the dazed man's skull. "You know who he was, this Gruener guy?"

"No," Seymour answered, "only that he had some papers. That constitutes the sum total of my knowledge."

Angelo turned to the man he was seated on. "What the fuck you doin' here?" Seymour stuck his gun into its holster and stepped out of the room.

"Nothin', nothin'. Really, man . . . . I got a wife and kids."

"What the hell were you looking for?"

"Nothin', man, nothin'."

"No? That box of coins yours, then? The one downstairs?"

"You take it, man. You take it. Aw shit, man, look, you take it."

Seymour came back into the room. He had a roll of tape around his index finger.

"Here," he said, "tape his hands." Angelo taped the man's hands behind him, then rolled him over onto his back.

"Where'd you get the tape," he asked.

"Bathroom," said Seymour. "Tape his legs too, then run a band tight across his neck and tape it to the bed somewhere." He faced the man. "Have you seen any papers, a box of papers dating from 1963?"

"No, sir. . . . No, sir, I sure ain't."

"Be certain now, my friend. You're in a good bit of trouble." Angelo had the man's ankles bound and was starting on his neck. The man lay passive, unresisting.

"I ain't, sir. I'm sure I ain't."

"Let's have a look then," said Seymour.

They went through the rooms upstairs first, in the closets, under the bed, through the boxes in the room across the hall. No papers. Downstairs next, flinging books onto the floor, lest the papers be secreted inside, through the kitchen cabinets, behind the refrigerator and stove. They slit up the carpet and tore apart the cushions of the couch, finding foam rubber, hitherto undisturbed. They went down into the basement, looked in the washer and dryer, in the tool boxes, under the steps.

"Maybe it's buried in the yard," said Angelo.

"If it is, we're certainly not going to find it tonight," said Seymour. "No, indeed." There was a pulse in his ear again. He clenched his jaw, flexing the muscles of his cheek and temple. "Let's go back upstairs and have another chat with our friend."

Seymour sat beside him. The man was supine now on the bed, lying diagonally as Angelo had taped him, his neck veins distended above the adhesive ligature around his throat. From there the tape ran up to one of the vertical posts of the headboard. The strip around his feet extended to the foot of the bed on the opposite side. He couldn't move much without making the band around his neck more taut. Angelo had taped his mouth as well, but Seymour peeled it off, with uncharacteristic deftness, when he came back in the room.

"What is your name?" Seymour asked him.

"Bill."

"Bill, my friend, it is imperative that my associate and I depart with the papers I have referred to in hand. Do you understand that?"

"I ain't seen 'em. I'm sure I ain't seen 'em."

"No? Well, Bill, that's most unfortunate for you. You see, if we are unable to find those papers, I'm afraid you are going to have a most unpleasant experience this evening. Do you understand that?"

"Sir, I ain't seen 'em. I ain't seen nothin' like papers like what you say."

"Most unfortunate. Let's see what we can find in the closet to entertain you."

"Come on," said Angelo, "let's just pop him and get outta here. He don't know nothin'."

"Let's just see." Seymour stepped over to the closet. "Let's just see. . . ." He picked up the knife on the lower shelf, sitting at eye level, then reached back up and brought out the jar.

"Did you notice this?" Angelo came over.

"The ear? Yeah."

"You saw what was in this jar?"

"Yeah, I said I did. It's an ear, for Christ's sake. You never seen an ear before?"

"Do you remember about ten years ago when Jimmy was killed . . .?"

"Jimmy, yeah. They mailed his ear. . . . Yeah! . . . Somebody mailed his ear to what's his name, the lawyer."

"Yes. Wasn't it in a jar, in alcohol or something?"

"Yeah, I think so. The boss went nuts."

"Yes, absolutely nuts. . . . Well, this is interesting, isn't it? I would propose that any papers of value Mr. Gruener might have had would have been right in that closet with the jar. . . . We'll have to let them know, tomorrow, first thing. . . . I'd love to have some fun with our young man here, but we really will have to be going. We've got a long drive ahead." Seymour turned to Bill. "You won't mind terribly, will you, Bill?"

"No, sir. No, sir!"

"Fine then. We'll have a little cookout first." He turned to Angelo. "Let's go get some lighter fluid."

"Lighter fluid?" said Angelo.

"Yes indeed," said Seymour, "I'll wager that between those two trucks and the car outside, we'll find a sufficient quantity of gasoline to get things started."

"Terrific!" said Angelo. "You want to pop him first?"

"No, my friend, no indeed. Why waste a bullet?"

CHAPTER 20

·

DAVID TOOK THE METRO BACK TO BETHESDA, LUMBERING UP AN INFINITE escalator a little after one. In this, the middle of the day, the trains were deserted; the stations too. But a food court at the summit of the escalator was brimful, from its ethnic food counters to the glass and neon windows, every seat at every table occupied. There was a good-size patio as well, outside the place, but that was just as full, diners inhabiting plastic chairs and tables, and even the deck of a granite fountain rim, for lack of more commodious facilities. He hadn't had a thing to eat all morning, nothing at all really—only that can of Coke at the museum with Sarah—and he felt it now, wrenching at his gut. The shortest line was at a sandwich stall with packaged food, staffed by a couple of kids in shirt-sleeves. He waited for a while amid the mayhem of the place, and got a tuna sandwich and two bags of chips to take up to his room.

Clinger came in sometime after three. The paired doors between the two adjoining rooms were both slightly open, and David was half awakened by the sounds of Clinger's presence. He must have been dozing, thus felt a little bit dazed when he awoke; uncertain at first about the time, and even the day; but it was early still. Less than two hours had passed since he'd come back to the room, eaten, slept. It was still Thursday, still the eleventh of July. He'd been dreaming—of Sarah, he thought. The old man was in it too, but he and Sarah were about as much of the dream as David could recall.

"You're back," said Clinger from their common doorway. "How'd it go?"

"OK. Good. . . . I've got lots to tell you." David sat up, putting his feet over the side of the bed, wiping his eyes.

"Me too, Doc. Hold on; let me just get rinsed off a minute and change my shirt. It's hotter than hell out there." He looked as hot as a steam bath anyway. His shirt, which was a brownish cotton print, short-sleeved, looking tight around the shoulders, though it was large enough by any other standard, was wet through, sopping below the sleeves and at the neck, clinging to his body like an extra coat of skin; as though it had united magically with its wearer through some titanic physical process or tortuous chemical reaction.

David felt uncomfortable just looking at him. He got up and washed his face, then went over to a chair and sofa at the far side of the room, near the windows. The sofa looked to be the more inviting of the two, so he dropped into it, putting his feet up on a low table in front of him. In five minutes or so Clinger emerged from his room through the adjoining doorway, walked around the second of the two queen beds each room contained, and sat in the chair facing David on the little sofa.

"So what happened, Doc? You go first. . . . Did you talk to her?"

"Yeah. Two hours worth. I don't even know where to start. . . . I, uh, caught up with her at the museum, in her office. Then we talked practically the whole morning. She's . . . um . . . she's a sweet kid with a . . . a kind of screwed-up life . . . which she's made the best of, I guess. She's a beautiful woman though, absolutely beautiful."

"Yeah, I could see that. So what did she say? Tell me what happened." Clinger leaned forward, elbows on knees, face open, anticipatory. His hair was still wet from the shower, combed tight against his scalp in orderly rows streaming back from the brow in perfect geometric linearity. He looked fresh and very clean, militarily groomed in a way, but for an armless tee shirt, ragged at the shoulders where the sleeves had been unevenly detached at their seams.

"She works at the National Gallery," David began, then filled in what Sarah had told him of her life, bouncing like a pinball from one fact or incident to another, one date or detail to the next, with no regard for order or chronology; just spitting out the things that she'd related to him: her job, her art, education, interests. Then her ancient tragedies and recent fears: the calls—Cindy's included, though that was demystified now; the old man's note, FedExed to her at work; his phone call—for now she knew that it was his. And last, the painful particulars relating to the death of her family, how much it was like . . . .

"Like what happened the other night," said Clinger. "That's no coincidence, the way the two cases were so similar, even ten years apart. . . . I mean, you've got two double murders, which is to say shootings, then arson. And you said they found a guy dead in a car then too . . . when her parents were killed?"

"Two, actually; a man who probably was involved, and then that boy she'd been dating."

"Yeah, well, they probably used him to get in the place. In Bakersville you wouldn't need a boy. Shit, people just about leave their keys in the door in case they happen to lock by accident."

"Well, Cindy was careful. I know that. And Alan, for sure. . . ."

"Yeah, you never know. . . . These guys are professionals, like I said. They got ways."

"I don't know, Brian. . . . Anyway, the kid has had a rough time of it. I felt a little guilty telling her about my problems, what the old guy dropped on me."

"You didn't tell her about . . . ."

"No, not that. I told her there was something, but not exactly what. It's bad enough that *we* know about what happened. I don't think Gruener would have wanted *her* to know about it too."

"OK. So what's next?"

"She's coming over here tonight, around seven. She had some things to do at work today that she couldn't get out of. But she's pretty spooked by all of this. . . . Not really frightened, I guess, just spooked. Uneasy, sort of. . . . Look, she's a good kid, a nice kid. We can't let anything happen to her. . . . I . . . I couldn't help Cindy. . . . Maybe I could have and didn't, I don't know. But I can't let anything happen to this one. She's my responsibility."

"Mine too," said Clinger. "You and her both. . . . Listen, I've got some stuff to tell you, too. I've been just as busy as you this morning. After you left, I walked over to the apartment, walked around for a while. There's a guy comes in at ten o'clock, then leaves around eleven. Drives an old beat-up car, Toyota or something. I got the license number. Nobody in a three-hundred-thousand-dollar condo's gonna drive a car like that, which is to say he's not a cleaning lady either. He stays maybe an hour and leaves, then the car comes back around noon. So I wait by the garage door, and when another car comes out, I walk in and find the guy's car. It's in space 2-D. . . . They've got a space for every condo, then some extra spaces if people have two cars, but this guy's in 2-D. I figure that must be where they're watchin' her from."

"You can't be sure though. . . ."

"Wait. It gets better. So I go out around and ring for the manager and say I'm interested in renting a place. He probably thinks I'm a gangster or something, the way I look, but he's friendly anyway: he tells me there's only two places that get rented, which is to say units that the owners aren't living in. One's 2-D and one's on eight, 8-F or something. I've got it written down. . . . . 2-D might be available in ten months, he tells me, which is to say that it was rented out two months ago, if it's a one-year lease. That's it, then. That's gotta be the place. Now I'm gonna call Phil and have him check out the license plate of that car and see if he can get us a name and phone number for apartment 2-D in that building."

"Can he do that?"

"Sure, just make some calls. . . . Everything's on computer."

"You're a pretty sharp guy, Brian. I ever tell you that?"

"Aw shucks, Doc." They both laughed. "Hey, if this girl Sarah's comin' over here, they—somebody—might follow her. You know, maybe it wasn't such a good idea. It's not like we can call her though, change the plans."

"No. It's OK. We thought of that. She's going to have a friend pick her up in his car and drive her to the next Metro stop; then she'll take the train back here. She can take the elevator right up to the Hyatt. They can't follow her like that, can they?"

"No. That's good, Doc, I'm impressed. You learn pretty fast. You guys are way ahead of me."

"Listen, Brian, you play the good old boy pretty well, but *nobody*'s way ahead of you."

Isacco called at three, precisely.

"Anything happening?" he asked Jake.

"With the girl? No. She don't even use the phone. She's gotta know something."

"It's a waste anyway. Nobody's gonna contact her now. I told them that. Those papers are gone. Burned."

"I hope so. I sure hope so," said Jake.

"What's all the fuss about anyway? You know what's in the papers?"

"Yeah. Yeah, I do. . . . Better you don't know."

"I guess. If they wanted me to know, they would have told me. Hey, Angelo and your friend are gonna check out the place tonight, Gruener's place. . . ."

"My friend . . . . My friend Caplan? You mean the asshole of the world?"

"Yeah, that's him, the *pompous* asshole of the world. Anyway, if they don't find the papers, they're gonna just level the house, you know, to be sure."

"OK, then what?"

"I think that's it. Then they come home. And you too."

"Good. They gonna leave the kid alone, the girl?"

"I guess. Why complicate things?"

"You know something, Carmen? I can't begin to think of a reason."

"So who's the guy?" asked Edward, turning onto Wisconsin. "The girls at the office said he was, like, majorly cute."

Sarah smiled. "He's not your type." It was six-thirty and the traffic had started to thin.

"You mean you're going to spend the evening with a *hetero*? How disgusting!"

"He's nice for a hetero." *He* is *nice, too*, she thought. A little paranoid maybe, with all these silly precautions, but he'd made her promise. And with all the things that had happened to her lately, and to him too—that fire at his house and all—you never could tell for sure what was reasonably safe and what wasn't.

Edward drove into the parking area under Mazza Gallery and dropped her off. She kissed him on the cheek, got out, took the Metro one stop to the Bethesda exit, then ascended on the elevator to the Hyatt.

She'd been there a score of times, occasionally with friends for a meal, but mostly when Francie and Mark had stayed there while her place was being decorated. She loved the pink marble, cut against the grain, Spanish pink marble like Trump Tower. The glass-backed elevator took her up to fourteen.

He opened the door within an instant of her knock, as if he had been waiting at the peephole. The room looked just the same as the ones her aunt and uncle had been in, two double beds, a little table, two chairs, and a love seat at the far end of the room, over by the windows. He led her over to a chair and she sat down, her back to the windows. There was a door open into the adjoining room and she saw some movement there, a moving shadow, though no one appeared at first

"Did you eat?" he asked.

"No, but I'm not really hungry. Not right now anyway."

"Well, I thought maybe we could call down for room service or something. We haven't eaten yet either, my friend and I." He turned toward the opening between the rooms. "Brian, come in and meet Sarah."

"OK, Doc, just a minute," came a slightly muted voice through the doorway.

"My aunt and uncle stay here."

"The ones from Cleveland?"

"Yes. It's nice. . . . I like the lobby, the marble."

"It's Rojo Alicante."

"What?"

"Rojo Alicante, the marble. That's what it's called, from Spain. It's in the lobby of Trump Tower too. I asked someone what it was once, when I was there . . . at Trump Tower."

"Yes. . . . Yes, I noticed it there myself." She hadn't expected that from him. Rojo Alicante . . . . How full of surprises this nice doctor was!

"Hi!" A big man came into the room, a mountain of a man, with a huge hand that he extended to her. When he held her fingers, he was as gentle as a child.

"Sarah Gruener, meet Brian Clinger. Brian, Sarah."

She smiled. Brian Clinger took the sofa, nearly filling it. The doctor, David, sat on a corner of the bed.

"I told you about Brian. He's the chief deputy sheriff of our county, Jackson County."

"Yes—Mr. Clinger. The doctor told me how you've been taking care of him the past few days."

"Please call me Brian, ma'am. Actually he takes pretty good care of himself."

"And I'm not in the office now, so I'm just David."

"O.K., I'll call you Brian." She turned left toward Clinger: ". . . and you, David . . ." She straightened toward him. ". . . if you . . . ," turning to the deputy again, ". . . don't call me 'maam' any more."

David smiled. Probably Mr. Clinger did too, but he was off to her left, at an obtuse angle, and she didn't turn around to see.

"How about if I order something?"

Clinger stood up. She saw his shadow move, then turned her head. "Doc, miss . . . uh, Sarah . . . I've got some stuff to do." He leaned over to David and said he had to call Phil, someone named Phil, whoever that was . . . not that it was any of her business. They'd tell her sooner or later, if it was important. "I'll pick up something myself," he said. "I know you two've got a lot to talk over."

David protested a little, but Mr. Clinger had his mind made up and went next door to his room. Then, in a minute or two, they heard the outside door squeak open and click closed.

"He's a wonderful guy," said David.

"Seems like it."

"What would you like?"

"Like?"

"To eat. Anything special? The restaurant's good here, but you probably have eaten here a lot more than I have. . . ."

She told him that yes, she had eaten there a lot, and that the pasta was very good, or at least well-reviewed, but that a burger was fine for her, and he said that sounded good to him too. So he called down and ordered cheeseburgers and Cokes, and hung up and came back to her, sitting where he'd just got up from on the side of the bed, with his knees within an inch of hers and his elbows on his thighs, leaning forward toward her, his eyes on hers. He didn't try to touch her again though, which was good. Not that he'd meant anything by it. He probably didn't even find her attractive, not that it mattered really. She'd have a bite to eat and then they could make their plans. Maybe she'd sit and talk a little too. . . . Rojo

Alicante! That was a surprise. He was an interesting man, not too taken with himself despite his looks. It might be entertaining to see what other tricks were

hidden in that handsome head of his. She wasn't in the mood to paint this evening anyway.

She was beautiful. Beautiful! The way the light fell on her cheek, the light from the window behind her and the lamp on the table beside the bed. He couldn't stop looking at her. Just a kid though, just a young kid.

"So tell me something about yourself. How old are you?"

"Twenty-six. How about you?"

"Forty."

"Really? Forty? You don't look it." She wore a fresh-looking pants suit, off-white, with a navy blouse open at the neck and a thin gold chain within the opening. She had a little lipstick on, light pink, almost indistinguishable, but not a spot of makeup other than that.

"No? I was thirty when I started my practice, and I've been there in Bakersville for ten years."

"How long . . . how long was, uh . . . Cindy... with you?"

"Just a couple of months . . . three months. We met about six months ago."

"I'm sorry. . . . About, you know, what happened."

"No, it's OK now. We'd had a fight. Things were pretty much over for a month or more. . . . It's just that . . . ."

"Just that what?" She sat forward a little.

"I felt responsible for . . . everything."

"Why?"

"I don't know. It's hard to explain. . . . Look, tell me some more about yourself."

"Me? I'm not very interesting. Just the art, that's all."

"Well, tell me about your art."

"OK. I do painting and sculpture. The paintings are mostly photo-realism. The sculptures are constructions, welded geometric shapes. Assemblages. Sometimes figurative though."

"Who does the welding? Not you?"

"Sure I do. Why not?"

"You know how to weld?"

"Sure. . . . My dad owned a Chevy dealership. A man in the shop taught me welding one summer. He did the most amazing lead work."

"That's wild! I work on cars all the time, and *I* don't even know how to weld."

"It's really not hard. . . . What kind of cars do you work on?"

"I'm halfway through a '58 Chevy convertible."

"Those are nice. That's the first Impala, right?"

"Yeah. Yeah, how did you know that?"

"I grew up with cars, Chevys. I used to have a whole shelf of those little promotional models. My dad saved them for me. I think he was a little disappointed that he didn't have a son. . . . Anyway, the '58 was always my favorite, even more than the '57, which is the classic."

"You're full of surprises."

"So are you."

"Me?" he asked.

"Yes. Rojo Alicante."

He laughed. Sarah showed him a little smile, almost a smirk, making her appear neither more beautiful nor less so, but, rather, insistently beautiful in a somewhat different way, mischievously beautiful, or whimsically beautiful. It wasn't flirtateous. *That* sort of look he could recognize, and *had* recognized a hundred times before with other women; that quizzical half-smile with eyes askance. There was no mistaking it, for it intensified with lack of recognition.

Sarah's face said something different: "I'm comfortable with you," or "You're an interesting person," without, however, the slightest hint of carnality; about what he'd expected: a girl like her would be going out with body builders, actors . . . diplomats, if she chose. What would she see in a forty-year-old doctor from a small town? Not that he felt insulted; he'd come to Bethesda to help her, nothing more. That she was beautiful was just a fortuitous circumstance.

"Tell me about your girlfriend," she said, the wry smile vanishing as she started to speak. "Cindy, right? . . . If you don't mind talking about it . . . . about her. She was really cruel to me on the phone. . . . You said you felt guilty about her. It wasn't your fault though. You couldn't have known."

"No, that's true. I didn't have any idea that . . . that something like that could happen. I mean, I didn't even know she'd called you. I didn't figure it out until we checked my phone records. . . . Yesterday, that was. Last night. They must have traced the call back to my house. . . ."

"So why would you feel guilty? I don't understand." She shook her head.

"Well, we'd been fighting; that is, *she'd* been fighting with me. Then, that night . . . Saturday . . . she must have found your picture in my wallet. I just leave it out usually. . . . Anyway, I should have tried to talk to her more, to see what was wrong, you know?"

"OK, I can understand that. I didn't kiss my mother goodbye before I left that last day. I felt bad about that for a year. . . . More than a year, I guess. . . . You must have loved her a lot." Sarah looked up at him, then downward, toward his knee, no longer interrogational, but almost shy, diffident.

"I don't know. That's what we were fighting about."

"What? What was it you were fighting about?" She looked up again, into his eyes. "If I'm being too nosy, tell me to shut up."

"No, it's OK, it's OK. . . . I . . . Apparently I didn't give her the kind of love she wanted. That's what she said. Not in those words, but something to that effect."

"Didn't you love her?" She tilted her head to the side, inspecting him; then, when he hesitated, weighing his response, she repeated: "Didn't you love her?"

"I don't know. . . . I really don't. . . . I didn't love her the way she wanted to be loved, I suppose. The guy that was with her when she died might have loved her that way."

"What guy? Who was with her? . . . Tell me if I'm asking too many questions."

"No. It's OK. . . . An old boyfriend. He followed her around like a puppydog; doted on her, you know? He was a good guy though. I feel bad about him. I really do feel bad about him."

"So what was he doing there that day, at your place?" She looked puzzled; perfectly attentive, but not quite capable of comprehending what he'd said, as though they were speaking similar but slightly different languages. He explained it as best he could, Cindy's coming and going, her weekend with Alan, her return.

"And you knew about it? About her going back to him after she'd been staying with you?"

"Yeah."

"And let her come back?"

"Yeah. . . . Sure. . . ." He shrugged. "I didn't own her. She was with him before, you know."

"I think she was right," said Sarah, putting on that little smile again, the wry one, not delightful, but cute and charming.

"About what?" he asked.

"That you didn't love her enough."

"Thank you, Oprah!" She'd made him laugh. What a sweet kid she was! Smart, funny, sincere. She kept that little smile on, more of a smirk really, mocking, but in a gentle way. Sharp as a razor this woman was: perceptive; a regular analyst!

"So, what about you?" he asked. "Tell me about this friend of yours . . . the one who drove you to the Metro."

"Edward?" The sun had settled to a point below the upper frame of the window, backlighting her face so that some auburn highlights showed through the jet-black hair. She smiled more broadly, no longer smirking, looking delighted; looking delightful: "You want to know about Edward? He wants to know about you, too."

"Jealous?"

"Yes, maybe. If he were here, he'd be jealous of me though, not you."

"Of you?"

"Yes, he heard you were cute and is dying to meet you."

David laughed. It wasn't so much funny as joyous. Yes, that was it: joyous. "OK, so if he's not the man in your life, who is?" *Let's get this over with*, he thought; *out in the open*. She hadn't volunteered a thing herself. Better if he just went ahead and asked.

She didn't answer right away. She was serious now, neither sad nor angry, but the happy smile was gone entirely from her face. Finally she spoke. "Edward's as close a friend as I've had, male or female, past or present. But to answer your question, there haven't been any men in my life the way you mean it, not since high school."

"High school!"

"Yep."

"High school?"

"Yes. High school. That's what I said." She seemed a little irritated, defensive. He hadn't meant to do that—upset her that way—but he couldn't stop now. He really had to know.

"So what happened in high school?"

"Death. Death happened in high school. The boy that I was seeing . . . the one I was with that night—I think I told you—that betrayed my parents, you know?" David nodded. "He led the men in, the ones who did everything. Then they killed him too. I guess he deserved it. He betrayed us, all of us. . . . He betrayed *me*."

So that was it. That was the story. No actors or diplomats. Nobody. "So . . . you mean you haven't dated since then? In the last ten years?"

"No. Yes, that's right."

"God!"

"Look, I'm sorry for the way I acted this morning at the Gallery. I don't usually get like that. I don't know why I did that, crying like that. That's not the way I am."

"I don't think it's so unreasonable to be frightened. I'm pretty apprehensive myself right now." *Jesus! What had she said? She hadn't been with a man in her adult life? This extraordinary woman?*

"No, it's really not that. I'm not afraid for my life. If anyone wanted to hurt me, it would have been easy enough to do before now. It's just that the . . . what happened to your . . . house . . . made me think about my family, my parents; that boy too, I guess. Seth was his name. . . . Usually I can keep it out of my mind, but . . . ." She paused, then just failed to resume, her eyes filling without the precipitation of tears, as she seemed to blink them away. *He couldn't believe it... from age sixteen on. Who would have believed it to look at her?*

There was a knock at the door, and David went to the peephole, seeing the waiter, a clean-cut young man who brought in the food and set it on the table. He passed the boy a ten-dollar tip, which he accepted effusively, leaving the room with an angulation of his head and neck that was midway between a nod and a bow.

They ate, he hungrily, she obligingly. She drank some wine though, from a bottle of something he had ordered with the burgers. "Whatever you recommend," he had told room service. It seemed to cheer her a little.

"So what are we going to do . . . about the money?" she asked when they were done.

"Whatever you say. It's yours much more than mine. I don't really need it, except . . . ."

"What?"

"I don't know if I can go home any time soon to get to the money I have, that I've saved, you know, stocks and investments. I don't even have a checkbook with me. Of course I have the money your grandfather left in that box. That'll help . . . some of it, anyway. I feel like it should be yours though."

"No, you've earned it, or deserve it at least, for what you've been through. But there's no point in us not collecting the inheritance, splitting it I mean. I definitely want you to have your half. There's no way to get it transferred here?"

"I don't know. Maybe we can call the man in the Caymans—Ansari is his name—and explain the problem."

"OK, let's do that."

"I'll call tomorrow," said David. Sarah nodded and looked up at him, the light reflecting from her cat's eyes, blue-green and crystalline, as familiar to him somehow as his own reflected image in a glass, with pupils every bit as black as her hair, now dilated a little wider than the incident lamp light would seem to require. They drew him in, those sea-green eyes and raven pupils, and in that one frozen moment he perceived that she was unquestionably the most exquisite creature he had seen in the forty undistinguished years of his life.

"I don't want you staying there by yourself." he said later, after Clinger had returned. They'd talked for a full hour, he about his family, his sister and parents, his practice, she about her art, about Edward, about the self-sufficiency of her life alone.

"Don't be silly. I've lived alone for years."

Clinger must have heard. He came from his room through the common doorway. "That's right," he said to Sarah. "The Doc is right. You oughtn't to stay alone now."

"So what should I do, check in here?" She had that little smile back, the wry one.

"Don't you have a friend who could move in with you?" asked David. "Maybe even Edward again."

"Probably," said Sarah, "but that wouldn't make me feel a whole lot more secure. I'm all right by myself—really."

Clinger sat down on the sofa, leaning forward a little, nearer to them; for emphasis, perhaps, or clarity, or a desire to be seen as sincere, which of course, he certainly was. "OK," he said, "how about if I just stay there . . . at your place with you. Doc here can't do it—that's for sure—but there's no reason why I can't. Nobody knows who I am—you know, to look at me. I can go back with you, if you've got the room, and stay a couple days, which is to say watch out for things until the two of you can make your arrangements to get a flight out or do whatever you decide to do."

"Yeah. Yeah, that would work," said David. "I'd feel a lot better about it."

She agreed finally, hesitantly, after twenty minutes of disputation. "If it'll make you happy," she told him. Clinger left with her after ten.

He didn't much like leaving the doc alone. It was probably safe, but you couldn't say for sure. No question this was the right thing to do though. The girl was the one they knew about, the one they were watching. Everybody would sleep better this way.

Then tomorrow morning he could get up early, come back to the Hyatt, and call Phil, who should have something for him by then: the name of the guy who owned that car; the tenant of the condo too, if it was someone else. Names, addresses; they'd be getting somewhere finally. Once you had that stuff, well, these guys couldn't do too much in public when you knew their identities. They liked anonymity, thrived on it. Professionals were like that, predictable, cooperative in a way. In a couple of days the girl and Doc would be the hell out of there. Then he'd clean things up a little for them, make sure nobody bothered them again.

"You didn't really have to do this," Sarah said when they were outside. The air felt sticky, especially coming from the lobby of the hotel, cool as it was. He felt the moisture accumulate on his brow and chest, then in his armpits, wondering if there was a separate place he could shower. He wouldn't feel comfortable using her bathroom, the one she used herself to bathe and stuff. That would be disrespectful.

"I think we'll all sleep better this way. The Doc is worried about you."

"Is he? Did he say that."

"Yep, sure did. He feels responsible for you. . . . I do too, I guess."

They walked down Old Georgetown Road toward her place. Clinger was sweating like a fountain now, his shirt sopping. He hoped she wouldn't notice.

"It's humid," said Sarah. "You're probably not used to our Washington nights."

"No, ma'am," he shot out automatically. She'd correct him in a second.

"Sarah," she said. "No more 'ma'am'. OK?"

"Yes, ma'am. . . . Sarah, I mean. Sarah."

"Which apartment is it?"

"Apartment?"

"The man you saw, the one monitoring my phone."

"Oh, that." Doc must have told her. "2-D. Just one floor up, to the right of the door." They were half a block from the condo now.

"What did he look like?"

"I didn't see him that well. Middle age, maybe a little bald, out of shape it looked like."

They got to Bethesda Avenue. "That's the one, there, up one floor, to the right of where the door is. There's a light on, see it?" He didn't motion. Nobody seemed to be looking though.

"I'd like to just go in and knock on the door. You know, just confront him."

"Not a good idea," he said. "They've left you alone so far. You and Doc just get away from here, and maybe if nothing comes out in a month or two, they'll just forget about it."

"No, I don't think so. They haven't forgotten about it in the last ten years. I don't think we're going to be done with this for a while. . . . Not for a while."

She unlocked the entry door and they went inside. The lobby was empty, the elevator too, and the hallway on the seventh floor. Not even any cooking odors. Her place was nice, big, with a separate guest area and bathroom across the living room from her suite. That made him feel a little more at ease.

"Want a beer?" she asked him after he had seen his accommodations.

"Great!" He was thirsty from the walk, hot as it was.

"Do you. . . . Do you have a gun? Do you carry a gun with you?"

"Yes, m. . . Yes, I sure do. I could take down an elephant with it if I had to, so you needn't worry about a thing."

"Well, I'm not worried really, but . . . does the doctor . . . uh, David . . . does he have a gun?"

"No . . . uh, yeah, he does. It's in my truck though. He found it at the old man's—I guess that's your grandfather—at his place. I'd say he's probably better off without it though. So's he doesn't shoot himself."

"I think he ought to have one," said Sarah.

"Yes, ma'am," said Clinger. Sarah stared up at him, sort of angrily, but not really that, because her eyes were brighter, glittering almost, the way a person's eyes look in a smile.

CHAPTER 21

SEYMOUR DROVE DIRECTLY TO PITTSBURGH, GETTING TO THE HOTEL LATE, trusting the Bimmer to a valet parking attendant with pimples and a bovine face, all eyes and nostrils. "Be careful," he said, smiling, not at the boy but at the way he looked, the pimples and the tawny hair. Chris was his name. "Guard it as you would your life, Chris. . . . Your *life*."

"Yes, sir," Chris said. His hand was shaking when he took the keys.

They checked into the Vista, using their proper names, paying with credit cards, taking adjacent rooms, he and Angelo. It was midnight when he switched on the television, knowing that the fire would not be on the news, but disappointed, a little anyway, when it wasn't.

He was tired, but exhilarated. It had been a splendid day! Action, adventure, a magnificent lunch. And that sluggard in the house—Bill it was—working-class to the bone, to the very air he breathed. Dirty and unkempt as a vagrant. What was it those highway placards admonished: "Help keep Pennsylvania beautiful"? Well, they had done their share in vaporizing Bill! Perhaps he'd cooked up into something prettier than his uncooked form gave promise of, like turbot, or sweetbreads *au beurre*. It was a pity they had missed the opportunity to see the final product after their little conflagration had brought about its salutary effect. Old Bill might have looked almost appetizing.

All in all it had been a diverting trip. Yet Seymour had had rather enough of it now: that last hurried meal, ill-prepared, shoddily served—at a truck stop no less. Old Bill might have tasted better. And then there was Angelo's company—now there was a true vulgarian, blue-collar to his toenails, which, by the way, were doubtlessly filthy and uneven like the rest of him. It made one sick just to sit beside him in the car, to watch those unkempt feet tread the spotless carpet of the Bimmer, even clad in shoes. Another day with Ange would test the utmost limits of a cultured man's endurance.

So he was ready—eager, in truth—for the eight-hour drive home the next day; well, not so much the drive itself as its completion; ridding himself and his estimable car of that slovenly peasant's presence; getting home to an immaculate bed with freshly pressed linen; sipping potable wine in proper glasses; supping on elegant food prepared and served with style and discrimination. Their work here was done. True, they hadn't uncovered the papers, whatever their content, wherever their location; those mysterious documents from 1963 pertaining to the Yankees or Cardinals or Celtics, or to the 1963 Kentucky Derby, for all he knew. They hadn't found anything like that in fact. But it scarcely mattered. If the papers hadn't been shredded or washed away or incinerated back in 1970 or 1980; if, indeed, they'd ever even existed, they were gone now, vanished, theoretical. Burned, likely, in one or the other residence the company had condemned. And all the people once involved had been eliminated too; all but that girl, and she was irrelevant now.

Their work was therefore done, and done brilliantly, *blazingly*—Seymour smiled a little at that. So he'd be back in Chicago tomorrow night, back to envy and accolades. Pittsburgh would be a transit point, a populated stopover with amenities sufficient to his needs—barely sufficient—until he spoke with Isacco in the morning and got the company's approval to head home. Back to his home, with its marble and crystal and mahogany. Tomorrow.

So Seymour slept from one o'clock on, contentedly, then woke on Friday to a preordered breakfast of croissants and coffee. At nine in the morning, carefully groomed and elegantly dressed, he called and left a message on Isacco's machine. Twenty minutes later the phone rang in his room.

"Seymour?"

"Yes?"

"This ain't a pay phone."

"Obviously."

"You know the rules."

"Yes, well, I'm not about to stand out on the street, you see. It's quite safe anyway."

"Safe, huh? That's crazy. Don't do it again, you hear me? We follow procedures, understand? Procedures."

"Thank you for your advice, Carmen. Thank you indeed. . . . Have you concluded your critique?" Isacco mumbled something incomprehensible, then kept silent on the line for twenty seconds, after which Seymour resumed: "Now, would you like some information?"

"Information. . . . You mean what the hell's going on. Yeah, go ahead."

"We found nothing of the . . . sort of documents we were told to look for."

"That's not good. They're not gonna be happy about that. . . . So what did you do? Did you get into the place?"

"Certainly. We had a nice . . . uh . . . what should I say? . . . Bonfire."

"Total? The place totaled?"

"I would say so. . . . Yes."

"OK, that's both locations. They've gotta be disposed of, then. I would guess they've gotta be. They had to be in one place or the other."

"Yes, perhaps. I believe so. . . . We found an ear in the house."

"What's that?" said Isacco. "Say again?"

"An ear, I said. An ear. Rather like Jimmy's ear, the one that Lesser received in the mail. I believe that it was preserved in a jar of alcohol, as was the one we found."

"Shit! Where was it?"

"In a locked closet with a plethora of weapons. Firearms and such. Uzis, a machine gun, grenades. . . ."

"In Gruener's house?"

"Yes, of course. Where did I say we were?" Seymour smiled. Isacco had lost his hearing, or possibly his comprehension of proper English. Auditorily challenged, or linguistically—what was the correct term now? Dumb and crude maybe. That was it, just plain dumb and crude.

"Which side?" asked Isacco.

"Side? Of what?" What the devil was he talking about now? Side of what?

"The ear. Right or left."

"I don't know." Seymour thought about the ear, submersed like a mollusc in its silted bath, visualizing the sediment, drifting dustlike with the currents in the jar, then that severed edge. . . . It was . . . a right ear . . . right, definitely .

"Right, I believe. . . . Yes. Right."

"Shit! Then that's it. That's it! They mailed the left one to Lesser; I'm sure of it. So that's gotta be the other one. Somebody said the both of them might have been cut off. Jesus, the boss went crazy back then. You know. You remember. Better he's dead now. I'll have to tell Little Joe. Jesus! You hold tight. I'll call you back."

"Would you prefer that I go out and look for a pay phone?"

"Fuck you, Caplan. Stay where you are."

Friday dawned sultry in Bethesda, with broken clouds upon a gray-blue sky, brilliance filtered by the low-slung pall of saturated air. Sarah woke at seven. At seven-twenty she found Clinger seated on a couch beside the steamy windows in her living room.

"Up early," she said.

"You too."

"Work."

He nodded. "I'll go with you." She didn't much feel like arguing or think that it would be of any use. Four hours she had slept, or five. The clock had said three-ten the last time she'd looked. There was a lot on her mind. Not the show so much: that was under control. But the strange man in her building, in 2-D, and then that story about the fire in . . . What was the name of it? Bakersville? . . . David's town. And all the details about her grandfather, all those things that David had told her. And David Arthurs himself. He was different from what she'd known of men, from what she had let herself know through these years of isolation, of loneliness really, though she hadn't accepted the fact that it was loneliness she felt. But now, the past days . . . but it was just one day, just one, though it seemed a week, a month, since yesterday morning when everything in her life had changed completely.

They left at eight-fifteen in her car. Clinger drove: wanted to get the feel of the city, he said. She asked him about his wife, his family. He seemed lonely, sad, the way she had often been and was still, from time to time. A kind man though, kind and smart and an exemplary father, judging from what he said and what he didn't say. She thought his kids would probably be gentle and respectful too, having learned those traits from him.

He dropped her at the entrance. "You can come up," she offered.

He declined. He'd meet her later, at whatever time she said. He had to make some calls, look around a little, see that no one else was following her—or maybe him now. OK, she told him, one-thirty, by the entrance.

"Wait," he said, when she was ten feet from the car. She came back. "Just in case I miss you for some reason, we need a place to meet."

"Well, right here," she said.

"No. No, someplace else. Someplace other than here. A rally point—you know what that is?" She shook her head.

"A place to regroup after a battle or something. That's the first thing they teach you in the military, and in law enforcement too. A place agreed upon to meet if something goes wrong. Understand?"

She nodded.

"You name it," he said.

"Well, I meet people at the Smithsonian Metro entrance. It's convenient either for the Metro or for cars to get to. A street runs right by it where a car can usually stop to pick somebody up; even park sometimes, if they're lucky."

"OK, show me on the map." She pointed and he made a little mark there with a pen. "Good," he said. "One-thirty here, right?"

"Here, or at the rally point if we're attacked, General." She was laughing, but Clinger just shook his head and drove off, slowly, looking back. They were so serious, those two, serious and paranoid, both of them. With David she could understand it, after all he'd been through. Clinger too, maybe, dealing with criminals every day. As for her, if someone wanted her hurt in any way—threatened; killed, even—it could have been done long ago. All right, she was upset about those strangers in her building, monitoring her calls, watching through the window. But she had protection now, protectors, David and this smart, enormous deputy, big enough to take on half the Russian army by himself.

He'd pick her up at half past one, here, by the door. She should be done by then; before then really. They wouldn't need her much today. The show was almost ready, Boucher and Fragonard and the dozen contemporaneous portraits; still crated, but in a week they'd all be hung, labeled, analyzed, and reproduced with perfect accuracy on pages of the lovely catalogue in which her name was prominently featured.

She headed to her office, nodding to someone's new secretary, then walking in on Lisa, typing. Lisa seemed subdued, deferential. Jonelle was nowhere to be seen. Or heard either, which was a first for her. Perhaps she'd been too hard on them, scowled too angrily, spoken too brusquely. They hadn't deserved that really, having meant no harm. She'd make it right. Later maybe, if she had a chance, or Monday.

It was noon when Dr. Spivak drifted in. "Sarah, you've done us proud," he said. She thanked him. "Lunch?" he asked. No, she had a little more to do and had to leave early for . . . an appointment. He looked disappointed—no; crestfallen—then lingered inappropriately, stepping around her desk, leaning over her shoulder to look at the catalogue a bit too long. Maybe Ev was right: maybe. . . . It hadn't occurred to her before, but now. . . .

"Well, the reception tomorrow," he said, having reached the door. "See you there."

Yes, the reception for the sponsors. Tomorrow in the East Wing. She could bring David. . . . No, no, he wouldn't come, not insanely paranoid the way he was . . . as the two of them were really, he and Clinger. . . . And if he did come, how would she introduce him? A friend? Her grandfather's doctor? She wasn't sure. She wouldn't know quite what to say.

At twenty after one she headed out. Clinger was waiting at the exit door, talking with Cyrus. "Anything I can do for you," said the guard to the deputy, "let me know." As she passed, Cyrus stopped her.

"I'm sorry about that man, Miz Gruener. . . . I hope I didn't do wrong in lettin' him through yesterday."

"No, Cyrus. It's all right."

"He had a picture . . . a picture of you. . . ."

"No, uh . . . yes. I know. It's OK. We're friends."

"OK, Miz Gruener. Thanks. Thank you. You ...you take care now."

Clinger walked beside her to the Mustang, unlocked the door, and helped her into the passenger seat, respectfully, diffidently, like an adolescent boy on a first date.

"We didn't have to use the rally point," she teased, then remembered how safe he made her feel, how protected. "Sorry," she said. He shook it off.

"I made some calls," he told her when they were in the car. "A friend of mine, guy named Phil, one of the other deputies. He checked up on the man I saw in that Toyota. I got a name and address. Name and phone number for the apartment too."

"That's good, I guess." So they had some information now. They could go to the police, except . . . except for the money, the estate. There wasn't any will now, not since the fire. That could be a problem. And those papers, whatever was in them. They would be a problem too. People had died because of them. Maybe there was some way just to turn everything in. Just call the man and offer him whatever he wanted, the money even, if need be. David would figure it out. If not, Clinger would. Maybe he had it half solved already.

"What now?" she asked him.

"I'm not sure yet. I gotta think. Gotta talk to the doc too. We'll come up with somethin'."

"Did you talk to him today?"

"Ma'am?"

"The doc... David."

"Yeah. Yeah. Everything's OK. He asked if you were all right."

"Right at the next corner."

"Yes, ma'am, I remember. Back to your place?" She didn't want to go home. Not to be alone. Not now.

"Uh, if David is at the hotel now, why don't we go right there?"

"Sure. We don't want to take your car there though." No. She knew that.

"No; I know. But you can drop me at the Friendship Heights Metro stop and I can take the train like yesterday. Then you can drive the car back to my place and meet us there. At the Hyatt."

"OK, that'll work . . . give me a chance to look around a little more too. Around the building. Give you guys a chance to talk some more. You got a lot to talk over."

"Yes, we do," she said. "A lot."

"How long we gotta wait?" asked Angelo. He looked cleaner, but not a whit less disheveled. Refreshed or fatigued, morning or night, Angelo always looked disheveled, unkempt as a vagrant.

"Until he rings us back."

"Come on. It's an hour already. Hey, we're done. Let's get outta here."

"All right, all right. Go and collect your things, and we can leave as soon as he calls."

The phone rang seconds after Angelo departed.

"I talked to the family," Isacco said. "They figure it's the other ear. Jimmy's. They figure Gruener saved it all this time. You got it?"

"What, the bottle? Certainly not. I'm not apt to be found driving around with a disembodied ear in my car. I'm sure it burned up with the house. 'Poof,' you know, with all that alcohol."

"OK. That's OK. Look, the family went nuts. Little Joe, you know. He and Jim were close. You know. They weren't gonna tell the old lady. It's lucky Mr. Joe is dead. Anyway, they want you to go to Washington as planned."

"Why so? The house is burned. You said yourself the papers they wanted are probably nonexistent."

"Yeah, they think so too. But that ear of Jimmy's flared everything up again. They want the girl dealt with."

"Dealt with? They want her questioned?"

"No, they want her gone. They want her dead."

Blazes! thought Seymour. Another day or two with Angelo would practically do him in. Disputing orders though . . . that was not permitted even from a man of his importance, a man a rung or two below the very summit of the corporate ladder. The girl would take them two more days; three perhaps. Two days or three of sleeping in substandard rooms, eating common food at diners, cohabiting with working-class scum. And Angelo beside him in the car to Washington and back! This little journey wasn't entertaining anymore.

He felt a pulse in his temple, heard it in his ear, growing faster, louder, until it made him bite down hard, over and over, pumping out the muscles of his jaw. It was all that bitch's fault, that Gruener bitch, emaciated blonde or redhead, or plump; whatever the blazes she was; sleeping in her low-class shack, fornicating with paupers, riding public transportation to her fast-food restaurants. She was laughing at them, at him and his employers; laughing at keeping him two or three more days from his crystal and mahogany at home. Funny, it was to her. A monumental joke. Pimply-faced bitch! He was going to get a knife and cut out a little piece of bitchy flesh for every bite of greasy food he had to chew, every second in the car with Angelo. Yes, a long and pointed knife with a serrated blade. Perhaps he'd bring an ear or two back with him for good measure.

She dialed his room from the lobby on a house phone. "Hi, it's me . . . uh, Clinger dropped me at the Metro. I'm coming up, OK.?"

"Great," he said. "I'll be at the door."

He was. Same as yesterday. The door popped open almost before she had a chance to knock.

"You're here early." He was smiling. He had a beautiful smile. The shirt he had on was the one he'd worn yesterday. Probably didn't have too much with him, maybe one change of clothes. He had put on jeans though, which made him look athletic, trim. He led her over to the chair she had sat on the day before, then sat himself on the bed facing her.

"I got done early. The show we're working on is just about ready." Daylight from the window behind her was in his eyes. Deep brown, they shone sepia in the glare.

"The show?" he asked.

"'Boucher and His Times.' I organized most of it. That's my job. That's what an associate curator does at the Gallery. Part of the time anyway." She looked at his cheek, wondering what it felt like in the early afternoon: a man's cheek several hours after a shave. Rough or smooth?

She'd touched her father's cheek so many times, but that was long ago, difficult to remember. Roughness she recalled, but that was mostly in the evening, when he'd come home from work. And smoothness in the morning. Yes; yes, it had been smooth then. She remembered now. . . . But midday: what did beards feel like then? In between morning and evening? Gently gritty, like a stiff towel? She would have liked to touch his face with the backs of her fingers, lightly, for curiosity, on the smooth skin where the beard was shaved down to an olive-stippled hue.

" . . . Isn't he the one?"

"The one? I didn't hear what you said."

"Boucher. Didn't he paint for Louis XV?"

"Yes. Yes, he did. That's pretty good, for a doctor. . . . You like art?"

He shrugged. "I took art history in undergrad. . . . I like most of it. Not the crazy modern stuff though. . . . Maybe I don't understand it."

"Yeah. A lot of it is pretty strange." She crossed her hands, resting them on her lap. He probably wouldn't like her art, the sculpture anyway. Maybe the paintings. . . . "I do some metal sculpture. It's not as off-beat as some of the new things, but I don't know if you'd like it."

"I bet I would if you explained it to me . . . you know, taught me about it." Teach him about it. . . . Yes, that would be fun, teaching him about her art, about art in general. . . . But they wouldn't be doing it any time soon. Not any time soon, the way things stood at the moment.

"I won't be showing you any of it soon." She sat forward, lowering her eyes.

"No. You can tell me about it though."

She looked at him. "Yes, I can do that." When though? He was in trouble, in fear for his life. He'd get his share of the money and leave soon. . . . Not that it made any difference. They weren't tied to each other in any way. God! They'd only met the day before. What was she thinking? In a day or two more he'd be gone . . . unless . . . unless maybe the three of them could find a way out of the trouble he was in, get the papers, whatever they were, back to the parties concerned. . . . At least they had a name now, some information on the people they were dealing with. . . .

"Did you talk to Mr. Clinger about what he found out?"

"Yeah. What did he tell you?"

"He got the man's name. The one who owns the car."

"Yeah . . . good. . . . That might help. At least we know how to get in touch with them."

"You don't know who they are? The people behind all this?"

"No. Just a lawyer's name. He's out of town till Monday. . . . I can't really call him though, not since we got into those papers. No, that option's out now. . . ." David shook his head, looking preoccupied, suddenly somber.

So that wouldn't work either. They couldn't even call the people, give them what they wanted. He'd be gone in a day or two. Not that it mattered all that much. . . . He probably didn't find her particularly attractive in the first place.

She seemed a lot more withdrawn today, almost sad in a way. Maybe something he'd said, since she'd come in cheerful. "Hi, it's me. . . . I'm coming up, O.K.?" Then she'd been warm and open for a minute, but after that turned quiet, pensive. Something that he'd said, no doubt, but he couldn't think of what: only a word or two about her art, the exhibition, not much more. But now she hardly even looked at him, staring down instead at the bed or out the window.

"Are you OK today?"

"Me? Sure, why?"

"I don't know, you seem a little sad."

"Do I? No, I'm fine, I'm fine."

"Are you hungry?" he asked.

"I didn't eat. . . . A little hungry, I guess."

He called down for sandwiches, then stepped over to the closet, took out the metal case, went back to where she was sitting, and set it on the bed.

"This is what I found in the house, what your grandfather told me in the note to use for expenses." He opened it.

"God!" she said. She put out a hand and ran her fingers over the packs of bills. "How much is in there?" she asked him.

"About four hundred thousand. . . . Look, I can't possibly keep it. It's yours more than anyone's. . . . I need a few thousand for immediate expenses; then I want you to take the rest. Just decide what you want to do with it . . . where you want to keep it, you know?"

"No, no," she said, "let's not argue about that now. He wanted you to have it. You hold on to it for now. . . . We'll . . . we'll talk it over once everything else is settled."

"So, what do you want to do about the money in the bank?"

She reached over and closed the case. "Let's do what my grandfather wanted us to do."

"What? Go and get it you mean? I don't know. . . . I had pretty much decided not to take any of it myself, but I might have to revise that a little. I guess I could be in sort of a bind here."

"Yes. Yes, I understand. . . . Look, he wanted you to have half—my grandfather did—and I think you should take it. . . . What about . . . . Did you call the guy? The banker?"

"No, not yet. You want me to?" "Yes," she said, nodding, looking at him now, finally, into his eyes.

He went to the phone and dialed, first the hotel operator. "How would I get a number in the Cayman Islands?"

"I'll check, Sir." She did, then took care of everything else. Probably knew about the prodigious tippers on the fourteenth floor. Within ten minutes Mr. Ansari of the Caribbean International Bank was on the line.

David explained who he was, who *they* were. "Yes," said Mr. Ansari, "I was expecting you to call. Adam is . . . . He has died, then."

"Yes."

"That is a personal tragedy for me, but a kind of relief as well. I know he was in great pain. You were his doctor, I believe?"

"Yes."

"And the woman—Sarah—she is with you now?"

"Yes."

"Well, congratulations are in order. You are both very wealthy young people."

"Sure," he said, then held the receiver up in her direction. She stepped around the bed and took it.

"Hello?"

"Are you Sarah?" the voice asked. It had a thick accent, Persian, as she understood.

"Yes."

"Your grandfather was a great man and a good, good friend of mine."

"Yes, that is what I . . . what the doctor has told me."

"I will be honored to help you in any way I can." "Ownourrred," he said, and "holp."

"He wanted me to see you before transferring the money," continued Ansari. "He sent me a photograph." Another one, she thought. Another picture . . . .

"So you need us to come there? Both of us?"

"That would be best, but I can transfer to your name and to the man's name the separate funds if you fax me signed documents."

"If it's better for us both to come, we can."

"It really isn't essential, unless you wish to do so." "Rrreeahllee," it came out.

"Well, how do you know it's me? That I'm who I say I am?"

"Your grandfather sent me a recording too. Your voice and the man's. A phone recording. I have listened to it many times. I recognize your voice. If I have the signatures, I can release the funds."

"What recording? I didn't . . . . I mean . . . what was I saying? I can't think of any recording he might have made, unless . . . ."

"Oh, he was talking on it too, Adam was. He asked you if you were happy, and you said 'Yes, I am.' You sounded very sure about it. Very charming, like Adam. You said some other things too. Enough things for me to recognize your voice. The man too. He was talking to Adam about the disease, about the tumor." "Too-mour," Mr. Ansari said.

"He took care of everything, my grandfather, didn't he?"

"Yes. He always did. As long as I have known him. Everything is all arranged."

"So that's all there is to it then?"

"Yes. Certainly. Now that I have heard your voices. I hadn't thought it would be so easy to distinguish them."

"All right then. Can we call you back in a day or two to let you know what we plan to do?"

"Certainly. . . . I am at your service."

She set the phone down in its cradle and went back to her chair. David came and sat in front of her, sitting on the bed, his knees almost touching hers in the two feet of space between.

"What did he say?" he asked. "He has a recording?"

"Yes, our voices. My grandfather sent a tape."

"From the phone, I bet."

"Yes," she answered.

"What else did he say? Does he need us to come to the Caymans?"

"Yes," she said. "He can't release the money unless we go there together."

Clinger came in at three, after they had eaten. It was good to see him. David dragged him over past Sarah to the sofa, then sat down again on the corner of the bed, facing some point between the two of them. He was feeling awkward, self-conscious now, with this woman, this girl. Doctors didn't do that. They were used to dealing with exceptional people objectively, dispassionately, the hideously malformed and the inordinately attractive, ministered to alike, with total and complete neutrality.

But Sarah was so beautiful, so sweet and beautiful that he couldn't force his eyes from her face or his ears from her voice, though he was sure that she looked at him as a protector and nothing more. And he *was* her protector, with all his heart and mind. He'd never let anything happen to her, no matter what. Not because of Cindy. Not the old man either, though a last and only request. Sarah was the reason he had come, not the money; never for the money. Maybe it was her picture that had beckoned him. But he hadn't felt quite this way when he first saw the pretty photograph under Gruener's mattress, or even a little later, looking at that other picture in the packet, the one he'd slipped into his wallet for Cindy to discover. He wasn't really sure *how* he had felt then or how he felt now. Everything had happened so suddenly.

So he was glad for Clinger's presence. His emotions were becoming too intense for him to stay alone with her for very much longer. If not for Brian, he might say something, do something, to make her ill at ease, frighten her, the way he had the other day—yesterday it was—at the Gallery. He mustn't touch her; she'd made that clear. But the radiance of her face and the sweetness. . . .

"Everything OK?" asked Clinger, interrupting the uncomfortable silence.

"Yeah. Sure." David looked at Sarah, at her face in quarter profile. Her eyes were on a lamp beside the bed, its light inconspicuous within the daylit room. Still, it played on her features, illuminating them subtly, gently, yet catching on the oceanic greenness of her eyes.

"You sure, Doc?"

"Huh? . . . What, Brian?"

"You sure you're all right? Nothing's wrong?"

"Oh . . . yeah . . . no, I mean. Everything's . . . . uh, everything's fine. . . . We, uh . . . we called the bank . . . the man there. Ansari."

"What'd he say?" asked Clinger.

"I guess we'll have to go there. We . . . I figured that though. . . . He said we're rich. "Congratulations, you're rich." Something like that. . . . Uh, how about you? You find out anything else?" Sarah leaned forward, toward him. He could smell her hair, a fresh smell, like scrubbed skin.

"Yeah. Yeah, I talked to Phil. Maybe . . . uh, Sarah told you." David nodded. "OK, then I went back to the building and watched for a couple hours. There's two of them. That's all I saw anyway. The one guy that drives in—that old, beat up Toyota. His name is Siskin. I got his address and phone number too. Then I saw another guy come out on the balcony to smoke a cigar. He's shorter, lean, sharp looking, dignified sort of. That's all I think's there. I watched all day since I got back."

That other man . . . . Like the man he'd seen out on the balcony, looking out of place, smoking that long cigar. "The other man . . . he's got to be the one who rented the apartment. You've got that name too, right?"

"No, that'd be a phony name on the apartment. I've got it written down. Sounds fake. . . . I got the phone number though. Of the apartment."

"So what do we do now?" asked David.

"That's for you guys to decide. Me, I think you should get the hell outta here. I'll stay around after and take care of the two guys. I can do that a lot better if I know I don't have the both of you to worry about."

"No. You're going home, Brian. When we leave, I mean. Just as soon as we leave." He turned to Sarah. "What do you think . . . that you and I should do, I mean?"

She looked at him, directly into his eyes, her gaze green and penetrating. "I think Mr. Clinger's right. We should go."

"Well?" said Clinger.

"When?" asked David. Sarah was still staring, ocean-eyed.

She shrugged. "Right away. Tomorrow."

"OK," said David. "Let me make some calls. I'll see if we can get a flight. It should be empty on a plane to the Caymans in July."

He looked at her, searching for some sign of her thoughts, of what played in her mind when she saw him, thought of him. She glanced away for an instant, toward the lamp again, her eyes catching its light, then back directly at him, locking frozen into his stare. Her eyelids opened wide, then narrowed, green fringed luxuriantly with black, the skin crinkling a little beside the long lashes, her lips pursing in a hidden smile.

"I'll get my things ready tonight," she said. "Let me just give Lisa a call at the Gallery before she leaves, and then you can go ahead and make our reservations. . . . I've got a feeling . . . I don't know . . . just some crazy instinct tells me that everything's going to be all right."

"She works at the National Gallery. You can get her there, or here in the building. I figured on the parking lot downstairs, under the building, but she don't usually drive."

"I think we should bring back an ear," said Seymour. "Yes. They might like that. I'll have to get a knife." Jake peered at him, staring him down, but Seymour kept his eyes a little askance.

Angelo was over on the couch. He looked sleepy. At six o'clock that evening he had staggered in asking where to park. "Lot a block up," Jake had told him, and he'd gone back out to tell Caplan. Then, ten minutes later, Seymour had come in himself, prancing like a penguin with his poker spine and thousand-dollar suit, wearing pearl cufflinks for a murder.

"I don't like that about the ear," said Angelo from the couch. "It complicates things. Let's just take care of it and go."

Jake agreed. He didn't see why they had to kill the kid in the first place. She hadn't done anything. It was Gruener they wanted to punish, and he was dead already, beyond torment or insult. "There's no point, you know," he told Caplan. "The girl's not . . . ."

"Jake," said Seymour, "I fear you're getting old, soft and old. Why don't you just head out and leave us to our work?"

"Yeah. Yeah. I'm outta here tomorrow. Leonard can show you where to go, where to find her."

"What's the best hotel around here?" asked Seymour.

The place your mother hooks in, thought Jake. He would have said it too, but he was a professional, a skilled professional, and there to do a job, without let or hindrance. "You oughta stay here, if you want to see what's going on."

"Here? In this place? Incomprehensible."

"Well, there's a bunch of hotels out on Wisconsin, then. Take your pick." No place would be superb enough anyway. Not for Seymour and his iridescent suit.

Jake looked over at Angelo on the couch. He was leaning back into the cheap fabric, hands behind his head. Angelo winked and smiled back knowingly.

"Want a smoke?" Jake asked, taking out a wrapped cigar, asking neither man in particular, though surely more Angelo than Seymour, had he been pressed to choose.

"No, thanks," said Angelo. Seymour brushed at a pant leg.

Jake nodded, took out a fresh cigar, and went out onto the balcony to clear his throat and lungs. He kindled the cigar's cut end with a pocket lighter, flaming it for an instant, then blowing the incipient smoke out of his mouth, recapturing it instantly in his nose. Across the busy street, choked with peak-hour traffic, three men stepped into a pizzeria, swinging its glass door in, then out again, closed. Scents arose from it, from the door, the roof, bursting forth uncontained: the fundamental sweetness of baking dough, the pungent smell of melting cheese. Coalescing, they so engorged the early evening air, already thick with Potomac vapors, that even the fresh cigar's insistent smoke was powerless to obliterate them.

They walked back after eight. The sky was blue-gray overhead, but streaks of orange sunlight, visible to the west a quarter-hour earlier, were gone. Sarah said little. Just that she was tired and would have to pack in preparation for tomorrow and their quick departure. The flight left Dulles at a little after five.

He was going back to Bakersville, Clinger had said, telling half the truth. He would go—that was the valid half—but not yet. First he had some work to do. There were three burned bodies now: Cindy and her friend Alan, and, when he'd checked in again with Phil, it turned out that Bill Gallagher was missing too; well, not missing, but not identifiable, since it was probably him that they found in the old man's house, or what was left of him, incinerated to a skeletal ash.

He'd told the doc, but not Sarah. Why alarm her any more? She wasn't sleeping much as it was. Besides, the two of them would be out of there in a day. If Doc wanted to tell her once they got where they were going, well, that was his business. They could buy a lot of protection or distance, or both, with all the money they'd have then. There wasn't much point in worrying her now.

The two of them were perfect together, as though they'd been together since childhood. Couldn't get enough of each other. It was amazing, after only a couple of days, but that's the way human attraction worked, disdainful of time and circumstance, even of beauty sometimes. Not with these two though. They were a handsome pair, remarkable when they were together. He and Linda had been like that back in high school, when he played on the football team and she was prom queen. Everybody'd envied him then.

There was a man out on the balcony when they turned the corner, but he disappeared right away behind the closed curtains. Sarah didn't see him, or didn't say anything if she did.

"Don't look up there," he told her.

"Did you see someone?"

"No," he said. "No. Just don't look."

Once upstairs, she went into her room to pack, humming some tune he didn't recognize. He turned the TV on and grabbed a beer. Everything was pretty well arranged now. Doc would head out to the airport in the morning, take a cab with the two boxes beside him—the cash and the papers—check them in a storage bin, pick up the tickets, and get back to the hotel by noon.

He'd be busy tomorrow too: first check in with Phil in the morning, then meet Doc back at the hotel. At two he'd get the truck out, pick up Sarah at her door, and follow Doc to the airport so they could leave the

Buick there. Their flight would be at five. He'd stay to see them off, just to be sure.

He was supposed to leave for Bakersville after that, but he'd made his mind up now. First he meant to give those folks in 2-D a little surprise, whoever they were, Feds or crooks or hired guns. He'd have a little fun with them, teach them a lesson, courtesy of the boys in Jackson County. No reason the doc had to know.

Sarah's door was closed. He took out his gun, the snubnose .38, and checked it. Six shells, safety on. He put it back in his calf holster. Tomorrow he'd wear the shoulder strap with a thin jacket. Better if it looked like rain for that. It wouldn't be conspicuous that way.

CHAPTER   22

O N SATURDAY MORNING JAKE SLEPT IN. AT TEN, EMERGING FROM THE
shower, a towel around his hips, the spreading lines of peppery
hair slicked back upon his scalp, he came upon Leonard, busy at
the tape machine.

"Forget it," said Jake. "Phone didn't ring all night." Leonard grunted,
acknowledging or affirming, popped the tape anyway, and went through
the futility of scanning it.

For Caplan and Fontana it was to be a day of observation. Jake had
run it by them Friday night, and to his amazement they seemed to listen.
One day of surveillance—two maybe—then you made your move. That's
the way it was done. Forty years in the business had taught him that. Oh,
there were situations where you couldn't wait, circumstances when you
had to move right in, like the day in Bakersville, but if you had the time
to prepare, even so much as a little time, the job was easier, more controlled, less eventful. Watch her for a day, he told them, then you set it up,
like a billiard shot.

His travel case was laid out on the bed. Some dirty socks sat in an
open dresser drawer, and he tossed them in, then stepped back into the
bathroom for his toiletries. His hair looked thinner wet. He combed it
back, first sponging the misted mirror with the towel he undraped from
his loins. He stood nude before his image, an altogether shapely man of

sixty-three, flat and tan, not inordinately haired, though subtly gray upon the chest commensurate with his threescore years. *Not bad*, he thought, inspecting. *Not bad at all.* Seymour and Angelo had twenty years on him; and both with flab enough to lubricate a battleship. Their minds were flabby too. Too much coaching from the sidelines, not enough getting in the game. They moved slowly, thought slowly. No doubt about it, they'd screw things up. Oh, they'd manage to get the girl taken out, all right, but then proceed to leave a trail a Cub Scout could follow. This one extra day was all he needed. By tomorrow he'd be four hundred miles away from here. Whatever they did after that would hardly concern him, even this act, this utterly senseless act. He'd be in Chicago by the time they got it done. They could blow up the Capitol then, for all he cared.

"You seen anything of them?" he asked Leonard, once dressed. "My colleagues?"

Leonard said no. He was listening to static on the blank tape. Jake went into the kitchen and opened the refrigerator with the back of a knuckle, then lifted out a carton of juice with opposing surfaces of thumb and forefinger. He filled a glass and drank it the same peculiar way.

"I think that's them," said Leonard. There was a definite knock; Leonard went to the door, put his eye to the peephole, and pulled the knob inward, admitting Seymour first and, in his wake, Angelo.

"You get your beauty rest, Seymour?" asked Jake.

Caplan strutted toward the kitchen, resplendent in a blue silk suit, double-breasted, a crisp white shirt showing French cuffs and lapis links at just the proper distance below his iridescent jacket sleeves.

"Who shined your suit?" asked Jake. Angelo laughed aloud. He was standing over by the sofa. Seymour, who had reached a point perhaps eight feet from the kitchen, stopped and turned toward Angelo, who suddenly became silent.

"You're late," Jake added.

"We had some shopping to do," said Seymour, facing him now. Seymour took a jackknife out of his pants pocket and opened it. The serrated blade looked like a museum piece against the black enameled hilt. He lifted it to eye level, rotating the prow-shaped point longitudinally a quarter-turn or so, a pasty smile upon his face, leer-like, which rounded out his cheeks to the shape of a three-quarter moon. For a knife to have delighted Seymour so, it must have been the very finest of its kind.

"I bet you told 'em you wanted an ear slicer and put it on your Visa card," Jake offered, by way of jest.

This time Leonard laughed, effusiveively. But Seymour paid no mind to him, peering instead at Jake, his eyes mere slits, his lunar face no longer grinning. "My friend, you're going to get yourself in a good bit of trouble with that mouth of yours," he said.

Jake belched aloud, a guttural bellowing of air, flatulent, as though he'd swallowed a balloon. "Sorry, Seymour. The juice does that to me."

Seymour fingered the knife shaft, keeping its blade pointed toward Jake, then took a single step forward. Jake, still standing in the kitchen, picked up the carton of juice, folded its spout closed with two opposing knuckles, turned his back to the open knife, stepped to the refrigerator, opened it with the edge of a finger, and set the juice inside. Then he turned again and walked over to Seymour, slowly, but at a steady pace; stepped right up to him, so that his shirt was touching the point of the jackknife and his face stood directly above its point, his nose a hand-width from Seymour's nose, his eyes level with Seymour's, unblinking. He put a finger on the blade.

"Better put that away before you get yourself cut with it." Behind Seymour, over by the couch, Angelo stood now, stock still. To Jake's right, Leonard too looked frozen, rigid as a statue, the blank tape in his hand, his mouth ajar a good half inch. Five seconds passed . . . ten . . . . Then Caplan smiled. His mouth smiled, that is, though his eyes burned, slitlike, first threatening, then hollow. He folded the knife and dropped it in his pocket.

"Sit down, Seymour," said Jake, placing a hand on his shoulder and leading him to the couch. "Sit down." Seymour sat.

"You probably missed her this morning. Remember what I told you? You've got to watch for a couple days, pick up her patterns. I ain't gonna do this for you. I'm leavin'. Noon, I'm out of here. You saw what she looks like last night, her and that big guy with her, whoever he is. You'll have to find that out too, you know."

Seymour nodded.

"She works at the art museum, the National Gallery. I showed you on the map. Leonard says she sometimes takes the subway, sometimes drives. Saturdays when she goes there, she usually drives. That's what Leonard says. She don't go every Saturday, but she goes some.

"You got to watch her a couple days, check out the car, her movements, where she eats, who she sees. We can't do it for you. You do that, you'll be ready for Monday, when you *know* she's got to go to the museum and come back. You tap her then, Monday, maybe Tuesday. Now, I recommend you check to see if her car is here, downstairs, see what it looks like; then head over to the Gallery and look around. Check out the area around the building and the closest subway stop to it; figure where she'd park if she drives; watch her leave the Gallery if she went there; see what route she takes.

"If you see the car downstairs, you watch the subway, see what time she gets back, if she even went. Tomorrow's Sunday. You can't plan anything then, 'cause there won't be a pattern. So if you don't arrange things today or tonight, you'll have to wait till Monday, even to check things out. You got it?"

"The car's there," said Leonard. "I saw it in the garage."

"OK, good. Then the subway," said Jake.

"You know if she even left?" asked Angelo. "Maybe she's still here. Maybe she didn't go out today."

"Maybe. I wasn't watching for her. It ain't my job now. I slept till after nine. You guys should've been here. It ain't my job any more."

Caplan got up. "All right, Angelo," he said. "Let's go. We'll have a look at the Gallery anyway. In preparation for Monday."

"You using your car?" asked Jake.

"Certainly. I don't drive Fords." Seymour pulled his cuffs down to the proper point of display and straightened his jacket. It shone metallic in the incident light.

"Hey, what you need is one of those vanity plates, you know? C-A-P-L-A-N. They've got 'em in Illinois. . . . I know a guy who used to make them."

"Do you?" asked Seymour. "I'll look into it. Does he still make them, this friend of yours?"

"No," said Jake. "Not any more. They put him in the laundry for a while, and then he got paroled."

At eleven, Clinger gathered his things. "I'm gonna go now." Sarah was in her room, still packing.

"OK." she said. "I'll be ready."

"I'll pick you up at two. Out front. . . . It's a red truck."

"OK." She heard the door close.

The case on the bed was too big. She could see that now: way too much for her to manage. She'd never get it out to Clinger's truck. There was a smaller fabric bag in the closet and she pulled it out, hurriedly filling it with fewer things, indispensable things, enough for a few days.

David had even less, just a little carry-on, with one change of clothes and hardly that. It didn't matter though: they'd have more than enough money to buy whatever they wanted in the Caymans, minks and jewelry if she felt the urge, though that had never been her style. There had to be decent shopping there. They'd go together, help pick out each other's clothes. She liked the thought of that. Another nice thing to look forward to.

So all she needed were essentials: some jeans, a couple of tops, a bathing suit. Her toiletries were in two little bags: toothpaste, deodorant, shampoo. She threw them in the case and just began to close it when the phone rang. It startled her. She picked up the cordless at her bedside.

"Hello."

"Sarah?" The voice was. . . .

"Yes?"

"It's Dr. Spivak." Dr. Spivak! She couldn't talk to him. Not now, not with the line monitored. *Not now*.

"Yes, Dr. Spivak. Listen. I can't talk right now."

"I understand, Sarah. I just heard you were going away for a while, and I wanted to make sure everything was all right."

"Going away? No. No, I'm not going away. . . ."

"Your secretary said you were. . . ."

"No, there must be some mistake."

"But your secretary . . . Lisa, isn't it? . . . uh, she said you wouldn't make the reception, that you had to leave town for a while. She said . . . ."

"I'm sorry, sir, I've got to go. I'll check with you later or tomorrow, I'll call you. I'll call you." She hung up.

Oh God! This was bad. Now they'd know. Whoever it was down in 2-D would know now. God, this was bad. They'd know and maybe follow her, find them at the airport. . . . If she could only call and talk to David. Or Clinger. They'd tell her what to do. But the phone, the phone

... and they'd watch her too, if she tried to go outside to call. OK ... OK ... she'd wait. Once Clinger got here, she'd be all right. He'd be outside in a couple of hours. All she had to do was wait a little. Clinger would know what to do. He always did. He'd know.

She closed her case and took it into the living room, set it near the door. At one-thirty she'd go down, wait in the lobby with her things. What could they do to her in the meantime, locked in her apartment? Clinger would be there by two. Before two; he was always early. He'd figure out a way to elude them. He knew that sort of thing. Then, once they were on the plane, they'd be safe, she and David. . . . He liked her. She knew he liked her. It wasn't just the money. Not with him. Not with her either. She didn't even think about it. To be with a man who cared about her, a man she cared for too, an end to loneliness, that was all that mattered. Once they were on the plane, they'd be safe.

"Shit!" said Jake.

Leonard rewound it. "You want me to play it again?" He still had the other tape, the blank one, in his hand.

"What? No. No. . . . It's not my problem. I'm out of here." It *was* his problem though. Thirty years the Main Man made it his. He sat on a chair in the kitchen, his head in his hands, elbows on the table. Caplan and Fontana were gone, down at the Gallery, waiting for a woman who had been in her condominium all day. She was leaving. Leaving! They'd have his head for this.

"Let me think."

Leonard looked on, his finger on the play button. "I can run it again for you."

"She's got to take the elevator," Jake said, primarily to himself. "She'll be out of here right away now. . . . She knows something's up; she knows, damn it. . . . I figured that."

Leonard's jaw dropped open for the second time in ninety minutes.

"You'll have to help me. . . . There's money in it for you. A lot of money." *That or a bullet*, thought Jake, depending on Leonard's choice in the matter and the directives from home.

"I don't know," said Leonard. "This is some pretty heavy stuff. I don't know."

"Better decide now. . . . You're into it already, pal. You're into it big." Jake stepped into the bedroom and came out holding the Glock, as long as a carving knife with its silencer attached.

"OK," said Leonard. "OK, I'm in."

"Good. Come on." He put the gun into his belt and threw a light gray jacket on to cover it. They went out to the elevators, leaving the door open.

"What do we do?" asked Leonard.

"We wait."

Five minutes passed, then ten. They stood by the elevator doors. One green light said "L" for lobby. The other said "3". Neither moved.

"It may take a while," said Jake. The hall was empty.

At twelve-fifteen, the left-hand light went up to six, stopped, and came down. Then nothing for another thirty minutes. Two people came out of a door down the hall. Jake pulled Leonard back into the apartment. "We'll wait until they leave," he said. A little after one, an elevator went up to eight, then stopped at seven. Jake pushed the down button. In a minute the doors opened. There was a woman in the back, sixty-five or so, with a small dog in her arms. "Going down?" she asked. "No," said Jake, "up, actually. Must have pushed the wrong button." At one-twenty-five the green light on the left blinked off, no longer registering "L." "1" flashed on, then "2." It kept going. When "7" came up in green, the light stopped changing. Jake pushed the button for down and opened his jacket.

"This is it. The whole fuckin' family! I shoulda left yesterday." Leonard looked strangely blank, his mouth open again. He was trembling noticeably. Jake could see his hands shake.

A tiny bell sounded, and the doors slid open.

She looked scared, pathetic, a blue cloth case beside her on the floor. Jake stepped in, leaning against the sensor on the door edge.

"Get the case," he said to Leonard. Jake took her arm and led her out. She didn't resist. The whole fuckin' family! He should have left yesterday.

David came back at eleven, in plenty of time. The cases were checked in separate boxes, ones with no time limit, near International Departures. A month, he figured, maybe a little more. They could travel somewhere:

Italy, France, the Orient. After that, things would have died down, and it would likely be safe for them to come home.

There was plenty of time. He went upstairs to get his bag. Both bills were paid, his and Clinger's, settled earlier that morning in cash. He had enough now for any contingencies. Five thousand or six. He didn't count it all.

He tipped the parking attendant in advance: one thing he'd learned, if nothing else. The Buick appeared in a minute, its engine already warm from the morning drive.

They'd meet two blocks up, just past the post office, where there were spaces at the curb to wait. He passed a gas station on the corner, then a mail truck driving in. The standing zone was empty, as expected. He pulled over, leaving the car idling, the air on. It was nearly two. Clinger would come up the intersecting street a block behind him, then turn right on Wisconsin. When he saw the red truck pass, he'd follow. Four miles farther on, they'd pull into the parking lot at White Flint Mall, then pass through, cautiously, just in case someone was following. Clinger had thought of that.

He looked at the clock on the Buick's radio: two-oh-four. His watch said the same. He felt a tingling in the base of his spine, then forward, in his groin. Was something wrong? No. . . . No, it was still early. Two or two-ten: it didn't make a bit of difference. They had until five. At two-twelve he saw the red truck turn onto Wisconsin. You couldn't miss it. He took a deep breath and let it out. *Whew*! He lowered his window.

He turned his head left, putting the car in drive, keeping his foot on the brake. When the truck passed, he'd start. . . . But it didn't pass. It pulled off behind him. He looked in the rear-view mirror. Clinger was in the cab, but he couldn't see Sarah's face alongside. Clinger got out and ran up to the car.

"We got trouble! We got trouble, Doc!"

"What, Brian? Where's Sarah? Where is she?"

"Come on back to the hotel. We gotta talk."

They drove back two blocks to the Hyatt. An attendant drove the Buick into the garage, but they left the truck out front, accessible. David gave the valet fifty dollars.

Clinger wouldn't talk until they got upstairs. They gave the man at reception another fifty to get the key back, the one to David's room. When they stepped inside, Clinger led him to a chair and sat him down.

"They've got her. She wasn't there. I know they've got her. I called her place. . . ."

"Oh God, no! Oh my God, no!"

"OK, OK, we gotta think. She's . . . she's probably OK now. They wouldn't do anything there in the building right away. We gotta think though."

"We've got the number," David said. "I'm gonna call there. Look, maybe I can trade them the papers for her. . . . It's worth a try."

"Maybe . . . maybe. But it just might wind up getting both of you killed. Look, let me think a minute. Let me think."

"OK, we have the guy's name, the guy with the car. If he knows we have his name, he won't . . . he won't do anything that'll put him in jail."

"Yeah, but he might not be the principal. . . . *You* know . . . the one with the gun. That other guy looked like the professional. . . . Look, maybe . . . . We know where he lives. Maybe we can use that in some way." Clinger pinched the base of his nose.

"Can't we just call the police now? They've got to be able to help us. Look, I don't care about the money. I don't give a shit about it. They can kill me too. I don't care that much. But I'm not going to have that girl hurt because of me. I won't survive that, I promise you. If they do anything to her, I'll go in there myself. They'll have to kill me too. They'll just have to kill me too."

"Oh, they will. They will. . . . If we give them half a chance, they will."

"So what about calling the police?"

"No, the cops are out. These guys have killed too many people to let her live if we get the cops involved. The law won't care the same way we do. It's just a job to them. I know. I know all about it. I've been there."

"So what do we do?"

"Let's go over to the guy's house," said Clinger. "That's all I can think of. . . . See what we find."

Jake taped her to a chair, put her in the bedroom. He couldn't look at her. Whatever they did, they'd have to do it without him. Caplan would get back by five or six. Then she was all his. He'd get the hell out pronto. Pronto. Just give him some time and distance and he'd be fine with it, whatever, back to his old self.

But his mind took over then, the excellence, the subtlety of it. How did she know to leave? Now, today? How could she possibly have known that? Unless. . . . Someone outside would have to be . . . someone who understood more than she could possibly understand, knew more than she could ever know. Knew about the papers maybe; about their precious contents too. Yes, a person outside who understood it all. Something, someone, he'd have to find, uncover. That was his duty. His *duty*. There'd be hell to pay if those papers got loose. He'd be caught in it too. No doubt about that.

He drank another glass of juice and rinsed his face with water from the kitchen sink. There was no way out of it. Leonard couldn't do it. Caplan either; he didn't know shit about the contents of those papers. Asked if it was about the Yankees, for God's sake! The fuckin' *Yankees*!

OK, OK. He'd do what he could. He walked into the bedroom, leaving Leonard on the couch behind him. The girl was breathing softly through her nose, making a little whistling sound. Her body followed the contours of the chair, arms taped to chair arms, legs to legs. She couldn't move much, just her head and shoulders, but they were still too. Even her eyes were passive, fixed on the floor. She didn't look up when he entered. That was the way they always were, submissive. Sometimes it made things tough.

"Look, missy, I don't want to hurt you. . . . I'm . . . I'm not gonna hurt you. Not me. . . . I promise you that." She looked up at him now for a second, then averted her eyes again. He stepped over and peeled the tape from around her mouth, then pulled at the napkin he had stuffed inside. It was wet through.

"Spit it out," he directed. He took it in his palm and put it on a table, wiping his hand on the gray jacket, which he had left on. He took it off.

"Look, missy, uh, Sarah, right?"

She nodded very slightly, breathing through her mouth now, more deeply, in and out, huffing a little on the exhalation.

"I'm not gonna hurt you. I'm not. . . . Really I'm not." He put a finger under her chin, lifting her face toward him, then sat down on the bed beside her so as to lower himself into her line of sight. She looked at him, into his eyes. She was a beautiful kid, flawless. It was a shame to kill her. No reason for it. He'd have to be away from there, as far as the Taurus could carry him away, from the time that Caplan got back.

"You know who I am? Who we are?"

She shook her head.

"It's about your grandfather. He left some papers."

She looked blank.

"You know anything about them? Some papers, old papers he was keeping?"

She looked down, away from his eyes and shook her head no. *She knows something*, he thought.

"Listen . . . Sarah. There's some men coming back that won't be as nice as me. If you know something about what I said, the papers, you've got to tell me now. You understand?"

"I don't know," she said, so softly he could hardly hear her. "I don't know about any of that."

"Well, think about it. We've got some time, a couple hours anyway. Now I'm gonna leave the gag off, if you keep quiet. You gotta be quiet though, or I'll have to put it back on, understand?"

"Yes," she said, in a child's voice, muted almost to extinction. "It's hard to breathe that way."

"OK, then. I'll be back." He picked up his gray jacket from the bed and went back into the living room to Leonard, closing the door behind him. *The whole family*, he thought, *the whole fucking family*.

It was a modest house, yellow frame, siding maybe, set in the middle of a street of similar but distinct structures, spaced just far enough apart to admit a driveway between each home but nothing more. A middle-class neighborhood, though probably expensive enough in Alexandria. They'd made it there in thirty minutes in the truck, Clinger driving fast, David navigating from a map which his index finger had traversed at the same rapid rate as the vehicle, but on a different scale.

There was a car in the driveway, not the Toyota Clinger had seen, but another, blue, a Honda it looked like. A window air conditioner in a front-facing window to the far left of the facade was running.

"That's it," said David, "1442."

"Let's go." Clinger pulled in to the curb across the street. He lifted up his left pant leg and took a gun from the holster on his calf, stuck it in his belt, and pulled his shirt out to cover it. "You want to carry?" he asked David.

"What?"

"The . . . you know, the one in the case." He motioned with his thumb to a place behind the seat. The old man's gun, the box in the storage bin.

"No. No, not now. One gun's enough."

Clinger said OK. They got out and headed for the house. No sign of habitation other than the car and the air conditioner. Clinger rang the bell. They heard it inside. A living room window was open. The air conditioner was twenty feet to the left of the porch, humming, dripping. The ground beneath it was wet. In thirty seconds a face appeared behind a horizontal window at eye level in the door. It was a woman, late forties, early fifties, lumpy, unkempt.

"Can I help you?" she asked distantly, through the closed door.

Clinger held up his badge. "Police, ma'am. We need to talk to you. . . . It's about your husband."

Her face disappeared for a minute, a full minute. David looked at the door, pointed to the knob. Easy to break in. Clinger nodded. "No problem," he said, almost in a whisper. "Give her a while though. Sometimes they have to think a little."

The face reappeared, then the knob turned and the door opened.

"OK, come in," she said. They stepped in. David closed the door.

"I knew it," she said. "I knew it. I told him." She was dressed in a housecoat, her hair matted down in back by the surface she'd been lying against, maybe in the room with the air conditioner running.

"You know what this is about, ma'am?" asked Clinger.

"The tap, right? The phone line he's been tapping."

"Do you know about it? Who he's working for? . . . The reason why he's there?"

"No. No. . . . I don't know anything. He just took the job because of me . . . to pay some bills. I've been sick, you know? I've been really sick."

"Come on, Brian!" David prodded. He looked at his watch.

"He can't go to jail for it, can he? You won't put him in jail . . . ."

"Ma'am, he's about to get himself into a whole lot of trouble. Unless we can talk him down, he's about to get himself in bad trouble. . . . Homicide. You understand me?"

"No, that can't be! Lenny is a good man. He'd never do anything like that. You're wrong! You're wrong!"

"He may not be aware himself, ma'am. The men he's working with . . . they're killers. Professionals, you know? He'll be in the same boat they're in if we can't talk him down."

"Oh no. Oh God, Lenny!" She sat on a couch in the living room. The place was littered with papers and empty plates to the point of chaos, a random distribution of household objects and refuse that seemed to constitute a sort of domiciliary entropy.Clinger put a hand on her shoulder. "We need your help, ma'am."

"What? What do you want me to do?"

"Just get him on the phone for us. We'll take care of the rest."

"You've got to help him, officer. He's a good man. He wouldn't hurt anyone. It's just those people he's been working for. . . . I told him. I told him that. You don't make that kind of money for what's legal. I told him that. But I've been sick. . . . And we had bills to pay. You understand? Do you?"

"I think so," said Clinger. He squeezed her shoulder with his big hand, but gently, sympathetically. "We need your help, ma'am."

The woman's head was shaking, but her face remained masklike, her eyes dry, impassive. Finally she nodded: "All right, all right. If you can help him . . . us, I'll . . . I'll do whatever you say. I'll . . . . Just tell me what to do."

"Just get him on the phone, ma'am. We'll tell you what to do next."

"But I haven't got his number over there. He wouldn't give it to me. He never . . . ."

"We have it, ma'am. Just get him on the phone for us, and go sit in the back room there with the air conditioner on. We'll take care of the rest."

She nodded.

Clinger dialed for her, then hung up.

"What's wrong?" asked David.

"Busy."

They waited five minutes, then called back. Clinger listened for a ring or two, then winked at David. He handed the phone to the woman.

They were on the couch when the phone rang, the two of them, seated maybe an arm's length apart. Jake had shut the door to the bedroom when he left it, and the girl hadn't made a sound since. Jake hadn't either, speaking not a word, just leaning forward, cradling his forehead in his open hands a cushion-width away. So it had been quieter than a graveyard there in the apartment until that phone call startled Leonard, nervous as he was in the first place; in way over his head. He must have jumped enough for Jake to notice the movement.

"Take it easy," he said, putting his hand out. "It'll be Isacco." That was OK, thought Leonard. Isacco was OK.

"Come on back. I got her here."

No, it wasn't Isacco he was talking to. It was Caplan or the other guy, Angelo.

"Look, I'll explain it to you when you get here. Just get your asses back. I want to get on the road. You understand?" He clicked the phone off.

"They're on their way." That wasn't good. He didn't want to be alone with them when Jake was gone. His hands started shaking again.

"You want a sandwich?"

Leonard said no. He wasn't hungry; couldn't have eaten if he had been. Jake shrugged, got up, went into the kitchen and opened the refrigerator, but in an odd way, hooking the door edge with his knuckles. He took out some cheese and dropped it on the counter. Then the phone rang again, and he came back over to the couch for the remote.

"Yeah," he said, then listened. He covered the mouthpiece. "You give her this number? Your wife?"

"No," said Leonard. "Never." Betty? It was Betty?

"How'd she get it, then?"

"I don't know. Honest to God. She never called me here. . . . Look, maybe she found it in my pocket or something. If she's calling, it's got to be an emergency. She's sick. I got to talk to her. She's sick." Something was wrong for Betty to call him here. His hands were trembling.

"All right, go ahead, but keep it short." Jake handed him the phone, then went back to the kitchen for his food.

"Betty?" he said into the phone.

"Lenny? Listen, there's somebody here. You got to listen to them. Just listen, OK? Don't say anything."

"Yeah, OK."

A man came on. Jake was putting the cheese on some bread. He didn't look over. "Leonard?" the man said. "Listen to me. Don't say anything, you hear?"

He said yes, OK.

"We got your wife here, you understand?"

He swallowed hard. Betty. His Betty. He couldn't talk, but cleared his throat. The man must have taken it for a response.

"Listen to me. We know the girl's in there. If she's been harmed, you're in a lot of trouble. You understand me?"

"Yes."

"Is she all right? Yes or no."

"Yes. Yes."

"Good. That gives you a chance at least. Is anyone there with you beside the man we've seen staying there?"

"No. Not now."

"There's someone else, then?"

"Yes. Two."

"Two more men?"

"Yes."

"The only chance you have to see your wife again is to get to your home with the girl in the next hour. Otherwise you'll never see her again. Do you understand me?"

"Yes."

"We'll wait one hour. Is that clear?"

"Yes."

"After that, we're coming over there. If the girl is hurt in any way— *any way*— I will personally find you and kill you myself, along with all your friends. If there are any of them that aren't lucky enough to die, the police can have what's left of them. . . . Do you understand me?"

"Yes," said Leonard. "Yes. . . . OK." The phone clicked off.

"What was that about?" asked Jake.

"She's sick. I gotta go."

"Like hell you do!" said Jake. "Just keep your ass right where it is and wait till Caplan gets back. He'll tell you when to go."

"OK." He got up and went into the bathroom. Jake said he could. Maybe there was a scissors; something. But it was bare: tissue paper, a bottle of mouthwash. He put down the lid of the toilet and sat there for a minute, thinking. Betty! She was all he had. Twenty years they'd been together. What was there for him without her? What? And it was his fault. She'd told him not to take the job: "There's something fishy, Lenny, something isn't right."

He started to cry, sobbing softly, low enough that the sound of it couldn't penetrate the walls. In a minute or two he got up and rinsed his face. He flushed the toilet, though it was empty. His watch said three-fifty. Caplan would be back in maybe half an hour. He had fifty minutes left to get home.

Jake was sitting at the table when he came out, eating his sandwich, drinking a glass of juice.

"We got any beer left?" asked Leonard.

Jake turned. "Yeah, I haven't had any. There's a few bottles left. Take one. It might calm you down. Me, I'm outta here in thirty minutes."

He went to the refrigerator. There was a bottle of wine there, unopened, a green bottle with yellow foil at its top. That would do. Jake sat at the table, facing away from him. His plate was empty now. "How about some wine?" asked Leonard.

"No, thanks. I gotta drive."

Leonard brought out the bottle and lifted it up at arm's length, above his head, then above Jake's head. Jake picked up his cup of juice and took the last sip, emptying it. He set it on the table and dropped his hands, as if he knew. Almost as if he knew. Leonard brought the bottle down hard upon the silvery peppery hair. The bottle didn't break, but Jake did, going limp, falling over to his right, beside the chair. Leonard didn't look at him. Maybe he was dead. Leonard didn't want him dead, but it didn't matter all that much. What *did* matter was getting out quick with the girl and getting the hell home. Forty-five minutes he had now. He'd have to hurry.

CHAPTER 23

"MA'AM," CALLED CLINGER, IN A VOICE NEITHER LOUD NOR SOFT, BUT temperate. He tapped lightly, the sound of his knuckle nearly inaudible to him outside the door, though perhaps a little louder past it, amplified by the intervening wood. Her bedroom door was closed, but he spoke through it, through its junction with the jamb, resounding enough to be heard, subdued enough not to intimidate. "Ma'am," he said, "I wanted to thank you for your help. . . . Ma'am?"

"Yes," she answered. He heard the woman sniffle, then clear her throat. "Yes," she repeated, more distinctly.

"I think we got through to him . . . to your husband, I mean. . . . I think he's going to try to get out of there. . . . Ma'am?"

The door opened. She looked spent, disconsolate, her round eyes red and moist. There was a wad of tissue in her right hand thick enough to fill a whole dispenser box. She nodded and moved her mouth in a pathetic attempt to smile, but didn't say a word.

"I'm gonna be leaving now, ma'am, but Doc . . . uh, the other man will be here if he shows up—your husband, that is. He's supposed to be bringing a woman with him."

She sniffled. "The one he's been . . . . uh . . . from the place in Bethesda?"

"Yes, ma'am. I hope so anyway . . . that he can get out with her, that is. . . . ma'am, is your husband armed?"

"You mean a gun?"

"Yes, ma'am."

"No. Lenny? No, no, he never even owned a gun. No, not Lenny."

"OK, that's good."

"Are you going to press charges?"

"Ma'am, as far as I'm concerned, if your husband brings the girl here, and she's OK, we're done with him. I need to ask you not to show yourself until he gets her into the house, though. Can you do that for me?"

"Yes. Yes, OK. . . . I'll stay in here until the other man tells me to come out. Is that all right?"He told her that would be great, and the woman closed the door.

Clinger walked back down the hall. Doc was standing at the front window, looking out at the street, waiting for the guy. Too soon though. Way too soon. Nobody could have made it that fast in a rocket ship. The floor creaked a little under him, making Doc's head turn.

"Is she all right—the woman?" He looked like a man waiting for execution.

"Yeah. I told her to stay put. In the room, I mean. Not come out till the guy gets here, you know, her husband."

"Do you think he'll...? You heard him on the phone, Brian... What do you think he'll do? Do you think that . . . that he can get Sarah out of there?"

He didn't really. The odds were against it, even if the guy wanted to, which was questionable. They'd have to come up with something else themselves, some other plan. Pretty soon too. . . . *He* would anyway.

"Fifty-fifty," he said, trying to look convincing. "I think he'll try. . . . Look, I'm gonna go to back the building. If they don't get here in forty minutes, I'm gonna go in. I'll call here to see. We can't wait much more than that."

"I should go. . . . I should be the one to go, not you." He looked as if he meant it too, but that would be ridiculous. *Ridiculous.*

"You! C'mon, Doc, you ever shoot a gun?"

"Sure."

"You ever shoot at a person?"

"No, of course not, but. . . ."

"How about an animal? You hunt?"

"No. No, I guess I never shot at anything live, really, just a target."

Just what he thought, what he *knew*, in fact. *Shit!* "Look, I haven't got the time to argue. I'm goin'. You stay here. Watch the woman. See she stays in her room. You want the gun in the truck? The one in the case from the old man's house?"

"No. . . . No, I'd probably shoot myself." Or somebody else, thought Clinger, the woman, or some delivery boy, which would be just as bad.

"OK. She says the guy's not armed. Way he looks, you could beat the shit out of him anyway. Look, I'll call in forty minutes. If the girl's not here, we got nothin' much to lose. I'm gonna make those guys' day real unpleasant, *real* unpleasant. If she gets here safe, then I'll be back to pick you up. Anything else happens, get the hell out. Fast."

"You think it's fifty-fifty that she makes it here?"

"Yeah," he said, trying to look truthful. "Maybe sixty-forty."

"Sixty-forty? Sixty-forty which way?"

"Your guess is as good as mine, Doc. Your guess is as good as mine."

When they got upstairs, the door was open. Not wide open, but not closed tight, either. Maybe an inch ajar. Seymour turned his head clear around, raised his brows, took the gun from its holster under his left arm, then pushed the door in slowly, slowly. There wasn't a sound. No voices, no radio. Nothing.

Jake was lying on the floor, out cold, his face sideways down in the carpet. The top of his head had a red spot maybe an inch, maybe two, round. The hair was caked into it, but there wasn't any blood around any-where else, so they knew he wasn't shot. When they turned him over, his eyes were twitching, sort of, little twitches in the lids, like a pulse almost, but not so regular. Seymour slapped him, light at first, then harder, but Jake didn't come to. Not at first anyway.

They left him lying on the floor and looked around the place. There was no sign of the girl, no sign at all, just a wood chair in the bedroom with long strands of unwound tape on the floor alongside it. So they knew pretty well where she *had* been, where Jake had had her tied up, and they could figure out how somebody had come in and got her out, somebody without a knife on him, or he wouldn't have had to spend a couple of minutes unwinding all that tape, somebody smart enough to get into the place and slick enough to sneak up on old Jake, who wasn't the kind of guy you generally snuck up on. Knew how to take care of himself, that boy. First time either one of them knew of that he hadn't.

Good thing for Leonard he'd been gone by then. If Jake got bopped like that, Leonard probably would have got himself cut up in little pieces. That's what they'd expected to find, little pieces of Leonard, in a closet maybe, but no such luck. Jake said he never stayed around too long. Better for him. Bought him a few hours anyway. They'd finish him off themselves later on. Seymour would, for sure. He had that look in his eyes.

"Well," said Seymour, "shall we see how old Jake is doing?" Seymour buttoned his jacket, pulling the front hem of it down over his pelvis. The pistol, which he had replaced beneath his left arm, barely showed. Angelo wondered if he routinely packed a coordinated gun to his custom tailor to have each suit properly fitted, then thought, yes, he probably did.

They walked through the living room over to Jake, flat on his back at the opening into the kitchen. He hadn't moved much; maybe an arm, which was splayed out sideways at shoulder level and bent at the elbow. Angelo got some ice from the refrigerator and put it on Jake's head, up by the matted blood, then on his brow, but nothing happened. Jake was still out cold. He turned toward Seymour, who had gone over to the glass door of the balcony and stood there now, elegantly, looking out. Seymour wouldn't give a shit what he did to the old guy to wake him up. He could have unzipped his pants and pissed all over Jake's face for all Seymour cared. He had some urine in him, too, but thought better of it. After all, you never could be absolutely sure how Seymour might take to something like that, not to mention Jake, if he happened to wake up.

So he picked up a palmful of ice and stuffed it down Jake's shirt, onto his chest, thinking it might shock him a little. It started to. He sort of groaned, but still didn't come around. Not quite yet. So Angelo went to the refrigerator, took out a bottle of beer, drank a swig of it, ice cold, bitter, and foamy, then poured the rest in Jake's eyes, holding them open so the fizz would get in good. It ran down over his mouth and into his nose, yellow and frothy like piss, but cold. Jake put both hands up to his eyes and turned his head, coughing, probably from the beer in his nose and throat.

"Hey, what the . . . ." That was Seymour, strutting over from the window.

"He's coming to," Angelo told him, taking a last swig of beer from the nearly empty bottle to cover his smile. Jake looked funny, pathetic, all wet like that, the yellow beer, like urine, running over his cheeks and hair. Angelo wished he had a camera, one of those Polaroids, to take a picture for the boys. *Here's your Main Man for you, boys.* He dropped the flaccid head back down smack on the carpet and went to the refrigerator to get himself another beer. All this mental work made him thirsty.

"Ange, what in the blazes are you doing?" Seymour had come over to a point where his immaculate shoes bestrode Jake's head. His cuffs were adjusted and his jacket smoothed to photographic perfection. Only Seymour would have said 'blazes.' He was one for the books, Seymour was. One for the books.

"He's waking up. Look." Angelo pointed with the bottom of the beer bottle. Jake was moving his head from side to side. Seymour stepped back, avoiding either the movement of Jake's head or the oval pool of moisture around it. The beer gave off a rancid odor, mixing with some embedded foulness in the beige carpet, which it turned darker, into a shade of yellow-gray. Jake had a big round bubble in one nostril that expanded and finally popped when he forced some air out through it. It looked pretty funny. Angelo thought he'd like to have a Polaroid of that too.

Seymour went over and kicked Jake's head, lightly though, not enough to knock him out again, but probably just to see if he was conscious. Jake opened his eyes and looked around dazed, as if he didn't exactly know where he was.

"What did you pour on him—beer?"

"Yeah. I was drinking some, and I thought . . . you know, that it might wake him up. Looks like it worked."

Jake made a noise. Like he was trying to talk or something, but they couldn't understand the words.

"Let's get him up," said Seymour. They dragged him over to the couch and propped him up against the loose cushions. In a couple minutes, he shook his head and wiped his face off with a sleeve.

"What's goin' on?" he said, kind of slurred.

"You tell us, Jake. You tell us." Seymour sat down near him on the couch. Not right next to him, but about two feet away. Probably didn't want to get the beer on his clothes. He straightened his left pant leg so it wouldn't get creased. "Where's the girl?"

"The *girl*," said Jake. He shook his head again. "Wha-a-at?"

"The girl," said Seymour. " The one you had here, tied up in the bedroom. Sarah. The granddaughter, you know?"

Jake shook his head again. He was coming out of it, but slowly. "The girl . . . . Yeah . . . I was sitting over there." He pointed to the kitchen. "He must have hit me." Jake put his hand up to his head where the red spot was. "He must've knocked me out."

"*Who* hit you?" asked Seymour. "*Who*?"

"With that bottle." Jake was looking over at the table. There was a bottle at its edge, lying flat, sideways, a big wine bottle with foil at its top, unopened.

"*Who* hit you?" asked Seymour again.

"*Who* hit you?" asked Angelo.

"Leonard . . . . It was Leonard. . . . His wife called him, and . . . and . . . . He took the girl?"

"She ain't here," said Angelo.

Jake got up and went into the bathroom. Angelo heard the toilet flush, then the sounds of water in the shower.

"What the hell's he doing?"

"Washing up. What do you expect?" said Seymour. That was just what Seymour would probably have done too, if he'd had blood in his hair and beer in his nose. In five minutes Jake came out, chest bare, a towel about him from waist to knees. He looked lean and muscular, amazing for a man of his age. Someone said he'd been a boxer once.

He went into the bedroom on the far side of the living area, opposite the one the girl had been in. In five more minutes he came out, neatly dressed, with a clean blue shirt and gray pleated pants.

"You pour the beer on me?" he asked Angelo, his eyes narrow as a lecher's.

"It spilled," said Angelo.

"Yeah?" Jake took a wrapped cigar from the top of the coffee table in front of the couch, opened it in that funny way of his, dexterously, with his nails and finger joints, and stuck it in his mouth. He walked over to the sliding glass door and pulled it open, stepped out onto the balcony, disappeared from view behind the curtain, then came back in maybe thirty seconds later. Seymour was sitting on the couch, brushing off a pant leg. Jake went over to him, standing above him, looking down.

"You want the girl?" he asked. Seymour raised his head.

"You want her?" he repeated.

"Certainly," said Seymour. "Yes, of course."

"That big guy we saw with her, with the girl . . . .Yesterday, right? Walking in with her?"

"Yes? yes?"

"He's outside, downstairs, standing by a big red pickup in front of the pizza place. Stick with him; you'll find the girl."

He couldn't sit down, couldn't leave the window, couldn't peel his face from it, peering at the street outside. Outside would have been better, standing at the curbside, looking down the street, one way then the other, maybe to catch the first glimpse of it as it turned the corner, if it came, the beat-up black Toyota, with two heads in the front seat showing above the dash. Two heads, two occupants, the sick woman's husband and Sarah, driving to this little house from hopelessness to hope, from death to life, from despondency to exaltation. Standing outside would have been easier, but riskier, too, for both of them if the man became confrontational. Inside with the woman was the only place to be.

Twenty minutes passed, half the time allotted. In twenty more, Clinger would go in. To what though? Sarah might already be . . . . Oh God! The poor kid, poor, beautiful, sweet kid. What had she done to anyone? Had he brought this to her? He'd never be able to live with himself if he had. Never.

A couple of cars came down the street, neither a Toyota. But it was too soon, way too soon. Down the hall, in the bedroom with the air conditioner on, the woman lay silent, making the whole place unnervingly quiet. Some sound, any sound, would have been better. Cindy even, with her droning television. Even that would have been welcome right now, even that. He might have willed himself back, if he could have, to three months before, with Cindy in his commodious house. He hadn't been happy then so much as content, and he might have willed himself back there if he could have, had it not been for Sarah.

Ten more minutes passed. He looked at his watch: Just ten minutes to go now. Then Clinger would call . . . and then what? What would he do? That call would be the end of everything, unless his small-town deputy could pull off some kind of miracle. Sarah would be dead . . . Sarah . . . because of him. Then there would be nothing left to lose, and he'd go himself to that place and find whoever it was that had done these things, and kill them himself somehow, or die trying.

And as he thought about his vengeance, black thoughts such as he had not known in his forty years of contentment, though not unmitigated happiness; as he thought about Sarah, and where he might get a gun and how gain access to the building where Clinger stood, a sentry, waiting; as he thought, his eyes upon the shrubbery beneath the window, his hands clenched at his side, there came a shadow into his vision, out at the very extremity of his visual sense awareness, out where the street was at its farthest visible point, out to the right. And it was a car, black, unfamiliar, neither General Motors nor Ford nor Chrysler, and when he raised his eyes he saw that there were two people in it, coming closer, closer, until it slowed and turned into the driveway of the house. And now came a sound from the rear of the house, down the long hallway.

"Lenny! It's Lenny." A door snapped shut sharply, the poor woman closed within her room as she had promised.

He moved to the front door, restraining himself from opening it, but looking out through the little horizontal window. The man got out, then Sarah. He took her arm and led her to the door. David waited for something to move, the door or the handle, but it didn't. The man knocked. So David turned the knob and pulled it inward, toward him.

"Where's my wife!" asked the man, fiercely. "Where is she?" He had foam at the corners of his mouth like a mad dog.

"She's in the bedroom," David told him. "She's all right." The man ran past him down the hall.

Sarah stood in the doorway. She was shaking, pale, her eyes red; looking spent. He put out a hand and touched her cheek. "Thank God," he said. "Thank God."

"You saved my life." Her eyes were wet now. "They would have killed me."

"Clinger. It was Clinger."

She lifted a hand to his, the one against her cheek, then drew closer, closer, weeping now, following along his arm, her hand against its outer surface, her cheek against the inner as her face brushed softly along the skin, then onto the fabric of his sleeve and farther still until it reached his chest, nestling into it, her body trembling.

"It was you."

He folded his other arm tight around her, pulling her close, both of them trembling now, he no less than her. He closed his eyes and lowered his cheek until it touched her hair. She smelled clean, like shampoo. His chest felt strange, as if a weight lay in it, pulling downward, throbbing. It seemed as though he had held her to him like this before, though he knew he hadn't. She seemed to fit into him in some strange way, as though there'd always been a template for her there within his chest and arms, a receptacle shaped to engage her form precisely, her form and no other.

A minute passed before he found the will to speak, finally summoning the words from a maelstrom of confusion: "We'd . . . we'd better get out of here," he said, without, however, relinquishing his hold of her. The fabric of his shirt felt moist now where her face had been resting against it. He smoothed her hair, holding her head between his hand and cheek.

"We'd better go," he repeated.

The phone rang, startling him. "Don't answer it," he yelled down the hall, to the strange man and his strange wife. Sarah was shaking, holding close to him.

"It's Clinger," he whispered. "I've got to tell him you're OK." She let go, but moved in tandem with him to the phone, a step behind, close enough to touch.

"Doc?" said Clinger.

"I've got her, Brian. I've got her."

"OK. The two of you get the hell out of there. There's somebody moving in that apartment and they'll figure out where you are pretty soon.

I'll meet you down by the museum where Sarah said. You might still make a later flight."

"Brian, I love you for what you've done for me, for us. I mean it."

"OK, Doc. Shut up and just get the hell out of there."

Angelo and Seymour slipped out through the garage. Jake told them how: down the elevator to "G" and out a side door next to the entry ramp. Seymour went to get the car, while Angelo walked around the building to a place on the opposite side of Bethesda Avenue, diagonally across from the big man and a little down the street from where he stood facing the apartment. He was a mountain of a guy, easy to spot, as big as a fullback. Angelo watched him a while from behind, at an acute angle. Mostly he just stood by the truck, looking up at the window they had seen him through, not at all reluctant to be seen standing there watching, so sort of confrontational in a way.

In a couple minutes Seymour pulled up maybe half a block down and Angelo walked over and got into the car, going past the big guy on the other side of the street. He didn't seem to notice. Just stood around for a little while, leaning against his truck, looking up at the building, until, after a few more minutes, he went into a shop, the pizzeria it looked like, came out a little while later, got into the truck he'd been leaning against, and turned out into the spotty traffic on Bethesda.

Seymour started the Bimmer and followed, keeping a few cars back. The truck edged out onto Wisconsin, heading for the District, not moving fast, more like keeping up with traffic. They passed a big cathedral on the left and then some scattered residential and commercial areas. The truck kept on.

After about three miles it turned. Seymour followed but gave the guy some space, hanging back half a block or so. Now they were in the District. Angelo could tell that from the buildings, government type, marble, granite. Like Chicago, downtown. He saw the Washington Monument. The truck seemed to be heading for it, then went on past and turned again onto a smaller street where the museums were, maybe half a mile from the place they'd been that morning, where the girl worked. So what Jake had said was bullshit, about following this guy to find the girl.

She would have been nuts to go back there, to where she worked, after being taped up in a chair by some crazy man in her building. That didn't make sense. Jake was really full of shit on this one.

The truck stopped across the street from a fancy building that looked like an oversize bank, like the museums lined up along the grassy Mall but smaller. There was a big yellow banner out front that said "Chinese Bronzes at the Freer," so that must have been the name of the place. Seymour drove on past and parked half a block up. Most of the cars were gone, not like that morning. It was after five. Probably the museums were closed, just an occasional person coming out of a building or walking down the street. A few men were jogging along the Mall, maybe fifty feet away from the cars at their closest point of approach.

"This is bullshit. She ain't gonna come back here."

"Perhaps you're right," Seymour answered. "I can't really envision it either, but we have no other recourse right now."

"How about Leonard? We gotta find him anyway."

"Oh, we'll find him. We'll certainly find him. But let's keep an eye on this fellow for a bit. Let's say an hour; then if nothing transpires here, we'll see about old Leonard."

Angelo reclined his seat and closed his eyes. The sun was behind the car, but it somehow caught a window in a building a couple of blocks in front of them, reflecting harshly into the windshield. He lowered the visor, blocking it.

"You see him?" he asked Seymour.

"Yes. Yes, I can see the truck quite well in the side-view mirror, but I can't quite make out the man. . . . Perhaps it's the reflection."

Angelo raised his seat. He wasn't going to sleep now, not with all this commotion, not as hot as it was with the windows down and the humid air pouring into the car from the sunlit buildings and pavement to the right of him. He felt sweaty, grubby, washed out. The visor had a vanity mirror on it and he flipped it open, inspecting his face, the lines and the emerging shadow of his beard, and the diminishing hair, persistently retreating from the advanced position it had once occupied. Just past his right ear, where the hair had bushed out, as it normally did, making him look considerably older, he caught the reflection of a big man standing over by a sign on the opposite side of the street, in front of the museum, the Freer, if that was the name of it. It looked like the big guy from the truck.

"Hey, he's outside."

"What?"

"The guy. From the truck. He's outside, over by the sign there. Check your rear view mirror. Don't turn. Don't turn. I think he's looking this way."

"Son of a bitch!" said Seymour, his quasi-British accent abandoned solely for the sake of the phrase.

"You see him?"

"Yes, yes. Let me think. He must have noticed us following him."

"No! Who would notice a mother-of-pearl top-of-the-line Bimmer driving half a block behind him for eight, ten miles?"

Seymour turned and glared but said nothing. After a minute he started the car.

"I'm going to drive off and see if he follows us."

"Yeah?"

Seymour headed up the street. Jefferson Drive, the sign said. He turned right at the next intersection. Angelo looked back. The truck hadn't moved.

"He ain't moving."

"Yes, I see."

They went up another block to a main street and turned right again, circling around. Nothing behind them yet.

"I gotta take a piss," said Angelo.

"Not right now. I'm going to drive around to a place near him but where he can't see us. You get out and walk around behind the truck. Keep an eye on him but stay out of sight."

"First I gotta take a piss."

"All right, go in the museum."

"It's closed."

"Well hold it, then. Just hold it for a while. I can't just drive around now looking for a restroom."

Seymour turned again, onto a side street leading back to the Mall. It ran at right angles to the street the truck was parked on and crossed it at a place a full block behind the position of the truck. They turned once more, then stopped halfway down the street, at a point maybe a hundred yards behind the truck. The guy couldn't have seen them where they were.

Angelo got out. His bladder was an overfull balloon, ready to pop, a ripe peach sprouting through its skin. He had a thin jacket on, fastened at the bottom where the zipper started. Closed like that, it hid the gun tucked into his pants at the belt line.

The hot air was oppressive, steamy, sunnily hot, though the sun itself was hidden by the tall building. His shirt was pasted to his chest and to the small of his back beneath the jacket, and the gun on his left hip felt like a stone in his shoe. He walked along the row of scattered cars in the direction of the truck, beside some low shrubbery and trees. In twenty seconds he had reached a point where he could see the rear of the truck, then the bed, and finally the back of the cab. The man was in it, facing forward. Angelo watched for a while, three or four minutes. The man stayed still within the truck.

Behind him sat Seymour in the car. He turned around to face him, shrugging, his palms out, upward. *Hey, now what?* Seymour moved his head, nodding it looked like. The air was thick, intolerable, the gun like a goad in his side, and his bladder . . . his bladder primed and charged, incendiary, incapable of enduring one more minute of distention. Fine, then, fine . . . he'd piss in the truck. A sightseeing bus drove up and stopped just at the corner, one of those open jobs you could get off of and onto whenever you chose. There were two people on it. Neither got off, and no one was around to board. The bus moved up a little, to a position blocking his view of the truck. He heard the loudspeaker in the proximate distance saying something: "Freer . . . collection . . . Asian art . . . Peacock Room . . . Sackler . . . ." He'd waited enough, enough. Fuck it. He walked out alongside the bus, on the side opposite the truck. When it started to move again, he stepped out behind it, following its slow acceleration right up to the side of the red truck. The man didn't see him, couldn't have. The right-hand window was open. He reached inside his jacket for the gun. The bus was half a block up now, not a soul visible on the street. He put his left hand up, knuckles down, and pushed the button on the truck's passenger door latch. It was unlocked, and the door pulled open—he pulled it open, backhanded. The big man turned. Angelo pointed the gun at his face and slid into the seat beside him.

"Put your hands up on the steering wheel." The big man did it without a word or even an exclamation, without looking particularly frightened. Surprised, though. Boy did he look surprised!

There was a flat black case on his lap. "What's that?" asked Angelo.

"My manicure set," said the man.

"Smart guy," said Angelo, heartily irritated, his shirt adhering to his chest and back, his bladder in full contraction at the crescendo of a recurrent spasm.

"Naw," said the man, "not so smart. You've got the gun."

There were two of them in the car, hardly professionals, nothing like the wise guys he'd dealt with in Newark. Nobody in the business for very long would drive a vehicle like that, a pearl-white BMW, flamboyant as a peacock on steroids. It would take an idiot to tail someone in a car that was that assertively conspicuous. He'd spotted it when he made the last turn, but wasn't certain, wasn't absolutely sure, until they stopped in front of him, three cars up, then stayed in their vehicle, motionless.

This wasn't good. Nothing about it was good, except maybe that he'd lured them away from Leonard's place, where Doc and Sarah were. By now, though, they'd be out of there, likely headed this way. That would be the main problem, getting rid of these two if and when the doc showed up. Or before if possible. He didn't know how he'd do it yet, not just yet, but he'd figure a way. Give him a minute or two and he'd figure it out.

They'd pulled ahead of him, parking, like him, on the left side of the one-way street, leaving their back exposed. That meant they didn't have a clue he had spotted them. He could see the driver's eyes in the side-view mirror, watching the truck, the left side of it anyway. Clinger leaned over to the right. The cars in front blocked their view of the rest of the truck, the passenger door especially, if it wasn't opened too wide. OK, he'd slip out and have a look. If they saw him, so much the better. Maybe scare them off.

He slid out the right-hand door, opening it just enough to extrude his thick frame. A car drove by slowly. He stepped behind it across the street. From where he stood, neither man's face was visible in a side- or rear-view mirror. That meant they couldn't see him unless they shifted position or turned. The passenger was reclined in his seat, the driver upright, watching the truck, probably, in his left mirror. The BMW had Illinois plates. He memorized the number, using a mnemonic for the letters, the way they had taught him in school. The guys always wondered how he did that, recalled plates a month after he had seen them. He never told them though. Kept them humble.

He watched for a few minutes. Nothing much happened. Then the passenger popped the visor mirror open and must have spotted his reflection. He guessed that anyway. The BMW started and pulled out, down the street and around the corner. He thought of following on foot for a second, then realized how impractical that was. He knew the pattern anyway: they'd circle around and try to get in position behind him somewhere. He had ten minutes, maybe more. They'd have to be careful now. He would, too. He stepped back to the truck.

His gun had a full clip, nine shells, and he had another clip in his pocket. Maybe enough, maybe not. After all, you never knew what these guys carried. They weren't professionals, weren't predictable. Anything was possible, like the old man's house. Anything. He'd have to be ready for . . . whatever. The other gun was in the back, the one in the little black case from the old man's place. He reached behind the seat and pulled it up, placing it on his lap as he slid behind the steering wheel.

The passenger-side mirror didn't give a wide enough view of the street behind him. He adjusted it, reaching through the open window to wipe the surface clean. Now, with the three mirrors as they were, he could cover just about the entire width of the street. He turned his head and scanned the area behind the truck. Clean as far as he could see. Only thing to watch was a side street coming in around the gallery. The passenger mirror picked that up, so he was covered for a while. He'd have a look at the old man's gun, then step out and stand beside the truck, where he'd be heads up to anything that came at him, front, rear, or either side.

The little case was heavy on his lap. He opened it: an automatic of some kind. No manufacturer's name, but it looked exotic. There was a silencer for the threaded barrel, a full clip with hollow points, and lots of extra shells taped to the bottom of the case. He screwed on the silencer. Might come in handy. You never know. Then he snapped in the clip and cocked the slide back, putting a bullet in the chamber. Plenty of firepower now.

A bus drove up, blocking his view of the side street. He'd better get out beside the truck. He put the gun back into the case, closed it, and was about to set it on the seat beside him when the passenger door popped open and another gun was in his face, a long one like the one in the case, with a silencer, but more familiar, S and W .38, it looked like. *Son of a bitch*, he thought, *son—of—a—bitch*!

"Put your hands up on the steering wheel," the man said. The passenger, he thought. He'd had a better look at the driver, who wore a suit and had fuller hair. What was in the case, the man asked. "My manicure set,' Clinger told him. "Smart guy!" said the man, but he didn't feel so particularly smart at the moment and said so.

"Where is she, the broad? She comin' here? You wanna live, you'll tell me. Quick."

"Who do you mean?" He thought about going for the gun, then about alternatives. He couldn't think of any alternatives.

"Who do I *mean?* Look, I'm hot as hell and I gotta take a piss and you ask me who do I *mean?* Who the hell are you anyway? Who the hell are you?"

Yeah, going for the gun was the only way. "I'm the worst dream you ever had." He couldn't help saying it. Maybe it would make the guy pause a fraction of a second. He pivoted instantly and put both hands out toward the gun, pretty fast, too, but the guy got one off before he grabbed the barrel and pushed it away. The guy's wrist sort of snapped and the gun fell onto the floor, too far away to reach. He felt a burning in his side, in the side of his chest, up on the right side, away from his heart. He was glad of that. It didn't hurt really, just felt kind of hot and cold at the same time, and a little numb. He felt as if he had to cough, but held it in. The man looked mad. His eyes were narrow, hostile. His right hand looked limp, immobile. He started for the gun with his left hand, leaning down toward it, but Clinger grabbed him, pulling the man's shoulders toward him, so that the two men faced each other, head and torso, frontally.

"You shot me. You know that?" he said. "You shouldn't shoot people." His right side started to go numb now, and he couldn't suppress the cough any longer, but let it come, and a powerful spray of blood shot out, like an aerosol emission, onto the man's face and jacket. The man winced. Clinger felt breathless, clammy. The man looked scared.

"What were you gonna do to her, huh? What did you want her for? For this? For what you did to me?"

"Yeah. Yeah. You broke my arm, you sonofabitch."

The man started to struggle, but it was useless, so tight were Clinger's hands upon his shoulders. There was no way he could let the man go, no way at all. Not now. The man's foot slid along the floor of the truck, feeling for the gun maybe. He shouldn't do that. Clinger knew he shouldn't, though he had forgotten for a second exactly why. He shook his head, feeling faint now, struggling to keep his mind clear. There was fluid bubbling up from his chest as he breathed, metallic tasting. He couldn't let the man go though. No, no, he couldn't *permit* him. He moved one hand, then the other, to the man's head and started to turn it. The man said something. "Hey," it sounded like, but wasn't clear enough to be discerned. The head kept turning. Halfway around it snapped, then turned a little more and got flaccid. Clinger saw the bottom of the man's neck start to swell and turn purple. Then he moved his hands away and the head flopped down onto the man's chest, like a broken doll. It started to slide down onto the seat, the doll, or the man. Its crotch moistened with a small dark spot, which grew precipitately into a full round pool of gathering wetness. *He's going to get it on the seat*, thought Clinger, but just for an instant. He felt cold now, despite the heat of the afternoon and the beads of sweat springing out on his face and running down into his eyes. And a little breathless, with bubbles of something in his mouth and nose that tasted faintly metallic, like blood. And he was tired too, so tired that he had to rest. No matter what, he would have to rest, so he put his head down on the limp man's head, which felt soft and warm like a pillow, and put his arm about the man, down by his hip, despite the gathering moisture, then slumped over upon him as though upon the softest and most fragrant of silken beds and closed his eyes in sleep.

CHAPTER 24

S HE STEPPED DOWN FROM THE PORCH IN FRONT OF HIM, HOLDING BACK A little to maintain contact with his hand upon her shoulder, gentle but firm, urging her forward. "Come on; we've gotta go," he had said, hanging up the phone. Agitated, his voice and face, like hers, no doubt, though the trembling of her hands was much diminished from what it had been. His hand felt steady, if imperative. And good, reassuring. Appropriate.

It was just after five, a minute or two since Clinger's call. The street was empty: not a vehicle in motion, nor a person to be seen left or right down the long sweep of broken lawn and sidewalk.

"I've got to get my purse." She pointed to the old Toyota in the driveway. David nodded, then let himself be drawn with her to the car door, for she was reluctant still to let loose of his arm. She reached in through the open window, finding it there where she had left it on the seat, her big leather bag with its long strap. She slung it over her shoulder.

"He put my suitcase in the trunk."

"Leave it," he told her.

OK, she said, thinking that was best. Nothing in there she couldn't replace. She had her purse, anyway; which was more important: her license and passport and credit cards, and the money she'd taken for the trip, a few hundred in cash.

They headed up the street. "Which way?" he asked. She wasn't sure; she'd have to get her bearings. Left seemed better though. She pulled him that way, her hand crinkling the fabric of his sleeve. There was a Metro stop on King Street. They'd head toward it. They'd be safe there once inside, on the trains, with all those people. At the first corner a car full of kids cruised by, the first vehicle they'd seen; a convertible with the top down, two boys in front, three girls in back. She waved widely, both arms in the air. The car slowed to a slow roll thirty feet away.

"Which way's King?"

"King who?" yelled one of the boys. They all laughed.

"Five blocks that way," the girl nearest to her pointed. "Down there." The girl waved as the car accelerated.

They turned left, nearly sprinting now, a little breathless, though less from exertion than fear. As they reached the second block, the black Toyota passed quickly, heading out toward King Street, the man and his frantic wife, flying by without a sign of recognition. A few seconds later it swerved around a corner and disappeared from view.

That corner was King. They reached it just a minute after the man and his wife had turned away toward headlong flight. King Street, with its pedestrians and traffic, busily reassuring, making her feel less conspicuous, less vulnerable. The buildings looked familiar now. The tobacco shop she'd photographed was four blocks to the right. That meant the Metro stop was a couple to the left, and they headed for it. In three minutes more, they were there.

She had two fives handy and bought their fare cards, keeping David next to her, touching. Clinger would be at the Smithsonian Metro stop, she explained. He'd know what to do, where to go. "Did he tell you that: where to meet him?" David asked. Sure. Their rally point, he'd called it; turned out he'd known what he was up to all along. The Blue Line train went straight where they were going without a transfer: fifteen, twenty minutes at the most, station entrance to fellow station entrance, even now with peak commuter traffic.

They took an escalator down to the crowded platform, full of shoppers going home, climbing into the trains, or coming home, stepping from them. They were nice, the crowds, comforting. They entered a full car headed for the District, staying near the door, stepping aside to let people

enter or exit as the stations approached. She clung to his side, never letting go of his shirt or arm. They might have killed her, if not for David.
That man in the apartment and the other ones he said would ultimately
come. They might have killed her if this good, kind man hadn't figured
out a way to stop them.

She held her body fast to a vertical pole as the car jerked forward, then
back. Her other hand grasped his shirt, bunching it up within her fingers.
She could see the reflection of his face beside hers in the blackened glass
of the exit door, his eyes on her quarter profile. Then she turned, looking
at him, and he smiled paternally, put a hand up and smoothed her hair.

"Are you OK?" he asked. She nodded, but she was shaking again,
teary; not so much frightened as dazed. The aftershock, maybe. . . .

"We'll be all right. . . . I'm going to get you out of here. Tonight."

She nodded again. He put an arm around her shoulders. Strange: she
didn't mind that now, though it had seemed so intimidating just two days
ago. A man's touch, a good strong arm as reassuring as her father's arm had
been, and now somehow she felt almost as she had with her father, snug,
protected. Not uncomfortable at all. It had been years since she'd had that
sensation. When was it? Childhood? No. . . . Well, yes; she had felt
something like that in childhood too. But then there was another time,
later, much later, with an arm like this and a powerful feeling of . . . of joy
. . . . She was younger then, but grown, a young woman, somewhere in a
car. . . . Yes, and it was . . . a man's arm holding her close like this, eyes
locked into hers, and she had said something to him; something about home:
being home or not being home; and it was her parents who were not at home
and he not taking advantage of their absence that night. And it was *Seth's*
arm, not her father's, but . . . but . . . Seth's. And now she discovered that she
felt the way she'd felt with Seth, but more strongly, more maturely, the way
she *would* have felt with Seth, had he been stronger and more mature, and she
more a woman. It was protection and happiness she felt. And joy. And
she leaned into the body of this strange new man beside her, this good
strange man who had saved her life, her head against his chest, and felt joy.

They passed another station, "Metro Center," the voice said, "Doors
opening. . . ." Half the car departed, half the number departing entered

anew. He motioned toward an empty seat. No, she shook her head, only two more stops. She mouthed it, putting up two fingers. At Federal Triangle four people entered, no one left. Smithsonian was next, she told him. The train started, then slowed. "Smithsonian," said the mechanical voice, "Doors opening on the left." There were ten people or fewer on the platform, maybe twenty on the other side, across the double-wide concrete depression harboring tracks running north or south, east or west, to Van Dorn or Addison, as the overhead signs proclaimed.

They exited alone, past the people on the platform waiting to board. The museums would be closed now, Sarah had said. All but the Air and Space, and that was nearer to some other Metro stop. So the streets around the Smithsonian station would be quiet, the red truck conspicuous in its isolation. She dragged him toward the Mall exit, never letting go of his hand. Clinger should be out there by now, parked nearby.

He was. David saw the big red Ford from the escalator's summit.

"There. The red one." He took her hand and pulled her toward the truck in a frenzied walk. Clinger's massive head wasn't visible in the window, but that was OK. He'd be around the other side maybe, standing in the street. He was always doing that, leaning against one vehicle or another, never sitting still for very long. They didn't see him though, past the hood or over by the long rear bed with its black cover. So maybe he was in the cab after all, on the far side of the seat or slumping down, napping, having taken care of all their dangers in his unassuming way. In ten seconds they reached it. The side glass was down. David put his face into the opening, seeing—*Oh God!* he thought. *Oh my God, no!*—seeing Clinger there, slumped over to his right, his skin ashen, a pool of purple blood on the seat, inching over its rim toward the floor. Then another man too, underneath, his legs flaccid on the truck's black carpet.

"Oh my God!" he said, saying it aloud now, holding Sarah away. "Oh, Jesus, God!"

"What is it?"

"No. Stay back there. Stay back there." He pushed her against the side of the truck, gently but definitively. "Stay there," he told her. He opened the door. Clinger was warm. He leaned in. The other man beneath him was inert, a flaccid object. He felt Clinger's neck for a pulse, but there was nothing, no sign of life. He climbed up past the open door onto the floorboard, peeling open an eye, but the pupils were blown, wide as saucer rims, indicating death, irrevocable as nightfall, irrevocable as the passage of time. A car drove by, pearl white, looking frosty pink in the declining sunlight. It stopped fifty yards up; then its backup lights came on, and it started in reverse. David backed out of the truck, fumbling over an object beneath him, on Clinger's leg. It was the case, the black leather case from the old man's house. He took it up, full-weighted as it was, the gun obviously still inside. The car came nearer. A man leaned out.

"Angelo?" he said. "That you?"

David stepped down and closed the door, waiting until the car was just beside the pickup, blocking his view of it from where he stood, then took Sarah's wrist in his right hand, the gun case in his left, and ran toward the Metro stop.

"What is it? Who is it? Where's Clinger? Is Clinger all right?"

"Come on. Hurry. I'll tell you."

When they reached the escalator, he looked back. The pearl-colored car was parked just in front of the truck, and a man was stepping from it, a black-haired man, forty-five or so, dressed in a blue suit, satiny and iridescent like the car. They ran down the escalator. No one else was in the station now, just a uniformed man within a glass enclosure between two rows of automatic turnstiles. They shoved the fare cards in, he shaking like a frightened little girl, Sarah watching him, not quite comprehending, her hands steady enough to help him with his card, then slide hers in.

"Come on." He dragged her down a second escalator.

"This side goes back... toward Metro Center. Is that what we want?"

"Yes. Yes. Anything."

They got on the platform. It was deserted. Across from them, beyond the depressed tracks, a man sat reading a paper on a concrete bench. Twenty feet down from him, a woman with two children stood out toward the platform's edge. Otherwise the station was empty.

"How often do the trains come?"

"Five minutes, ten. It depends on demand. Probably ten now."

"We can't wait. Come on." He dragged her to the end of the platform. There was a noise, a rumbling, like a train. He looked up.

"It's on the other side," she said. "See?" She pointed toward the platform. "The lights aren't blinking."

He looked across. There, lights were signaling dully on the concrete floor, on and off, on and off. Then he saw the man, stepping around a pillar by the escalator, separated from them by the recessed tracks. The man saw him, too, and started running up the platform toward the other escalator. Instantly the train came in and blocked him from view.

"Come on." He got down on the floor and slid into the channel for the trains, down beside the tracks. It was four feet deep or so, shallow enough that his arms projected above it.

Sarah shook her head. "Don't," she said. "No, no, don't."

"Come on. It's OK. We'll go across. When the train leaves, we'll go across. He's coming over to this platform. Come on."

"Who?"

"Come on. I'll tell you." She slid down into his arms. They ran down the tracks, keeping between the lines of worn-smooth metal, down toward the rear of the train on the far track. Then he heard something else, low and rumbling, looked behind and saw a light, another train, heading toward them on the tracks beside their feet. He thought he saw the man on the platform they had left, running along the raised concrete, moving synchronously with the oncoming train, toward them. He couldn't be sure, but it looked like the suit, blue and iridescent, catching the flicker of the signal lights at platform's edge.

"The other train," Sarah said.

"OK, we'll get ahead of it. It's got to stop."

They ran up fifty yards, into the obscurity of the tunnel. There were lights every thirty feet or so, casting a dull pall over the tracks. The air smelled sooty, carboniferous, like the exhalation of a coal mine. They passed the point at which the train would have to stop. There was a yellow light, bright in the darkness, on the near wall. Beside it, faintly outlined, was a break in the wall, ten feet from him. They moved toward it, seeing better now, finding there a niche in the wall with a ladder leading somewhere. Anywhere. Maybe out.

"Come on." He led her to the metal rungs and they climbed up into a recess. The train across from them started off just as the other arriving train halted, its lights flooding the tracks below, bright even fifty yards out from the headlamps. Now they lit the niche too, enough to show a door above them, atop another ladder in a second, higher niche. He left her on the lower recess and climbed to the door. It was locked.

The second train started, accelerating toward them, then past, as he groped his way back down to her. He was trembling, but he found her composed, incomprehensibly calm.

"What's in here?" She put her hand on the case. The moving windows of the train gave an intermittent light as it passed.

"A gun, I think. It was in there before, anyway." He sat beside her in the recess and opened the case. The thick air had again grown dark with the departure of the train. To the right, the last car's terminal glow diminished in intensity down the tunnel. To the left, diagonally across from them, one of the occasional yellow bulbs along the wall gave a sickly emanation, just now becoming adequate to their dark-adapted eyes. Then, adjacent to the niche, a little bulb on the near side projected a hollow light that shone outward onto the wheel-burnished metal of the tracks, leaving the recess itself even more obscure for its presence. He took the gun from its case, holding it outward slightly toward the tunnel. The dim, claustrophobic illumination from front and side made it shine faintly gold. The silencer was fixed in place. *Clinger must have done that*, he thought, *then left it in the case on his lap*. For what? For him, in this tunnel? He looked up, through the sulfurous air. The place was silent now, the station and the tracks, absent the people and trains.

"Maybe he's gone now," David whispered. "He might not have seen us."

"Who?" she asked.

"A man back there. . . . Listen, Clinger's dead."

"Oh God! Oh no! What happened? Do you know what happened?"

"Yes, I think so. They must have followed him from the condo. Did he say he'd meet us here, at the museum?"

"Yes, at the Smithsonian Metro . . . outside . . . if we got separated. The rally point; I told you before."

"God, I feel bad. I feel so bad. He died for us, you know." There'd been no time to think, what with the man following them and their flight into the tunnel. But now, in the silence and the dark, with the man likely gone and Sarah safe beside him, the image of Clinger's inanimate form on the truck's seat weighed on his mind like the casket of a parent at a funeral. He felt cold, sick, the way he sometimes felt when a patient died, but magnified a hundred times, a thousand. "They must have followed him," he went on, in a voice no louder than a whisper. "He must have led them here, without knowing. . . .I killed him, you know? Just like Cindy."

"No," said Sarah, but he shook it off, as though she hadn't spoken.

"He shouldn't have stayed," he said, more to himself than her. "I didn't want him to stay. I told him not to, not to come here with me. It wasn't his problem. He made it his, though. He took my problem for his own. He was a great guy, really a great guy. The best. Kind and unselfish and very lonely without complaining about it, you know? And brilliant in his own way. You should have seen him with his kids. He was . . . he was . . . ."

"Yes. Yes. I know . . . . I know . . . Did he ...That man you . . . *we* . . . were running from, did he do it? . . . kill him? . . . kill Clinger?"

"I don't know . . . . One of them did. There must have been two of them. Clinger killed the other one himself, I think. There was a . . . ."

David heard a noise. Probably Sarah heard it too. She put her hand on his arm, sitting motionless now, listening. Then there was another sound, like a foot on cinders. Instantly the sickness was gone, Clinger's spectre gone too, transformed into fright, throbbing in his chest, pulsing in his ears, pounding in his temples. David probed his head outside the recess, one eye an inch beyond the wall, and looked back down the tunnel toward the station. Thirty yards away, at a point illuminated by the dull glow of another yellow wall lamp, an iridescent blue-green shadow passed, then darkened, becoming a faint silhouette against the yellow lamp and gray station beyond.

"He's coming." He pushed Sarah back farther into the recess. Her shoe scraped, making a gritty noise.

"I see you," said a voice, sounding hollow in the tunnel. "Whoever you are, send her out. All I want is the girl. Send her out and I'll leave you alone."

"Oh shit!" he whispered, mostly to himself. The gun in his hand was shaking violently. He rested it on his lap to quiet the tremor so Sarah wouldn't see.

"Listen, my friend," came the voice, distinct enough, perhaps fifty feet away. "I have no quarrel with you. I would much prefer not to have to proceed any further and dirty my clothes with all this soot. Send the woman out and I will leave you to your business."

"Tell me what it is you want." His voice was trembling too, like his hands, an agitated voice, strained and cracking. "Is it the papers? I've got them. Maybe we can make a deal."

The sounds of the man's shoes stopped. "What do you know of the papers? Who are you?"

"Who do you *think* I am?" said David. They were looking for him, weren't they? They'd burned his house down, for God's sake. Who else would have the papers? Who else?

"How in blazes should I know who you are? Listen, if you are in possession of the papers, I'll take them and the girl and leave you alone. I promise. You can trust me."

"Bullshit!" he said around the edge of the recess, his voice choking. It wasn't good for the man to hear that, the anxious pitch of his voice. He cleared his throat, to little effect. His mouth was parched and the air within the tunnel dusty and offensive, making his airway like sandpaper. "Bullshit. . . . Look, I'll give you the papers. You understand? All you're getting is the papers. Not the girl; she doesn't know anything."

"Listen, I'm through talking to you. Send her out. Send her out here toward me and tell me about the papers. Then I'll leave you alone. I have no quarrel with you, but if you think I'm going to wait here until another train appears, you're much mistaken. Send her out. Now. Or I'll carve the both of you up, then take some slices of your friend outside in the truck as a personal souvenir. You understand me?"

Sarah made a muted sound behind him, like a child whimpering. He would have reached back to touch her, had either hand been free, but both were on the gun, one on the grip, the other on the barrel, trembling uncontrollably, even at rest. The man's shoe moved again. He heard it scratch the gritty surface, closer now, half the distance it had been before. He lifted the gun from his lap, shaking visibly, and pulled the slide back. There was a bullet in the chamber, dancing with the movement of his hands like a nugget of gold in a flowing stream.

The shaking . . . the shaking. He'd have to steady himself. He took a deep breath in through his mouth. The air tasted of soot. His thumb was on the safety. It was down. Was that on or off? Up was off, he thought, or was it on? He decided off, and flipped it up. He would have to lean out. Then the light beside the recess would be directly on him, directly on the gun. He took the handle of the pistol and smashed it, blackening the tunnel in front of the niche. The only light now was from the yellow bulb opposite them and a few yards up toward the station. The recess itself was unrelievedly black.

"The darkness won't help you. I know where you are. Send her out or I'll kill you both. You've got five seconds."

The voice was very near, ten yards or so away. Behind him, Sarah made an indistinct sound, childlike, high-pitched, then a sniffling inhalation. He leaned around the corner of the recess, immersed in darkness. The man in the iridescent suit was opposite the yellow bulb, feeling his way along the wall. Somehow the suit absorbed the light, fluorescing, almost, like green neon in the velvety blackness. A shoe crunched again against the tunnel's granular surface.

David pointed the gun, steadying his hands against the wall. The man didn't seem to see it. He was ten feet away, the outer edge of his suit aglow like the corona of a lunarly eclipsed sun.

The man reached into his jacket for something, his cuff links like reflectors in the amber-black obscurity. "Perhaps I'll take your ears too, then go out and collect two more from that fellow in the truck. But first I'm going to carve up your girlfriend there."

"Fuck you," said David, not loud, but audible in the silent tunnel. His voice was steadier, deep again. He pulled the trigger. The gun kicked back, the force disproportionate to its diminutive sound, like a blowgun firing rockets. The man disappeared, then reappeared, displaced downward, lying on the tracks, fluorescing faintly, at a lower level, motionless. David leveled the gun and fired again, and again. One bullet was silent in its impact; the other rang musically off the metal track, sending up a bright orange spark. He climbed down and walked over to the man, his body splayed out on the tracks, his head faintly illuminated by the yellow light of the bulb and the gray glow from the station. There was a knife beside him, a jackknife with a black handle and a long open blade. The man's eyes were open. David leaned over him.

"Can you hear me?" he asked. The man blinked faintly in the dark.

"Yes?" David asked again. The man blinked faintly.

"My girlfriend wants to keep her ears, and I say if you don't like it, then *fuck you*." He pointed the gun at a spot on the man's brow, just above the place between his eyes. His hands were no longer shaking. He fired again. A dot appeared on the man's brow where the gun had been pointed, and the head moved a little. Then he walked back, got Sarah down from the niche, put the gun in the case, tucked it under his arm, led her back to the station, helped her up onto the platform, and got aboard the next outbound train for Metro Center.

They sat in the very first car, a bright orange seat not more than ten feet from the glassed-in compartment for the man who ran the train. Maybe the operator, encased in his little booth, was drowsy or inattentive, or had broken his glasses a day or two before then come to work anyway, optically impaired. In any case, he didn't seem to see a body in an iridescent suit upon his tracks fifty yards up. In mid-acceleration there came a bump, like a wheel passing over an animal on the highway, then another, as the rear wheels struck it too. There were twelve more cars in the long train to Metro Center, twenty-four compound metal wheels, each taking a swipe at the iridescent fabric, then wiping its oil and carbon upon the shreds. Funny, he hadn't wanted to get his suit dirty. David put his arm around Sarah's shoulders, and she leaned into him, her soft hair upon his neck.

"Nobody's going to hurt you. Nobody." He whispered, but the sound of it was somehow louder to his own ear than a whisper, aspirate and vocal both, heard above the rumble of the compound wheels and the clatter of the tracks where welded segments joined. There could be no safety here—ever. Not in the crowded Metro trains, nor on Washington streets, populous or empty, nor behind the door of a hotel room, anywhere, anywhere. It wasn't just the papers they wanted, but Sarah herself. Maybe the old man had known that all along. It was time to go, well past time to go. He'd get her out tonight, whether by car or plane, whether to the Caymans or Alaska, but tonight. Nobody was going to hurt her. Nobody. He'd see to that.

They came up the escalator in Bethesda, she on the step above him, her back against his shoulder. At the top of the second, smaller stairway to the surface, they turned toward the Hyatt. The keys to the Buick were in the room. He'd need them. Wherever they were headed, they'd have to have a vehicle. Halfway to the building they saw the patrol cars parked in front, one from the District, one with Bethesda Police Department lettered on its door.

They must have found the key in Clinger's pocket. He figured that was it. Sarah understood without him having to tell her, though he did anyway. "I can't go in there," he explained.

"No. No. . . . What about my car? They don't know anything about me yet."

"Maybe, maybe. . . . Let's have a look around."

They walked to her building, slowly, inconspicuously, taking three minutes to walk a block and turn a corner. The apartment on the second floor was dark, manifestly vacant.

"He's dead, you said, the man who tied you up?"

"Yes. That or badly hurt. Unconscious, you know?"

"Yeah. Well, that's all of them that we know of. At least for now. . . . There'll be more soon enough."

"But we've got time now, right...? OK, I'm going to run up and get my keys. Then we can go. Come with me though. I'm a little frightened at the thought of going in there myself—in the elevator especially."

No, he said, he'd get them. He told her to wait for him, to sit in the pizza place across the street, its window looking out on the building's east facade. She gave him her house key, told him where to find the set to the Mustang, on the breakfast counter beside the kitchen.

"OK. I'll be back in a few minutes. Seventh floor, right?"

"Yes. The first door to the left as you get off the elevator, on the right side of the hallway."

He unlocked the glass door and went into the lobby. The building looked empty, desolate. She'd never be able to live there again. No matter what happened, this place would be off limits to her forever. The elevator was open, waiting for an occupant. He got in and pressed seven. The car didn't stop on the way up.

Her hallway was silent, sterile, devoid of cooking smells and of sound, an apartment building tenanted by ghosts, noiseless and desolate. He slid the key in and opened the door. There was a light on somewhere inside, off to his left. It reflected in the windows, lighting the entry hall minimally. He made out a switch and flipped it, brightening the hallway. The kitchen would be to the left, where the light was. He went to it. The keys were there, on a ring with a pink plastic pony that said "Mustang." He put them in his pocket.

"Who are you?" asked a voice, off to the left. He turned. There was a man in the doorway to another room, a bedroom maybe. He had a gun in his hand with a silencer on it, like the one he had held in his tremulous hand an hour before.

"Sit down on the couch," said the man. He motioned with the silencer. David did as he was told. Sarah was safe at least. That was one thing he had finally done right.

"Where's the girl?"

"What girl?" asked David. "Some guy sent me here to pick up a car."

"Right! Put your hands behind you." The man ran a long strip of tape around his wrists with one hand, holding the gun to his ear with the other. When the tape was properly wound, he set down the gun and fastened the end of the tape. Then he pushed David over onto his side, gently though, which rather surprised him, and taped his legs. It looked like medical tape. David wondered why he would have had it ready, then decided he must have been waiting there for someone, probably Sarah.

"I'll need to know who you are," said the man. David hadn't seen him very well, dark as the room was. He sounded middle-aged, maybe from New York in his youth, with a vestigial Brooklyn accent and inflection. Maybe the guy Sarah had thought was dead, the one who dragged her into the apartment downstairs earlier that day and then a little later lay face down on the floor as Leonard led her from the place.

"You must have some idea who I am," he told the man.

"Suppose you tell me."

"Look, maybe we can make a deal. I know what you want. The papers, right? . . . . Look, I'll turn them over to you. You let us go, me and the girl. She doesn't know what's in the papers, and I won't say anything. If I planned to use them, I would have already."

"You know about the papers? . . . Who the hell are you?"

"Jesus, figure it out. You guys burned my house, for God's sake. Who do you *think* I am?"

"Not the doctor . . . . From Bakersville? Arthurs? He's dead. . . . I saw . . . ." The man bent down, turned him a little, and reached into his wallet pocket.

"Son of a bitch!" the man said. "Jesus Christ, so who . . .?"

"Look, do you want the papers or not?" He'd been in there eight or ten minutes. Then five more to get into the building and upstairs. Sarah would know that something was wrong, soon enough if not by now. What would she do? He tried to think. . . . Maybe call the apartment. Yes, she'd do that; then the man would have to answer or let it ring, and she'd know, either way. She'd call the police if she heard that voice, after what he'd done to her before, in the other place downstairs. All he'd have to do was wait.

"Where's the girl? What's going on?"

He didn't have to say a thing. In five more minutes she'd be on the phone to the police.

"You sure I can't get you sump'n, Sarah?" asked Tommy for the third time.

"A drink, or just some water, anythin'?"

No, she said, again. "Thanks, though." She looked at her watch. What was it now? Twenty minutes? There was something on the leather band. She scraped at it with a fingernail: a bit of adhesive from the tape. That man who had tied her up . . . . But he was dead now, dead or unconscious on the floor in there. And if not, if he hadn't been hurt as badly as he'd seemed to be, but was alive, alert, functioning, well, he'd be long gone by now. David had said so too. No question, he'd be either dead, immobilized, or gone.

Yes, but something was wrong. That was for sure. Twenty minutes was too long, way too long. OK, so maybe David ran into someone in the lobby, maybe the police; but there was no sign of a patrol car, so that wasn't it. He might have headed for the car; found the keys and gone straight down to get the Mustang. . . . OK, then he'd have to drive out and go around the block. She looked down the street through the window at her side. Still a little light out, the shadow of the building decoloring its masonry to various intensities of gray. Tommy came over to her booth again. "Here," he said, "on the house." He set a cup of Coke on the table, extra large. Sarah smiled.

No, it was really too long. Way too long. Something had happened.

She'd better check, although she didn't have her key now. David had it. David . . . . OK, the manager would let her in. She looked down the street again. Maybe the burgundy Mustang would come around the corner. A couple of cars drove by, one with its headlights on, neither burgundy, neither a Mustang.

The phone rang, somebody calling in an order. "You want oregano?" asked Tommy. "Fifteen minutes." He hung up. *The phone*, she thought, *the phone*.

"Can I use your phone?" she asked him. "Sure," he said.

She left the black case on the table with her purse.

"It's local," she told him.

"Yeah, yeah, go ahead. I'll bill you." Tommy laughed, then turned to shove his pizza into the oven. She dialed her number. It rang six times, then the ringing stopped. Someone had picked it up without speaking. David would do that. It would be David. What was taking him so long?

"David? Is that you?" There was silence. She felt suddenly cold and shuddered.

"David?" Tommy turned and smiled, then grabbed a flat plane of cardboard and started to fold it into a box.

"Hello, missy," said the voice. "I've got your boyfriend here. If you want to see him again, you'd better come up right away." She heard David yell something in the background. "No. No. Get away. . . ." The line went dead.

"What's wrong? You OK?" asked Tommy. Her eyes were wet.

"Yes, yes. It's nothing. I'll be fine."

She sat down at her booth. Her mouth felt very dry, so she took a sip of Coke, jarringly sweet and effervescent. "Hello, missy. Hello, missy." "No," said David, "Get away." He'd saved her life twice now, risking his own to do it. This was the third. That man, the one who'd pulled her from the elevator and tied her up. Hardly dead. Maybe it was all a sham, ketchup in his hair to fool her. But why, why?

Whatever—he had David now. Threatening to kill him if she ran away. No, that couldn't happen. Not if she could help it. She'd have a little surprise for the man this time, more than luggage in her hand. She opened up the black case and looked at the gun. Safety up, David had said, muttering to himself. There were bullets in it too. He'd only fired three or four. That left a few for her. Why not? If he could do it, she could too. She owed him that at least. She closed the top again, tucked the handle of it under her arm, and headed over to her building. The manager would ring her in.

"You son of a bitch!" David tried to stand but fell back on the couch, the tape around his legs considerably stronger than his will.

"You want me to tape your mouth? Hey, I'm not gonna hurt her, OK?"

"No, you're not. She's not stupid, you know. She won't come up here. She'll call the police. She isn't going to walk in here after talking to you, you dumb son of a bitch."

"We'll see," said the man.

"You're all alone in this, you know. Your friends are dead."

"Friends? . . . Seymour, you mean? What are you talking about?"

He told the man; about the subway and the other body in the truck, lying under Clinger.

"Well, I'll be damned! You two did pretty good for yourselves! You got Seymour, eh, pal? Well, that's no big loss. I'm sorry about your friend though. He must have been a decent guy. . . . But Seymour! I'll be damned!"

Then the man got quiet for a while, thinking maybe, hardly moving. A couple of minutes passed. *She'll call the police*, he thought. *Take them ten minutes to get here.*

"Seymour, eh? God *damn!*" said the man abruptly, coming out of his reverie. Then, almost as an afterthought: "OK, pal. We're heading out."

Finally. He'd finally come around. Sarah wasn't stupid. There wouldn't be a lot more time. The man came over and untaped David's legs. "We'll go down nice and slow. Tell me where the papers are and I'll try to cut a deal for you."

Just then there came a knock at the door, small-knuckled, a woman's knock. The man went out into the hallway, disappearing around a corner. "Go away!" David yelled. "Get away from here."

"Hold on, missy," the man said, distantly, down the hall. He came back into the living room.

"Come on, pal, time to get you moving." He put a piece of tape over David's mouth, then pulled him up. "See? She likes you more than you thought." His arms were still fastened behind him, but his legs were free. Now it would have to be. Now. He plunged a shoulder into the man, knocking him over. The gun flew ten feet away, but the man wasn't hurt. He scrambled over to the gun and picked it up. David stumbled and fell headlong over a coffee table, cutting his brow above the left eye. Maybe she heard the noise and left. *Go away, run away!* he thought, but couldn't shout it for the tape across his mouth.

The man came over to him, standing above him, looking down. "Listen, pal, don't press it. You make me shoot you, I gotta go out there and finish her off too. You want that? Maybe I won't get the papers, but you'll be dead, both of you. That's no good for anybody, none of us, but I'll be the best off of the three. Either you do it my way or I'll snuff the both of you. What's it gonna be?"

David turned his head away. *No*, he thought, but it was useless, useless. The man had it right. Nothing he could do . . . nothing.

"Come on." The man helped him up, then stood behind him, pushing him toward the hallway, holding the long gun to his temple. "The next time you try something like that, I'll shoot you in the head, you understand?" He nodded. There was something in his eye, blood running down from the cut on his brow. He shook his head, blinking, trying to fling it off. The man stopped him and wiped the eye with the palm of his hand, then got in back again, pushing gently forward toward the door.

"OK, steady." He reached around David and turned the knob, then pulled him back by a shoulder, facing the door three or four feet away, enough for it to open in. "OK, Missy, easy now. I got your doctor here."

The door swung in slowly. Sarah took a step around it, the gun from the case in her hand. David stood facing her, the man behind him holding the muzzle of the silencer against his temple.

"Easy," he said. "Easy, missy. Set the gun down. You'll have to shoot through him to get to me. Now set it down slow. It's the only way." Her right hand held the gun, shaking so violently that she couldn't have fired with much effect anyway. She started to cry, her shoulders convulsing in silent, uncontrolled sobs.

"I'm sorry, David," she choked out, barely audible. "I'm so sorry."

"Set it down," said the man. She kneeled and put the gun on the carpet. Her head was shaking now, but her hands seemed to quiet once they were empty. The man stepped around David and kicked the long pistol back with his heel, then led the two of them into the living room and onto the couch at the far end where David had been tied.

They sat passively while he taped their legs and Sarah's arms, then set them back gently on the couch. When he was done, he came around in front, facing them. David thought his eyes looked weary and sad.

"Now let me make a phone call in peace," he said, "and we'll try to cut a deal."

CHAPTER 25

IT WAS HORRIBLE TO LOOK AT THEM, TAPED UP THE WAY THEY WERE, WRISTS and ankles, half-leaning sideways on the pretty couch, like a couple of bodies in a garden, the ornate leaves and pastel flowers of the fabric twining about them the way vines did around a corpse in a vacant field or along a roadside. As if they were dead already. It tore your heart out. The girl especially, as sweet as she seemed, uncomplaining, though caught up in something she didn't even comprehend, entrapped for the second time today, on death row as far as she could tell. She hadn't even looked up at him, just bent her head in resignation, then stuck her hands out behind her for the tape to envelop her wrists. Kill her, they'd said. Not him, not now. Orders or not, professionalism or not. They wanted her dead, they could do it: Little Joe could take care of it all by himself, look into those big green eyes and pop her in the head. Not him though, not Jake DiLorenzo. Fuck no. He'd officiated at the last Gruener family tragedy he cared to be a part of, ten years ago. They wanted her dead, they could do it all by themselves.

He had an idea though. A little bit of a stretch, but it just might work. Maybe yes, maybe no, whatever; anyway, he'd feel better if he tried.

"The Queen" they called her, the old-timers did, out of respect. To the young ones, who hadn't seen her thirty-five years before, she was "The Old Lady." Shit, what did they know? Helen she'd always be to him.

He was twenty-eight back then. "Pleased to meet you, Mrs. C," he'd said, nearly bowing. "Call me Helen, and I'll call you Jake." She was a wonder, then and now. What better person to appeal to over the heads of the Bosses?

He'd thought of it when the girl came into the place. Something about her reminded him. He wasn't sure what, but something . . . the girl's black hair or extraordinary face, like Helen's when she was young, when he'd first come to work for the Family. Old Joe would stare at her for hours back in those days, never leave her side. Crazy jealous he was, insane.

A wonder she was, then and now. If anyone could fix things, if any person had the humanity, the grace, to do it, it would be Helen. First he'd have to get them there, though. She'd need to see them, the girl in particular. That would do it if it could be done. He'd have to track Isacco down tonight, soon enough for him to arrange transportation, then a meeting. There wasn't any question of a pay phone: you couldn't leave the two of them tied up that way, not unattended like that. That meant using the girl's phone to call, which was absolutely forbidden. Well, nothing was absolute. He'd have to break a rule or two, for a change. Worst that might happen, Isacco gets a new office and a new phone. It was just about time for that anyway.

He glanced over from the kitchen counter, the phone in his hand notched snugly between the web of his thumb and the palm opposed. The two of them sat immobile on the sofa, looking at each other, leaning slightly toward each other, their mouths taped, communicating with their eyes. It tore your heart out. Jake shook his head. *The whole goddam family.* Not him though, not this time. He used his knuckles to dial. "Call back," he said after the tone, "we got a situation." Into the running tape, area code and seven digits, he read off Sarah's number.

He put the phone down and went into the living room, pulling a chair over so that he faced them on the sofa. Neither looked up.

"You OK?" No response. Not that he blamed them. Somebody did that to him, he would have been the same way, not just pissed, but vengeful.

"Missy, you OK?" He put a finger under her chin and lifted it. She didn't resist. There were tears at the corners of her eyes. She closed them as though to avoid seeing his face. *If Helen got a look at her. . . .*

"You need to go to the bathroom or anything? . . . Missy?" She shook her head almost indiscernibly, still looking downward, her eyelids all but closed. She had long velvety lashes on a face that was just about as magnificent as any he had ever seen. Like Helen's thirty-five years before.

"How 'bout you, pal? . . . Doc?" The doctor shook his head no.

"Look, I've got some stuff to tell you." Their eyes turned toward him, which was a start at least. OK, he said, he'd take the tape off their mouths if they'd be good, quiet. They didn't protest, didn't even look that angry, just sad, resigned. He peeled the strips off gently, first the girl's, then the doctor's, using his fingertips, smoothing the skin at the zone of separation.

He had a plan, he told them. They were both looking at him now, fully attentive. The girl's eyes had dried, leaving them soft but hollow, passive.

"Here's what we do," he said. He was going to take them somewhere—he didn't say Chicago—to meet Helen. He didn't say "Helen," either, but someone: a woman, "this woman," actually. Someone who might be able to help.

"Look, mister," the doctor said, finding his voice again, "can't you just let us go?" He went on like that: he wouldn't say anything, tell anyone. Jake could have the papers. Everybody would live happily ever after. Jake sort of shook his head, not definitively, but the doctor must have taken it that way. He straightened himself, nodded, then changed tack: OK, then why not let the girl go anyway? She didn't know a thing about what was in the papers. Why would they want to hurt her? She hadn't done anything.

It wasn't that, he told the guy, who didn't seem to understand. "It's that thing with Gruener. They want vengeance. That's what it's all about. Vengeance. That's what Gruener wanted and got, and now, well . . . you know how those things work."

But it turned out the doctor *didn't* know. That was Gruener for you, always in control, cards up tight to his chest until he laid them all out on the table, arranged in precise and calculated groupings, right under your nose. "You lose," his hand said; "you're screwed." Like this guy. Never told him a thing, just left him a Goddamn note to find the girl, give her some money or something. Right! He might just as well have given him a gun to shoot himself, and the girl too. It broke your heart to see them there like that, nice people, pretty people, a couple of models or movie stars caught up in a script they had never read and weren't quite prepared for. It didn't seem fair, the two of them sitting there, tied up like convicts, condemned to something—death maybe—without even knowing their offense.

So he told them. A little of it anyway. How Gruener had tracked down the Boss's son, his older son, Jimmy. What with the security, nobody ever quite figured out how he got in. But he did it. "You lose, Jimmy; you're screwed." He got to him way up in his high-rise condo and killed him quiet as a ghost, then mailed an ear back to Mr. Joe for good measure, after burning the body just the way his own son's body had been burned. Payment in kind, first born son for first born son, blood begetting more blood, until the world is inundated with it.

The girl looked straight at him now, unblinking, with those bright green eyes that were so much like her grandfather's, penetrating, hypnotic. It was Adam Gruener's face diluted one part in four, then made emphatically feminine. It jogged his memory.

Jake had been a courier then, sent to Dallas with a box of money and a sealed contract. He hadn't known exactly what was coming down, what exactly the money and the contract were for; hadn't thought to ask, fresh as he was from having his head pounded in the ring, then taking a couple of dives for the right price and the proper people. Gruener was charming, magnetic, a superhuman who showed him life at the top the way the chief of surgery might have taught heart operations to an intern. A month he spent in Texas, following Gruener around like a baby duckling. Who'd have thought back then that he would wind up eventually icing people on his own? Jake DiLorenzo, who had cried all night when he beat somebody up too bad with those quick gloves of his! And then to kill a person! Who'd have thought it? But by the time he got to victims, they were all low-lifes anyway. All of them, without exception, up until that day ten years ago, when the Gruener family had made a wiser man of him, as circumspect and cautious as an old stag.

". . . Yeah, I guess I had an idea. There were some comments in the note about revenge." The doctor was talking to Sarah. She had asked him something: "Did you know about this?" Something to that effect. Jake hadn't been paying attention, but he must have caught a little of it. She didn't ask any more, just shook her head, gazing at the floor again, with those long black lashes strewn against her cheek

"We've got some time," Jake said after a minute. "You want to eat something? It'll be a long trip."

The guy shook his head, less hungry than disgusted it seemed. The girl just sat there crying, her shoulders shaking, but quiet about it, resigned, the way her mother had been in that last second. It broke your heart to look at her.

"Why don't you make something to eat? You can feed him too. We got a couple hours anyway. We won't be able to stop for food after that." She nodded and tried to wipe her eyes on a shoulder but couldn't manage it. Jake untaped her ankles and wrists. She turned a little and raised her legs to help him. Then she dried her face, got up without a word, and went to the kitchen. Jake followed her in, opened the drawers, took out all the sharp knives, wrapped them in a towel, and set them over by the balcony windows. He sat back down in his chair facing the doctor and unloaded the other gun, the one the girl had come upstairs with, putting the clip into his pocket. There was a bullet in the chamber and he popped it out, then slipped it into the clip. That made five bullets out of nine.

"You shoot four rounds?" The doctor didn't respond.

"You've got to talk to me if we're gonna get through this, pal. I'm trying to help. Honest to God I am. Look, you told me about wasting the guys. What were you trying to do, impress me?"

"No," he said. "Just to let you know you're all alone in this."

"Good. At least I got you talking again."

He nodded. "Yeah, OK, OK. You expect me to be happy?"

"No, pal, I understand. . . . So you popped old Seymour, eh?"

"If that was his name," said the guy, the doctor.

"He was an asshole anyway. He had it coming." The girl, Sarah, put something in the oven. "He killed your friend?"

"I don't know. Him or the other guy, the one in the truck with him, underneath."

"Angelo. Squashed him maybe, your friend did. He was no loss either. . . . You did OK for a novice. Really. Seymour was a pretty nasty guy sometimes. . . . Most of the time."

Sarah came back into the living room and sat on the couch next to the doctor. There wasn't any need to tape her up again, as submissive as she seemed.

She had balls though, real balls for a woman. Passive as she was, she leaned forward, looking right into his eyes. OK, if he was such a good guy and wanted to help them, then why not let them go? Why had he gone to so much trouble to catch them anyway? "Why are you doing this to us?" she asked. "You know we haven't hurt anyone . . . any of the people you work for. . . . Look, we'll give you back the papers and never say a word about them. . . . Nothing. . . . I don't even know what's in them. David never told me, or Clinger either. Clinger's dead, and David won't say anything. I know he won't, and I won't either. We have no reason to. Can't you just let us go? You said yourself that the revenge part of it was wrong."

He tried to explain it to her, about him being on the line now too. You couldn't disobey orders, nobody could, even a Main Man like him. They'd kill him too, sure as night comes after day, him and them too, sooner or later. Wherever they went, anywhere: some place in Africa or a Russian prison, it didn't matter. There were ways to arrange it. Look at the things they'd done already.

"You both oughta be dead by now, you know? I'm not supposed to be talking to you, telling you these things. Look, my ass is on the line here, just like yours. I'm trying to . . . . Hey, I really don't want to hurt you, either of you. Honest to God I don't."

"Why?" asked Sarah. "You killed all those other people, didn't you? How many people have you killed?" He didn't answer her. Not that he felt guilty or anything. Why should he? Fuckin' low-lifes, all of them . . . most, anyway. He was good at what he did. Everyone looked up to him for it, for his skill and knowledge. It was just hard to wipe out a whole family like that. He stared at the carpet. He'd answer her if he could just find the right words, the perfect words.

"Did you kill my parents? You killed my parents, didn't you?" Jake felt her eyes on him, burning into him. She had balls, this girl. Tough as nails. Maybe he had done that to her, made her self-reliant when she was still a child, a survivor, like an animal cub orphaned by hunters. Real balls she had. He wouldn't have put up with it from anyone else.

"You did, didn't you?"

"Look, I'm trying to help you."

"Why? Why do you want to help me? Because you killed my family?

Because you killed my whole family?" She spoke in a soft voice that was almost emotionless, but the verbiage, the content of her speech, was hard, cold. The conjunction made it jarring. It unnerved him.

"No. No, I didn't do it. I didn't do that."

"But you know who did, don't you? If you didn't do it, I bet you know who did."

Jake nodded. Her green eyes were on him, on his face. He glanced up at them, then down again. She had brown shoes on, lace-up shoes that she held close together, juxtaposed as tightly one to the other as they had been when her legs were taped.

"Who was it? What was his name?"

"Martin. Martin something. I never knew his last name."

"That was the name of the man they found dead in the car with the boy, with Seth," said Sarah. "Was that him, the same Martin?"

Yes, he told her, that was him.

"So who killed *them*?" she asked. "Who killed Martin and Seth?"

"There was another man there. . . . I can't tell you who."

"I'm glad," she said. Her eyes were wet now, glistening, motionless, burning into him. "I'm *glad* he killed them. They deserved to die."

"They?" asked Jake. "The boy too?" Tough as nails, this girl. His creation, his progeny in a way.

"Yes. . . . He betrayed me . . . us. He worked with them, Martin and whoever, got them into the house. I never knew why. Maybe you do. They must have paid him something."

How could she have figured that? The kid had been crazy about her. Not that it really made a difference. Martin shot him anyway. Said he wanted to talk to him, then shot him in the head. "Why'd you shoot the kid?" Jake had asked him. "Are you kidding? He could have identified us," Martin told him. So Martin had to go. He took care of it then and there, which was a pleasure. Another low-life. . . . But she shouldn't be allowed to think the kid had done anything to hurt her. No, that wasn't right.

"No," he told her, shaking his head, putting up a finger and shaking it too, for emphasis. "No . . . I heard it different. That's not right. I know what happened. . . . They told him, the two guys, Martin and the other one . . . they told him they were FBI agents or something, that there was some kind of union corruption, stuff like that. He thought your family was in danger, you and your parents. The kid was trying to help. That's all. He never would have hurt you. . . . That's what I heard anyway. That's what the guy told me, the other guy that was there. He had no reason to lie about it."

Sarah didn't say a thing, but sat rigid, staring past Jake at the far wall. Her face stayed masklike for a while, then grew softer, and finally, after thirty seconds or so, her eyes dissolved into great drops of moisture that first accumulated, then spilled down her cheeks in continuous channels, as copious and regular as a weeping doll's.

"He thought ...? Seth thought ...? What are you saying? Are you sure? Are you sure? He wasn't ...?"

"No . . . no, he didn't know anyone was going to get hurt . . . nobody did."

"Nobody!"

"Yeah, that's right, nobody. Nobody did."

"How can that be?" she asked. Her eyes were wide open, liquid-looking, though the tears had been superseded by a kind of amazed stare.

"How? I'm saying nobody meant for them to be killed."

"But . . . then what happened? Why *were* they killed, my parents . . . why were they killed?" She spoke with a little girl's voice now, a tiny voice, as though so frightened by the prospect of an answer that she muted the question almost to the point of its extinction.

"For the papers," he told her. "They were killed for the same god-damn papers."

"The papers! But . . . but they didn't have them. Did they? . . . They couldn't have."

No. Nobody thought that. Adam Gruener had them. Jake tried to explain it to her. They were after her grandfather, Jake's employers were. Where the hell *was* he though? Not in Iran anymore; that's about all they knew. Then all of a sudden here was this son of his with a lot of money, paying cash for a car dealership, an expensive house. Where else would he have come up with that kind of money, if not from Adam Gruener? Perfect! A perfect way to get the old man's attention. Just start a little fire in his son's home, a signal that they meant business. Next time maybe somebody gets hurt. But not this time. No, not this time, since nobody would be home. The kid told them that, mom and dad out to a party or something, and he'd get the daughter out too, so the place would be empty. Just a Goddamn message. The two men, Martin and the other one, went to deliver it, as ordered, then nearly shit themselves when they found that mom and dad *were* home. What could they do? What else could they do? It was an accident really, as crazy as that sounded, just a tragic Goddamn accident.

"An accident."

"Yeah."

"You're telling me that killing my family was an accident?"

"Yeah. Yeah, that's what it was. It wasn't supposed to happen like that."

She'd been pretty calm before, but now she started to sob, silently, into her cupped hands. This was a Goddamn shithole he'd gotten himself into. Revenge they wanted; payback. Yeah, they didn't have to do the work, never got their fuckin' hands dirty. He did, though. "Call Jake,' they said, "he'll take care of it." Fuck that! He got up and untaped the doctor's wrists. Let him comfort her if he could. She really got to him, this girl. She really had gotten to him.

He put his arm across her shoulders, and she tensed, maybe thinking it was the man's arm on her. She moved the cupped fingers from her face, wiping her eyes and cheek with the back of a hand, then with her wrist, across the other side, looking over at him, seeing his arms free, one on her neck and shoulder. Blinking once, twice, then wiping her face again, she leaned toward him, into the crook of his shoulder, closing her eyes, her hair against his cheek.

How long had he known her? Two days? Three? It seemed all his life. How could that be? Probably it was everything they had been through together, the uniqueness of it, the threat of death, the sensation of his murdering a man, though in self-defense, or maybe mostly to protect her; and the sight of Clinger dead, shielding her from that as well, holding her away from the truck door, back away like a child at a funeral. Then this, the imminence of death again, and her coming to him to share in it, with that silvery gun in her hand, flapping about like a luffing sail, uncontrollably, much too much to be of any service.

So they had risked their lives for each other. Inexplicable. But what was strangest of all was that it seemed perfectly natural, as though they'd been tied together forever. Maybe she felt it too, as odd as that seemed. Yet here she was taking up the threat of death alongside him, walking into it like a lamb to slaughter. To be with him? Was that kind of devotion reasonable after two days or three? For him it was. So why not for her, though it hardly seemed possible.

The man had said something that had moved her. He wondered about the boy, her feelings about him then and now, now that she had learned she had betrayed herself in feeling herself betrayed. Had she loved him? Not that it mattered, with him dead these ten years, but somehow it rankled in a way he didn't understand. He would have asked her had he dared, but he was frightened at what might be her answer. What difference did it make, this recollection of some boy she had known in high school? Yet somehow it bothered him. Somehow it grated in his mind.

The phone rang at eleven. The man picked it up without saying anything at first, then sort of cleared his throat, but artificially: in an intentionally artificial way. "Yeah," he said, in response to something. "Yeah. . . . Her place. The girl's place. . . . I couldn't help it. It's an emergency. . . . So you'll get another office. You were due to change anyway." He stood facing them as he spoke, the gun on the kitchen counter. "I need a van and driver. . . . Yeah, closed. . . . Yeah, medical's good. . . .OK, yeah, good idea, something short-acting. I need them alert in the morning. . . . Now. . . . Yeah, both of them, the doctor and the girl. . . . No. No. He knows where they are though. . . . Yeah, I want them to talk to Helen. . . . No, they gotta talk to Helen. See if you can fix it. . . . OK, OK, great. . . . Yeah. Yeah, OK. Thanks."

He came over to them. "There's a van coming," he said. "We'll be out of here in maybe a couple of hours."

They got there late, around one o'clock. The man buzzed them in, two of them, wearing white lab coats, a big burly guy with short hair and a mean face, and a smaller man, lean and shaven, with protruding cheekbones. They conferred for a while in the vestibule. Not the big guy, who didn't respond to English, but the lean one, who spoke with a thick Russian accent, or maybe Polish, David thought. He made out some of it, a sentence here and there. "It's a closed van?" asked the man. Yes, said the other, the skinny one. "We'll have to carry them down," the man said. "No problem," the lean one answered. "Ve have stretchers." All the while the burly man stood apart, out of the general conversation, but responding to the little guy when addressed in his own language. That turned out to be Russian. "Da... Da... Chorosho," he said laconically from time to time: Russian, unquestionably. Sergei was his name. The other man called him that three or four times. Sergei was manifestly threatening, a bruiser with a vivid scar on his upper lip, so that he seemed to sneer when he spoke. There was a bulge on the left side of his lab coat just the size of the gun Adam Gruener had left in his leather case for use in the Metro.

"I don't like the looks of that guy, the big one," he whispered to Sarah.

"No," she said. "The other one seems all right though, the one we were talking to. I think he means well. Anyway, whatever they're going to do, well, we can't change it. *Har che pich amad, khosh amad.* That's what my father used to say. It's Persian. *Que sera, sera* it means. . . . I'm just tired of this now, just tired of the whole thing. I just want to get it over with."

He didn't answer. What could he say? The men were still talking, their man and the smaller one. Sergei walked over to the far end of the living room and stood there, staring at him or at Sarah. He couldn't tell which, for Sergei's eyes were too distant and half-obscured by shadow.

After a few minutes, the man—their man— came over to the sofa. Beyond him, at the far end of the room, Sergei remained dead still, facing them, staring unremittingly. At Sarah, David thought now. Trouble, no question about it. The man bent down. "You'll have to take these," he said. He put a vial of pills on the coffee table beside the uneaten food Sarah had prepared. "One each is enough."

"What is it?" David asked. He knew though. A sedative, fast-acting: midazolam or something similar. It was used in the hospital as a cheap pre-operative medication, and on the street, at a considerably augmented price, for date rape. Sergei stood across the room, immobile, staring.

"Nothing that'll hurt you. We've gotta get the both of you out to the van. It'll make you sleepy. It's safe."

David glanced up at Sergei, whose stare was clearly confrontational.

There was no mistaking it. The man—their man—turned around for a second, then back. "Yeah, I know," he said, quietly. "Don't worry, I'll get rid of him when we get down to the van. Nobody's gonna hurt you while you're with me. Either one of you. OK?"

OK. What was he going to say? If the man had wanted them dead, they would have been shot by now. Sarah's can of Coke was sitting on the table, still two-thirds full. They washed down one pill each with it. Sarah took hers first, unhesitatingly, then leaned closer against his arm.

"Hey, Mister," said David, once the drug was swallowed.

"Yeah, pal? Call me Jake."

"OK, Jake. . . . Don't you want to know where those papers are?" Sarah settled into him, her hair upon his cheek again, the way it had been a little while before. It smelled clean, fresh, like shampoo.

"Sure. You want to tell me now?" Might as well, he figured. Better to show up bearing gifts, sort of an act of good faith on their part. Maybe it would help Sarah, anyway. As for him, he'd been into the papers. That would likely be a death sentence.

"They're checked at the airport. Two cases—a smaller one full of money and a big one with the stuff you want. They're in the lower level lockers near international baggage. The keys are in my back pocket. Inside the passport. The box numbers are on them."

"OK, that's good, we'll pick 'em up. It's better that you told me." Sarah snuggled closer, linking arms with him. She seemed sleepy, but not from the pill. It wouldn't be working that fast.

"What if I hadn't? What if I hadn't told you?"

"Oh, you would have . . . you definitely would have, in about fifteen minutes when that pill kicked in. . . . It's better you told me now though. Now the two of you nice kids go use the bathroom before you fall asleep, and I'll see you in Chicago."

There was motion, a kind of floating, weightlessness, flat on his back. And once his eyes opened and there were lights above, passing jerkily, halting, then shifting again, backward, then a slow descent. Ping! And the sound of a door sliding, then the motion again, jerky and then smoother. There was someone above him, above his head, seen vertically a long way off, just the bottom of his jaw, a big man who turned downward once, sneer-ing from a scar on his lip. Then a door snapped open and he rose again, then dropped flat down and so came to rest. And when he turned to the left, he was alone, but then a second later she was there where vacancy had been, beside him, her eyes closed, sleeping, breathing, and he was happy to be there with her, wherever he was, moving now forward and up and down a little, feeling starts and stops that blended into one continuous motion, as the smell of a cigar came to him, sweet and pungent.

"Airport," said a voice, familiar, the man's voice—Jake's—it was. "Sergei gets off there," he said, "then straight on to Chicago."

It was light when she awoke, full day, though overcast, gray-bright. They must have been on secondary roads for a while, with sinuous swerves and angled turns, rolling them gently side to side in their litters. Some min-utes, she thought, perhaps longer. The drug had been so powerful, the sleep so comfortable, that the sense of passing time had quite vanished, leaving her disoriented, though perfectly at ease. She was alive, at any rate; they were, for David's breathing sounded softly in her ear, like the flutter of a breeze. It had been there the whole night long. That she remembered, if nothing more.

She notched her head a little to the right. Beside her, an arm's length away, David lay asleep, though commencing to move a bit now, one hand folded beneath his cheek, his closed eyelids fibrillating with revivified con-sciousness. Below her cot the man—Jake it was—sat on a canvas chair at their feet, awake but immobile. Five minutes passed, or ten, her thoughts clearing to perfect lucidity. The van came to a stop. Jake rose, swung the doors open, and got out, taking a big metal case with him. The other case, the one she had seen filled with money, still sat on the floor of the van by the side of David's cot, near his left arm. Past the open van doors, gray day-light played upon a flat course of shaven lawn, even as the surface of a lake, with a border of shrubby trees in the distance. Then the doors closed, fold-ing her again into the cool half-light of their confinement.

Five minutes passed, a little less or more; the back of the van swung open again. David had moved, though silently, languidly, sitting now on his litter, one leg on the floor. There were two men outside. "OK, come on," said one of them, a short, stocky man with a thick mustache. Sarah climbed out first. To her left was a mansion, a palatial house of three stories, faced in cut stone, eighteenth century English country in style. There was a semicircular drive along the facade, with two Lincolns and a Mercedes limousine parked within its arc. The van was in a turnout thirty yards from the nearest angle of the house, an extension of the driveway leading toward detached garages forty or fifty feet away.

The air was warm, humid. It smelled fresh, like cut grass. They went in through a side entrance, David beside her, holding her arm. The man with the mustache opened the door and passed in first, the other man behind them, entered after. They stepped through a pantry stocked with shelves of cans and jars, then through a restaurant-size kitchen to a flight of stairs. David was behind her, then a man behind him, and the stocky man in front of her, leading the way up.

At the top of the stairs was a group of rooms. It looked like a section of the house reserved for servants' quarters. A woman came up to her, thin, severe, with linear lips and black hair pulled into a tight bun at the back of her head. "Would you like to get washed up, miss?" she asked. Yes, she would. She left David in the upstairs hall and went into a small room with the woman. It had a bed and dresser, comfortably appointed but not luxurious, a maid's room probably. There was a bath adjacent, through a door beyond the bed. "Everything you need should be in there, miss," the woman told her. It was, down to a fresh robe and five kinds of shampoo, all unopened.

She showered and blew her hair dry, then put on her clothes, the slacks and blouse she had worn for a full day now. The door to the bedroom was slightly ajar. When she had finished dressing, she opened it fully. David and Jake were at the end of the hallway, over by the stairs, talking. She went out to them.

"We were waiting for you," said Jake. "She'll meet with us any time."

"Who?" she asked.

"You'll see," he said. "You'll see." The odor of coffee came up the stairwell. Jake sniffed at it noisily. "I asked them to feed you both a little first. You'll need your strength. Just don't let the kid scare you. He's a hothead, but he'll listen to his mother. That's the way they are. Both of them were, even the one who got killed. He was mean though. This one's not. Now, be good, and we'll get you out of this. I hope so anyway. If not, my ass is right there in the pot with yours."

He led them down the steps. Outside a big mullioned window on the landing, sun had broken through the clouds, turning the level grass the color of emerald sea-water. As she passed it, descending the stairs into the gray hallway, Sarah wondered if she would ever see sunlight on water again.

CHAPTER 26

I T WAS A LONG HALLWAY THEY ENTERED, RUNNING THE DEPTH OF THE mansion, paneled in laboriously wrought oak, paved in checkered marble, lit at either end by grand and much-divided windows. Jake led them halfway down, then stopped before a double door carved of oak, like the walls and coffered ceiling. He turned and made a face, quizzical, hopeful maybe, then nodded. "I'm in this with you," he had said at breakfast. Well, if Jake could be upbeat, why, so might they. Yet nothing was certain, not their futures, not their very lives. David's mind struggled through the weight of it. But it was for Sarah, really, just for Sarah. A week before, he hadn't heard her name, yet now she populated all his waking thoughts, and half of those at night in dreams, for all he could remember.

Jake knocked lightly on the door and entered, not waiting for a response, closing the door behind him, leaving them nearly alone. Down the hall, thirty feet away, the mustachioed man sat on an upholstered bench, inattentive. It was the first time since the horror of the subway that they had enjoyed a moment of privacy. There was so much to say, David's heart was overflowing with it, though he scarcely knew where to begin, or how much diminishing time he might have to speak uninterrupted.

"Are you OK?" he asked, turning to face her.

"Fine . . . I'm fine. . . . The shower helped."

"Yes." He nodded. His had too, the shower and the breakfast both, but those were not essential things he felt obliged to tell her then. There wasn't time for such talk: seconds, minutes. "Look ..." He put his hand up to her cheek, touching it with the outsides of his fingers, brushing away a strand of hair. "Whatever comes of this, whatever they do . . . . I'm not sure how to say it exactly, but . . . . I don't know, something happened to me these past few days. With you, I mean. With us. I don't know if you understand what I'm saying. . . ."

Her face turned somber. He felt it too, the sadness, like a final separation of two people who were not meant to be apart. "I do . . . I do understand," she said. "I do understand. I'm. . . ." She took his hand. "I know."

"If we get out of this . . . ."

"Yes. . . . Yes." She looked up at him, her green eyes reflecting the frontal daylight, bright above the pupils from the ornate window at the far end of the hall, checkered below from the patterned floor, as though the beauty of the space around them, and of the world beyond, had been absorbed within her, and her bright green eyes were two tiny lenses opening in upon it. There were endless words to say, but so little time . . . so pathetically little time. And he would have held her to him, but the physical parting so soon after their embrace would have made his sadness unendurable.

The door opened, startling him. Jake came out, angling a hand inside, usherlike. "OK, kids, you're on." He seemed cheerful still, a good omen. This was it, then. Jake walked past, over toward the bench where the other man was sitting. Through the open doorway daylight issued unallayed, shimmering through a wall of facing windows across the splendid room. David passed through the door, Sarah behind him, her hand soft and dry within his own. He had told her, at least. Not everything he might have wanted to say, but enough. Enough.

The room was bright and pleasantly cool. There were two people inside: a woman seated with her back to the door and a man on a sofa perpendicular to the windows, so facing the center of the room. Both turned toward them, the woman full around, the man just a quarter. It was an extraordinary place, like a period salon in a gallery, filled with antique

French furniture, Louis XVI and Empire style, arranged in eclectic juxta-position by some gifted decorator or borrowed curator with no less money to buy things than he had leisure to seek them out: a grand room, elegant and commodious, inviting. No fit place for villains to dwell.

"Come sit down," said the woman, standing now as they approached. She looked to be in her sixties, with silvery hair worn short, a handsome woman with fine features, unsullied by age, tall and straight, dignified, elegant and graceful. There were two empty chairs within the grouping, arranged around an inlaid coffee table. Sarah took an armchair facing the woman, David a carved-back seat opposite the man.

"They've fed you, I hope. . . . Sarah? And Doctor. . .?"

"Arthurs," he said. "David Arthurs."

"Yes, Dr. Arthurs, then. . . . And this is my son, Joseph."

Joseph was about thirty, dark, with slightly thinning hair and even, youthful features; ten, maybe twenty pounds above his ideal weight, so that his face was rounded subtly. Joseph nodded, clearing his throat, a reluctant sort of gesture, brusque. He didn't say a word, this Joseph, but sat there nearly still, his arms folded, legs crossed, staring over toward the window, as though that was the place he would rather have been, outside, out of this room, away from this meeting. *That's bad*, thought David. Maybe Jake was wrong. Maybe it wasn't such a good day, after all. Joseph looked irritated. Not angry, in particular; certainly not evil. Just distant: a bland, distant man.

The woman turned leftward to this Joseph and said something, some indistinct words in a low voice, low both in volume and in pitch, so that the words were mostly unintelligible: ". . . our guests," she said, ". . . con-sideration . . . ." Joseph raised himself on the couch and nodded a second time toward some untenanted space midway between David's chair and Sarah's, looking at neither of them, though, but rather at the coffee table or over toward the wall of windows, just as distant, no less bland.

"My name is Helen, if Jake hasn't told you that. Call me Helen." She smiled at each of them in turn, politely. "I had a chance to speak with him—with Jake—this morning . . . while you two were getting washed. You've been through a lot, I hear."

"The hardest part is not knowing what to expect next," said Sarah. Her voice sounded remarkably normal, soft and composed.

"Yes, I can understand that." The woman gave them another smile, a kind smile, genuine from all appearances. "We'll try to straighten that out today. That's why I called Joseph to come here this morning. He's the one we'll have to appeal to." She turned to her son. "Isn't that right, Joe?"

"I suppose so," said Joseph offhandedly. He was looking at her now, at his mother. His expression had changed from mild hostility to profound detachment. An improvement of sorts, the best that could be expected under the circumstances. After all, this was the brother, the younger brother, of a man whom Sarah's grandfather had killed, immolated, and anatomized for trophies.

"Well, let's go one step at a time." Helen spoke without gestures, sitting bolt upright like the mistress of a charm school, but naturally, elegantly, her hands in her lap, palms down. She wore black satin slacks and a white silk blouse, with fine pearl strands about her neck and more pearls on small silver earrings accentuating the shimmering brilliance of her hair. "We know about the two other men, about their . . . their *accident* . . . Seymour and—Joe, who was the other one?"

"Fontana."

"Yes. Well, Joe, is that a problem? Were they very important people for you? I don't think Seymour was."

"No," said Joe, "Seymour's nothing. Lesser's nephew, that's all. Lesser might be a little upset, I suppose." *Lesser*, thought David. *That was the lawyer. I shot his . . .*

"Angelo was useful, but he can be replaced," Joe continued. "The main problem with that was damage control, but we've got some people in Washington who can take care of it." Joe uncrossed his legs and sat forward, palms on his thighs, elbows out. The bland expression of detachment vanished. "Look, Mother, we're talking around the problem here. I'm going by Dad's request. His dying request, that last week before he died. . . . Hey, I can't talk in front of these strangers. This is crazy, bringing them here. This whole Goddamn thing is crazy."

"All right, Joe. All right." The woman—Helen—was getting agitated too. You could see it in her eyes. But her posture, the arrangement of her hands upon her lap, kept constant, betraying nothing. She turned her head a few degrees toward her son: "You're a man now and the head of the Family, and you're going to do what you think is best, but I want you to understand what happened, what's behind all of it. And these people too. They're part of it now. Not of their choosing, but they've been drawn into it the way *we* were . . . *I* was. . . . The way your *dad* was, God rest his soul. Things work like that sometimes. Sometimes the world twists our actions around in strange ways, so that what we started out doing, what we meant to do, gets distorted into something we never wanted, something we never intended. Love into hate, life into death, good into bad. . . . You don't know what happened, Joe, just some of the incidents, some of the superficialities. It's time you understood it all. Your dad didn't want that, didn't want for you to know. I promised him you wouldn't, too, that last week. . . . After his heart attack, I mean. . . . But it's time now, before more wrong is done. Before the wrong goes on forever."

"*What*, Mother? What are you talking about that you don't think I know?" Joe sat facing her. He looked uncomfortable, half assertive, half diffident, so that his expression was a mixture of the two, neither entirely authentic. "Hey, I run the business now. You think there's something about it that I don't understand? Something that you want to talk about in front of these two strangers and then expect me to let them walk out of here like a couple of dinner guests? I'm in charge of the Family now, and I say that's not going to happen."

"Wait a minute, honey. These people aren't exactly strangers to what I want to tell you. . . . When you hear it, you can decide between right and wrong. I've taught you that much. . . . Not like your brother . . . ."

"Yeah, my brother! This woman's father killed him, remember?"

"Her *grandfather*, I believe," said Helen. "Is that right, Sarah?"

"My grandfather, yes. Jake just told us about the . . . about what he did."

"Yes, what he did. . . ." Helen turned toward her son again. "He did just what your father did. . . . Your father arranged for his son—Adam Gruener's son—to be killed. His wife too, Sarah's parents. So you're— we're—not the only bereaved ones here. Did you know about that, Joe?"

"No, but . . . . No, I didn't know about that. . . . I never knew that."

"There's more, too. You don't know about those precious papers either, do you?"

"I know enough. I know Dad wanted them destroyed. He told me that before he died. The papers and Gruener. He wanted them both found and eliminated. I promised him on his deathbed."

"But what's *in* the papers? Do you know that?"

"I want to say something. . . . Ma'am?" David interrupted. "Look, Sarah doesn't know about the papers, ma'am... Helen. She doesn't know what's in them. I read most of it, but I haven't told her anything. The other man didn't either, the one who got killed. Look, ma'am—Helen—if you talk about it in front of her, then your son, Joe there, is going to . . . well, he may not want her to walk out of here. Shouldn't we send her out now, before any of this stuff is discussed; send her away from here? Can't you just let her go? She's got nothing to do with any of it. . . . It . . . it isn't fair."

"And what about you, Dr. Arthurs? You're willing to stay and answer for it?" asked Helen, but in a friendly tone out of keeping with her words.

"Yes, ma'am. I'll personally do whatever you say, whatever you and your son decide, if you'll let Sarah go out of here safe. Whatever you want me to do, Helen . . . . Joe." Joe looked at him now, a little softer perhaps, a little less distant.

"I see. Well, Sarah, it looks to me as if you've got yourself a pretty good guy here. Hold on to him. . . . David, let's do this my way. I want the four of us to talk it out. I'm the only one here who knows all the facts, the only one anywhere, I guess, except maybe Jake. I think it's important for Sarah to learn about them too, to keep things secret. After all, we've gone to great lengths to keep this information private, more for shame than fear. If it gets out, she'll suffer from the same shame, won't she? It was her grandfather, after all."

Joe got up and took a step forward to the side of his mother's chair. He reached down and took her shoulder in his fingers, gently though. She turned her head slowly, gracefully, maintaining the same posture as before, hands on her lap as before, acknowledging his touch as though she had anticipated it, turning her head as though she had expected her head to turn just so.

"What are you talking about, Mother? Those papers . . . they're just some company business. I know that. You can't tell me there's something critical about the Family that I don't know. I run things, you know . . . . I run everything."

"Sit down, Joe, please. . . . Sarah, listen to me. The doctor there knows some of it. I'll tell you all the rest. Then we'll see who lives and who dies. . . . Maybe we'll all walk out of this room a little wiser. There's been enough blood spilled. Maybe we'll all be smart enough to stop it all right here and now. Here's what happened. . . ."

Sarah watched Joe. He was oblivious anyway, sitting there elbows on knees, his mouth a quarter-inch ajar, listening to his mother. Helen had paused and not yet resumed, collecting her thoughts maybe. There was something terrible that Adam Gruener had done, worse even than murdering that man, Joe's brother, Helen's other son. Something worse than that, something unimagined, more horrible than murder. Sarah didn't want to hear it but knew she would have to. Sooner or later—sooner, rather than later—the quarter of her that was Adam Gruener would need to know what fabric it was made of.

Helen turned a little toward her son. "I was younger then; like Sarah here. . . . Joe, honey, get that picture on the table."

Joe got up, suddenly docile, went over to a carved table by the window, picked up a portrait in a gilt frame, and brought it over. Sarah examined it, then passed it on to David. It was a photograph of Helen, maybe thirty or so at the time. Black hair done up in a French twist, abundant jewelry, a low-cut gown, all surrounding a remarkable face with the same delicate features gracing Helen now, but with the smoothness and glow effected by the erasure of thirty-five years of aging. It was the portrait of an extraordinarily beautiful woman at the peak of her glory.

"That was taken at the time, or I think a year or so after. I hadn't found out about it yet. . . . I know, because my hair went gray after that. A year after, I think.

"Joe's father—his name was Joe, too. . . . We were going to name our first boy Joe, then I miscarried, so when our first living child came, we called him James . . . Jimmy . . . then, after a couple of years . . . well, you understand. It seemed OK to use the name again, but on our second-born, Joe here.

"Anyway, Joe, my husband, had some business in Las Vegas. We used to fly out, sometimes for a weekend, meet the celebrities. The best of everything, you know?

"One day, he said to me, 'Baby, I've got a surprise for you.' We used to travel in a limousine, get dropped off at a private entrance for security, so I didn't know half the time where we were, which casino, even, or resort. It was late, a couple of hours after dinner, and we went into a back entrance somewhere, maybe the Sands, and up the elevator to a suite. There were thirty people, maybe more. Dean Martin was there. I wanted to meet him, but Joe took me into the bedroom, and there was John Kennedy. There were a dozen people around him, but Joe pushed through to introduce me to him. He had . . . I don't know how to describe it . . . this sort of magical bearing, magnetic, like a little mischievous boy in a man's body. People would just mill around him. You might say that it was because he was the President, but I think it was how he *got* to be President. I think he had that quality before, maybe even back when he was a child.

"Anyway, he asked me to sit down next to him. And we sat and talked for an hour, just the two of us. Everyone in the place was envious. Hostile about it, in fact. I felt a little funny myself, but he put me at ease. He had that ability. Mostly we talked about him: the frustrations of being President, the loneliness. I didn't know about his personal life then. Nobody did, I suppose, not in our circle of acquaintances. So I didn't think much of his attention. Joe didn't either. He was proud, in fact, that his wife had captivated the President like that. We left at one-thirty or two, and I didn't think a lot about it until around six months later."

Joe hadn't moved, neither a finger nor an eye, watching his mother like an obedient child. Sarah glanced to her left. David was just as still, just as riveted. Her mind ran ahead, trying to imagine where the story might be going. Had Helen's husband and Adam Gruener done something during the 1960 election? They were from Chicago, Helen and her husband. She had read somewhere that illegal votes in Chicago might have pushed Kennedy past Nixon that year. Had Adam been a part of it, fixing an election? That made sense, something people might kill to keep from getting out. Still, it wasn't so horrifying. If that was the limit of her grandfather's sins, it wouldn't keep her awake nights.

Helen took a sip of water from a glass in front of her, then went on: "So about six months later, Kennedy made a trip to Chicago, just for a day, one of those fund-raisers the politicians do, you know. Joe was in

New York on business—my husband Joe, you understand. I'd found out that I was pregnant with Jimmy, and he didn't want me traveling; after the miscarriage, you see. Just a month or so pregnant, but Joe was like that. I think he was more worried about me than the baby. That was how he was with me.

"So that morning, the morning Kennedy flew in, one of the aides called the house and asked if I wouldn't mind coming downtown to meet with him, with the President. I didn't think I should, but the man made it seem like such an honor and an obligation at the same time that I thought, well, what can it hurt? Remember, I didn't know about his private life then.

"So they sent a limousine to pick me up, and some men—agents— took me up to his room at the Drake. Nothing happened between us. It never occurred to me that something might. We talked for an hour or so. *He* talked, mostly. I think he was a lonely man, a sad man, despite every-thing. Maybe I made him feel a little better for having someone to listen. He was very polite, a perfect gentleman. We shook hands, and I left. The limousine brought me back home, and I never saw him again."

"I never knew about that, Mother. You never told me, or Jimmy either, about it. God, the President! I bet Dad fixed that election. . . . Is that what this whole thing is about? That's it, isn't it? Kennedy's election."

"No, Joey, no. . . . No, your dad came home from New York the next day. Someone had called him and told him where I had been. I guess Kennedy's reputation was out by then, not to the public, but to the Families. They were coming down hard on some of the bosses then, and a lot of personal things were circulating. He didn't say a word to me about it. Not then. We talked about it later. I guess he just assumed that I had slept with Kennedy. He was like that, too proud to ask. He loved me, your father, unconditionally. I never suffered from want of love. But he was jealous, and crazy when he got jealous. He must have made up his mind then and there. I didn't find out about it, didn't even suspect it, until a year after it happened, when I heard him talking on the phone to Jake. I picked it up by mistake. In retrospect, I should have guessed it. The way he reacted to the assassination, with that sick little smile. . . . I'll never forget it."

"Mom, what are you saying? What do you mean?"

"Your dad killed Kennedy, Joe, bought it, paid for it, and did half the planning with Sarah's grandfather there. And he did it for nothing, for jealousy, for a misunderstanding. . . . Because he loved me too much."

"Oh Jesus, Mom! Oh, God!" Joe got down at his mother's knees and put his head on her lap. For the first time, she moved her poised hands, setting them on his head, caressing his slightly thinning hair. She had tears in her eyes, though her posture was as straight, her chin as erect, as they had been from the first. Helen motioned them out with a head gesture, nodding toward her and David with a distinct though dampened look of sorrow on her face. When they left the room, Joe was sobbing, childlike, into his mother's impeccably satin-clad thighs.

Jake took them to the airport. He didn't drive, but rather rode with them in the back of the limousine, facing them in a jump seat. He had the metal case of money on the floor beside him.

"Well, you kids must have made a hell of an impression. Better even than I thought."

"No," said David, "we didn't say much. The lady, Helen, did all the talking."

"Did you see the picture of her, the one on the table?"

"Yeah, she showed it to us."

"What did you think?"

"She looked a lot like Sarah does. When she was young, in the picture."

"I thought you'd notice that. I'd bet seeing missy here made a big impression on both of them."

"Maybe," said David. "It did on me."

They weren't far from the airport, and reached it in twenty minutes. Jake got out with them.

"You want to take some money with you now? You can take ten thousand through customs each way."

"No," said David. "Why don't you keep the money in the case? You saved our lives. Sarah thinks you ought to have it, too. We'll have plenty from what Gruener left us—left Sarah, anyway."

"Left *us*," said Sarah.

"No. Thank God I don't need it. You and missy there got me a promotion. Helen asked me to stay on at her place and be the head of her security. It's a cushy job and pays however much you care to make. I don't need much though, a bachelor with no kids, you know. No, I don't need the money. I'm gonna drive out to your place, Bakersville, and put it in a box for you. I'll send you the key. First I've gotta go to Washington again, so I'll get it to your place in a week or so."

"Why to Washington?" asked Sarah.

"We've got some cleaning up to do. They're looking for whoever made all that mess. I've got to find the perpetrator . . . you know, find someone to be the perpetrator. We don't want them questioning Doc here. We gotta make sure the both of you get left alone. You *are* going back to Bakersville, aren't you?"

"I guess," said David, "if it's safe."

"We both are," Sarah added, "if it *is* safe."

"Oh it'll be safe . . . it'll be safe. Don't worry about that," said Jake.

"I don't know how to thank you." Sarah put her arms around his neck and kissed him on the cheek.

Jake smiled, but his eyes were strange: solemn perhaps, or pensive. "Don't thank me. I owed it to you."

"*Owed* it? How could you *owe* me anything?"

"I, uh . . . . It's a long story."

Sarah's arms were still around his neck. She tilted her head to the side and up, looking into his face. "You were the one, weren't you? With Martin."

"Yeah, missy, but . . . ."

"I know you didn't do it, Jake, not the bad part. I know you now. You're too good a man to have done that. It wasn't your doing. I know that. . . . I know that."

"I'm sorry, missy. Forgive me." Her arms hadn't moved. He took them gently off his shoulders and set them at her side, then turned from them and walked out of the terminal to the limousine. Sarah ran to the window, but when she got there, he was gone.

He stopped at a pay phone, one of those clustered sit-down cubicles halfway down the concourse.

"I've got to make a call. . . . My sister."

"OK." she said. "I'll meet you at the gate." He watched her walk toward it, thirty yards away, close enough to keep an eye on her.

"Hi, baby," he said, when she answered.

"David! Where are you? I've been worried sick!"

He told her a little, though nothing of substance. "We'll be back in Bakersville in a month or so."

"*We?*"

"I met someone, someone special."

"Not another one! Special though? What do you mean by special?"

"Just special."

"You're not thinking of ...? Remember what happened with Lynnie!"

"Lynnie! Do you still hear from her?"

"Sure," said Karen. "Two cards a year, Christmas and my birthday. Then I have to send her two in return."

"So you have her address."

"Sure."

"And phone number?"

"Somewhere."

"Get it for me."

She lived in Baltimore now. Lynnie Garber, a new last name, at least. The phone rang twice before she answered. David smiled, remembering her always within reach of a telephone, even in the bath.

"Lynnie?"

"David? David, is that you? Oh my God! What's wrong? Is something wrong?"

"No, kid, I just wanted to say hello."

"God, you sound so friendly! I thought you'd never want to talk to me again."

"No, Lynnie, I never felt that way. Look, I just wanted to say . . . to tell you that I'm sorry for everything that went wrong with us. It's something I need to get off my chest. I know now that it was partly my fault. . . . No, *mostly* . . . mostly my fault. I understand that now."

"You've met someone, haven't you?"

"Yes. . . . Well . . . yes, just lately, someone special. How did you know that?"

"And you're in love. . . . Good, I'm glad. Now you'll find out how miserable the rest of us have been all these years."

"Maybe."

"It's OK. It's worth it. I felt that way about *you* once. Imagine that!"

"I know, Lynnie. I understand. . . . I think I really do now."

"Well, it's about time! Should I put you on my Christmas card list?"

"Yeah. . . . Yeah, let's both do that. It's really good to talk to you."

"More than good, David. Be well."

Ansari met them at the airport. A short man, weathered and pockmarked, fitted aptly with a nose like a beak, clean-shaven and scented heavily of cologne, he was unmistakable among the sparse receiving crowd in the terminal. An honor to meet them, he said, in his Persian accent, deferential as a debtor. He had kind eyes, thought David, trustworthy. Adam Gruener would have required that.

They drove to the bank in his shiny white Cadillac. Ansari had done well for himself. Carefully groomed, with manicured nails, a blue silk suit, iridescent, yellow tie and handkerchief in his breast pocket, he dressed like the man in the Metro—Seymour, Jake had called him. David thought about it for a moment, the lurch of the train passing over an impediment on the tracks. Two days ago, but it seemed a month, a year. Sarah had not been a part of him then—or perhaps she had, perhaps she had always, in a way.

The office was large and impressive, paneled in imported wood, and with an immense desk that made Ahmad Ansari inconspicuous against its surface, notwithstanding the blue and yellow grandeur of his plumage. "Sit down," he told them, and they took the pair of leather armchairs facing him, separated from him by the immaculate and empty walnut desktop. What were their plans, he asked. David thought for a moment, looked at Sarah, shrugged, and said he really didn't know.

"Well, whatever you decide to do, you will have a great deal of money to do it with."

Seven million was a lot, more than they'd ever need. David told Ansari it was too much for them even to think about now.

"Well, you will have a lot more to think about then. At the last annual report, it was about that, seven million. The past year though, with what the U.S. stock market has done, and with going short on Japanese and Korean equities, there is about fifteen million dollars in the account."

"Fifteen million?" asked Sarah.

"Yes, perhaps that will alter your plans. You need not rush right back to work, for instance. You can stay here in the Caymans for a while; maybe. . . ."

"We were planning to," said David. "A few weeks anyway, until things, uh... settle down a little at home."

"Good. Then we need not take care of everything today. I will get the forms to transfer the money, and we can put it anywhere you like. It can be done in a matter of days."

"What if we didn't transfer it?" asked Sarah. "What if we just left it here?"

"Yes, you may. I would consider it an honor. Adam let me manage his money for many years."

"Well, we will do the same—if it's all right with David, that is. What do you think?"

"Fine," said David. "It's much more your money than it is mine."

Sarah arranged it: one account for now, which Ansari would continue to manage, keeping ten percent of the profits, as her grandfather had insisted, despite his protests. "I will be honored, Miss Sarah." Ownourred, he said, trilling his r's. ". . . Oh, I nearly forgot. There is a parcel for you."

"A parcel?" Sarah asked.

"Yes. I kept it in the vault. I will just get it. Please excuse me for a minute."

Ansari went to the door and stepped out, leaving it pulled to, but unlatched, a sliver ajar.

"Well, what do you think?" asked David.

"About ...?"

"About being alone with me on an island for a couple of weeks."

"What do I think? I can't think of a single person I'd rather be on an island with. . . . My whole life, there hasn't been one. You know that. I've told you that."

"What about . . . . What about that boy . . . Seth . . . The one . . . ."

"I was a child then, a different person. . . . It's hard to know what I felt then. . . . Hey, I thought you never got jealous."

"I never did."

Ansari came in, closing the door behind him. He had a small parcel in his hand, a little box wrapped in khaki-colored packaging tape. Sarah took it, then held it to her right for David to examine. It had passed through the mail and was addressed to Gruener and Arthurs, C/O Ahmad Ansari, Caribbean International Bank, Georgetown, Cayman Islands.

"What is it?" asked Sarah.

"I don't know," said Ansari. "It came a couple of months ago. I never talked to Adam again, so I never had the chance to ask him. Why don't you open it, and we'll all find out." He gave her a pair of scissors from the drawer, and she cut the tape and wrapping. There was a paper box inside, thick gilt cardboard, and inside that a small velour bag with a drawstring. She undid the cord and poured the contents of the bag onto the desk. Three rings clattered onto the wood surface: an engagement ring with a prodigious diamond and two gold wedding bands.

"That was Pari's! That was Pari's ring, the diamond."

"My grandmother's?"

"Yes. I saw her wear it. Nobody had a diamond that big. That was hers."

"And those must have been their wedding rings, my grandparents'."

"I believe they were."

"Why would he have sent them to me . . . to us?"

"Well, you would know that better than I, but Adam had a reason for everything. . . . He always had a reason for everything."

Ansari dropped them at the Intercontinental, the nicest hotel on the island, he said. The place looked empty, a Caribbean resort in summer.

"May I help you?" asked the woman at reception.

"Yes," said David, "a suite, if you have one." They were millionaires now. What the hell.

"We'll have to do some shopping," Sarah said, once the door was closed and locked. David had tipped the bellman exorbitantly for carrying up a one-ounce key.

"Yeah, toothpaste at least."

"I don't even have a change of underwear." She smiled, looking down at the floor, her hands on his waist.

"Maybe you won't need it."

"Oh, you! . . . I'm a little worried about that though."

"What, underwear? We'll get you all you want."

"No... No, seriously, I mean . . . I'm not going to be . . . You'll have to . . . you know. I don't even know what to do."

"And you think that's bad?"

"Isn't it?"

"You are something! Look, maybe you want me to make an honest woman of you first. I mean, we've got the rings."

"Don't tease me."

"You think I'm teasing? I'll buy you a new ring if you want."

"No, those are fine. We've got time, though. . . . Do you think . . .? You knew him. Do you think my grandfather meant anything by sending those rings to us?"

"Yeah. I do. I really do. I think he picked me for you and you for me. And I think he was right on the money."

"I do too, only . . . ."

"Only what?"

"You said you never got jealous . . . you know, when we were talking before, and the other day, too. You said you'd never been jealous with anyone. Like your wife, I mean, and . . . and Cindy."

"I guess I never was."

"Well, does that apply to me, too?"

"To you? What do you mean?"

"Oh, I don't know. How would you feel . . . if it were me . . . you know, with another man? Would you feel the same as you had with Cindy, and with your wife . . . what was her name?"

"Lynnie."

"OK, Lynnie. Would you feel the same if it were me?"

"No. No, I wouldn't feel the same."

"How would you feel, then?"

"Angry, I guess. Yeah, I'd be angry."

"Angry at me?"

"Sure. And at the guy, too."

"And what would you do if you caught us together?"

"Look, why are you asking me this? You're getting me upset."

"I'm sorry. I don't mean to. I just want to know . . . . Just tell me that, what you'd do if you caught me with someone."

"What I'd do?"

"Yes. What would you do?"

"I'd kill him."

"You would? You really would?"

"Yeah. . . . I'd think about it anyway. Now that I'm a killer, you know."

"You'd want to kill him, like . . . like Mr. Joe with Helen."

"Yeah, I guess I would."

"That's what I was hoping you'd say." She looked up at him with her deep green eyes, as magnetic and mysterious as emeralds in moonlight. There was a strange sensation in his chest, a vacuum and a fullness both at once, paradoxically, as he bent to kiss her, and her lips were electric, tingling, and her exhaled breath in his nostrils, sweet and earthy. And his heart turned on its axis for the very first time in his life, delighted, at last, that he might hold the greater part of his being, trembling and patent, close within his arms.

EPILOGUE

BAKERSVILLE, PA.
AUGUST 1996

I T WAS SORE WHERE HE WAS PRESSING, TENDER. HE COULDN'T HELP IT though. Something there that had to be checked. She knew that.

"Does it hurt you? Underneath where I am pressing?" he asked.

"Just a little. . . . It's not bad."

"Well, I told you; we had to open it, cut it, you know. I explained. When a stone moves down like that, it isn't possible to do it with the scope, the way I told you before. . . ."

"Yes, Doctor, I know. It's all right." He was a nice man, trying to be nice, only a little hard to understand. That was all. The words, the way he said them. You had to concentrate real hard. Then you could follow what he was saying but you needed to listen so carefully, each word an individual effort, so that it exhausted you just trying to get at what it was he said. Not like Dr. David, who talked real plain, so you could follow everything, even the medical explanations. Still, he was nice, this Dr. Nouri. Kind. And his hands were gentle too, the way a surgeon's hands were supposed to be.

"I am going to just check with the hospital, with the lab . . . to be certain that the the your pancreas is OK. You can get dressed and go out into the waiting room and I will tell you in a few minutes, when I find out the values."

He closed the door behind him, leaving her alone in the little room.

"Values," he had said, as if her organs were for sale, a funny way of talking. Her clothes were on the chair. She took off the paper gown and started dressing, standing before a mirror. However many times she saw her face and body reflected, however many times a day, putting on powder or fluffing up her hair, what she saw was not her form, not a form she recognized as hers, accepted as her face and body. What was her, what was really her, was the form she had seen thirty years before, or thirty-five, younger, thinner, with hair of a different shade, though the color suited her now. Her face was smooth still, though rounded. Not a wrinkle anywhere. George had always loved her skin. She looked down at her abdomen. There would be a scar now, her first scar ever, though George wouldn't mind so very much.

The waiting room was half full, younger people mostly, a boy with a cast on his arm, sitting between his parents. She guessed that was who they were. Then a few other people who looked familiar, a girl from the bank with someone, her husband maybe, and another man she had seen somewhere in town. George was seated opposite the doorway she stepped through, across the room, right next to Stella Daly from church. He rose to help her over, taking an arm.

"I'm all right, George. I'm not a baby." She told him what the doctor had said, about her "values." They'd have to wait a while, till he phoned the lab. So George led her back toward the seats they had vacated, lowering her clumsily, at quarter speed, then sitting down in the adjacent seat. To her immediate right, just beyond the angle of the room, was Stella, her knees perpendicular, close enough to touch.

"You had an operation," Stella told her. *Told* her, as though she might not have known about it herself. Stella was forever into everyone else's business. Still, one couldn't be rude to her, what with Stella a recent widow and all.

"Gall bladder," Dora volunteered. "They had to do it like they used to, not with the laser. They had to cut."

Stella nodded. "That's bad. Some people die from that."

She was mean, Stella was. Or not so much mean as pessimistic, always looking at the bad side of things. She'd be a terrible patient. They said she hadn't been a very nice wife, either. But it wasn't really kind to think that, not with what she'd just been through.

"Do you have to have an operation too?" asked Dora.

Stella shook her head. "No. This doctor is taking care of Dr. Arthurs' patients. While he's gone, you know. They put me on some medicine. Depression, they said, since Clarence died. I don't know. . . . I'll be glad when Arthurs gets back."

She would, too, though Dr. Nouri had been kind and gentle, fixing her up the way that Dr. David had said he would. That first day, three weeks before, when the town had heard about the fire, and she had too, just as soon as anyone else, thinking that Dr. David might have been inside with the woman; that was a scare, just like her own son being lost, missing. She told Stella how she had felt, how worried she'd been for the doctor.

"I know. I was in Pittsburgh with my son. He didn't want me to come back here. Didn't think it was safe. But when they caught that man, you know, the one they said did all those awful things . . . ."

"Yes," said Dora. "They say it was drugs. He had Dr. David mixed up with somebody else, another person with the same name. David Arthurs, just like him."

Stella shook her head. "Well, that's the story anyway, but I don't know. . . ."

"No. No, they had his picture in the paper. A real mean-looking man with a scar on his lip, a funny name. What was it, George, that man's name?"

"Sergei. Sergei something," said George. "Russian. He come from Russia, accordin' to the paper. Somebody tipped the police off to where he was, and they went there and found him deader'n a skunk. Shot hisself. Found a note too. He wrote a note like a kind of confession, then shot hisself. They found him when they went to his place, around Washington, it said."

"Terrible," said Stella. "I never saw anything like it in Bakersville. It's getting just as bad as the city now, but at least they caught him. Still, I don't think that's the end of it. There's something fishy about that deputy too, the one that got killed."

George turned all the way around, staring at her. He never got excited much, but when he did, it was for something special, something really bad. "Look, Mrs. Daly," he said, "I knowed Brian Clinger, and he was as fine a man as I've ever knowed around these parts. I've never heard no one say a thing against him since the day he come to Bakersville."

"Yes, well, that may be so, Mr. Chilcott, but I heard different. Do you know Ruth Byerly? You do, Dora. She works down at the courthouse."

"Ruth? Yes, yes. What about Ruth?" Ruth was a bit of a busybody too, though not nearly as bad as Stella could be.

"Well," said Stella, "she's mother to Larry Byerly. You know, from the repair place." Dora nodded. Sure, everybody knew Larry. She glanced over to her left. George was looking off toward the other side of the waiting room, as far away from Stella as he could have looked. Once you got that man mad . . . .

"You know who Larry's with now," Stella continued. Dora didn't know. He'd left his first wife ten years before.

"No, I knew his first wife though. She used to do the billing for the garage."

"Yes, maybe. But now he's with Linda: used to be Linda Clinger. Now you know?" Dora shook her head. George, to her left, was incommunicado.

"Well, she used to be married to that deputy, the one that got killed. His kids live with her, her and Larry. And you know what Ruth told me?"

"He was a good father. That's all I know. Them kids had a good father." George had turned around again. His face was purple. Dora worried a little about him. His heart wasn't as strong as it once had been. Dr. David had told her that, not to let him get too excited when he watched the Steelers.

"OK, honey, we know he was good. Stella's only saying what she heard."

"He was a good father to them kids. I know that. You talk to them about it. They'll tell you, same as what I say."

"Well, maybe he was a little too good," said Stella. "Too good to be on the up and up. He left those kids a lot of money. Drug money, I'd guess, from the company he kept."

George was turning a darker shade of purple, and his neck veins were standing out. "I'd say whatever he left them was honest money. He made a good living as a deputy, and I never knowed him to throw it away on frivolous things like some folks do. If he left 'em money, it was honest money. I'd bet on that."

"Well, where'd he get a million dollars then, working as a deputy?"

"A million dollars!" said Dora.

"A million! What do you mean, a million? Where'd you get that from?" asked George.

"From Ruth, that's where. From Ruth Byerly. Look, I heard he left them each, both of his kids, he left each one of them a million dollar trust fund. Ruth said they heard from a lawyer or somebody . . . somebody at a bank in the Cayman Islands, where they have all that drug money. . . ."

"A million dollars?" asked George, lighter purple now.

"*Each*. A million dollars *each*. That's what Ruth said. A million each in a trust fund." Stella looked triumphant.

Just then the inner door opened, and Dr. Nouri leaned through it with the top half of his body, holding onto the doorknob for balance. "Mrs. Chilcott!" he called, pronouncing each letter in that odd foreign way of his: *Cheelcohtt*. "Come in, back to my office, Mrs. *Cheelcohtt*. I have the values."

She pushed herself up and started toward the doctor, George right behind her, not wanting to stay alone with Stella most likely. The office was at the far end of the hall, thirty feet or more past the room she'd been in before. The door was open, and the doctor ushered them both in, then shut the door behind them.

"Your pancreatic levels were a little high, the amylase . . . ." He went on some more, but what he said was medical talk. And even the other words. Well, between his accent and the technical business, you couldn't get too much of it straight.

"Am I going to be all right?" she asked. She wasn't much worried about herself, but what about George? Who would cook for him?

"Yes. Yes. It will take a month or so, then the values should return to normal. We will have you in perfect shape by the time your regular doctor returns."

"Dr. David?" she asked.

"Yes," said Dr. Nouri, "first of September, he will return. I spoke to him this afternoon."

"Well, what happened? Can you tell me where he's been?"

"Yes, yes. He's on his honeymoon."

"Honeymoon! He's married? The doctor got married?"

"Yes. To a very nice lady. I talked to her as well."

"Another one!" She couldn't help but say it. "He goes through women like those rubber gloves of his. I wish he'd make up his mind and settle down."

"I believe he has, Mrs. Chilcott. This time I believe he has."

George led her out through the waiting room, past the place where Stella had been sitting, vacant now. Probably they had called her back to be examined. The car was parked in front, not fifteen feet from the door. She was tired now. All that unaccustomed exertion. George opened the door for her, then held her arm as she lowered herself onto the seat. It was funny how life was. Not so long ago they had been young like the doctor and his new wife, she and George; newlyweds, excited about a better job or a baby on the way. You never really appreciated good things when you were young, just took them for granted. Those kids sure wouldn't though, not with what their Dad had done for them. A million dollars each! What did it matter where a person got the money if it bought a better life for his family?

"Was he really a good man, that Mr. Clinger, the deputy who got killed?" she asked George.

"Sure was. Good man and a good father."

They drove through town, stopping at the traffic light by the court-house. Someone waved from the curb and she waved back. Estelle Gallagher, the nurse, she thought it was, but the light was in her eyes, so she wasn't certain.

"I'm glad the doctor's coming back, Dr. David."

"Yep. He's a good man too. You can see it in his face."

"You know what I'm going to do . . . when he gets back?"

"What's that Dora?"

"If I feel better by then . . . if I get my strength back. . . ."

"Yep? Then what?"

"I'm going to bake him a big tray of cookies."

George started laughing. Why she didn't know, but he did, a great exhalation of broken chuckles burgeoning into thunderous laughter, so that he lost his breath for a moment and had to stop the car, pulling it into the herringbone pattern of Main Street's unattended vehicles, whereupon he loosed the wheel and held his stomach with his left hand, wiping his wetted face with the right, a livid face again, but magenta now rather than purple. And as he looked over at her, it started again, in rolling corporate waves, a laughter so infectious, so immoderate, that it started a little in her too. George was like that once you got him going, though what it was that had struck him so funny in the first place, she couldn't imagine for the life of her.